ASYLUM

ASYLUM

THE CIRCEAE TALES

ASHLEY HODGES BAZER

WestBow
PRESS
A DIVISION OF THOMAS NELSON

WestBow Press books may be ordered through booksellers or by contacting:

WestBow Press
A Division of Thomas Nelson
1663 Liberty Drive
Bloomington, IN 47403
www.westbowpress.com
1-(866) 928-1240

This book is a work of fiction. People, places, events, and situations are the product of the author's imagination. Any resemblance to actual persons, living or dead, or historical events, is purely coincidental.

Because of the dynamic nature of the Internet, any web addresses or links contained in this book may have changed since publication and may no longer be valid. The views expressed in this work are solely those of the author and do not necessarily reflect the views of the publisher, and the publisher hereby disclaims any responsibility for them.

Certain stock imagery © Thinkstock.
Any people depicted in stock imagery provided by Thinkstock are models, and such images are being used for illustrative purposes only.

The Scripture quotation is taken from THE HOLY BIBLE, NEW INTERNATIONAL VERSION®, NIV® Copyright © 1973, 1978, 1984, 2011 by Biblica, Inc.™ Used by permission. All rights reserved worldwide.

ISBN: 978-1-4497-6224-7 (e)
ISBN: 978-1-4497-6223-0 (sc)
ISBN: 978-1-4497-6225-4 (hc)

Library of Congress Control Number: 2012914901

Printed in the United States of America

WestBow Press rev. date: 8/17/2012

For my mother, Janie.
The Lord will always see us through.

ACKNOWLEDGEMENTS

First, I would like to give a big thank you to the panel of judges for the WestBow Press/Munce Group 2012 Writing Contest. You made my dreams come true by taking a chance on an unpublished author.

To the amazing staff at WestBow Press—coordinators, designers, editors, marketing team—I appreciate your time, patience, and dedication. Without your guidance, I wouldn't have been able to make this journey. Thank you all.

To my brother. You made the best visual aid of the Circeae System! I am most grateful for your ongoing love, humor, and support.

To my mom. My biggest fan! Thank you for reading all my stories and giving helpful feedback. And for encouraging me to keep at it.

To my husband. For all the times you took the Dingoes outside or downstairs. For believing in me when I stopped believing in myself. For holding my hand through the ups and downs. Thank you. You are the best. I love you.

To my sweet Dingoes. Thank you for letting Mom work when she needed to. You guys are awesome! I love each of you!

To the readers of *Asylum*. Thank you for choosing my book. May you fall in love with these characters as much as I have. There are more stories, and hopefully more books to follow.

And finally – to an awesome God, without Whom none of this would be possible. *Soli Deo Gloria*!

"May the LORD answer you when you are in distress;
may the name of the God of Jacob protect you.
May he send you help from the sanctuary
and grant you support from Zion."

Psalm 20:1–2 (NIV)

PROLOGUE

"Aram!"

Jarred from a deep, meditative prayer, Aram Zephaniah lifted his chin. The little prayer room, hollowed out adjacent to the broad stone corridors of the underground living area, had been silent. Aram whispered another quick prayer before he twisted around to look behind him.

Barrett Grayson stood breathless and waiting. From the wide eyes and drawn brows upon his young face, Aram could tell the news was dire. He rose carefully, his eyes on the boy. "What is it, son?"

"A shuttle just arrived," Barrett said, then hushed his voice to a whisper, "from Regiam. I-I mean Reticulum. Constable Engrell has requested your assistance. Come quickly."

He ran from the room, spurring Aram to follow him through the torchlit caves that had served as a temporary home for many Lumen and Logia since the fall of Prince Ternion. A shuttle from Regiam, the fallen royal city now renamed Reticulum, meant refugees of one sort or another. Once Aram found out who they were and their condition, he could place them in safe houses, away from the reach of the Progressive Legacy.

Water seeping through the bronze-colored stone reflected the outer lighting system of the two-person craft. It was really too small for interstellar travel and should not have made the journey from the central planet of Crenet to its moon, Archet, where the Logia chose to hide. It had obviously taken quite a few hits. The damage was so extensive that the ship would have to be destroyed or abandoned. The Crown Himself must have carried the shuttle to them.

As Aram stood on a ledge jutting over the wide, open cave below, attendants paced all around the ship, waiting for the passengers to emerge. A few others scattered about, quellers in hand should the shuttle reveal an adversary. Aram's eyes caught the gaze of Stu Engrell, former member of Prince Ternion's Praesidium. Concern lined the man's haggard face.

The hum of the shuttle's engines dwindled into a panicked cry of a baby. Barrett glanced nervously toward Aram. To calm him, Aram held up a hand and murmured, "Trust the Crown, son." The ramp extended, lowering to the ground as the hatch popped open. A woman's whimper joined the baby's crying, echoing off the surrounding stone. The men with quellers closed in around the ship.

Aram whispered a prayer as he moved down a set of stairs cut into the rock. He passed the crowd of attendants to Stu's side.

"Who is it?" Aram asked.

Stu shook his head. "No contact was made prior to landing. But look." He pointed to the open hatch. The symbol of the Logia—a circle vertically divided in half by a curved line, and again horizontally by a jagged line—was carved into the bulkhead.

The woman, swathed in robes of deep jewel tones, stumbled down the ramp a few feet, clutching a howling bundle close to her. The people who had run onboard followed her, trying to slow her down. She crossed to Aram and Stu before she collapsed. Reacting quickly, Aram moved to catch her, careful to keep the baby from falling. Stu helped him lower her to the ground. It took Aram a moment before he recognized her bruised and bloodied face.

"Sasha ..." he gasped.

The young woman sobbed as relief passed through her eyes. "Aram. Stu. We ... we made it?"

"Aye," Stu confirmed gently. "What happened?"

Sasha Leighton was the daughter of Harlan Cromley, a well-respected Logia and head of Justice under the Praesidium. She had married Dorsey Leighton several years back. Dorsey, one of Harlan's advisors, was also Logia. They'd had a son, Chase, nearly a year ago. It really shouldn't have surprised Aram to see her here, but he couldn't avoid the shock.

"My father … and D-Dorsey …" She wept, clinging to the child. "They killed them, Aram."

He held Sasha close, sharing a pained look with Stu. They both knew that she spoke of the Legacy, and the news was beyond devastating. "Oh, my child, my heart grieves for you," Aram said.

She panted for breath, and Aram realized she was much worse off than he had thought. "They hurt you too," he murmured.

"Barrett." Stu stepped back, calling out to the young man who still watched from the ledge above.

Aram shook his head. While Barrett was skilled with the gift of restoration, Sasha's injuries were beyond him. "It is her time," he said solemnly. "Barrett cannot help her."

"I had to—to …" she coughed, shifting the crying child into his arms, "… get the baby to safety …"

"*Soli Deo Gloria*," Aram whispered, looking down at the infant boy.

"Please, Aram—please take care … of him," she pleaded through tears and body-wracking coughs.

Aram nodded, his heart deeply saddened. It had taken much courage for this young woman to survive such an attack and pilot a shuttle that great a distance only to bid her child good-bye. So much pain the Legacy had caused.

"I promise," he said.

The baby cried, tiny fingers reaching for his mother. She smiled tenderly at him, lifting a weak, shaky hand to touch him. A final sigh closed her eyes, and as her head lolled against Aram's arm, he felt her pass from this life.

"May you find comfort and rest in the arms of our Creator King, my child." Aram spoke the blessing as he drew her closer in a final embrace. The baby's crying intensified into an urgent wail.

Aram gently transferred Sasha's body to the waiting arms of two men standing by. He stood, cuddling and shushing the baby. Stu watched with despair in his eyes. "I've alerted Redic and Callum."

With a nod, Aram pulled the infant to his chest. "It's time for all of us to disappear. The Legacy is ruthless. I am taking the child to Etta. Harlan's grandson will be raised Logia. He would have wanted it that way."

Stu nodded. "That's what Callum hoped you would do. He suggests you leave immediately, in case they were followed. We'll take care of Sasha."

Looking back at Sasha's body, Aram sighed. "Protect us, my King," he murmured, turning his eyes to the tiny, questioning face in his arms. "Protect us all."

CHAPTER 1

Day 9092 PLR: Revenant

Captain Chase Leighton stood at the bottom of the ramp of his ship, the *Halcyon*. The crew had already boarded and was now waiting for him. But he couldn't leave just yet. He had something more important than an on-schedule run launch.

The loud, bustling Ghost bay faded into the background as he saw her. She ran across the prep strip, ducking around mechanics and shipmates. A load of pallets rolled into her path, but she whipped around the other side to get to him. She'd only been gone since yesterday, but by the Crown, he'd missed her.

"Come on, Captain," his first officer and medic, Nicodemus Church, urged from the craft behind him. Nic was several years older than Chase, brawny, with light blond hair and blue eyes. The two had a tight-knit friendship, and because of that, Church often razzed Chase about his rank. He now emphasized the title with a full dose of sarcasm. "Lancaster's already got permission to take off."

"Give me a minute, Nic," he murmured, walking a few steps to greet his beautiful wife, Trista.

1

He wrapped her in his arms, pressing a kiss to her forehead. Her long, soft brown hair tumbled over his hands as he pulled her close. "Thought you'd forget," he said.

"I'd never forget. This is our tradition." She smiled up at him, her brown eyes sparkling with a touch of gold and a good dose of spirit. Over his shoulder, she waved at his officer. "Hi, Nic."

Church grumbled his acknowledgment and slipped back into the ship. Chase chuckled, shaking his head as he looked down at Trista. "Everything all right?" he asked.

"Yes," she answered, her fingers playing with the wedding band on her opposite hand. It was a mannerism that Chase loved, simply because he knew how much that ring meant to her. "I just got back from that routine run to Doppel. I'm glad I made it home before you left."

Before every run, as often as possible, Chase and Trista met on the floor of the docking bay to kiss good-bye and wish each other Crownspeed. He normally would have met her as her ship docked, but with his mission scheduled to head out, he had been unable to do so. He'd spent a few moments delaying his crew as he paced in front of the *Halcyon*, waiting and hoping that she'd come. And here she was. It was worth the scolding he'd probably catch from Redic—head of the Ghost movement—by way of his son, Seraph.

"Where are you headed?" she asked.

Chase brushed a stray lock of hair from her face. "We're going to check out the possibility of a Logia in hiding with his family on Ossia. One of our contacts alerted us that the Logia was on the books for interrogation but somehow slipped away."

"Stay safe," Trista whispered.

"Always. I have you to come home to." Chase smiled, reciting the words they always said to each other. "Do you have any scheduled runs?"

Trista shook her head. "But if someone links ..."

Chase pressed his forehead to hers. "You stay safe, then, too."

"Always." She smiled playfully, snuggling into his arms again.

"All right. I have to go." Chase rested his chin atop her head. He wanted to stay close and not leave her. "I've kept the crew waiting long enough, and Church just might take off without me if I don't get up there."

"Would that be so bad?" she asked, lifting an eyebrow as she glanced up at him.

"Oh, tempting woman!" Chase grinned at her, placing a tender, loving kiss on her lips. "I love you, Tris."

"I love you too, Chase. Crownspeed."

"Don't forget," Chase said as he withdrew from her, stepping backward toward the ramp. He pointed at her with a grin. "We've got that anniversary dinner Lila and Echo are planning for us when I get back."

A look of surprise flickered over Trista's pretty features as she tilted her head and folded her arms over her chest. "You weren't supposed to know about that."

With a wink, he jogged back to her for another quick, close hug before running up the ramp of his ship. "Come with me," he called out from the doorway.

"You know I can't," she answered with a smile, backing away from the ship as the engines started to roar. She shouted, "Redic would fire us both."

"It was worth a shot!" Chase shouted back with another grin, waving to her.

Her shoulders rose with a soft chuckle as she lifted her fingers to her lips, blowing him a kiss. He gave her another wink before he ducked into the spacecraft, swallowed whole by the ramp. Dashing to the bridge, he dropped into the pilot's seat, saluting Trista through the viewport. She waved again, her eyes glued to the ship. He knew she'd be there until the *Halcyon* rolled out and took off.

"You two make me sick," Church muttered, leaning forward in the copilot's chair to initiate low thruster control. The ship rocked gently in reaction as it glided to the prep strip.

"Yeah," Lancaster, the communications officer, added from his station. "Just because you're married ..."

"Shut it," Chase said, settling back in his chair with a smile. "You guys are just jealous, and you know it."

"Whatever, Captain Lovebird. Strap in," Church replied. "We still clear?"

"Yeah," Lancaster said. "Although Junior wants to know what the delay is all about. I told him that we had an internal issue that was already under control."

Chase smiled, grateful for his crew's solidarity and loyalty. He'd talk to Seraph later and explain the real reason for the delay. Junior could certainly cut him a little slack. After all, when they returned, he and Trista would be celebrating their first year of marriage.

Chase situated the mesh harness over his chest, attaching it to the affixed joints on both sides of the seat. Happiness reigned in his heart today. Nothing was going to change that.

◆

Day 9094 PLR: Revenant

The corridor that ran behind the sacrarium was empty, allowing Trista to take her time. The walls served as a memorial to the Ruler Prince and those who had sacrificed their lives in His name. Redic had insisted that it not be a place of sadness, but of gratitude and hope. Trista paused for a moment before the image of her parents, Antin and Kylea Carlisle. She really didn't remember them, as they had died when she was very young, but her sister Lila had told her many stories. She felt like she knew them well.

The Reserve on Revenant was indeed a unique base and headquarters, perfectly suited for the Ghosts. Built underground years ago, during Prince Ternion's reign, it held every possible accommodation necessary for making life comfortable. It had been intended as a hidden sanctuary for the Ruler Prince Himself, should He face violent opposition. The location was off the system map, only accessible through a wormhole—the Pathway—that the Crown had provided. Few of Ternion's men knew the coordinates. Ternion had never made it that far, having been executed by the Tribunal before anyone could help Him. Redic Clairet had made his escape from the Progressive Legacy to the Reserve and eventually established it as the Ghost base. Shortly thereafter, Trista's sister, Lila, had made it their home when their parents were killed by the Legacy. Trista had grown up here.

The northwest atrium was Trista's favorite place. Not only was it where Chase had proposed, but the setting was serene and inviting. Silvery-gray marble tiled the floor. In the center, a charming fountain trickled softly into a small circular pool. The lip of the pool, built from the same marble as the flooring, was knee-high and wide enough to sit on. Medium-sized trees and bushes surrounded the large room, giving it a vibrant atmosphere. Large, cube-shaped planters scattered in various spots burst with colored blooms. Delicate black iron tables and chairs were placed neatly around the room.

Next to the pool, Trista's friend, Selah Grayson, waited for her. Selah, on an errand for Echo, needed to discuss with her a few more details for tonight's anniversary gathering. Selah was Redic's daughter, and the first to bear him a grandchild. As Trista crossed the atrium, she saw Selah cradling her handsome infant son, Quinn.

"Ooh, Selah," Trista said softly as she approached. "May I?"

Selah greeted her with a smile, offering the swaddled baby to her waiting arms. "Certainly," she said.

The child slept soundly, completely unaware that the arms that now enfolded him were not his mother's. Sunlight poured in from the thick, double-layered glass ceiling above, streaming natural warmth into the room. Trista smiled as she held the baby, dreaming of her own. The day was coming, she knew.

Selah shared in Trista's smile. "It's hard for me to put him down."

"I can imagine. Do you want him back?" Trista asked.

"Oh, no. I have to learn to share," Selah said with a soft laugh. "Have you and Chase thought about …?"

"Oh, yes, especially now that Lila and Sterling have Blane. The aunt and uncle card isn't cutting it. We both want at least two, but we'll take whatever the Crown gives us." Trista sat down next to her friend. "We've just held off because one of us is usually out on a run somewhere. And I think we're hoping that someday soon, we'll have victory over the Legacy."

"Here, we do." Selah smiled gently. "I can't imagine raising a child under the confines of the Legacy. I wouldn't do it. But here, Quinn will know the freedom and sovereignty of the Crown."

Trista's finger ran tenderly along the baby's cheek. "He's so handsome, Selah."

"Thank you," Selah murmured, leaning over Trista's shoulder to look down at her son. "I think so too."

Trista joined Selah in her laughter, causing Quinn to stir a bit. Bouncing him lightly, Trista settled him back into his cozy slumber. The ladies sat in thoughtful silence until Selah's husband, Cam, her brother Seraph, and their friend Brax passed through, deep in conversation.

"But Chase wouldn't do it, anyway. I don't know why they are calling for him. That makes no sense," Seraph said.

With a casual shrug, Cam replied, "All I know is that Remy received the request this morning, and it came across the proper channel."

"Could it be a snare?" Brax asked.

Cam shook his head. "I don't think so. Frisco is usually pretty careful. And Bruiser has always followed orders."

The men paused as Cam's gaze fell on Selah. His look of concern dissolved into one of joy. "Ah, excuse me," he said to his friends before crossing toward his wife and child.

Trista greeted Cam by offering Quinn to him. Cam carefully tucked the baby boy into his arms, looking down at Selah. "How's my little family today?" he asked.

"Quinn decided to sleep in after his long night." Selah smiled, rising to slide into Cam's embrace as well. "And that allowed his mama to sleep a little, too."

"Good." Cam kissed the top of Selah's head. "Your doctor will kill me if I don't let you get enough rest," he said with a playful smirk toward Brax.

"That's right. Use me as an excuse." Brax laughed.

Trista stood, angling her head as she peered past the others to Seraph. "Did I hear you say something about Chase?" she asked.

Seraph's smile twisted into a backpedaling mask of nonchalance. "Oh, it's nothing about him, really, although the *Halcyon* is en route and set to arrive this afternoon. When they land, I have to have a little talk with him about holding up his ship a couple days ago to bid you farewell."

With a blush, Trista dropped her gaze and fiddled with her ring. She hated that Chase would get in trouble. The delay had really been her fault. Seraph nudged her, offering a forgiving smile.

"No big deal, Tris. I'm just going to hassle him a bit. And by the way, Echo is expecting you at nineteen hundred hours in the central atrium. She and Lila have everyone at the Reserve in on that dinner."

Brax cracked a grin. "She asked me to sing."

"She did not," Seraph bantered, popping Brax in the chest.

Trista smiled, both in response to Brax and at the idea that her husband was on his way home. Tonight was indeed going to be a night to remember. Even if Brax *did* decide to warble for them.

Seraph continued, the mask ebbing away into concern, "But we were just debating what to do about this link Remy received."

"What's going on?" Trista asked, tucking her arms around her middle.

"Bruiser said they're having some sort of computer malfunction in their shuttle's navsys. They are stranded on Viam and want Chase to come unravel the situation," Cam said, rocking his little one gently.

Trista frowned. Chase never made runs to fix computer issues. He was a ship captain. That meant that his Logia gift had somehow been exposed. "How does Bruiser even know about Chase?"

Brax pointed at her. "See? I say it's a set-up."

"And like you said, Ser," Trista said, tilting her head in confusion, "he doesn't use his gifts lightly. He wouldn't just go out on a routine run like that. Besides, we have people to do that kind of thing. Like me."

Cam glanced to Brax and Seraph. "I don't like the sound of it."

Seraph nodded. "Me, either. I'll alert my dad and Remy. We'll just tell Frisco to contract someone local."

"I'll go. I'll check it out," Trista offered.

Seraph narrowed his eyes. "I don't think so, Trista. It sounds risky. Besides, you're not a mechanic."

"A mechanic isn't required if it's a navsys issue. Viam's not far. In fact, Lila's making a run in about an hour. I can ride with her to the Junction and meet up with Frisco and Bruiser." Trista frowned at Seraph's uncertain expression. "I can handle myself. I can get in and out of there quickly. If I see something shady, I'll duck out."

The men shared another silent exchange. Trista tapped her foot, waiting for someone to say something. It seemed silly to squander resources on a contracted computer specialist when she could do it just as easily.

"I'd say get approval from Redic first," Cam advised Seraph.

Seraph nodded. "Yeah, Trista. Let me talk it over with my dad. I'm hesitant to say yes."

"I've done it a million times before, Ser. I'll be okay." She smiled.

"I'll keep that in mind." Seraph winked at her before nodding to the others. "I'll link you, Trista," he said as he headed for the opposite door.

"Don't bother. I'll come with you," Trista said, waving her good-bye to the others.

◆

"You think this is a good idea?" Redic asked, leaning against his desk as he spoke with Seraph, Trista, and Remy Sullivan, Redic's assistant and right hand.

Redic Clairet, with his silvering reddish-brown hair and sturdy physique, usually gave a daunting impression. Trista, however, had a different view of him entirely. As leader of the Ghosts, she admired and respected him, but she also knew the tenderhearted side. He was really more of a patriarch, acting as a father to those he commanded. She loved him as such.

"Were I in Chase's shoes, I'd say no," Seraph answered, reclining in his black leather chair.

"But you're not," Trista responded, straightening in her own. She wasn't trying to be difficult, but Seraph's air of authority, particularly speaking for Chase, frustrated her. "Sir, I've done this kind of thing many times. Really. I can handle it."

"It's a little different this time, Trista," Remy said in her soft way. "Especially in light of the fact that they know about Chase's gifts. He's made sure that only the Crew and select others know about that. Something is up."

Redic blew out a breath, pushing off the desk to walk around to his chair. "What do we know about Frisco and Bruiser?"

"Frisco is solid," Seraph responded. "He and his sister joined up with us when they were teenagers. Lost their parents to the pandemic on Gravatus years ago. We've never had issue with him."

"Bruiser?" Redic asked as he lowered into his seat.

"He's fairly new. Frisco brought him on a couple of months back," Remy answered, crossing her arms over her chest with subtle grace. "Said he was a Zenith who became disillusioned with the Legacy and wanted to serve something with purpose."

Redic cocked his head, looking at Remy. "You don't believe him."

While Redic was the patriarch of the Ghosts, Remy was the matriarch. She and Redic had been lifelong friends, and many Ghosts pondered the true nature of their relationship, although there had never been even the slightest hint of anything romantic between the two. But where Redic was, Remy was there too. She often spoke for him, and he trusted her word over anyone else's.

Remy held Redic's gaze. "I'm cautious to go one way or the other. I've not had much interaction with him, aside from the initial assessments. He came across as rather honest, though."

"Mmm," Redic said, pressing his lips together in thought. He tipped his head, taking in a slow, steady lungful of air. "I'm on the fence on this one, Trista. I don't want you to take any unnecessary risks."

"I'll be careful and watchful, sir. Trust me. I don't relish the thought of becoming a Legacy prisoner," Trista assured him.

"All of our CSs normally go out with an escort. I'll go with her," Seraph suggested.

"Um …" Remy said, shaking her head.

"No," Trista insisted. "No. If it is a setup, it would be much easier to get one person out than two. Seraph, I'll be all right. I promise."

Redic nodded, clasping his hands before him as he leaned back in his chair. "She's right, son. All right, Trista, you have my approval. But safety above all else. At the first sign of anything suspicious, you get out of there. Understood?"

"Understood," Trista said, rising. "Thank you, sir."

With a smile, Redic nodded again. "Bring our men home, soldier."

"You got it." Trista gave a quick salute, along with a wink.

"And we'll see you tonight. I understand that Brax is slotted for the entertainment portion of your dinner," Redic said, lifting an eyebrow.

Trista laughed softly. "I might just have to sabotage something else on Frisco's shuttle, then."

Redic chuckled, shaking his head. With a respectful nod toward Remy and Seraph, Trista turned and headed for the door. As she exited, she heard Seraph say, "Dad, this is a mistake."

CHAPTER 2

The trip to Viam wasn't far, given the Pathway. Trista enjoyed the ride with her sister and the crew of the outbound *Vanguard*. They dropped her close to the docking bay from which Bruiser had reported to Remy. It wasn't the usual bay the Ghosts used for the Junction stop.

As planned, she'd hitch a ride home with Frisco and Bruiser. She shouldered a tool pack and strolled casually through the streets that led to the bay. Finding the ship wasn't terribly hard. Most of the bay was empty. Trista swallowed back the notion that perhaps it wasn't so much empty as abandoned.

The docking lights around the field were dark, and no light shone from within the two-man shuttle. As Trista approached, she looked around with uncertainty. If she were any kind of smart, she would walk away now and link Rev One or Ghost Three. Seraph would just love to hear how right he was. But surely Frisco and Bruiser wouldn't have ditched their shuttle. Well, if they had, Trista would just get the navsys running and pilot it home. The shuttle's console model wasn't much different from the one she and Chase used for getaways.

Trista pulled out her link and connected to the signal that Bruiser had used to reach Remy. Speaking low into the device, she tried to raise either of the men, but to no avail. Maybe they just went to grab a bite to eat. She'd give them a little time to get back before she took off for home.

Adjusting her tool pack, she stepped to the door of the shuttle and placed a seal override on the outer hull. It was a handy little tool that the Ghosts had put together for their shuttles. It sometimes worked on Legacy ships too. Before she input her code, though, the door shifted open and the stair unit unfolded, allowing her access.

Oh, boy. Trista swallowed, patting her tool pack for a screwdriver. It wasn't much of a weapon, but it might buy her just enough time to get away, should someone be waiting. She gripped it tightly in one hand and held her link in the other as she eased onto the dark ship.

Blinking her eyes to adjust them to the sudden darkness, she skimmed the shadows. She resisted the urge to call out the men's names. If they were on board, they could be either dead or injured. She really hoped that wasn't the case. She didn't know if she'd be able to handle that.

The shuttle consisted of a small middle cabin, a compartmented cargo bay to the rear, and the cockpit. She brushed past the bulkhead that separated the cabin and the cockpit and settled in the pilot's chair. The tool pack slid along her arm and onto the floor, which was exactly where she needed it. Giving the console a once-over, Trista frowned. Everything seemed in order.

Deciding that she could work a bit quicker with her hands free, she shoved her link into her pocket. She then knelt down, replaced the screwdriver in the tool pack, and rummaged through her tools to retrieve her hand torch. Activating it with a flick of a switch, she angled it toward the navsys processor. Nothing looked out of the ordinary on the outside. She'd guessed it was an internal issue, anyway. Placing the hand torch aside, she popped the casing off the box, and a jumble of wires blossomed out in wild tangles. Yeah, that's what she hated about working on navsys processors.

Craning her neck to get a good look at the wires, she worked herself down under the console. Something on the floor caught her eye. She reached behind her, grasping at the hand torch. The shaky light danced and flickered under the console before coming to rest on a human face. A swollen, bloodied, gruesome face.

Trista screamed and rose up, dropping the light as she smacked her head against the underside of the console. She didn't care about the pain. She just wanted to get out of there and report back to Revenant. She—

Meaty hands grasped her around the waist and lifted her off the ground.

Screaming again, Trista pummeled her fists against the muscular arms that held her. She wriggled and kicked until the man eventually released her.

"Bruiser!" she cried, surprised, but relieved to see him.

His wild eyes narrowed on her as his hand slipped around the back of her neck.

"Bruiser, wh—?"

Power tensed his muscles as his fingers gripped her hair. In complete control, he slammed her head against the console twice. Trista cried out, grabbing at his hand, but it was no use. He whirled her around and sent her careening into the bulkhead. She landed on the floor in a whimpering heap.

He left her there as he flicked the console into its active mode. She curled onto her side, knowing she should get up and at least try to fight. Or run. The throbbing in her head disagreed, though. Bruiser was three times bigger than she was. Fighting would only lead to further pain. And she probably couldn't run fast enough. What could she— Her link. She could use her link.

Bruiser grumbled into the ship's comsys. "Leighton didn't show, but he sent someone in his place."

"We're not interested in common prisoners, Mr. Bruiser. We're only interested in the Logia," came the reply.

"It's Leighton's wife."

Silence met Bruiser's offer. Trista wondered if perhaps the contact had severed the connection. She patted her pocket for her link. On the floor across from her, the bloodied face opened its eyes. Trista recognized Frisco. Oh, by the Crown, what had Bruiser done?

The strong, chunky hands hoisted Trista from the floor again, shoving her in the chair. Her link slipped from her fingers and rolled under the console. Blast.

"We'll have none of that. No distress calls. Understand?" Bruiser said.

Unable to stop herself from trembling, Trista asked, "Wh-what do you want with me?"

"We want nothing from you," Bruiser answered with a growl. "We want your husband."

"W-we who?"

The comsys fizzled with static. "A regiment of Zeniths are on their way, Mr. Bruiser. You are to stay with the prisoner until they arrive."

Bruiser's attention returned to the console. "And my compensation?"

"You will not receive the full reward, but you'll get a portion. Come by my office tomorrow morning."

A look of disappointment flickered over Bruiser's puffy features. "Yes, sir."

"Out." With that, the link terminated.

Trista looked up at the wide man. She hadn't known him for very long, but she suddenly understood Remy's hesitancy in trusting him. "You—you betrayed us for money?"

"You wouldn't understand."

"Try me, Bruiser," Trista said, offering him the benefit of the doubt. There had to be a reason. And maybe in talking it through, he'd realize how wrong he'd been. "The Ghosts are good people. Why would you do such a thing?"

Bruiser slammed his hands on the arms of the chair, leaning in inches from Trista's face. "You're trying to get me to let you go."

"Y-yes," Trista whispered. "This is crazy. They helped you, took you in. Even Frisco—"

Bruiser's hands flew from the chair and threateningly squeezed Trista's neck instead. "Shut it. Unless you wish to die." He growled, close enough for her to smell some form of intoxicant on his breath.

Trista gasped and lowered her eyes, only to see a shaky hand reaching for her link on the floor. She held her breath as she watched the quivering, frantic fingers press the button to signal a distress call. Bruiser's eyes followed hers, but not before Frisco flicked the link away from his hand. Bruiser let her go, then lifted the device, holding it before Trista. "The Zeniths will find use for this."

"Bruiser, please," she squeaked out with a cough.

Metal-on-metal rapping indicated the arrival of the Zeniths. By the Crown, they were fast. If only she'd had more time, she might have been able to convince Bruiser to let her go.

"Enter," Bruiser shouted, staring at Trista.

She closed her eyes, murmuring a soft prayer. The Ghosts sprang people from Legacy prison ships on a regular basis. And with no contact, they'd be looking for her. At least Chase would. He would come for her. She just hoped she'd be processed swiftly so that he could find her.

A single Zenith, armed with the brigade's standard slayer, stepped onboard. "Mr. Bruiser?" he asked.

"In here," Bruiser answered. "The prisoner is unarmed."

"All right, Ghost, hands in the air," the Zenith said, stepping in front of Trista. He gestured toward the exit with the barrel of his gun. "Outside."

Trista stood, raising her hands as the man instructed. Bruiser led them out, and the Zenith behind her pressed his gun into her back. It was more a matter of humiliation than security. Trista wisely held her tongue.

As she stepped from the ship, two other Zeniths grabbed her and slammed her against the hull of the shuttle. They patted her down before wrestling her arms behind her to place them in cuffs. She watched Bruiser hand the lead Zenith her link, explaining a few of the details of its customization. Blast. That meant a security breach back home.

"The ship is now the property of the Legacy, Mr. Bruiser. Do you have alternative transportation?" the Zenith asked.

"Yeah. I'm on my way to Crenet," he answered. "I have bounty to claim."

"And we have a prisoner to process. Thank you for your loyalty, sir," the Zenith said, bidding good-bye to Bruiser.

Bruiser glared at Trista, giving her a mock salute. One Zenith sealed the little ship while the others surrounded her, herding her toward a larger shuttle docked next to the Ghost ship. They, thankfully, hadn't seen Frisco, and apparently Bruiser had forgotten about him. Perhaps the Ghosts would respond to her distress signal and get to him before the Zeniths did.

◆

Chase stretched, adding the final detail to his report. He had slipped off the ship as soon as it touched down, but there was no sign of Trista. He reminded himself that she might have gone out on a run, or maybe she was helping Echo prepare for this evening. Either way, he'd find her after he submitted the required information to Remy.

Several members of his crew had searched high and low for any sign of the reported Logia and his family, but the home on Ossia had been abandoned and ransacked. He and Church even scoured the place, looking for a hidden door or something that might have led to a concealed shelter. Nothing. The venture was discouraging. It meant the family had been captured and the information had not gone public, or the raiding Zeniths had executed them on sight and the announcement had not yet been posted on their lexical upload matrix. That would be surprising, though, as the Legacy loved to use the LUM to brag about their forays.

He transmitted the report to Rev One and then rose to leave the bridge. The maintenance crew was already onboard, shutting down the various systems and running their standard checks. He nodded to each one as he passed, thanking them for caring for his ship.

His link went crazy in his pocket. Pulling out the tiny device, he peeked at it. Trista's distress signal. What the blazes?

Dashing down the ramp, he scampered to the nearest operations console, tapping into its DDL. His eyes scanned the list of registered runs, and found what he was looking for:

CS: Trista Leighton
Outgoing Craft: *The Vanguard*
Drop Location: Viam, sector 09.24-43M
Status: Emergency Run
Priority Level: Three
Reason: Navsys issue

The *Vanguard* was Brendan Faulkner's ship, of which Lila was first officer. And with the Pathway, Viam was a heartbeat away. *Blazes, Trista, hold on.* He clutched his link and ran for his personal transport, located in the smaller bay.

His mind ran every possible scenario. Could Trista have tripped her distress call accidentally? Was she in serious trouble? He considered trying to raise her, which was against policy following a distress signal. Instead, he tried Lila, but couldn't get a strong enough connection. So intent on his next move, he nearly plowed into Seraph, who had entered the bay with Cam and Brax. They all seemed to be in a hurry.

"Hey, Chase. You okay?" Cam asked.

"Trista," he said, holding up his link.

"We're already on it, man," Brax answered, pointing toward Britt Lockhart's ship, the *Lambent Stallion*. The shuttle was open, engines started.

"I'm going, too," Chase said, moving toward his shuttle just another field beyond the *Stallion*. "She's not had any experience with the Legacy."

"No," Seraph replied, following him. "Let us handle this, Chase. You just came in from a two-day run, man. There's no way you'll be able to stay alert enough to fly."

"And there's no way I'll be able to rest, knowing that Trista might be in trouble," Chase said, lifting the hatch.

"They wanted you," Seraph said, staring at him. "They know, Chase. They know what you can do."

Chase paused, dropping his eyes to the ground as he released a heavy sigh. It was why he'd kept his gifts quiet to begin with. He'd had a feeling they would someday land Trista in a load of trouble. The day had come.

"You got organized awfully quick," Chase commented. He couldn't help but wonder why. Her distress call had only gone off moments ago.

"We were on standby," Seraph said with a sigh. "I kind of expected something like this to happen."

Chase stared at his friend. Expected? That meant he'd knowingly placed Trista in danger. "Did you send her?" he asked.

"She insisted on going. I did everything I could to stop her," Seraph answered.

Trying to remain calm, Chase closed his eyes. The link alarm sounded again, saving him by refocusing his thoughts. He scanned the readout. The location had changed. Glancing at Seraph, Chase said, "Same docking bay, two levels up."

Seraph scowled, squeezing his eyes closed. "Fine," he said, giving in to Chase. "Cam and I will take the first site. You and Brax take the second. Let us know if you run into trouble."

Chase climbed onboard, strapping in as Brax followed him and sat down in Trista's spot. Chase hadn't flown this ship without Trista next to him. Although he normally enjoyed Brax's company, it irked him that Brax was there instead. Chase frowned as he started up the shuttle. "Forgive my lack of small talk. I'm just not in the mood."

"Understandable, man," Brax said, pulling the harness over his head. "I know how you feel."

Chase gripped the throttle, perhaps a bit too tightly. Yeah, he'd heard the stories. He even remembered when the *Valor's Fool* crew flew its mission that ended up restoring Prince Ternion to His glory. Brax had nearly lost Belle during that time, so yes, he probably did understand. But this was Trista. His Trista. Blast. He yanked back on the throttle, speeding the little shuttle out of the bay and onward to Viam. The *Stallion* wasn't far behind.

CHAPTER 3

In his years serving ExMed, Dr. Reid Terces had never felt nervous. Through all the procedures, all the demonstrations and presentations, nerves never bothered him. Today, however, his mentor and partner, Dr. Cyndra Niveli, by way of her husband Admiral Altus Niveli, had dragged him into a meeting with the Spokesman of the Tribunal. Reid had to remind himself to remain cool.

The conference room, located on the upper level of the Justice Center, had no windows. A long black monolith served as the table, surrounded by dark-gray, cushioned chairs. The walls were painted the same charcoal, giving the room a foreboding air. Terces hadn't ever really noticed until today.

Cyndra had suggested that they take a seat close to the Bands screen, where the Spokesman would make his appearance. They swiveled a couple of the chairs around, facing the wide screen mounted on the far wall. Cyndra activated it, then sat to wait.

Before long, the Spokesman stared back at them. It was the first time Reid had encountered him personally. The man before them—Reid was fairly certain that he was human—had no hair on his face or head. No eyebrows, no eyelashes. The Spokesman's features were angled and pale, almost as if he had been crudely carved from stone. His eyes, black as night, held nothing but disinterest. The word that came to Reid's mind was soulless.

Dr. Niveli rose, glaring at Reid. He understood. He quickly got to his feet as well, hoping that the Spokesman would appreciate the show of respect.

"Thank you for seeing us today, Your Excellency. As my husband, Admiral Niveli, may have told you, we have a proposal that we would like to bring before the Tribunal. We are seeking approval for a new ExMed procedure," Cyndra said.

The Spokesman's voice graveled along his words. "ExMed procedures do not require approval from us, Dr. Niveli. Why do you waste our time?"

"I'm afraid that your approval is required for this one, my lord. The Agency of Justice and the Agency of Medicine have both banned this particular procedure, as it has failed on every subject we have used. The results have been consistently fatal. But we believe we've found the source of the problem, and we'd like to try again," Dr. Niveli answered.

"Explain."

Niveli gestured to Reid. It was his turn. Filling his lungs, he stepped forward. "Using hunter technology, the procedure involves the surgical implantation of three transputer units in the back of the skull. We began with only two, but Dr. Niveli and I believe that the third one is crucial for proper functioning. Once the implantation is complete, by using varied impulses, we can take away and create memories within the person's mind, sculpting, if you will, the model citizen we desire."

The Spokesman's black eyes closed momentarily before he resumed his imposing stare. "Why not just turn them into hunters, Doctor?" A second voice had joined his deep one. Terces realized that another member of the Tribunal had asked the question.

"Hunters are, by nature, violent and often unstable. While they provide invaluable service to the Legacy, we want to create a breed of citizens who can function in our society without the outer biomechanical devices. Citizens who can contribute to the daily process of our lives," Reid said, forcing calm into his voice.

The black eyes narrowed. "You wish for us to override the agencies and authorize this based on your *theories*, Doctor?"

"We'd like an opportunity to proceed with a single prisoner, my lord," Cyndra said, stepping in. "If it doesn't work, we will abandon this method entirely."

The Spokesman lifted his square chin, looking down on the two doctors for a long moment. His eyes rolled back in his head before he closed them and said, "We have a particular prisoner in mind." He looked at the doctors once again. "We will give the information to your husband, Dr. Niveli. Our one condition is that you officially pronounce this prisoner deceased and give her a new identity."

Reid nodded his agreement to the condition, as Niveli confirmed, "Yes, my lord. Immediately."

"Good. We expect a full report when it is done." The screen winked into nothingness.

Dr. Niveli turned to Reid with a smug smile. "Congratulations, Doctor. You sold him on the project."

"I think it had far more to do with their desire to get rid of this prisoner," Reid said, "but no matter. We've got our subject and permission to go forward."

"As soon as I leave here, I will hunt down Altus and get the information regarding the prisoner. We'll send a Zenith to deliver her to ExMed Acquisition. Do you have any preliminary preparations they can do for you?"

Reid shook his head. "No; it's all done by the technicians. I have some things to pull together as well. Just tell them to link me as soon as she's arrived."

"Do you require any additional staff?" Cyndra asked. "The reason I ask is I have a group of doctors who might be interested in your work. They could assist."

"Aftal and I have it under control," Reid said. "But they are welcome to observe the procedure."

"Excellent," Dr. Niveli replied, clasping her hands together. "All right, Doctor, let's get to work."

Reid gave another nod before gesturing for Cyndra to go ahead of him. The lights snapped off as they reached the door, leaving the conference room submerged in shadow. Reid's thoughts returned to his new subject. She would soon find herself in a similar, sudden darkness. He just hoped that his theories would prove right this time.

The bay looked as though it hadn't been operational for some time. Containers sprawled about, crumpled and collapsed, splintered pallets scattered recklessly, docking lights bent or even toppled over. It was a hazard just to fly through it. Chase shook his head. "She should have known better," he muttered to no one in particular.

Brax glanced at him. "Maybe the other levels are in better shape."

Chase began to flick on the outer lighting system, then thought better of it. If the Legacy was waiting to ensnare him, he wasn't going to advertise his presence with beams of light. And he didn't imagine Trista was skulking around the shadowed edges of the bay anyway.

The comsys crackled with static before Cam asked, "You got anything, Chase?"

Chase was glad Cam didn't use their call signs. Regular first names gave a sense of anonymity. Among the Ghosts, he was known as Logia Three. That would be a dead giveaway to anyone listening in. And from the looks of the bay, no one would hesitate to blow his craft—and him—right out of commission.

"We're doing a slow flythrough along the prep strip," Chase answered. "So far, we've got nothing here, but I'm going to put down for a more intensive search. Brax will stay close to the shuttle, but I want to—"

"Negative!" Cam replied, his tone changing to one of urgency. "We need Brax immediately. We've got a casualty onboard."

"Tell him to get up here now!" Seraph shouted in the background.

"Is it Trista?" Chase asked, shoving thruster control into reverse to slow them down.

"Negative, Chase. It's not Trista," Cam said, adding a touch of compassion to his words. "It's Frisco, and he requires Brax's immediate attention."

"Sounds serious," Brax commented.

"On our way," Chase responded with a sigh. It was a bittersweet mix of relief and panic that he felt. He was thankful Trista wasn't hurt, but that meant she was still missing. Well, he would drop off Brax and return to this level to scour it for a sign of her. She had to be here. He had to reach her before they ...

Chase blew out of the bay, circled around, and re-entered two stories down. He ignored the dull red lights that surrounded the Ghost shuttle and its field, indicating that the Zeniths had claimed it as Legacy property. Apparently, they hadn't left any soldiers behind to guard it. Or those soldiers had already been taken care of by Cam and Seraph.

Brax hopped out as Chase settled the shuttle on the prep strip. "You comin'?" he asked.

"I want to look for Trista," Chase answered, staring out the viewport.

Brax nodded as Seraph appeared at the top of the steps of the other shuttle. Seraph dashed down, exchanging places with Chase's passenger.

"Frisco's onboard. He's pretty beat up. Said that Bruiser sabotaged the ship and made the call for you to come. Bruiser then attacked Trista when she arrived, and called to report her. Frisco thinks they arrested her. He said that Zeniths took her from the ship at gunpoint," Seraph said. "Apparently, they wanted you. She was just a happenstance. As you can see, Zeniths have claimed the shuttle and could come back at any time. You should get out of here. Now."

"I'm going back to look for Trista. For a few minutes, anyway," Chase countered. "She's never gone up against the Legacy before, Ser. I'm not leaving her here to face them alone."

Seraph hung his head a moment, obviously disagreeing with Chase's choice. "I don't think she's here, Chase, but I'll grant you a few minutes. Then get yourself back to Rev. We'll meet you there. And if you don't find anything, I'll help you look for her."

Chase gritted his teeth, shifting the thruster control. "See you at home."

"Crownspeed, man."

Chase nodded again, closing the hatch as Seraph returned to the other ship. Bruiser had better hope never to cross paths with Chase. He'd kill the traitor with his bare hands.

Swallowing hard, Chase reminded himself that he shouldn't think such things. He was a Ghost, after all. And first and foremost, a Logia and a devoted follower of Prince Ternion. But maybe he could kill Bruiser just a little. He spun the tiny ship around and returned to the upper levels to search for Trista.

◆

"Trista Leighton."

Trista stood from among the weary and worn prisoners and walked toward the Zenith who had called her name. The processing phase hadn't taken long, but she had been instructed to wait—for what, she didn't know. The Legacy hadn't followed their standard operating procedure, from what she understood. Others who had survived Legacy imprisonment said they were asked basic questions, the answers were logged and submitted, and then they were stripped of all personal property and given the shameful red Legacy prison uniform. The Zeniths had asked her a few questions, but placed her in a cell immediately.

She thought they might send her to the interrogators for a more intensive round of questioning. Throughout the night, she'd prayed that she would be able to avoid interrogation. The stories she'd been told frightened her to the core.

She had seen the Justice Center before—from the outside. Plain gray brick buildings in the shape of a U loomed several stories above, blocking the sunlight. The Legacy had tried to dress it up with trees and other foliage, but they couldn't hide the formidable sense of doom that encompassed its campus. The inside was even worse.

When she arrived, only a handful of prisoners occupied the holding cell, but during the course of the night, many others had joined them, leaving little room to move. The room smelled foul, and while the chill in the air should have helped diminish the odor, it didn't. Her fretful prayers turned from escaping interrogation to complete salvation as she stared at the door, imploring the Crown to allow Chase walk through.

Two other Zeniths positioned themselves nearby as the first one unlocked the door to the cell. Trista guessed they anticipated escapees. No prisoners attempted such foolishness. The stingers in the Zeniths' hands ensured that.

"I thought court hours began at oh-eight-hundred hours," Trista said softly, hoping that she wasn't next on the interrogators' list.

The clock hanging on the opposite wall indicated that it was only oh-four-twenty, a time when most people were sleeping. She realized how exhausted she was, but adrenaline kept her going somehow. There was no way she could sleep in this place.

The Zenith laughed as he grabbed the chain between her wrist binders, leading her out of the cell before connecting it to a second length of chain attached to his belt. "You don't get a trial, honey."

Trista stopped walking, frozen with terror. The Zenith paused momentarily, looking at her. "What do you mean?" she asked.

He yanked her forward. "ExMed is waiting for you."

Trista's heart nearly stopped. She tugged back on the chain, and the binders cut into her wrists. It was futile, as the Zenith could easily overpower her, anyway. The ones guarding the entrance to the cell angled their stingers toward her. Her captor lifted his hand toward them and shook his head. "Orders are not to harm her in any way."

She found some relief in that. If they weren't to harm her, then perhaps ExMed would be compassionate as well. She decided that, at this point, obedience would probably be her best option.

The Zenith led her to a waiting lift and forced her in before taking his place next to her. He smashed his access card to the reader, then flipped it up and down while they waited. Trista held her breath and watched as the floors passed.

"What are they going to do?" she asked quietly, her fear stripping away every ounce of confidence.

"Don't really know," the Zenith said, pocketing his access card. "But you know ExMed. I reckon it will be painful, one way or another."

His words erased any thought of obedience, instead kicking in Trista's survival instinct. Her focus on his slayer, Trista pulled the chain between her binders tight and leapt onto the Zenith's back. He shouted, whirling around as his hands grabbed at her. She tried to get the chain over his head, but he rammed back against the lift wall.

Trista cried out as the force of the movement thrust all air from her lungs. In one quick motion, he unchained her from his belt and flipped her over his shoulder, pinning her to the floor with her hands at her sides.

"I can hurt you in ways to make it look like I haven't touched you," he hissed in her ear.

The Zenith then pulled her to her feet and wrapped her chain around his hand, holding her close. They rode in silence the rest of the way. The ExMed facility was located at the top of one of the structures, just above the medical unit. In addition to her other worries, Trista found it bothersome that the Justice Center had its own hospital ward.

As the lift opened, the Zenith clamped his other hand on the back of Trista's neck and shoved her toward a tall counter, the chain still firm in his grasp. He squeezed her neck a little tighter than necessary. He'd proven that she couldn't best him. Now she had to find some other way.

Behind the counter, a woman sitting at a DDL desk looked up at them. "Yes? May I help you?"

The Zenith leaned over the counter, looking down at the woman. "Prisoner one-one-eight-three-seven-two-one Trista Leighton, requested transfer from Zenith custody."

The woman studied her DDL. "Trista Leighton," she repeated aloud as she scanned the monitor for the name. "Room six. I'll let Dr. Terces know she is here." She gestured down a long corridor to their left.

With a nod, the Zenith resumed his hold on Trista, pushing her down the sterile hallway to the room. A black six was affixed at eye level on the door, which stood open to reveal a single wheeled bed table at the center, surrounded by all sorts of monitors and machines. Cabinets lined the opposite wall. Trista noticed the room had no windows.

"On the table," the Zenith instructed. He'd obviously had enough of her.

Trista stared at the bed in horror. She had placed confidence in the idea that one of the Ghosts would appear. Someone in disguise. Someone who would aid in her harrowing escape. If she took to that bed of her own will, she'd be giving up on that hope. "Not a chance," she whispered.

"Do I have to get rough with you again, Ghost?" the Zenith asked, his fingers twining in her hair to pull her head back.

"There's no need for that," a gentle voice said from behind them. "Thank you, Lieutenant Ziebleman. That will be all."

The Zenith muttered, "Yes, sir," and stepped away from Trista, leaving her in the custody of a tall, silver-headed man in a pristine white coat, flanked by two other men wearing similar coats. The tall man gestured to the room, smiling at Trista. "Shall we?"

"I'm not going in there," she said, stepping back from the man.

"Oh, come now, Mrs. Leighton," the man said as his lackeys moved behind her to take her arms. "It's only the preparation room. Be reasonable."

"I—"

His hand touched her back, sliding toward the center of her neck. A sudden pinprick to her spine made her knees buckle. The other men caught her and carted her into the room as the first one kicked the door closed behind him. Before she could get her bearings, they placed her on the gurney and removed the cuffs, replacing them with thick, padded leather restraints attached to the bed itself.

"I am in complete control, Mrs. Leighton. The sooner you accept that, the easier it will be for you," the man said. "I suspect you have been told nothing of what is about to happen here, which is exactly what we wanted. This is a classified procedure, and few people know about it.

"My name is Dr. Reid Terces. I am a neurosurgeon. Everything that I am about to tell you, you will soon forget, thanks to the procedure you will undergo in approximately one hour. I am ..." He paused, inputting something on his PDL. "... pronouncing you dead as of ..." He adjusted the watch on his wrist to look at it. "... oh-four-thirty hours. Cause of death: cardiac arrest, due to ordered execution by means of lethal injection."

Trista had to force herself to breathe. Death announcements, particularly those following execution orders, went public on the LUM, which meant that the Ghosts would receive that information. What would Chase think? Oh, by the Crown, she missed him. She blinked as tears formed in the corners of her eyes.

"Now, being a Ghost, you have no health records logged with us. Have you any health problems or issues, Mrs. Leighton?"

"Why should I tell you?" Trista muttered.

"Well, you could tell me, or I could invite one of our interrogators up here to get the information from you. You choose."

"No," Trista said softly. She wouldn't be able to handle the torturous, brutal things the interrogators did. "No health problems."

"Good girl," Dr. Terces responded, making another note on his PDL.

"What are you going to do to me?"

"We're going to change who you are, Mrs. Leighton." Dr. Terces placed his PDL on his lap, smiling at Trista as if he were telling her a children's story. "We're going to remove some of the bothersome memories that you currently retain and give you a set of new ones. You will become a servant of the Legacy and forget all about your Ghost friends."

Utter fear spun Trista's mind in a million tiny circles. "So that pronouncement of death wasn't far from the truth."

"In a sense, I suppose." Dr. Terces smiled again. "The technicians are here to prepare you for surgery. They will insert your IV, and then I will give you a muscle relaxer. That won't put you under, but it will give the techs enough time to cut your hair and shave your head without you thrashing about and making it difficult. Can you take that ring off?"

She glanced down to her wedding band. "I won't," she said, appalled by the suggestion.

"Then I'll have the techs cut it off as part of the prep."

Trista swallowed a gag. She felt hot tears rising again as her eyes darted from face to face. "You can't do this."

The men chuckled, as if she had told some inside joke. Dr. Terces stood, allowing one of the techs to take his place. The other tech pulled a cart close as the seated one rubbed her wrist with a tiny, moist square. He studied her hand for a moment before he turned and removed a large needle from the cart.

"Please! Let me go! Don't do this!" she begged, tugging on her restraints.

"Just relax, Mrs. Leighton. It will all be over before you know it."

Trista cried out as the IV needle pricked her skin. She squeezed her eyes closed, allowing the tears to fall freely. This was far crueler than imprisonment. Even more so than death. Would she forget Chase? And Lila, her sister and best friend. Blane. She'd never see her nephew grow up. *Oh, Ruler Prince, protect me …*

CHAPTER 4

Seraph hopped out of Frisco's shuttle onto the deck below. As he yanked off his flight gloves, he was met with greetings from the docking attendants and questions from the mechanics. "It's functioning normally," he said to the team of mechanics. "We're going to need to scrub the codes and reprogram our entire comsys, in case the Legacy pulled anything from it."

"Yes, sir," the mechanics said in sync as they moved past Seraph to board the shuttle.

Stu Engrell, a member of Redic's Crew, and Sterling Criswell, brother of Seraph's wife, Echo, stalked toward him. A severe frown lined Stu's face. "Are we compromised?" he asked.

With a sigh, Seraph glanced back at the shuttle. "Hard to say. The ship was at the Junction, but in a completely different bay, so I'd like to believe not. As pilot, Frisco was the only one approved to input the Rev coordinates and access the Pathway. Bruiser shouldn't have been able to decode the encryptions."

"I'll talk with Frisco personally. I'd like to get an idea of what we're facing here," Stu answered, looking across the prep strip to where the *Stallion* had landed.

Brax, Cam, and another medic gingerly unloaded the injured Frisco, who lay on a gurney. Bruiser sure had done a bang-up job on Frisco. Praise be to the Crown, Frisco had held on long enough for the Ghosts to get to him and rescue him. The men had decided it would be safest for him to travel back on the *Stallion*, so they had carefully moved him to one of the passenger seats, which had a reclining feature. The moment they landed, the medic ran onboard.

Redic entered the bay, crossing immediately to Frisco. As his dad spoke with the man on the stretcher, Seraph turned back to Stu. "Has Chase made it back yet?"

"Came in behind you," Sterling answered.

"Yeah; I expect to see him any second." Stu's brows dipped together. "Your dad wasn't happy when he heard that Chase went out immediately after his scheduled run. I'm supposed to speak with him."

"I know. I wasn't exactly thrilled about it myself." Seraph joined in Stu's frown, tucking his gloves into the pocket of his flight suit. "But listen, cut him some slack. This thing with Trista is hitting him pretty hard."

Stu rested his hands on his hips. "He's got to follow our rules and policy, regardless."

At that moment, Chase dashed toward Seraph from a different part of the bay. He greeted Stu and Sterling with a nod before turning his anxious eyes on his friend. "Did you find anything?" he asked.

It was the question Seraph expected, but dreaded. He hadn't searched the bay after they found Frisco, but he had kept his eyes open as they made their escape. Releasing a heavy breath, Seraph shook his head. "No. Did you?"

Chase shook his head, staring toward Frisco. Stu cleared his throat. "Listen, Chase …"

"I'm sure we'll have time to chat later, Stu," Seraph said, trying to postpone the chastisement.

"All right," Stu answered, sharing an intense gaze with Seraph. He raised a hand to excuse himself, moving on to join the medics who crowded around Frisco. Seraph gave him a tight-lipped smile of thanks as he and Sterling stepped away. As they passed Chase, Sterling clapped him on the back.

Rubbing his forehead, Seraph suggested, "Why don't we head to ops and check the Crenet records again?"

"I pored over them all the way back home, Ser," Chase said. "I even contacted Armand. He said nothing's shown up."

Seraph bit his tongue. While everyone in the Crew had emergency access to Armand's secure link, only Redic, Remy, and Stu were authorized to contact him. Redic would be livid with Chase after hearing about this. Of course, Chase considered the situation an emergency, but he still should have gone through the proper channels. Seraph decided not to pursue that argument right now, though.

"She wouldn't have just disappeared. That's not like Trista," Seraph reminded his friend.

"I know. That's what disturbs me." Chase's expression held bewilderment and fear. Seraph had never seen him like this. "Whatever they are doing, they are doing undercover."

He hated to bring it up, but it was a possibility. "ExMed?"

Chase frowned, shaking his head. "Logs are on the intra-LUM. I've already checked. I'm going out again. With Church. We're going to try the Justice Center on Crenet, just to be sure."

Seraph's focus centered on Remy, who had entered the bay and crossed quickly to Redic and Stu, as they spoke with Cam and Brax. The medics had taken Frisco to the medbay. Remy spoke into Redic's ear. Redic peered toward Seraph and Chase with a heavy frown. Whatever news Remy had delivered, it was terrible. Seraph could see it in his dad's eyes.

"Did you hear me, Ser?" Chase asked.

He'd heard, but with the scene across the way, he played it off by shaking his head and looking back at his friend. "Sorry, Chase. Distracted. Now, what?"

Redic parted from Stu, Cam, and Brax, and crossed the bay with Remy to where Chase and Seraph stood. Seraph's frown matched that of his father as the older man stepped close to the two. A pit in Seraph's stomach grew as he anticipated what was about to be said. Remy stayed slightly behind Redic.

"I'm taking anoth—" Chase said.

"Son," Redic interrupted firmly, "I need a moment with Chase."

"Sure, Dad. We'll talk more in a bit, Chase," Seraph said, nodding toward Chase as he walked to Cam and Brax. Stu and Sterling had disappeared.

Cam greeted Seraph with the customary handshake as the three of them stood together watching Redic and Chase. Seraph's heart sank as he saw the color drain from Chase's cheeks. Blast the Legacy. What had they done?

Redic squeezed Chase's shoulder as he gestured for Seraph to join them again. Seraph and the others moved in quickly, surrounding their friend. Redic and Remy slipped away silently.

"Chase?" Seraph said, reaching out to touch his friend's elbow.

Chase stared straight ahead at the floor in front of him. Gone was the puzzled, fearful look. He was obviously in total shock. "She was pronounced dead early this morning."

"Chase, I'm sorry," Cam whispered as Brax gasped in disbelief.

"Did they …?" Seraph started to ask, but couldn't bring himself to finish.

"Lethal injection," Chase choked out.

Seraph closed his eyes, biting his lip to swallow a curse. Trista hadn't even been granted a trial. The Legacy had been in the regular practice of trying all criminals, but it seemed now that they were foregoing such courtesies. How far would things go before they eliminated that process altogether?

"Excuse me," Chase mumbled, darting past the small group of men.

Cam set off after him, but Seraph grabbed his arm. "He needs to be alone. He's not going anywhere. I'll find him in a little while."

"This can't go on. They are going to whittle away at us until there are none left," Brax murmured.

"That's exactly what they are trying to do, Brax. And they've done far more damage with this than they ever hoped," Seraph replied, his eyes following Chase. "Far more."

◆

Trista stared at the lights as they passed above her in a hypnotic pattern. The technicians—the two males who had accompanied Dr. Terces—guided her gurney and intravenous setup through a series of corridors. According to the identifiers that hung on their chests, the blond one was Berreks and the darker-haired one was Matlen. She wasn't sure where they were taking her, but she couldn't squelch the fear and absolute panic that dizzied her mind.

The techs slowed before entering a chilled room tiled in white. Two large domes, each containing five lamps, were mounted on the ceiling. Oh, by the Crown, it was the operating room. Tears eked out of Trista's eyes. They were really going through with the surgery.

"Go ahead and place her in the handling keep. Make sure she's secure. We'll need to insert the breathing apparatus before I administer the paralytic," she heard Dr. Terces instruct over an intercom system.

The men locked Trista's gurney before releasing the side panel in order to move her. They worked efficiently to unstrap her. Berreks guided her IV while Matlen lifted her with ease. The awaiting keep sat in the center of the room, directly under the looming lamps. It looked like a bed contorted into the shape of a chair. Square blocks of black plastic lined the chair, and Trista realized that they contained monitors and other medical equipment.

A shrill beep sounded an alarm as Berreks disconnected her IV line from the pump and walked the pole around the far side of the keep. Trista took her chance. She thrashed against Matlen, her knee making direct contact with his jaw. Desperation strengthened her as she broke free from his grasp. He dropped her on the floor with a loud curse. Scrambling away, she ran for the door.

Berreks leapt over the keep, tearing after her. His menacing arms grabbed her waist and pulled her against him. She cried out, throwing her hands into the air to squirm from his grasp. In a low crouch on the floor, she launched her foot toward his middle. The light-haired man doubled over in pain as Trista jumped to her feet.

Matlen marched toward her, shaking his head. He closed in and circled around to position himself between her and the door. Trista's wary eyes watched him, preparing for his strike. Instead, from behind, thick fingers grasped the IV port on her wrist, causing her to cry out again. Berreks had recovered far sooner than she'd hoped. He whirled her into Matlen's waiting embrace.

She kicked at Berreks, screaming for help, but the pinprick hit the back of her neck again, slackening her body instantly. Her fight was over. Her head fell back against Matlen's chest.

"Two hands on the patient at all times when the patient is not restrained," Dr. Terces reminded the techs in a stern voice. He must have entered during the failed attempt to flee.

Matlen lifted Trista's limp body into his strong arms, allowing Berreks to return to his work with the IV. He attached the solutions hanging on the pole to the far side of one of the black blocks. Matlen settled Trista into the keep, roughly placing her arms into the restraints. Berreks checked her peripheral line before attaching it to one of the blocks below. With a couple of keystrokes, the keep's internal pump clicked, and the flow began again.

"You're lucky the other doctors were not here to witness your incompetence," Dr. Terces said, scolding the techs. "Retrieve cart number one."

Matlen stepped from view as Dr. Terces moved to Trista's side. "We'll have to wait for the torstatim to wear off before we can start her on the proceptum," he said to Berreks. "Give her another five minutes to let that cycle through, then add the first bag on the cart."

"Please don't do this," Trista whimpered.

"Try to keep calm, Mrs. Leighton. Just relax and let the machine do its work." Terces looked toward the door as Matlen entered, wheeling the cart in front of him. "Good. I'm going to prime her with a little somnoctis, just to take the edge off before we insert the breathing apparatus. I want a twenty-percent serenidor flow in the mask. Then we'll give her the paralytic and get underway. Have Dr. Niveli and our guests arrived yet?"

Matlen grunted, locking the cart into place next to Trista. "Yes. They are waiting outside."

"Bring them in. She wanted them to witness the entire procedure. Then link Dr. Aftal, and tell him we'll get underway within the hour."

Trista watched in horror as, at Matlen's prompting, two women and three men entered, all dressed in white lab coats. Dr. Terces greeted them briefly, shaking hands with one of the men.

The woman with silver hair pulled back at the nape of her neck stepped forward. "Doctors Caultin, Sainne, and Tuscane, this is Dr. Reid Terces, under whom Dr. Caiman served his residencies. Reid is also largely responsible for the development of many of the drug therapies we use." The doctor turned to Terces. "This team of doctors will be leading an upcoming project focused on the psychiatric rehabilitation of Legacy prisoners. We're very excited to get it off the ground, so to speak, although it's only in its planning stages."

"Very good, Dr. Niveli. Welcome, doctors." Terces nodded politely, as if he was at a téchaud party.

"Please help me!" Trista cried, hoping one of the doctors might have an ounce of pity for her.

Dr. Terces raised a hand to excuse himself as he walked back over to the cart, then to Trista. "Now, Mrs. Leighton, I've asked you to relax. Yelling like that isn't going to help you."

He held up a thin syringe, flicked the vial, then slipped the needle into her wrist port. "I'm giving her a light dose of somnoctis," he said to the doctors as they gathered close. "Once it has taken effect, and she's feeling a little sleepy, we'll insert the breathing device, which will provide not only oxygen, but serenidor as well. The MRP requires the use of a heavy paralytic to slow brain activity, which means the patient can't breathe on her own. I don't want to give her too much somnoctis as it could react with the paralytic."

"Why not just give her the serenidor then?" one of the doctors asked.

Trista's muscles began to feel heavy. She felt more lethargic than sleepy. Not that she could move much if she wanted to. The restraints held her firmly.

"The somnoctis makes her more comfortable. She won't fight us as much," Dr. Terces answered, pointing in the direction of the cart. "Berreks, start the flow. Matlen, the mask, please."

The dark-haired man glowered at Trista as he brought a fistful of tubing and a mask to the doctor. Berreks slid his fingers along the back of Trista's neck, lifting her chin with his other hand. He eased her mouth open, murmuring, "Continue to breathe normally."

She whimpered again, trying to shake her head free from his grasp.

"Go ahead and connect it to the keep's flow," Dr. Terces instructed.

Trista closed her eyes, hearing the constant current of air through the mask in Terces's hands.

"This particular design was modeled after the breathing component of the cradle," Terces commented. The other doctors mumbled their unified acknowledgment. "We can alter the flow between pure oxygen, which we will use with the breathing apparatus, and a variety of gases, like serenidor."

Plastic tubing poked into her mouth, causing Trista to gag. "Keep breathing," Berreks whispered, his fingers stroking the back of her neck in encouragement.

With a final push, the tubing lodged into place. Trista tried to swallow, but that resulted in a second gag. Berreks patted her arm as he stepped back. Terces took his place and secured a clear plastic mask over her mouth, slipping the band around her neck. She struggled to hold her breath as the heavy mist filtered through the tubing and into the mask, but before long, she gave in. The sickly sweet smell instantly enticed her into a drowsy stupor.

Despair filled Trista's eyes with more tears as her thoughts flew to Chase. He'd always protected her. Always kept her safe. And now, she was out of his reach. He probably thought she was dead, as the LUM indicated, according to Dr. Terces. She still held on to the hope that Chase would burst through the door to save her. Yet she was here, in the clutches of absolute evil. Could the Ruler Prince even help her?

She felt the technicians working on her body, but the medications ensured that she no longer cared. Her eyes grew heavy as she caught a final glimpse of Berreks looking her over. "She's ready, Doctor," she heard him say. And that was all.

CHAPTER 5

"Miss Carlisle, open your eyes, please. Compliance."

Krissa blinked into the reality around her. Confusion blurred her thought as she focused on the face before her. She saw icy blue eyes set in chiseled features, complemented by distinguished gray hair that was taking on tinges of silvery white.

"Good girl. Follow the light, please."

An intense light eradicated the face from her vision. She blinked again, her eyes surprised by the brightness. The light danced to the left, then to the right and back again. It moved up, down, out, and in toward her nose. It winked out, and the face returned.

"No loss of visual control. We'll need to check that again in a week." The man spoke to someone else as he stared at Krissa. He gave her a hint of a smile. "Do you know where you are, young lady?"

"I—"

"She needs to verify the programming, doctor," the other person interrupted.

"Yes. Thank you, Dr. Aftal," he replied. "Give me your full name, please."

Without much thought, the words came out. "Kr-Krissa Carlisle."

"Where do you live?"

Easy. "Crenet."

"What do you do for a living, Miss Carlisle?"

"I serve the Legacy as an SA. A systems analyst. I fix computers." It's what she'd always done. Probably what she'd always do.

"Tell me your story."

That question threw her a bit. She didn't have a story, really. She just lived her life day to day. "My st—?"

"Your background. Your family."

Family? Oh boy, was she being asked about Lila again? Wait, who was Lila? "I, um—"

"Take your time."

"Sister." Krissa closed her eyes, trying to think clearly. Why was he asking, anyway? Her brain felt so fuzzy. "Lila Carlisle. Raised me."

"And where is Lila?"

"Dead," she said quickly. "I think. She disappeared years ago."

"Any others?"

Krissa shook her head. "No. My mother and father died during the rise of the Legacy."

"Were they Logia?"

A dull pain twinged in her skull, causing her to cringe a little. It disappeared instantly, though. "Um, no. They were followers of Ternion, but—"

"Note that," the doctor instructed the one he called Dr. Aftal. "How did they die?" he then asked Krissa.

"They contracted the illness on Gravatus." Shadows of the past that she'd tried to put behind her rose up at his questioning. She hadn't spoken of her parents in a long time. A long time.

"Did you and your sister get sick as well?"

"Yes," Krissa said, lowering her eyes to her clasped hands, "but Legacy doctors were able to save us."

"Are you married?"

Married. Krissa thought for a moment. She—was she? She couldn't remember. Another shadow. A ghost ... of a man. He was just out of reach, but he was there. She looked at the doctor, blinking. "I—"

"Yes?"

"I don't know."

"Note that," he directed to Aftal. His penetrating gaze fell on Krissa again. "What do you mean you don't know? You don't remember?"

Closing her eyes to seal off his gaze, Krissa answered, "I see ... someone ..."

"Can you think of his name?"

His name. His name would be her name. But for some reason her name was different. His name. "Lee ... Lee ..." she stammered.

"Lee was your *husband*?"

Krissa's thoughts fired rapidly, barraging her with confusion. With a bright flash, everything vanished into inky darkness. She felt her body flinch as clarity returned, along with the hospital room and the two doctors.

Swiveling around on his stool, the doctor spoke again to Aftal. "Schedule the lab. We'll run another round of IIS this afternoon to clean that up. There's still some residual memory of the husband and a physical reaction to the reset. I don't think I'll have to go in to adjust. Should just be a matter of aligning the impulses. Contact the pharm and have them send up ten units of proceptum and twenty units of deleouxor."

Aftal nodded, keying information into his PDL. Krissa stared at the doctor as he turned back around. She had no idea how she had landed in a medical facility. The last thing she remembered, she was on Quintus, assigned to fix an issue with a residential craft. Important clients, Streuben had told her. Um ... Streuben? Who was Streuben?

"What's happened?" she asked softly.

"I am Dr. Reid Terces, Miss Carlisle. I'm a neurosurgeon. And this is my assistant, Dr. Aftal. It seems you had a little accident."

Krissa took a short breath. "Accident?"

"Record for this afternoon's treatment," Dr. Terces directed over his shoulder. He looked back to Krissa with a frown. "You were on the job, complained of a headache and dizziness, and passed out after a severe seizure. The people you were helping linked Zeniths, who brought you to a care center on Quintus, who then transferred you here. Have you experienced anything like that before?"

"No. N-never."

"Miss Carlisle, the symptoms that were described to us led me to run a neurological scan." He paused, a look of sympathy replacing the concern. "The results are pretty startling. Do you have anyone we could contact? Anyone who should know where you are? Who could be here to support you?"

"Just my—" Krissa looked down at her body, immobile on the bed. Oh, yeah. Streuben. "—my boss, Finnegan Streuben," she whispered. "But no, there's no one else."

"And this Mr. Streuben, he's here on Crenet?"

She nodded, wishing Dr. Terces would get on with telling her what had happened. Streuben would be livid with her for missing assignments.

"Good." Dr. Terces looked at Dr. Aftal. "Note that." With a nod, Dr. Terces turned his gaze back to Krissa. "Then I will let him know. And since you have no one else, I'll try to arrange for a counselor to stop in to check on you later. But I imagine you'd like to know what's going on with your body."

She stared at him, listening intently. She'd never had any problems or lapses in memory. No previous chronic medical issues. What the blazes was going on?

"I'm going to be frank," Dr. Terces said, leaning forward to prop himself up on his knees. "You had a large growth just above the brainstem that could have been fatal. It's my belief that the growth was a result of the illness you suffered years ago. We took you into surgery immediately. I was able to remove the tumor, but you're now looking at a lifetime of prescription medications and visits with me. It is quite possible that the growth will return.

"I don't want you to be shocked, but we had to shave part of your hair for the surgery. It will grow back, of course, but seeing yourself in the mirror might disturb you a bit." Dr. Terces added a gentle, thin-lipped smile.

"How long have I been here?" Krissa whispered.

Dr. Terces clasped his hands together. "Close to a week. As I said, we performed the surgery right away, but we encountered a few complications. I can tell you more in greater detail, but another time. Right now, you need to remain calm. Our next step is to run a series of tests. Some are physical; others involve your mental capabilities. We'll get you put back together, Krissa." Dr. Terces smiled with an air of paternity. Krissa couldn't help but like him.

"All right," she answered. She'd already missed nearly a week of assignments. Streuben would be—

"Good girl."

Krissa's eyes closed as she bowed her head momentarily. She then looked back up at Dr. Terces.

"Note that. Physical reaction to program reinforcement, as well. We'll need to eliminate all outward signs," he said to Aftal. "In the meantime, Krissa, I'm going to get you going on your drug regimen. Up until now, we've been giving these to you intravenously, but your body needs to adjust to the pill form. These medications are intended to keep you quiet. The initial doses tend to make you drowsy, but that's all right. Resting is good for you right now. Your brain still needs to heal."

He presented her with a large green capsule, two white pills, a smaller red one, and a cup of water. She hesitated a moment. She didn't like the idea of taking medicine, especially something that affected her mind. He lifted the pills to encourage her. "Take them," he insisted.

"What are they?" she whispered.

"We'll talk about that during one of our visits. You're still in recovery, and I want you at full capacity before we discuss your treatments, all right? You need to learn to trust me, Krissa. Compliance."

With her eyes on his, she took the pills from his hand and placed them on her tongue. The water washed them down. Krissa leaned back into her pillows and closed her eyes.

"Good girl," Dr. Terces repeated, patting her arm. "Good girl."

Redic's voice broke the miserable silence. "Chase."

Chase glanced up from the console that operated the *Halcyon* to see the Ghost leader standing in the doorway. He wasn't too keen on visitors right now, but he knew it would be very rude to send Redic away. "Evening, sir," he muttered with disinterest.

The older man stepped into the cockpit, taking a seat opposite from Chase in the copilot's chair. "That was a beautiful service and tribute," he said.

"Yeah …" Chase said, fidgeting with the arm of his chair. He knew the memorial was meant to honor Trista, but he felt as if they were forcing him to say good-bye to her after only a week. And he didn't want to say good-bye. Ever.

After a moment, Redic asked, "Reminiscing?"

"Tinkering," Chase answered, folding his arms over his chest. "We've had a buzz in the system for several weeks now."

He could feel Redic's eyes on him. Why didn't the old man just go away? Seraph at least knew him well enough to leave him alone when he was in a mood. So what that he'd been in a mood since the news of Trista's execution? They'd finally dragged him out for the memorial service. That should be enough.

"The techs could take care of it," Redic said softly.

"Well, I'm a little mad at the Crown right now, and I feel like squandering what He's given me," Chase replied heatedly, glaring at the board full of lights. They flashed into a frenzy with his thoughts.

Redic watched before he murmured, "Aram is worried about you. We all are."

Propping his elbow on the arm of the seat, Chase leaned into his hand and shook his head. "I'll be all right."

"You never are," Redic countered, staring out the viewport. "I was just a little older than you when I lost Caelya and the kids. I didn't speak to anyone for two years, not even Remy. Once I gave up being mad at the Crown, I prayed for death to take me. And as the days—the years—pass, it never gets any easier."

"Thanks for the pep talk, sir."

"I was fortunate. Selah and Seraph were returned to me, but not before I experienced that grievous sense of loss." Redic turned to him. "You find moments of joy, Chase. You have to. And you have to cling to those moments with all that you have. Don't lose sight of who you are. Bitterness will destroy you."

"It's all part of the game, isn't it, sir?" Chase chuckled bitterly, flickering his eyes toward Redic.

"Losing someone is never a game, son. Particularly someone as special as Trista."

Chase closed his eyes. Hearing her name brought up too many heart-wrenching memories. Her smile. Her laughter. Her eyes.

Redic took a slow, steady breath. "Seraph tells me that you accepted a run."

"Not a long one," Chase whispered.

"I want you to know something. I didn't create the Ghosts as an act of vengeance. I've never sought to use our crews and ships as a means of getting back at the Legacy for what's been done to Ternion's people. We represent the Ruler Prince, and we will act in accordance with His nature."

Chase looked at Redic. "What are you getting at?"

"Never choose vengeance, son." Redic's commanding gaze blazed with complete solemnity. "As hard as it is, as badly as you feel, never choose it. It will betray you and hurt you far more deeply than the initial pain. Allow the Crown His day. You just serve Him to the best of your abilities, with might, nobility, and honor. He will reward an honest, pure heart."

Blast. Redic was right. Chase lowered his eyes. "I'd almost lost sight of that."

"I know," Redic said, rising. He placed a fatherly hand on Chase's shoulder. "You're not alone. Don't act like it."

Chase nodded, placing his hand atop Redic's. "Thank you, sir."

"*Soli Deo Gloria,*" Redic murmured before exiting the cockpit.

Leaning back in his chair, Chase closed his eyes and bit his lip to keep from screaming. As tears stung his eyes, he slammed his fists on the arms of the chair and rocked forward, hunching over his legs. He pressed his palms into his eyes, then leapt to his feet, kicking the console. After several heaving breaths, he sank to his knees and prayed—first for forgiveness, then for strength. He had to get past this anger, and the only way he could start was with help from the Crown.

CHAPTER 6

From his office, Dr. Terces watched Krissa through the one-way mirror as she ran through the circuit of physical challenges with the trainer. She seemed in excellent condition and not at all affected by her surgery. The door opened behind him. Admiral Niveli and his wife stepped in and greeted Dr. Aftal. Reid had nearly forgotten that Aftal was in the room with him.

Cyndra crossed to the table and chairs set in front of the window, dropping a load of files next to Terces. "These require your approval. The *Straightjacket* project has full support of the board and the Agency, however before we launch, you must sign off on each treatment plan."

Dr. Terces glanced down at the files, then nodded before returning his attention to Krissa. The trainer tossed Krissa a pair of padded gloves. He held up a wide foam shield and called out instructions to her as to where to hit. Krissa nailed each target.

"We are eight days into the experiment, and she is processing without a problem. Her eye-hand coordination has improved greatly," Aftal commented.

"Have you tested her mental aptitude?" Dr. Niveli asked.

Terces reached across the table to turn off the audio feed coming from the training room. He nodded. "In all categories, she scored well above excellent. She's retained her intellect, her education, and her skills."

"Very good." Cyndra lowered herself into a seat next to Dr. Terces. "Any noticeable dissonance?"

"None. After we got those preliminary issues straightened out, she's taken to the implantation better than I would have thought," Terces said as he gazed at his patient.

"Better than the previous candidates, anyway." Dr. Aftal laughed.

"She's a striking one, Terces," Admiral Niveli stated, staring at Krissa. Her nut-brown hair had filled in a bit along the back, covering the scars from her surgery. She wore the longer portion of her hair in a ponytail. Color had returned to her cheeks with the physical exertion. The admiral raised his eyebrows as he watched her. "You have a romantic interest to keep an eye on her?"

"Not a romantic interest, no. Those kinds of feelings tend to interfere with our work. And because of that exact reaction, we've actually included a deterrent in the system to prevent any form of those feelings from arising." Terces turned from his focus on Krissa, meeting Niveli's gaze. "As for a watchful eye, she'll be serving under Finnegan Streuben. The ITCs require little downtime, so she only sleeps a few hours each night. With the regular work Streuben has system-wide, he'll be able to keep her busy and report to us on a daily basis."

Cyndra crossed to the window, watching Krissa for a moment. "Any trouble with the programming?"

"At first, yes. We had difficulty removing the husband. It took two additional intensive rounds of stim to lose him. But now, no problems of note. She verified the programming immediately, and every answer matched the encoding. And like I said, she's retained all of her mental faculties and her skills with computers." Dr. Terces scratched his forehead, giving a little chuckle. "In fact, she took a look at our DDL in the lab and did something to make it run ten times faster."

"Why is that funny?" Admiral Niveli asked.

"There wasn't anything wrong with it," Aftal answered.

All four looked out at Krissa again. She had pummeled the trainer up against the wall. He dropped the shield and raised his hands in surrender as Krissa bounced back with a sheepish grin on her face. The trainer shook his head, also laughing, and guided her to a different activity.

After a moment, Admiral Niveli asked, "How do we keep her from the Ghosts? Surely they will come for her."

"She's dead to them," Cyndra declared. "Reid gave the official word upon her arrival at ExMed."

"And we've managed to keep her a secret for over a week now. Anyone who's had contact with her has been in service for over five years," Terces said. "I'm not about to let any Ghosts waltz in here and abduct my subject."

"Besides, that's the beauty of the MRP," Dr. Aftal added, leaning over his desk. "Theoretically, she could walk into their base and not recognize them. And she's loyal. The Legacy takes care of her, so she has no reason to dispute them."

"Takes care?" Admiral Niveli asked, lifting an eyebrow again.

"We provide housing, food, work. And health care," Dr. Terces replied.

"He means," Dr. Niveli filled in, explaining to her husband, "that should complications arise, the patient will be cared for."

"I mean, I had to come up with a cover story for why she woke up in a hospital, why we'd cut her hair, and why she'll experience headaches and dizziness for the rest of her days," Terces countered.

"I suggested a brain tumor." Dr. Aftal grinned.

Dr. Terces gestured toward Aftal. "Which is the story we went with."

"But she is healthy?" Admiral Niveli asked.

"Completely," Terces confirmed.

Niveli turned his attention back to Krissa. "And should the Ghosts capture her? If the implants are removed?"

"Reid implanted a fail-safe. Attempted removal of the chips will trigger violent impulses throughout her brain, causing severe rupture. To put it bluntly, she will die," Cyndra said, smugly folding her slender arms over her middle.

"Dr. Aftal also programmed a pain mechanism within the ITCs," Terces added. "It can be triggered remotely."

"Who is in possession of the remote?" Admiral Niveli asked with concentrated interest.

Dr. Terces smiled. He was quite proud of their new toy. "Anyone with a slayer. A minor adjustment to the frequency, and Miss Carlisle is rendered immobile."

"Will that require every Zenith and Zephyr to be briefed on her existence?"

"Not necessarily," Terces answered. "I am confident Miss Carlisle won't give us any trouble. We incorporated this particular mechanism with the future of the procedure in mind. Once we are allowed to broaden our scope with other prisoners, the rate of success may fluctuate. With the accessibility of slayers, we insure that our subjects remain under our control."

"Excellent." Admiral Niveli smirked, sharing in Terces's pride. "The

Tribunal will be pleased with your work, doctors. When do you turn her over to Streuben?"

"She will be discharged tomorrow, and start to work the next day. I have an appointment with her at the end of the week to monitor her progress, unless I hear something from Streuben beforehand," Dr. Terces said. "And from what I understand, Lieutenant Blouter is dedicating a Zenith or two to watch her functionality for a few days."

Admiral Niveli nodded, clasping his hands behind his back. "Very good, Reid. Very good. The Tribunal suggested that we put together an advisory board, especially with the idea of going public with this MRP treatment. I'll schedule the meeting within the month to hear your report."

Terces shared a look with Aftal. "Give us six," he said.

That was obviously not what the admiral expected to hear. "I'm sorry?"

Tapping his pen on his desk, Terces lifted his chin toward Krissa. "I want to ensure success with this subject before we bring others into it."

The admiral narrowed his eyes, looking down his nose at Terces before agreeing to his wishes. "Six months, then," he grumbled.

"Thank you, sir. How much level of detail does the board need?"

"Full disclosure, Doctor. With your success, we have nothing to hide." Admiral Niveli smiled. It was the smile of a man who expected a miraculous triumph, only because he knew how very deadly failure could be.

With a guarded nod, Dr. Terces rose to bid good-bye to the admiral and his wife. After the couple left, Dr. Aftal stepped toward him, leaning against the wall as he looked out at Krissa. "You didn't tell him everything."

"No," Terces answered, sitting back in his chair to plod through the *Straightjacket* files. "No sense in worrying them. We just have to keep a close eye on her. And a solid wall between her and the Ghosts."

"And you're relying on Zeniths to do that?" Aftal chuckled with a skeptical shake of his head.

"No." Terces leaned forward, his gaze intense on Krissa. "I want to expand the auditory program control. Broaden words that will reinforce her programming."

"Should I incorporate the pain inducing procedure?"

"Yes," Terces said, smiling at Dr. Aftal. "Let's get on that."

Aftal tilted his head, his expression questioning. "You're talking mind control."

"In a sense, that's what we've already done. We're just taking it to a different level," Terces answered.

Crossing back to his desk, Aftal hit several keys on his DDL. "You'll have to go back in, but it should be surface-level implantation. Easy. It's the programming that takes a little more fine-tuning."

Dr. Terces placed both elbows on the table before him, leaning on his hands as he watched the girl exit the training room. "I trust you, Dr. Aftal."

◆

Day 9294 PLR: Crenet

"Report," the Spokesman said from the Bands screen at the back of the room. He stepped away, disappearing from view. The Tribunal always maintained their distance before larger audiences.

Armand Lyria shifted forward, angling the DDL display before him to shield the glare from the overhead lighting. His eyes connected with Zak Sinclaire across the table. Armand gave a curt nod, as did Sinclaire.

"We'd like to welcome you all as part of the advisory panel regarding ExMed subject Krissa Carlisle," Dr. Niveli said, standing from her place at the table. "You all were chosen as integral parts of the Legacy to participate in the rehabilitation of this subject. Doctors Terces, Aftal, and myself represent the medical team who is in charge of the subject, although Dr. Terces is handling the brunt of the interaction. My husband, Admiral Niveli, is acting as the Tribunal's representative when they are unavailable to attend these meetings.

"We've asked Zephyr Captain Zakaris Sinclaire to join us. The captain is known for his ethical viewpoint." Dr. Niveli smiled at Sinclaire. Armand noticed an underlying insult in her words. She continued with the introductions. "Lieutenant Gib Blouter is in charge of the regiment of Zeniths that regularly patrol the sector of Crenet where our patient resides. His reporting officer, Zephyr Commander Armand Lyria, is here as support."

Armand met the eyes of the others with a lift of his chin. He didn't want to be here. He'd accepted the invitation—well, it was more of a command than an invitation—because the name of the patient rang with familiarity. He only hoped that he wouldn't have to deliver bad news to the Ghosts. He hoped that he was wrong.

"Finnegan Streuben," Niveli gestured to a man at the end of the table, "operates a systems assistance business. He is our patient's direct daily contact and supervisor. We also have two representatives of the Elite, who are financially backing this project: Lady Mischa Saxby and Kalislyn Carter.

"I will now invite my husband to give a bit of background on the patient, and then Doctors Terces and Aftal will elucidate the procedure itself. We will allow for questions at the end of our meeting." She clicked a button on the device she held, activating the smaller individual screens on the DDLs in front of each person. An image of a young woman popped up. Her data file information scrolled below the picture, "Name: Krissa Carlisle; Legacy ID: 02C1917—ExMed patient."

Admiral Niveli leaned forward, speaking from his chair. "I will quickly bring you up to speed, as I think you will find Dr. Terces's report far more interesting. Before you is Trista Leighton, wife to Logia and Ghost captain, Chase Leighton."

Armand's heart sank. He wasn't wrong. It *was* Trista.

"Leighton is the grandson of the late Harlan Cromley, former head of justice under Ternion's Praesidium, and is the product of two Logia parents. Leighton is gifted with the ability to manipulate electronics with his mind, so you understand why it is imperative that we apprehend him. For just over six months now, we've had his wife in custody. Eventually, she might be used to lure the Ghosts or even Leighton himself to us, but for now, she has been integrated into a daily Legacy routine. Dr. Terces, please continue with your presentation."

Blast. They knew a whole lot more about Chase than he'd thought. He would definitely have to get in contact with Redic tonight, although risking the signal probably was not the wisest choice. This information would have to be hand-delivered.

"Thank you, Admiral Niveli." Dr. Terces gestured to the picture of Krissa. "Miss Carlisle is not in traditional custody, such as a prison ship. We are using a new method, developed by ExMed, that allows us to penetrate the parts of the brain that hold memories and recreate them for our benefit and use, thus establishing healthy, functioning, contributing citizens instead of lazy, ineffective prisoners.

"Mrs. Leighton, or Krissa, as I will now refer to her, has proved most receptive to this treatment that we call MRP, or the memory restructuring program. We began working with her when she was arrested last year. I was told to disclose all details, so if this gets a little incomprehensible, I apologize.

"Phase one of the MRP involves the surgical implantation of

microcomputer devices developed by ExMed called integrated transmuter circuits, or ITCs. These are implanted—" Dr. Terces tapped a key on the console in front of him, changing the image to a rendering of the back side of a human head. He crossed to the front of the room to point out the surgical entry points. "—here, here, and here. Each ITC contains two telescoping arms the width of a thin wire. The arms route to the necessary locations—the hippocampus, the temporal lobe, and the frontal cortex."

A third slide shifted into place—a diagram of a brain, the mentioned areas highlighted.

"In our preliminary trials, we left out the frontal cortex. The subjects died. Upon further research, Dr. Niveli and I theorized that the frontal cortex was key. Our work with Krissa has proved such."

By the Crown, they had tortured her. Put her life on the line and tortured her. Chase would be beside himself. Armand clasped his hands before him.

"Following surgery, the patient is kept on a paralytic while receiving a treatment of antirejection medication. High doses of proceptum, an antirejection agent developed by ExMed, are given intravenously. Once in recovery, the patient is required to continue a full drug regimen, including proceptum in tablet form.

"After we reach a stage of stability, we can move on to phase two of the MRP, which involves IIS, or intracranial impulse stimulation. This gets a little more complicated. It is here where the patient's memories are accessed, decoded, and then deleted or recreated. Impulses from the ITCs restructure the neurons and allow us to manipulate memory.

"A crucial component of the IIS is the hardware." The image changed to a drawing of a complex chair system. "The handling keep is a specially designed chair that shifts into a surgical table or a bed. It has a self-contained life support unit, similar to that of the cradle. Used in conjunction with the shroud, the IIS can be done in the same space as the MRP.

"The shroud," Dr. Terces tapped the button again, changing the picture to show a frightning metallic ring, "can be used separately from the keep. This apparatus encircles the patient's head and connects with the ITCs to manage the IIS. There are nine points of contact, including the base receptors, where the shroud interacts with the ITCs. For design, we connect the shroud to our main terminal, allowing us to manipulate the memory structure. For maintenance, we are able to reinforce the structure using the readout along the front.

"In Krissa's case, we deleted her memory of her time with the Ghosts.

And although this method is thorough," Dr. Terces changed the image to one of an actual brain scan, "there are still parts of the brain that retain echoes of such memories. Our fabricated memories, or programming, must contain pieces of that information so that we don't encounter neural dissonance. That is one reason, for instance, that we retained her maiden name of Carlisle, and chose a rhyming sound to correspond with Trista. I will turn the floor over to my assistant, Dr. Aftal."

Armand folded an arm over his middle and rubbed his forehead. This was ghastly. ExMed had taken their mission to a new low. In the past, they had done some pretty evil things—including to his wife, Vivienne—but this surpassed them.

Dr. Aftal rose with a nod to Dr. Terces, who took a seat. Dr. Aftal leaned forward over the table, his hands supporting him. "Our initial round of IIS removed Mrs. Leighton from her identity as a Ghost. As Dr. Terces mentioned, we returned her to her maiden name, as we could not completely, for lack of better words, scrub away who she was. Krissa Carlisle was, in essence, reborn."

A new image of Trista popped up. She looked mournful. Her hair cut just below her ears, she wore the uniform of Legacy service personnel. Her eyes were lifeless, void—like someone had cut out her soul instead of memories. Perhaps that's precisely what Dr. Terces had done.

"She has a talent with computers, so we latched on to that, connecting her with Finnegan Streuben," Dr. Aftal gestured to Streuben, "as a system analyst. Mrs. Leighton had a particularly close relationship with her sister, Lila. Because of that, we had to retain a few of those memories. I programmed Mrs. Leighton with the idea that her sister had disappeared years earlier, and that she herself experienced a difficult but complete grieving process. Although our records show that Lila Carlisle was executed, I chose to make her disappear in Krissa's fabricated memories, to prevent any anger toward the Legacy. As Krissa Carlisle, she is loyal to us." Dr. Aftal nodded to Dr. Terces, and they once again exchanged positions, Dr. Terces taking the floor.

"What about the husband?" Lady Saxby asked.

"I'm sorry?" Dr. Terces responded.

"If she was close to the sister, I would imagine that she was closer to the husband. You said that you couldn't eliminate all memories of the sister. I want to know if you had to give her some memories of the husband as well."

Dr. Aftal began to rise, but Dr. Terces held up his hand. He would field the question. "The memories with her sister, because she'd known her a longer time, were deeply ingrained. The memories with her husband, while they were strong, were removed. It was a difficult experience—intense for me and painful for her—but it was done. Leighton is no longer in her head."

Armand covered his mouth to hide his disgust. Not only had they taken Trista away, but they had made it impossible for Chase to get her back. It would have been far more humane had they just killed Trista, like the report months ago claimed.

"We've maintained our efforts through biweekly visits with Krissa. Her treatments include the drug therapy, as I indicated previously. She takes proceptum daily. I have her on a memory blocker called deleouxor. She takes imperactium and mensviscus, which are inhibitors that allow the ITCs to function without neural or cognitive obstruction. Side effects of the MRP and IIS include headaches, dizziness, confusion, and disorientation, which we manage with another medication named capustatim. In order to substantiate these symptoms, as well as ensure that we could keep a close medical eye on Krissa, Dr. Aftal came up with the idea to tell her that she has a brain tumor."

"Is that true?" Sinclaire asked. "Does she have any kind of growth?"

"Not in the least. But she believes it and operates with the full faith that it is fact."

Lieutenant Blouter raised his hand. "You said she has a talent for computers. Is she Logia like her husband?"

"No."

The Logia. Maybe Chase … or Selah … one of them could help.

"Could a Logia restore her?" Armand asked. *Cover yourself.* "Theoretically?"

Terces scoffed, shifting his weight. "Were there any Logia—"

"Come on, Doctor. Let's not kid ourselves. We both know that there are still Logia out there. Our job isn't finished." Armand chuckled a bit, meeting Terces's gaze. "If they get hold of her, could they heal her?"

"I don't believe the level of healing skill that the Logia have available to them would be able to reverse the MRP, no."

"Is there *any* chance of reversal? Failure?" Armand pressed. "Of something coming loose and all the memories flooding back?"

"No," Dr. Terces said. "The memories have been deleted from her mind completely. There is no chance of remembrance. As I said, she might feel that something isn't connecting somehow, but she will never remember the Ghosts or Chase Leighton as she once knew them.

"As a precaution, we established an auditory program control. Trigger words that reinforce the programming. Should she encounter Ghosts and/or Logia, certain words that might come up in persuasive conversation will activate pain inducers that have been implanted at surface level. Should she encounter Leighton himself, and he try to remind her of her identity, the program will reset itself. I also have a directive word that refocuses Krissa's immediate concerns to follow my will."

"Why did you wait six months to bring this forward?" Sinclaire asked. "ExMed usually has a habit of jumping the game."

"Precisely why we held off," Dr. Terces answered. "We wanted to make sure Krissa could function as we theorized before we announced the practice."

"Thank you, doctors. Your efforts will be recorded," the Spokesman said before the screen fizzled to black.

"And I guess that is the end of our meeting." Admiral Niveli stood, nodding to the doctors. "Gentlemen, we expect your weekly updates and bimonthly briefings, as usual. Good work. Thank you. You are all dismissed."

The doctors both nodded as the people in the room stood. Zak rose, once again making eye contact. Armand could see the fury and disapproval in his eyes. Sinking back in his chair, Armand tapped on the DDL keypad to return to the image of Krissa. With a sigh, he closed the file and removed the datadisk. Clutching it in his hand, he left the room to seek out Zak Sinclaire.

CHAPTER 7

Redic swallowed hard as he stared at the DDL in front of him. He ran a hand over his face, holding his jaw as he read the information. It couldn't be. It just couldn't be. Glancing up at the Legacy officer standing before him, he narrowed his eyes. "This … has already happened?"

Armand bit his lip and nodded. "I'm afraid so, sir. Months ago. It's been kept quiet. The only reason I know about it is that I was asked to participate on an advisory board and given this file. I was going to decline, until I heard the name. The meeting confirmed it. It's Trista."

"How heartless," Redic said, hitting the keypad to deactivate the DDL. He leaned back in his chair, staring at the wall beyond them as he thought through the next step. He'd broken difficult news before, but this one was tough. After a moment, he tapped the link built into his desk. "Remy, link Chase and Lila. Tell them to drop everything and get down here now. Then assemble the Crew. I want to talk with them in ten minutes."

"Lila and Brendan are scheduled for a run in thirty." Remy's cool response eased through the speaker.

"Negative. Cancel that run," Redic answered. "I want all outgoing runs grounded until after I brief the Crew. I imagine we're going to have to make some schedule changes."

"Copy," Remy said. The link clicked back into silence.

Redic gestured for Armand to sit in one of the chairs across from him. "Thank you for bringing this to us. I know it's not easy for you to get away."

Armand gave a nod as he took a seat. "It had to be done, sir. Zak and I conferred and determined that it would be less noticeable for me to come. We didn't want to risk blowing the signal."

"I can't believe that the Legacy would stoop so low." Redic frowned, his fingers running along the keys of his DDL.

"ExMed is vile, sir. They've been doing terrible, unthinkable things for too long." Armand lowered his eyes. Redic knew he was thinking back to a time when his wife, Vivienne, was a subject of ExMed. "Zak is looking into shutting them down for good, but he doesn't wish to reveal himself. He knows he can make a bigger difference in the downfall of the Legacy from the position he's in. Like me."

Redic nodded. His voice softened as he changed the subject. "How *is* Viv?"

"Enjoying retirement. I never pegged her as one to live quietly, but I've not seen her happier," Armand said with a conservative smile. "The candlestick house has been a good move for her."

"Glad to hear it. We certainly miss her around here," Redic replied.

Viv had assisted the Ghosts for a number of years, alongside her childhood friends, Cam Grayson and Brax Hughes. Armand was part of their group too, but, proving himself an effective spy, remained in the dedicated service of the Legacy. After Prince Ternion's return, Viv chose to operate a small household on Caelum—a candlestick house, part of a network of safe houses for the Logia. So far, the Legacy hadn't caught on to the candlestick houses, which also allowed Armand to visit regularly with his wife.

"Well, she was happy to work with the Ghosts for as long as she did, but I think she feels a stronger sense of purpose in helping the Logia. She has really dedicated herself to learning more about the Crown. There's a new peace about her."

Redic smiled before turning to Remy, who had just entered the room. "Lila and Chase are on their way. The Crew will convene in the Turret in a few moments," she said quietly.

"Thank you, Remy," Redic said, nodding to her.

"I'll wait in the Turret," Armand murmured as he rose.

"Why?"

"Do you not wish to talk to Chase privately?"

Redic shook his head. "You've witnessed the news firsthand, Armand. I need you here to corroborate the information. After we've told both Chase and Lila, we will meet with the rest of the Crew and hash out a plan. I just wanted to give Chase a few moments to collect himself before we let everyone know what's happened."

A knock on the door halted the conversation. Without being asked, Remy moved to the door to allow Chase and Lila to enter. Lila looked worried, while Chase, carrying a PDL, strode to Redic's desk. "Sir, I've run this over and over again in my head. I think they've falsified information. Church and I have already been on numerous runs. Now, I want you to let me go in—"

"Chase, the outpost issue isn't important at the moment," Redic interrupted as he stood. "Please have a seat."

Chase glanced to Remy, whose eyes were on Armand. Chase followed her gaze to the Legacy officer who served the Ghosts. He blinked, looking back at Redic as he slowly sat in one of the chairs. Lila sat next to him, which apparently tipped him off. "Oh, by the Crown, you've heard something about Trista," Chase murmured.

"Yes. She's ... alive." Redic furrowed his brow as he frowned. He was still struggling with the proper, most sensitive way to break the news.

"*Soli Deo Gloria*," Lila said with a relieved smile.

Anxiety overtook Chase's expression. "There's more. What is it?"

"Armand tells us that she's undergone a new treatment developed by ExMed. Their name for it is the MRP."

"MRP?" Chase's eyes darted between Redic and Armand.

"Memory restructuring program. They played with her mind, Chase," Armand said with a note of gravity. "They took some memories away. They added some. They created for her a completely new identity. And they have retained her as a servant."

"We have to help her," Chase said, rising quickly.

"We're going to do what we can," Redic replied. He knew that Chase would expect the Ghosts to put everything on hold to get to Trista, but that just wasn't feasible. He had to make the boy understand that.

"That's not enough." Chase's fist met Redic's desk. "We have to move. Now!"

Armand's quiet voice hit home. "She won't remember you, Chase. She doesn't remember any of this."

"The Logia can help her. Restore her. Aram, Selah, Seraph ..."

Armand shook his head. "It's not a block. They went into her brain. Surgically. They are using computers and impulses to cut out these memories.

I don't really understand it all, but they are saying that it's permanent and that not even the Logia could heal her. I asked that very question."

Chase's words sizzled with anger. "You *asked*? Did you see her?"

"No, I—"

"Then who did you ask? What part do you have in this?" Chase demanded, stepping closer to Armand.

"Cool off, son," Redic advised, his own temper flaring. "Armand is our eyes and ears on this right now."

"I'm part of a panel ExMed gathered to prepare and launch this procedure for general use with many of their prisoners," Armand explained. "Trista was their test subject."

"How long ago?" Chase's voice dropped to a whisper.

"Six months. They faked her death and performed the surgery just after she was arrested," Armand answered.

Chase fell back in his chair, his hand covering his face. Lila sniffled, closing her eyes. Redic pulled a handkerchief from his pocket and offered it to her before sharing a pained look with Remy. He said, "The Crew is on their way. We're going to formulate a plan."

"A plan for what?" Chase asked, despair sapping the color from his cheeks.

"We're going to bring her home, Chase. Whether she remembers or not," Redic said.

"I beg that you be careful, sir," Armand said. "If the information is correct, she will consider herself a prisoner among us. If she survives. Worse damage could be done."

Chase pressed his eyes closed. Redic knew the man's heart was breaking for his wife, but they had to play this smart. It was obviously dangerous, not only for the Ghosts, but according to Armand, for Trista as well.

"Love conquers all, Chase," Redic reminded him. "And we serve a mighty King."

"*Soli Deo Gloria*," Chase muttered through gritted teeth. Redic knew it was said more out of obligation than what he felt in his heart.

Redic rose, glancing to Lila. She looked inconsolable. She'd watched over Trista since they were just children, not to mention they were best friends. But Lila reacted to things far differently from Chase. She knew to trust the Ghost leadership to find a way to reach her sister.

Touching her arm with paternal tenderness, Redic said, "We must part from you. Are you all right?"

Lila nodded. "I'm relieved to know that she is alive, but fearful of what they will do to her." She pressed the handkerchief to her mouth, closing her eyes again.

"I'm afraid it's already been done. But for now, she is safe. As safe as she can be, anyway." Redic knelt at Lila's side, gripping her hand. "Be prayerful, Lila. Not only for your sister, but for Chase and the others of us who will do everything we can to get her back."

Lila nodded again. "Thank you, sir."

Redic embraced Lila, then stood, offering her a hand. Lila took it and pulled herself to her feet. Redic shifted her into Remy's waiting arms. "Link Sterling. Have him meet his wife down here. Then join us in the Turret."

Remy nodded acknowledgment to Redic as he and Armand stepped out of the room. Chase lingered behind, whispering soft words to his sister-in-law. The two had always had a tight-knit relationship, and Redic figured he was assuring her that he would bring Trista home. Chase caught up with them in a matter of seconds.

The Turret, a conference room adjacent to Redic's office, held the Crew—Redic's appointed leaders and advisors. They were also friends, colleagues, and family members. Everyone sat in their usual places. Next to Redic, on his right, sat his son Seraph; his son-in-law Cam Grayson; and their friend Brax Hughes. To his left, just beyond Remy's empty chair, sat fellow Ghost founders Aram Zephaniah, Stu Engrell, and Avalyn Marari. Cole Rose sat next to her, closed in by his brother-in-law Britt Lockhart. Armand took his seat next to Brax, and Chase sat across from Redic, next to former Legacy captain Brendan Faulkner.

"Gentlemen, ladies, thank you for coming on such short notice. Our friend Armand has brought some pretty devastating news from within the Legacy," Redic started, looking out across the Crew as Remy slipped in silently. Redic's heart went out to Chase, who was once more cradling his head in his hands. "As you know, months ago, Trista Leighton was caught and arrested during her last mission. We waited for news of her sentencing, expecting her to be placed on the *Bastille* or the *Oubliette*. However, information went out on the LUM alerting us to her execution. That information was evidently put there to throw us off. After six months, we've discovered that Trista is alive, but it seems that the Legacy getting creative in their methods of imprisonment. ExMed has found a way to use the mind as a form of prison. Legacy doctors have 'scrubbed' Trista's memory, turning her into a completely different person. This enables them to use her however they wish. Armand is monitoring the situation closely. He is now part of an advisory panel that focuses on Trista, and he will bring that information to us."

Armand cleared his throat. "Zakaris Sinclaire is also on the panel. Following each meeting, we plan to talk, in case we receive different information."

"Excellent," Redic commented.

"It sounds as if you're going to sit this one out and let them continue to do things to her," Chase whispered, staring at Redic.

Redic had expected the confrontation, but he had hoped to deal with it privately. In a firm tone, he said, "Quite the opposite, Chase, but we have to play it safe. The Legacy is using her talents with computers, calling her a systems analyst. I say we replay Bruiser's strategy—plant a ship, pull a few wires, request her expertise, and bring her home once she's onboard. If we can."

"Let me go," Chase insisted.

Redic shook his head. "Too risky. Britt, I want you to take this one."

Chase stood, leaning over the table. "She's my wife."

Holding Chase's stare with equal intensity, Redic answered, "The precise reason I can't send you."

"I have to—"

"He's right, Chase," Remy said, stepping in as the voice of reason. "The Legacy is on to you. They want you. If things go awry, they'll have you. And that makes Trista inconsequential. Who knows what they will do to her at that point?"

Armand rose, placing a hand on Chase's back. "They've not only taken her memories. They've made it so that if she encounters you—any of us, really—the devices in her head cause her pain. There are verbal triggers that reset the information she's been fed. Some of those triggers can hurt her. If we try to make contact, or worse yet, remove those devices, we might do more damage. She could die. For now, she's safe."

Chase rolled his eyes and shrugged off Armand's hand. "Safe ..."

Armand continued, "She's not physically injured or incarcerated. She's functioning—"

"She's a Legacy zombie."

"She's protected by several doctors and others who are watching over her every move."

"She's their prisoner!" Chase slammed his fist on the table.

"Chase," Seraph said softly as he rose from his seat to move to his friend's side.

The troubled man collapsed in his chair, leaning over the arm to cover his face. Seraph touched his back. "Dad, will you excuse Chase and me for a bit?"

Redic nodded, feeling for the boy. He knew what Chase was going through. All these years later, he remembered the very moment Remy broke the news to him that Caelya and their children had been captured by the Legacy. And despite Remy's warnings, he had done everything in his power to get to them. How could he expect Chase to feel any differently?

Seraph led Chase from the room, and the Crew waited respectfully before they resumed the discussion of their next step. Redic was grateful for the Crew's input. At this point, he wasn't sure what to do. But he knew they had to reach Trista before it was too late. For her. And for Chase.

CHAPTER 8

Day 9302 PLR: Pavana

Britt scurried toward the ramp from the cockpit, ready to greet Trista. She stood on the deck of the docking bay just outside the ship. He touched the moustache above his lip to make sure it was still in place. It was a lame disguise, but he wanted to give Trista every opportunity—short of blatantly telling her who he was—to recognize him.

They'd planted Cole at the pedestrian entrance to the rarely used bay. He was to keep watch for Trista and alert Britt when she arrived. Somehow, he'd missed her. Britt swept aside the thought that Cole might have been apprehended by Zeniths. Cole knew how to handle himself.

"Ya late," he said in his drawled Duke accent, folding his arms over his chest as he looked down the ramp at Trista.

She appeared different. She'd always been a pretty thing. Reminded him a lot of Laney when she was younger. But this girl who stood at the bottom of his ramp wasn't the Trista he had known back at the Reserve. Her entire countenance was changed. Almost like she was nothing more than a drone.

"I believe I am actually ten minutes early. My readout tells me I am expected at eleven thirty hours," Trista replied, staring up at Britt with an even gaze.

"'Deed. Well, don' jus' stahnd zer. I've a 'puter zat needs fixin'." Britt waved her onboard, his eyes noting the attendants who waited for ships that probably wouldn't come. They should be leaving in a few moments, as the lunch hour approached.

It irked him to see her wearing the Legacy garb and the short hairstyle. If he'd understood Redic and Armand correctly, the ExMed doctors had cut her hair prior to performing that awful surgery on her. He hated to be the one to confirm that. Chase was having a hard enough time.

"Where is the problem?" Trista asked, having climbed aboard, tool pack in hand.

"I wahn' ID befuh I let ya tinker wiz mah ship," Britt said, pasting a smirk on his face. He knew he was being obnoxious, but he had orders for reconnaissance, and he was determined to get as many details as possible.

She held up a Legacy issue identifier. "Krissa Carlisle, registered SA," she recited as he took the card. "Legacy-issue ID zero-two-C-one-nine-one-seven."

"Ya look familiuh. 'Av I seen ya somewhuh befuh?" Britt asked, lifting an eyebrow. *Come on, kid. Remember something. Anything.*

"It's possible. You requested me specifically," Trista said, staring directly into his eyes. "I might have provided service for you in the past."

Britt cocked an eyebrow. "Ya don' r'membuh?"

With a little shrug, Trista answered, "I work on a lot of computers, sir. After a while, they all look the same."

"I'z see," Britt said, handing back the identifier. Her eyes looked hollow. As she pocketed the identifier, Britt found himself feeling wave after wave of pity. Anger toward the Legacy coursed through him as well.

"The computer?" Trista asked. It was a shallow attempt to get the conversation back on task.

Britt pointed to the small room up a short ladder. "In ze cockpit."

"Thank you." Trista turned and crossed to the ladder, pulling herself up. Britt followed closely.

"Yeah, we wuz goin' 'bout our bizee-ness, and alla sudden, we'd a *ghost* in the muhchine," Britt said, emphasizing his words in hopes of a reaction. He didn't like the idea of those triggers hurting her, but he had to know what might set her off.

Trista's forehead twitched slightly as she tossed her gear on one of the seats and knelt down in front of the console. "What was it doing?" she asked.

"Well, I'z *chase ghosts* fer a livin'. Ya ever do zat? *Chase … ghosts?*"

Britt watched as Trista squeezed her eyes closed, angling her head a bit as if she was fighting an oncoming headache. After a moment, she shook off whatever the pain was, returning to her bland, passive state.

"Don't believe in them. To me, that's just a bunch of nonsense," Trista answered, apparently not grasping Britt's references. "The problem?" she asked again as she removed the casing cabinet from the console.

"Blasted zing won' transmit, an' I cain't get ze engine to sta't up," Britt replied, lowering his eyes. He would only have bad news to report. But now there was the question of whether or not to nab her and bring her back to the Ghosts against her will.

"Should be an easy fix," Trista said, poking around the open console with her fingers and a hand torch.

"Great," Britt muttered as he started to sit down in one of the passenger chairs to watch. Perhaps a bit more conversation …

"Um, Mr. Hazelton," she said without even looking his direction. "I work better alone."

Another strike. Trista hated being alone. If she wasn't with Chase, she was with one of her friends. That was one reason she always caught rides with outgoing runs when she took on assignments. Blast, the Legacy really had changed her.

Britt frowned, scooping himself up. "All right. I'll jus' be in here," he said, gesturing toward the main cabin. From his sleeve, he pulled out a Ruli card—the prince. It was marked with the Ghost symbol. Maybe it would spark something in her. He slipped it in her open tool pack. "If you need me," he added.

Double blast.

◆

Krissa shook her head as the buffoon hopped down from the cockpit. Who did he think he was fooling with that moustache, anyway? Anyone with eyes would be able to tell that it was fake. And the accent. By the end of their conversation, he had dropped it completely. And if he'd only bothered to look under the console, he would have seen that the ignition flux had been disabled. What an idiot.

He was a ghost chaser, after all.

"He chases ghosts …" she whispered with the thought. A sharp pain crackled through her forehead, causing her to whimper, but it went away as quickly as it came on. She dismissed it.

He couldn't be that bright. Did people still do that anymore? Science had proved that ghosts weren't real. Just electromagnetic imprints left behind. Krissa shook her head again. Besides, the Legacy hated talk of ghosts. Wait! Was he …?

She brought the console online and scanned through his transmissions. All encrypted with some sort of unrecognizable coding. A familiar pattern amid the symbols stood out—a small t, an E on its back, and a U with a line across the top. Immediately, she knew the E stood for the Crown, and the t U combination meant the Ghosts. Their symbol was a sword and a shield.

How did she know that?

Blinking, she held her breath as she peered toward the main cabin. Oh, boy. He wasn't a ghost chaser. He was a Ghost. Surely he wasn't trying to recruit her.

The glitch was an easy fix, as she had guessed. Improper sequencing blocked transmission. As soon as she cleared that up, the signals went out without a problem. Less than five minutes. She wanted to get out of there before he spewed any Ghost propaganda on her. She believed in the Legacy. And it was her duty to report him.

She packed up her tools and climbed out of the cockpit. "I, um, don't have the proper tool to access your ignition flux. I'll go fetch it and be right back."

"If you'd wait just a moment, I may have what you're lookin' for," the man said, his moustache twitching. He seemed flustered.

"I imagine one of the docking techs has one," Krissa said, holding her tool pack close to her. The ramp was secured. He'd locked her in. She forced calm to her face.

"There's no one out there. They've all gone for lunch. Really, I have a bunch of stuff back here," he answered, waving her toward a small cargo area.

"I'll be right back," Krissa insisted, nervousness dancing in her knees. "Open the ramp, please."

"Just a moment," he said again, popping his head out of the cargo area.

"*Now*, sir." She couldn't control the sense of panic that rose in her throat.

"I, uh—it should be right here."

Krissa yanked the panel from the wall, immediately disabling the ramp. The metal walkway fell open with a loud clatter, and she ran from the shuttle. She couldn't put enough distance between them. Whether the man wanted to hurt her in some way or take her back to the Ghosts as their prisoner, she couldn't tell, but she wasn't about to stick around long enough to find out.

The man appeared behind her, calling, "Wait! Come back!"

The bay blurred by her as she ran through it. Her legs carried her over the prep strip and through another docking field to a Zenith reporting station along the opposite wall. She picked up the link.

"Go, bay B twelve three-oh."

"Ghost ship," Krissa gasped, ignoring the shock of pain in her head that accompanied her words. "Field one-oh-two."

The link buzzed before the voice cut in again. "Zeniths are on their way. Name and ID?"

"Krissa Carlisle. Legacy ID zero-two-C-one-nine-one-seven," she recited.

"Thank you, Miss Carlisle." The buzzing returned before the voice said, "Given your status, Miss Carlisle, you will be expected to remain at the scene until you are released by the Zenith commander. If you do not, you will be apprehended. Do you understand?"

Status? Must be something to do with her medical situation. "Yes, sir," she answered. She'd feel better when she saw the uniforms approaching.

"Out," the link buzzed once again, then terminated.

Krissa sauntered back into view of the ship. Her wary eye scoped out the scene as she neared. Sure enough, as the Ghost man had said, all the attendants had moved off. Hazelton now stood at the top of the ramp, trying to piece back the panel as he obviously waited for her. "Any luck?" he asked.

She almost felt sorry for him. He'd been nice. A little weird, but nice. Except for not opening the ramp, of course. And possibly arranging for all the attendants to take off for lunch. And maybe trying to kidnap her or turn her Ghost. Movement caught Krissa's eye, drawing her gaze to the far corner of the bay. A man clad in a black flight suit ran toward the ship, shouting, "Get 'er up! Zeniths are coming!"

Hazelton stared at her for a moment before he ducked back into the ship. The other man leapt onboard and cranked up the ramp manually. They weren't going anywhere, though, with that igni—

The engine started right up. It had been a ploy. The man must have known about the ignition flux. Why would he do that? It was almost as though he had sabotaged his own ship. And if he had, then he *was* there to capture her. Why? She wasn't important. She was a no one in Legacy society.

A siren blared through the bay. "Attention, bay sector B, level one. Lockdown commencing." The automated announcement came across as Zeniths filtered into the bay.

The Ghost ship lifted off the ground, turning midair. It zoomed past the group of Zeniths, who quickly activated their slayers and shot at the shuttle. Krissa hid behind a pile of crates to avoid ricocheting blasts. She tucked her tool pack under her arm, squeezed her eyes closed, and covered her ears.

Shouting and cursing eventually replaced the loud whirring of the ship. "Find this Krissa Carlisle!" someone called out.

Whoever it was sounded angry, but of course, the Ghosts had just made their escape. The Zeniths hated the Ghosts for that very reason. They always made the Zenith Brigade look like incompetent fools.

Krissa peered out from the crates, rising slowly with her hands up. "I-I'm Krissa," she said, barely loud enough to be heard.

Two slayers snapped in her direction, taking aim at her head as the Zeniths who held them closed in on either side of her. Their commander stepped forward, demanding her tool pack and identifier. She offered the pack to him before fishing out her identifier.

"Did you assist in their escape?" he questioned, glaring first at her, then her card.

"No. I reported them as soon as I—" Krissa tried to defend herself.

The commander handed off the tool pack to another Zenith, who immediately rummaged through it. Krissa didn't know what they might be looking for, but they would find nothing but small tools specifically for use with computing hardware. She wrapped her arms around herself as she watched.

"They were logged as needing repair. How were they able to get off the ground?"

"I don't know. All they had to do was enable their ignition flux," she said.

"Did you tell them that?"

"No, I—" She stopped herself. Oh, no. She *had* told Hazelton that the problem was with the ignition flux.

"Commander," the inspecting Zenith said, holding her tool pack in one hand and some card in the other.

The commander took the card, examining it before flipping it in his fingers to hold up in front of Krissa. "What's this?" he asked.

It seemed to be a gaming card, marked with those same symbols in the Ghost code. Where had it come from?

"I-I don't know," she answered, allowing her confusion to show.

"I think the interrogators can get better answers from you."

"No! Please! I—"

The commander gestured toward Krissa, and the two Zeniths who stood near lowered their guns and produced a pair of binders. They grabbed her, roughly placing the cuffs around her wrists.

"Please! I didn't do anything!" Krissa insisted.

"We'll find out for certain," the commander sneered, walking away. "Aiding and abetting Ghosts is quite the crime, Miss Carlisle. As is being one."

The Zeniths shoved Krissa forward as the commander led them from the bay. Another flash of pain in her skull. She knew that resistance would only lead to brutality or worse punishment, so she went willingly. Perhaps the interrogators would be merciful. Their reputation suggested otherwise, but Krissa hoped she could convince them of her innocence and loyalty. She hoped …

CHAPTER 9

Dr. Terces scanned the chart on his desk before signing off on the requested procedure. He understood why Dr. Niveli insisted that the other doctors report their treatment plans, particularly in the case of ExMed, but he wished she would find someone else to review the charts. He simply hadn't the time. This approval had been sitting on his desk for a number of weeks, delaying the procedure.

The door to the office burst open, revealing a harried Aftal. His red cheeks indicated that something was wrong. Very wrong. Terces stood, a frown lining his brow. "What is it?"

"You haven't heard?" Aftal asked, skittering to the desk.

He tapped on the keypad of the DDL, bringing up the LUM. A few more keystrokes produced the news Aftal intended to share. A list of prisoners currently involved in interrogation three floors down. Aftal pointed toward the top of the list.

Detainee: Carlisle, Krissa
Legacy ID: 02C1917
Affiliation: Legacy (claimed), Ghost (suspected)
Date, Time, and Location of Arrest: Day 9302 PLR; 1145 hours; Pavana: Voler: Dock B1230: Field 102

Reason for Detention: Aiding and abetting Ghost escape
Status: Processed, Preliminary (failed), Interrogation
Stage 1 (failed), Interrogation Stage 2 (in progress)
Approved Interrogation Threshold: Stage 5 (maximum)

"Wait here," Terces ordered, stepping to the door. "And link Matlen and Berreks. Have Matlen meet me at the interrogation facility immediately. You and Berreks prep the lab."

"You think they've hurt her?" Aftal asked.

Terces just shook his head, dashing down the hall. Fury seethed from every cell of his body. He didn't bother to wait for the lifts. He flew down the stairs instead, his lab coat whipping behind him.

Matlen waited for him at the reception desk. Terces blew past the woman who stood to greet him, her welcoming words turning to idle threats of alerting Zeniths. He gestured for Matlen to follow him.

He knew exactly where Krissa was being held. ExMed had begun as an offshoot of the interrogation program. In fact, he had helped create and structure the interrogation methods when the Legacy first took power. They wanted a quick and efficient way to get answers from their prisoners. Long ago, Terces had discovered that most people respond best to pain.

Storming into the interrogators' surveillance room, Terces shoved the monitoring officer out of his chair. The Zenith on guard reached for his slayer, but Matlen, quite a bit larger and far more foreboding, advised him to stand down. Dr. Terces typed in a series of codes on the keypad, shutting down the interrogators' equipment within the adjacent room.

One of the interrogators, clad in the protective interrogation suit and helmet, glanced up toward the mirror, shrugging as if to ask what was going on. Terces lifted the console link. "A word, please," he said, allowing his rage to creep into the tone of his voice.

The interrogator raised a hand to his partner and handed off his interrogation rods before stepping from the darkened room. Terces frowned, his gaze falling on Krissa. She was strapped to their table, her eyes closed. Under the black light, he could see multiple, angry cuts that lashed her cheeks and trailed down her arms. Stage one of the interrogation had obviously been ineffective.

The interrogator stepped through the door into the observation area. He removed his helmet, staring with annoyance toward Dr. Terces. "What is this intrusion about?"

Flashing his identifier, Terces pointed toward the interrogation room. "You have my patient in there. You neglected to cross-reference your records."

"No, we did not," the interrogator answered. "That's part of our normal operating procedure. I assure you, that step was completed."

Terces leaned forward, clenching his fists. "If you had properly cross-referenced, you would have seen that this subject has undergone a major ExMed procedure and is under our authority. Any issues should have been reported to me straight away."

The interrogator squared his jaw, a smug expression settling on his face. "None of our techniques conflict with ExMed procedures, Doctor," he argued. "You saw to that yourself."

Bowing his head, Terces released a heavy sigh. The interrogator was trying to disarm him. He knew when the Legacy established the interrogation program as priority, there would be an issue one day. This man before him, Interrogator Gamead as his identifier read, outranked him. Gamead had Zeniths at his disposal. But Terces wasn't about to give up. He wasn't going to lose Krissa and all his work so easily.

"This is a new procedure. She is the first to undergo the treatment," Terces explained, trying to stay calm. "I demand that you release her at once."

With an air of defensiveness, Gamead crossed his arms over his inflated chest. "We have her in custody for Ghost interaction. It's quite possible that she assisted in a Ghost escape. Sorry, Doc. She's not going anywhere."

Dr. Terces dug his fingernails into his palms, looking again toward Krissa as her entire body twitched. It was possible that the interrogation, as well as Krissa's contact with the Ghosts, had interrupted his work. He'd have quite a bit of mopping up to do.

"Matlen, link Niveli and ask her to join me here immediately. And then link Aftal. Tell him we'll be in the lab within ten minutes." Terces glared at Gamead. "I'll get the clearance you need to release her to me."

An impatient chuckle shook Gamead's shoulders. "I can't leave her waiting much longer. She is thick in the midst of truth sleep, and we are in the middle of a line of questioning that—"

The interrogator obviously didn't get it. And he certainly didn't care.

"You will halt your questioning immediately. You've already caused enough damage." Shaking his head again, Dr. Terces pushed past Gamead and into the interrogation room. It was a move that he knew Gamead wasn't expecting.

Gamead followed, his white suit glowing a brilliant purple under the ultraviolet bulbs. "You can't come in here!" he insisted.

Ignoring him, Terces took Krissa's hand, trying to rouse her. "Miss Carlisle, can you hear me? Respond. Compliance."

Her jaw slackened, Krissa rolled her head to look at him and opened her eyes to slits before allowing her head to loll back. She was thoroughly incoherent, beyond the range of the truth sleep—a sure sign that dissonance had set in. At this point, no amount of interrogation would get answers. Terces clapped his hands to get Matlen's attention. "Tell Aftal to meet us now," he said, shifting the brakes on the table to allow it to roll freely.

"Doctor," Gamead all but shouted, grabbing the end of the table, "you cannot take my detainee."

Raising his voice over Gamead's, Terces said, "She will be brain-dead in a matter of minutes if I don't. You don't seem to understand. This is a point of crisis for this subject. Dr. Niveli will give you the authorization codes as soon as she gets down here, but for now, you must release Miss Carlisle to me. I have to get her back to ExMed *now*."

The interrogator glanced at his partner before he shoved the table back from him. Terces managed to hold it steady. "Fine. Take her. If those auth codes prove false, you're in a world of trouble. I'll not only take it to our commander, but to the Tribunal if I have to," Gamead snarled.

"Don't threaten me," Dr. Terces countered, spinning the table around to wheel Krissa out of the interrogation room. Matlen took his place, allowing Terces to check her out as they ran toward the bank of lifts to get up to ExMed. Terces hoped he had gotten to her in time. Before any real damage was done.

◆

Seraph nodded his gratitude to Remy as she placed a mug of kaf on the table before him. Cole and Britt followed suit. None of them wanted to be here in Redic's office, but Remy managed to make the situation almost pleasant with her hospitality. If only the circumstances were otherwise. Redic thanked her as she took her usual seat next to him, before he looked at the men.

"Tell me what happened," he said.

"She came," Britt answered with a shrug. "She wasn't Trista, though. She called herself Krissa Carlisle and rattled off some Legacy ID code. Throughout our conversation, I dropped hints, as you suggested. I tried to keep her onboard, at least until Cole showed up, but I didn't want her thinking I was trying to kidnap her or something."

Cole sat back from the table, shaking his head. "She must have thought that, though, because she pulled the ramp panel apart to get off the shuttle. I had to draw it up by hand, and Grease is having a blasted time trying to put it back together."

"And I'm guessing that she was the one who reported us, because that's when the Zeniths arrived. We had to get out of there." Britt frowned, swirling his kaf around in his cup. He was obviously distraught. "And I had to leave her behind."

Redic sighed, rubbing his forehead as he leaned heavily on the arm of his chair. "Which landed her in a heap of trouble."

Shifting in his seat, Seraph's gaze bounced from Britt to Redic. "What do you mean, Dad?" he asked.

"Remy ran Trista's pseudonym through the LUM as soon as she received Britt's report," Redic replied, glancing to Remy.

"Zeniths arrested Krissa Carlisle following the escape. They took her back to Crenet and processed her immediately into interrogator custody for aiding and abetting Ghosts. The interrogation log shows that they ran her through preliminary and stage one last night and moved into stage two," Remy said, reading the information from a PDL, "but she was released to Dr. Cyndra Niveli within just a couple of hours."

Seraph closed his eyes, shaking his head. This got more and more complicated as the days went on. Trista was worth their efforts, though. And they wouldn't stop trying until they got her back. He certainly hated having to be the one to tell Chase what he'd just heard. But knowing Chase, he'd probably already run the reports.

"Where did they take her?" Cole asked quietly.

"We don't know. The LUM doesn't give us anything, and all records of Trista end with her death announcement. Armand's trying to dig up something more on her or Krissa, but even he's getting very little on the inside," Redic answered.

Leaning forward against the table, Seraph looked at his dad. "As part of the advisory board, could Armand ask about her?"

"Neither of us feels that he could without risking his identity as a Ghost."

"Sticky situation," Britt commented.

"I still don't get this whole thing," Redic said. "Is it about Chase? Do they want him that badly?"

Seraph frowned, encircling his cup with his fingers. "I don't think so, Dad. I don't think it's about the connection between Chase and Trista at all. Sure, they'd like to get their hands on Chase, but even the Legacy wouldn't torment his wife like this just to get at him. They know that he'd have sacrificed himself for her freedom weeks ago. There's been no offers made, no bargains …"

"I agree with Seraph," Britt said. "There's more to it than what we think."

"Then we have to find out what it is. And put an end to it," Redic said, looking at Remy. "Let's get with Armand and Zak. See if we can't get a few people in strategic places to be our eyes and ears for a bit."

Remy made a note on her PDL, looking back at Redic. "What do we tell Chase? When he's not out on assignment, he's been in here every few hours, asking what we've heard. I purposely didn't tell him about this meeting."

Redic shook his head, blowing out another heavy breath. "Nothing we tell him will make it any easier. If I were him, I'd be looking for every opportunity to make a run. Seraph, keep him close to home. Any runs you assign to him, make sure they are simple. Keep him busy, but focused."

"Yes, sir," Seraph answered. "And I'll tell him something. I won't disclose everything. This news will destroy him. I'll just say that we'll continue to monitor the situation and look for any opportunities that we can to get to her."

"Very good. Gentlemen," Redic straightened in his chair as he addressed Britt and Cole, "thank you. I'm sorry it was so close, but I'm thankful you made it home."

Britt stood, followed by Cole. "Anytime, Redic," Britt said with a regretful, yet cordial smile. "I'm just sorry that we failed. Let us know how else we can help."

"It wasn't failure. We have more information to go on, and the two of you are safe. I'd count that as success." Redic smiled, placing both hands on the table as he rose. "But I will let you know when we make our next move. Dismissed."

With nods all around, Britt and Cole left. Seraph took a long sip from his mug before he looked at Remy and Redic. "I suppose I should go find Chase," he said, pushing himself to his feet.

Remy stood also, collecting the mugs from Seraph's side of the table. "I imagine you won't have to look very far. Try my office."

Seraph chuckled. "He already told me that he was heading to the sacrarium this morning. Felt like he needed some time with the Crown."

"Not a bad idea," Redic replied, handing off his cup to Remy. "I'll ask Aram to convene a formal service. It's been too long since we've done so. It's all too easy to forget that we don't have to go this alone. I think everyone could use that reminder."

"I just hope that Chase can make peace with the idea that we may not get Trista back," Seraph said, staring down into his mug.

"I hope he doesn't have to," Redic murmured. "I'm trying to remain optimistic."

"And that's why you're the leader." Seraph smiled, offering his mug to Remy, whispering his thanks. "You've got far more confidence than I do."

"It's not a matter of confidence, son," Redic said, clapping his son on the back. "It's a matter of faith."

CHAPTER 10

The immaculate, sterile room seemed strangely familiar. She'd been here before—waking up just like this—without a clue as to how she got there. She blinked, taking in the small black screens next to her, lit with green bars and graphs. Her every breath, heartbeat, and movement charted out in computerized lines, chirping with mechanical rhythms.

"Good afternoon, Miss Carlisle," Dr. Terces greeted her with his usual down-to-business tone. "And how are you feeling?"

"Dr. Terces?" Krissa whispered. Exhaustion enveloped her in a bewildering grogginess. With a groan, she tried to lift her head from the pillow, but it felt heavy and cumbersome. She just didn't have the strength. Instead, she closed her eyes again. "My head feels ... so heavy. What happened?"

"Do you not remember?" he asked, adjusting something that pressed against her forehead. "Note that."

"It's all a little muddled," she murmured, floating between reality and unconsciousness. The beeps of the machines reminded her that something important was happening. With some effort, she managed to ground herself on the reality side, clinging tightly to the outside world around her.

A female, out of Krissa's line of sight, said, "Looks like that round didn't take. We'll have to run her through another bout of IIS."

"But I want to allow her some time to rest," Dr. Terces replied. He shifted to address someone else behind him. "Have Dr. Aftal join us, please."

The weight on her head bore down against her shoulders as awareness settled in. Icy metal pressed against her neck before she heard the brittle ripping sound of hook and loop fasteners. The heaviness lifted from her skull. She opened her eyes to see Dr. Terces removing a complicated metal device, placing it on a table next to her. Perhaps she should have asked about the frightening equipment, but dehydration prickled her throat and crumpled her tongue into a useless mass. Water seemed more important.

"May I—" she started, her words sticking along the desiccated tissue.

"What is it, Miss Carlisle?" Dr. Terces asked, massaging specific spots along her forehead with his fingers. She winced with each touch. The spots were tender.

"M-may I have ..." she paused for breath, "... a sip of water?"

Dr. Terces indicated his approval with a nod. In the background, Krissa heard movement and refreshing water trickling from a faucet. A blond-haired man—someone she felt she should recognize—took Dr. Terces's place at her side. His gentle hand lifted her head and angled her neck to meet the crisp paper cup.

She closed her eyes again as the wetness touched her lips and washed down her throat. Too much water filtered into her mouth and went down the wrong way, causing her to sputter. Spasmodic coughing split her head in two, heavy pressure squeezing her brain. As the spell faded, she dropped back against the pillows, whimpering. She grasped for any sort of cohesive thought, but the commotion in her head raged with agony.

Dr. Terces berated the man who had offered her the drink. Something about undoing all that had been done. Compromising his work. She didn't understand. Dr. Terces's tone suddenly changed. "Ah, Dr. Aftal."

Krissa forced her eyes open a little to see a man, slightly younger than Dr. Terces, with dark hair, standing next to her bed. She felt like she should know him, too. She'd seen him before, hadn't she? He nodded toward her, then lifted his gaze to Dr. Terces. "Complications?"

"I'm afraid so. The interrogation obscured the ITCs, but I was able to get them back online with this round of IIS. Nothing ruptured, fortunately, but the programming seems slightly skewed. She doesn't remember what happened." Dr. Terces held up a finger, then turned to Krissa. "Miss Carlisle, where are you?"

Krissa blinked, focusing on Dr. Terces. "Um ... a-a medical facility somewhere," she said. She really didn't know beyond that. She knew who she was. She knew her doctor. But that was about it.

"Why?" he asked. "Why are you here?"

"I don't know." Panic robbed her of breath, and her mouth felt dry. "May I have a sip of water?"

Dr. Terces pressed his lips together, sharing a concerned glance with Dr. Aftal. "Note that." He lowered his eyes to Krissa. "You just had one."

She didn't remember. "I did?"

Dr. Aftal gestured for Terces to move. He took Dr. Terces's seat, shining a bright light into her eyes. She blinked, but he placed a cool hand on her face and forced one eye open, then the other. He pocketed the light, looking up at Dr. Terces. "I don't think the ITCs are damaged in any way, but we'll need to juice up the IIS to a pretty intense level. You'll have to put her under and monitor her closely."

"We can do that," Dr. Terces said, gesturing to the blond man. "Contact the pharm. I need ten units each of morisentia and anisceptrum. And the usual pre-IIS cocktail. We'll start her with serenidor and somnoctis."

"Going all out, huh?" Dr. Aftal chuckled.

"Not taking chances. We can't lose her," Dr. Terces replied, crossing to the opposite side of Krissa's bed.

"Still," Dr. Aftal said as his eyes met Krissa's. He gave her a quick smile before looking back at Terces. "Seems a bit much."

"Only ten units each. They'll work together for the effect we're seeking," Terces replied.

The woman asked, "No deleouxor?"

"No. Her memories are under control. It's now a matter of getting the story straight," Terces answered.

Krissa wished she understood what they were talking about. It sounded important. She should remember why it sounded important. The memories were there. She just couldn't grasp them.

"Retain some of what occurred, particularly with the interrogators," the woman ordered. "If she has deep-seated fear of them, she will do all she can to avoid them."

Dr. Terces now stared at a monitor above Krissa's head. "And I want that same fear regarding the Ghosts. We will have no more encounters like this."

Krissa winced in pain. She closed her eyes as the sharpness winked out of her brain.

"Note that," Terces said.

"So Miss Carlisle serviced a Ghost ship without her knowledge, reported them, but was arrested and spent some time with the interrogators. They eventually found her innocent." Dr. Aftal sounded like he was spinning a story. A story she was on the brink of remembering, had the pain not interfered again.

"Yes," Dr. Terces confirmed. "But there is lingering question regarding her loyalty. She will be watched, and I want her to know that. Perhaps that will keep her away from the Ghosts."

"He chases ghosts ..." Krissa whispered, remembering what the Ghost man on the ship said. "Chases ..." No, not chases. Chase. A man's face, kind and loving, pierced her memory before fire roared through her head, erasing all sensibility.

"Let's get on it. Now," Dr. Terces said. "The interrogation also affected the pain inducers. The concentration is too strong. We need to dial it back a bit. It has to be more subtle. I don't want the pain to be obvious to those interacting with her."

Krissa opened her eyes again as the throbbing settled into a dull ache. She wondered if the doctors would give her a sip of water. Her tongue felt heavy and dry, and her throat tickled with thirst. "May I have a sip of water?" she whispered.

"Right," Dr. Aftal confirmed, ignoring Krissa as he made more notes on his PDL. "Your directive word is still 'compliance,' and it's programmed to recognize only your voice. I'll make it so that every time she hears you say that, the ITCs will defrag her memory and clear out anything that is blocking the programming. It will also wrench her neural net into absolute obedience."

"Water?" she asked once more, barely able to hear herself.

"Good," Dr. Terces continued. "Once the IIS finished, I'm going to veer from procedure so that we can see where she is. I'll stimulate her cortex and try to bring her back to a state of lucidity. Cursed interrogators."

"And gentlemen," the female's voice sounded terse and angry, "not a word of this to anyone. It stays off the record. I'll clean up the mess between the interrogators and us. Altus is already holding off curious members of the advisory board so that you have leeway to do as necessary with the subject. If it comes to it, we abandon the project and rid ourselves of the evidence."

"It won't come to that, Cyndra," Dr. Terces said as he removed a vial from his pocket, attached a needle, and stuck it into the intravenous port affixed to Krissa's wrist.

No. She tried to pull her hand away, but he held her firmly. He didn't understand. She needed water. And there was something she had to tell him. Something about Chase.

Her tongue couldn't form the right words. "Ch-chases ..." she finally stammered.

Dr. Aftal placed his PDL next to the large apparatus on the table. He would listen to her. He'd been nice to her so far. With efficient motion, he reached above her to pull down a mask to place over her mouth and nose. He didn't even look at her. Please. "Water ..." she murmured as a misty gas filtered into her lungs.

Clouds of night blanketed her thoughts, causing her eyelids to droop. She felt the bed underneath her move. The doctors were whisking her away somewhere. "He chases ghosts ..." she whispered into the mask, hoping they would hear her before she blacked out completely.

◆

Day 9339 PLR: Revenant

Weeks had passed since the disastrous rescue effort. As Seraph had guessed, Chase didn't take lightly to the news that Britt and Cole were unsuccessful in bringing Trista home. In fact, he wasn't even acting like himself. He disregarded orders, ignored run assignments, and quit speaking to Seraph altogether, which was crazy because they had been best friends for a long time. He'd instead grown closer to his first officer, Nicodemus Church.

While Seraph had no problem with Nic, he didn't like the idea that Nic went along with Chase and fed into the frenzy of finding Trista. They'd pirated a ship from the fleet and set off about the system, trying to find any leads on her. Seraph had learned by way of hearsay that their journeys were as futile as the botched rescue, and that they'd returned home empty-handed. He'd also heard that Chase took out his anger on the ship and disabled it beyond repair. Redic was furious with the men, especially Chase. During the Crew's last meeting—which Chase had blown off—the topic of discipline arose, and Seraph had begged Redic to let him be the one to talk with Chase. Redic's anger could sometimes bury his compassion.

Seraph crossed the darkened operations room to the observation desk where Chase sat, staring at an array of computer monitors. Most everyone else was taking advantage of the sleeping hours. Chase, though, had just landed an hour or so ago. Man, he looked rough. His dark hair, normally kept neat, had grown shaggy. Add to that the scruffy chin and lost eyes. Seraph had good cause for concern. Pure obsession had taken hold of his friend.

Seraph leaned on the hutch of the desk, glancing down at the screen that was capturing Chase's attention before turning his gaze to Chase. Chase wouldn't even look at him. The silence between them was more than uncomfortable and had to be broken.

"What's going on, Chase?" Seraph asked.

"I suppose you're here to tell me how much trouble I'm in with the old man," Chase muttered, still concentrating on the monitor.

"I think you already know that," Seraph answered. "But actually, I was hoping maybe you'd remember we're friends and that you can talk to me."

Chase tore his eyes from the screen, bowing his head into his hand. Seraph watched him, wanting to speak words of comfort, but also wanting to give Chase the time to come to grips with whatever was bothering him. He heard Chase take a deep breath and release it in a heavy sigh.

"She can't be gone," he finally whispered with an edge of grief.

The barrier between them was gone in an instant. Seraph knelt at Chase's side, placing a hand on his shoulder. He wished he could offer encouragement, what Chase wanted to hear, but the realist in him just couldn't do it. "Britt said she was different. That she didn't recognize him at all."

"He was in disguise," Chase argued.

"Not completely," Seraph replied. "If she had known him, she would have seen past that stupid moustache. He did everything but outright tell her who he was."

Chase shook his head. "I should have been there."

"You couldn't have helped her, Chase. She's not Trista anymore. And Brax, or Selah, or even I may not be able to change her back. You're going to have to accept that."

"No," Chase said, turning to look at Seraph. "No, I don't have to accept that. She's my wife, and I love her, and I'm not letting her go that easily. You wouldn't, were it Echo they sliced into. I seem to recall you going to all lengths short of ending your life to help her."

Seraph sighed back into the silence, uncertain of how to console Chase. He was absolutely right. If Echo were captured by the Legacy, he'd take them on single-handedly to get her back. And he had done just that two years earlier.

"Do you think—?" Chase stopped himself.

"Do I think what?" Seraph asked softly.

The question obviously perturbed Chase. It must have been one he'd been struggling with for some time. "Blazes, Ser, do you think that the Crown would deny her eternity because of what they've done?"

Seraph's heart ached for Chase. "No," he murmured. "She saw Ternion. She knew the Ruler Prince and believed. And the Holy Book tells us that once someone is in His hand, they cannot be taken away."

"I'm being punished—" Chase's brows knit into a somber frown.

"You're not being punished."

"—for not being faithful to the Crown." Chase's fist slammed against the arm of his chair. "For intentionally turning from Him to find her."

"That's *not* how it works, Chase," Seraph said in a raised voice. He immediately softened his tone. "The Crown is not about punishment and bedlam. He doesn't use events like this to hurt us. Even when we turn away. He wants you to cling to Him."

"I've clung, Ser. I've grasped. I've clutched. I've held on until my proverbial fingers bled." Chase covered his face with his hands. "But He didn't bring her back."

"Don't give up on the Crown." Seraph now whispered his plea. "He takes us to moments of complete brokenness sometimes, and we may not fully understand why. I've been there, Chase. I've forsaken Him, and believe me, you don't want to go there. But we give Him that little extra measure of faith, and He accomplishes miraculous things through that."

"If she doesn't remember us, would it be kinder to ..." Chase squeezed his eyes closed.

Seraph placed a hand over his mouth and rubbed it along his face. He couldn't believe Chase was suggesting such a thing. "We're not going to kill her, Chase."

"I'm not leaving her to the Legacy," he said, his words full of pain.

Seraph's eyes flickered toward the monitor. An image of Trista wrapped in Chase's arms smiled back at him. On another screen, the death order and announcement blared from the LUM. Chase desperately needed a change of scenery. He also needed a shower, solid rest, and some good food. He was dwelling on things in a most unhealthy way.

"Come on, man. Let's get out of here for a bit. Make a run to Serenata or something," Seraph suggested lightly, hoping a recreational run would tempt Chase away from his fixation.

"I can't—" he started before a shrill beep interrupted him.

"What's that?" Seraph asked, sliding into a seat next to his friend.

"By the Crown," Chase murmured, his attention turning to a map of the system.

"What?"

Chase leaned forward over the keypad and began to type furiously. "I ran a trace on her link." He then sat back and pointed to a flashing red dot on one of the screens. "That's her distress signal."

Slumping back in his chair, Seraph shook his head. "It's not her, Chase. Frisco used her link to contact us, remember?"

"But he said he dropped it on the floor before he passed out," Chase explained, holding up a finger as he made his point. He opened his hand as he filled in the possibility. "She could have picked it up."

"Or a Zenith could have picked it up. It's been too long."

"It's her, Ser. She needs me to help her. Don't ask me to give up on her," Chase said, looking at Seraph with beseeching eyes.

Seraph frowned, a frustrated sigh rolling from him. "It's a suicide mission, Chase."

"And what if it's not?" Chase returned his focus to the map. The light flashed from near Crenet. "Assign me a run, Ser. I'll take the *Halcyon* crew and check it out."

Seraph again shook his head. "I won't put additional lives at risk. And if you were thinking clearly, you wouldn't, either."

"They won't be at risk. I'll dock them and go myself. Alone."

Pressing his lips together, Seraph growled, "Zoom in. See what we're looking at."

Chase's fingers flew across the keypad as the computer zeroed in on a more specific location. "A Zephyr base, abandoned," he said, "on Soubrette."

Folding his arms over his chest, Seraph rocked back in his chair. "No way. And why would Trista send a distress signal from there, Chase? Think, man."

"You look like the old man, sitting like that," The old Chase surfaced, teasing Seraph. He quickly gave way to the fanatical Chase. "A number of reasons, Ser. She could have remembered something while she was doing a job. They could be holding her prisoner there. She could—"

"It's not her." Seraph pushed back his chair and stood, looking down at Chase.

"Please, Seraph." Chase's eyes met his, filled with tears. "I need to do this."

"You just came in—"

"I can't sleep," Chase confessed. His hands collapsed over his chest. "My heart ... is out there somewhere." He gestured to the screen. "I have to find it before it stops beating and kills me completely."

After a moment of internal debate, Seraph returned to his seat with another sigh. "You'd better make it quick. And I don't want you flying alone. I'll send your crew, as long as you promise me that you'll try to rest along the way. They're not too happy with you for grounding them the last few weeks."

"I'll talk with them," Chase said.

"And when you enter the base, at least make sure Church is with you." Seraph brought up the orders menu on the screen, typing in the assignment for Chase and his crew. "It's a ludicrous mission, and if my dad sees it, he'll know something is up. You haven't taken on one of your assignments in a while. He's going to think this is a waste of our time and resources ..."

"It won't be a waste," Chase assured him. "Thanks, man."

"You owe me," Seraph muttered with a scowl. "Big time."

CHAPTER 11

Chase gripped his queller and peered around the corner. "Church?" The lights flickered above, the dim fluorescence blinking into the even dimmer green emergency lighting that lined the walls. The corridor was empty. Blast. Where were Church and the others?

What was supposed to be a simple mission had quickly turned complicated. Although the true mission was to investigate Trista's distress call, Seraph's made-up plan involved Chase and the *Halcyon* crew infiltrating the former Zephyr outpost and sending a message back to the Legacy. The message was intended to confuse, in hopes that the Legacy would send a dispatch of Zeniths to investigate. At that point, the rest of Chase's crew would greet the arriving Zeebs, as Chase called them, and walk away with a new set of uniforms. It wasn't much, but definitely worth the humiliated faces they would get to see. Before they left, Seraph had demanded to go with Chase, but Chase refused, promising to rely on Church and the other men.

"Church!" Chase hissed down the hallway.

The mission brief had reported the base as abandoned. However, when Chase and his crew debarked from their shuttle, and Lancaster entered the comm room, slayer blasts were fired. It was then that the lights began to flicker. The base was a trap, as Seraph had expected, and the Zeebs were toying with their prey.

Chase heard a click behind him, immediately followed by the cold, steely touch of a slayer under his ear. He stiffened as an abrasive voice ordered, "Drop the queller, Ghost."

Freezing into position, Chase hoped to buy himself just a second or two to think about his next move. He cautiously raised one hand, situating himself to outdraw the Zenith. He could easily smack the weapon away and quell the guy. As long as—

"Don't even think about it," a second Zeeb sneered, stepping into view. His slayer trained dead on Chase.

Blast. Zeeb One wasn't alone.

With a sigh, Chase allowed his queller to clatter to the floor. He wouldn't be able to help Trista if he was shot to pieces. Zeeb One pushed Chase against the wall and jerked the sword from his belt. Zeeb One passed the sword to Zeeb Two, who exchanged it for a pair of binding cuffs. Zeeb One pulled Chase's arms behind him and clamped the binders around his wrists.

"They are holding the others in ops," Zeeb Two said, admiring Chase's sword.

Zeeb One yanked Chase from the wall and shoved him forward. "Move," he commanded, jamming the slayer into Chase's back.

Chase squared his jaw and marched down the corridor, following Zeeb Two. He watched for an opportunity to take down the two Zeebs, but they soon escorted him into a wide room, full of control panels and his men. An entire squadron of Zeebs stood guard throughout the room, their various slayers activated and ready to take out anyone who made the slightest motion.

A Zephyr officer spun around as they entered the room. A cruel smile licked his lips, catching Chase's gaze. The officer's eyes flickered toward the Zeniths, asking a silent question.

"He's the last one, sir," Zeeb One answered.

"Good," the officer said as he sauntered toward Chase. His tone slipped into a deliberate, taunting lilt. "Could it be that we've ensnared the brilliant Ghost captain Chase Leighton? How in the system could that be?"

Chase quickly scanned the room, counting heads. His entire crew was accounted for. The only good thing about that was it meant no fatalities. Lancaster had taken a hit to his arm, but the others seemed to be untouched. Church's eyes locked onto Chase. As second-in-command, Church had whipped the more inexperienced men into a seasoned crew. Chase was at once saddened and relieved to see him here.

The officer stepped between the two men, glaring at Chase. "No witty response, Leighton? I'm surprised. I've heard that you were quick-tongued. But perhaps you've changed since ..." He smirked as he held up Trista's link.

His nerves quaking with anger, Chase took in a measured breath through his nose. He couldn't let this man get under his skin. "Let the men go free. I'll surrender willingly," he said softly.

A derisive cackle scathed Chase's ears as the officer laughed. "You're joking, right? We have you in chains, Leighton. You have no ground for bargaining."

Chase knew the officer was right. He shot an apologetic look to his men. He'd just won back their loyalty and had been working on earning their trust again. This situation wouldn't help that one bit. The officer instructed his Zeniths to recall the prisoner transport. They were all to be taken to the Justice Center on Crenet for processing. From there, their fates would be decided by the courts.

◆

"The court will not acknowledge your rank, Mr. Leighton, as it is falsely granted. Ghost ranks are not recognized within the confines of the Progressive Legacy," the judge stated, shuffling through a stack of papers. He made it obvious that he was too busy to focus on the proceedings. He hadn't even bothered to show up in person. His image was being broadcast over the Bands.

Chase stood in the tiny room, shackled in the criminal's stall. The Zeniths who had hauled him from his cell stationed themselves on both sides of the stall. Two legal representatives of the Legacy were present to display the evidence against him, sitting at a desk adjacent to the judge screen. The room couldn't even be called a courtroom. It was more like an office that had been restructured to accommodate quick cases.

"With that said," the judge waved his hand toward the representatives, "let's get on with it, gentlemen. The charges have already been recorded."

Bowing his head, Chase closed his eyes and whispered a prayer for strength. He'd already endured the taunting of the Zeniths and the miserable stares from his crew on the way to the Justice Center. And he knew if he ever made it back to Revenant, things would never be the same. But right now, he had to make it through this ordeal.

One of the representatives stood and circled around the desk. "Yes, your honor. Chase Leighton has perpetrated a number of crimes against the Progressive Lega—"

"Enough," the judge interrupted. "I have more pressing cases to oversee, and I've heard plenty already. Mr. Leighton, your reputation precedes you."

"I didn't realize my reputation was at the mercy of the court," Chase interjected.

"We shall now move on to the sentencing."

"Your justice process grants me a fair trial, your honor, although I understand that is no longer the Legacy's practice," Chase said. He knew there would be nothing fair about it, but skipping the proceedings altogether and receiving only the sentence made the trial a mockery. Just as they had done with Trista.

"I think you misunderstood the process, Mr. Leighton. This isn't a trial. It's a sentencing. You are a criminal, plain and simple. You forfeit any rights when you choose such a path." The judge stared at him as he pressed a button affixed to his desk. A red light under the screen indicated that his words were now being recorded for the official transcript. "The Legacy has recently instituted a new rehabilitation program. You will receive treatments, and if your behavior progresses, you may earn free time and perhaps, someday, release. Mr. Leighton, you are hereby, for an indefinite amount of time, sentenced to the *Straightjacket*, the Legacy's new prison ship for the criminally insane."

Chase's jaw dropped as panic lit fire through his chest. "I am not—"

"The doctors will, as stated previously, administer treatments at their discretion in hopes of rehabilitating you to proper citizen status."

Terror tumbled through Chase's head, sending the room spinning. He jerked on his chains, knowing it was a futile effort. They couldn't do this, could they? It was unjust. It was cruel. It was the Legacy. "Your honor—"

"When they feel you can and will comply with Legacy standards, your sentence will be reevaluated. Court officers, remove the criminal and escort him to prison transport," the judge ordered.

"You can't do this!" Chase shouted as two Zeniths grabbed his elbows. "I'm not insane!"

The judge's lips turned up in a callous and cruel smile. Chase could see the malice in his eyes. The red light faded back into the wall. "By the time they are done with you, you will be," the judge said before the Bands screen fizzled to black.

The Zeniths unclamped his shackles from the floor and yanked him from the courtroom through a door on the far side of the room. Chase struggled against them until one produced a stinger. A single zap to his ribcage was enough to bring him to his knees.

"Get up, Ghost," one Zeeb jeered at him, threatening him again with the stinger.

Groaning, Chase slowly pushed himself up and stumbled behind the leading Zenith. He'd have to place his hope in his friends now. And the Crown. But at this point, would the Ghosts compromise themselves for him? When missions were accepted, the risk was understood. No promises of rescue were ever made. And although some effort had been made to help Trista, they hadn't been able to get her home. Chase could very well be on his own too.

The transport was smaller than Chase expected. Most of the staff had already boarded the *Straightjacket* and were awaiting the inmates. From the port, the inmates would be taken to the Vetus rotation and delivered to the ship, which remained mostly stationary just on the very edge of the system. Vetus was a dying star, its red light not nearly as bright as the other two suns. Desolate, isolated, void of life. Chase was sure that the Legacy had that in mind when they anchored the *Straightjacket* in order to prevent ease of escape.

The staff consisted of a team of four doctors and sixteen orderlies. The crew was minimal and, after teaching the staff how to maintain the daily operations, would return to Crenet. The staff would tend to the daily needs and "treatments" of the thirty inmates, ten of whom were Leighton's crew. The others were Ghosts who had been apprehended or other prisoners who had, at one time or other, opposed the Legacy.

The Zeeb who escorted Chase onboard shoved him into a seat and affixed his shackles to the installed hardware on the floor. Chase glanced around, recognizing most of his crewmates. Hal Lancaster—arm bandaged and in a sling. Wes Torin. Ben Reiger. Seth Declan. Thad Newell. Jared Kern. Lem Duncan. Old Joe Weller. They all looked beaten and conquered. Remorse joined the links of Chase's chains, along with fear, panic, and anxiety.

A final prisoner was brought in and placed in a seat near the ramp. The blond-haired man had a patch covering a square of white gauze over his right eye, and a long gash down his cheek. Chase swallowed a gasp as he recognized Church behind the patch. What had they done to him?

A man wearing the traditional white coat of a medical doctor stepped onboard, followed by several others, including a woman. The men were big. Stocky. Plucky. Ready for a fight. The woman appeared delicate but dangerous. They were all dressed in the disturbing white uniforms.

"I am Dr. Adam Caiman, and this is Dr. Sainne, Dr. Caultin, and Dr. Tuscane," the doctor said, gesturing first to the woman, then to each of the men in turn. "We control the *Straightjacket,* and your souls belong to us. Do as you are told, and you might be shown mercy. Fight us, and you'll discover new levels of pain."

As a few burly-looking orderlies wandered onboard, Dr. Caiman instructed, "Administer the initial dose. We will not begin our journey with a riot."

Before Chase could blink, one of the muscular men was at his side, jamming a thick needle into his arm. "Hey!" Chase shouted, squirming in a vain effort to escape.

The man gripped his arm tightly and tapped the vial of bright pink goo that traveled into the needle. Chase struggled against his chains, protesting, "You can't do this! Come on!"

A sudden tingling sensation slackened his jaw and crept into his brain. His muscles turned to jelly, and nothing seemed to matter except for the pretty purple spots that danced on the wall in front of him. His entire body went limp as he slumped in his chair, his head rolling back against the neck rest.

"And that's how we play," the orderly said to him as he removed the needle and tousled Chase's hair.

◆

Redic looked around the Turret before focusing on the empty seat across from him. As the Crew gathered, Chase should have been sitting there. Redic breathed through his nose, trying to control his outrage. He'd already lost a loyal soldier to the Legacy. Now he'd lost a powerful leader, the *Halcyon,* and its crew.

His anger wasn't directed at Seraph, who'd apologized profusely for scheming with Chase behind his back. His anger wasn't directed at Chase, who in his focus on Trista had evidently lost all common sense and ability to protect himself and his crew. No, his anger was directed at himself for being blind to the notion that Chase would do anything for that girl, short of handing over the entire Ghost faction. And at the fact that Redic had sat back, just as Chase had suggested months earlier, and allowed the Legacy to do this.

"Gentlemen, ladies," Redic began in his usual manner, "we don't have a lot of time, so once again, I am turning this over to Armand." Redic gestured across the table to a screen on the wall.

"Leighton's been arrested, along with his entire crew," Armand said, via the secure visual link.

Everyone froze. The grim news lodged a heavy burden on each of their shoulders. Aram's expression, usually one of hope, fell with paternal concern for the boy he had raised. Redic empathized, remembering how he'd felt when he had heard about Seraph's imprisonment years ago. Granted, that had been after the fact. The others knew that this was a great victory for the Legacy. Now that they had Chase, they could find a way to harness and use his gift, particularly if they involved Trista in the mix.

"Let's get moving," Seraph suggested, leaping to his feet.

Armand shook his head. "They've been processed and sentenced. The word hasn't even gone out about the trials, as they don't want this to become public knowledge. If my information is correct, the Legacy condemned the Ghost prisoners to a ship called the *Straightjacket*."

A frown betraying his alarm, Brendan leaned forward over the table. "The *Straightjacket*?"

Armand nodded.

Cam opened his palms in frustration. "What does that mean?" he asked.

Brendan took a deep breath as he sat back in his chair, disbelief mingling with his worry. "In my Legacy days, the *Straightjacket* was nothing more than a glorified torture chamber."

"I'm afraid it will be again," Armand replied. "I'd never heard of it until recently because the Legacy kept it hidden along the outer rim of the system. Apparently, it was a prison ship for those with what the Legacy deemed as a mental deficiency. They pulled it from the fleet after a horrific massacre took place between the staff and the 'inmates,' as they called them. They've remodeled the ship and recommissioned it under its previous directive as a rehabilitation facility for the criminally insane. Their words, not mine."

"They are accusing Chase of insanity?" Brax balked.

"Not just Chase. His men, as well as other Ghosts who have been captured along the way," Armand answered. "And insanity is the plea, concocted by legal representatives to get him beyond the normal realm of the prison ships. The charges are stacked against him."

"I was aware of the things that occurred on the *Straightjacket*," Brendan added. "I've heard the stories. If those men are taken aboard, they will be changed forever. If they survive."

"Dad," Seraph whispered in distress as he looked at their leader.

Redic lifted a hand. "I know. The situation is dire. We have to come up with some way to get those men off that ship. Where will it anchor?"

"Vetus rotation, beyond standard planetary orbits. But an all-out attack is not the way to go," Armand said. "The *Straightjacket* has no defense systems or weaponry, but a warship has a direct trajectory plotted in case of a distress call. They are ordered to destroy the ship if that call goes out. Not to mention the staff, which has a two to three ratio with the inmates, has orders to kill the prisoners in case of such an attack."

"Gruesome," Cam murmured.

"Legacy," Britt countered with a disgusted growl. "It's how they do things."

"They know about Chase," Armand confirmed quietly. "That's one reason they are placing him on this ship. They want to find out what makes him tick."

"So why don't they just hand him over to ExMed?" Stu asked. "That would be far more direct."

"The *Straightjacket* is one of ExMed's projects," Armand answered, shaking his head. "This is carefully calculated. They not only want to get to Chase. They want to strike us in the heart by toying with these men's minds."

"And if they ask the right questions, they can strike us even deeper. May I remind us all that Chase has access to the Pathway and could lead them here?" Stu said, raging redness tingeing his cheeks.

"Chase wouldn't give up that information," Seraph said. Given Chase's service and loyalty to the Ghosts, Seraph shouldn't have had to defend him, but his actions since Trista's disappearance warranted question.

"They have ways of finding out what they want to know," Stu replied, staring down Seraph.

Aram heaved a great sigh, sharing a glance with Avalyn. "We will petition the Crown for His guidance and intervention."

Redic frowned heavily, running a hand over his graying hair and back before settling it on his chin. "And we will keep our eyes open for an opportunity. Armand, thank you for bringing this to us. We need a plan, folks. I am not losing the *Halcyon*."

"The ship itself we can get," Armand said. "I can put people in place and orchestrate it to look as if it's off for inspection or something."

"Do it. Britt, Cole, and Brendan, I want you on it. Make arrangements to rendezvous with Armand on Crenet as soon as we adjourn," Redic commanded. "Take who you need."

"The smaller the number, the better," Armand advised. "The typical crew is what—ten in number?"

"Yes," Remy confirmed, along with several bobbing heads.

"I'd say try to operate with half that. Five or less. A standard inspection team is two, three people at the most. A pilot. Maybe a supervisor. Any more than five would be too obvious."

"What about Chase and the others?" Seraph asked, looking at his father.

Redic raked his hand through his hair again. His son wanted a promise that he just couldn't give. Exactly like the previous conversation with Chase regarding Trista. Perhaps Seraph would be more understanding. Still, he couldn't easily dismiss the lives of nine men and a Logia. "That's a tougher call, Ser," he murmured quietly.

"We can't let them rot on that ship," Seraph argued, his gaze locking with each of the Crew.

"It's too tight to get anyone onboard," Armand said. "And that warship could easily take any vessels we send."

"Then we'll have to trust Chase to make a move." It wasn't the answer Redic wanted to give, but it was all he had at the moment. "Remy, scour all Legacy channels for anything out of the ordinary. Put extra people on it if you have to. I want them monitored night and day," he ordered.

"Of course, Redic," she acknowledged, keying the information into her PDL.

"Ser, assign routine runs. Business as usual, but Vetus rotation is off limits," Redic said. They'd had very few dealings in that rotation, anyway. Due to the darkened star, the planets were mostly abandoned or crawling with Crepusculum. "If we pick up something, we'll detour our closest ships to check it out."

"All right, Dad." Seraph sighed. Redic could see in his eyes that he wasn't satisfied with the plan. But Seraph would also go along with whatever Redic thought best.

"I know, son," Redic said gently. "I want them home too. This is beyond us, though. We have to give it all over to the Crown."

Seraph submitted with a nod. "And I'll be joining Aram and Avalyn in prayer, Dad. For guidance, for protection, and for intervention."

"As will we all, son," Redic offered his Crew a sad smile. "As will we all."

CHAPTER 12

Day 9352 PLR: The Straightjacket

"Gentlemen," Dr. Caultin said as he entered the room, greeting the two orderlies who had yanked Chase from the isolation chamber only moments earlier. He stepped to the table that now held Chase firmly strapped to it. His eyes scanned Chase's file before he looked down at him with a cold stare. "Well, let's begin this prisoner's conditioning."

The table under Chase spun and anchored into position, holding him upright. His head had just started to clear from the sedatives they regularly administered. Too bad the restraints were already in place. He would singlehandedly annihilate those in the room. "Conditioning?" he asked. He couldn't help the growl that accompanied the question. His body was already beginning to crave the drugs that were being imposed upon him, even after being in treatment for only a week.

Dr. Caultin positioned a small box attached to a contraption that held it at Chase's eye level. "A way of controlling you without the use of drugs. If and when you return to society, you will be expected to behave without medical help."

"If and when I return to society, I will not be under anyone's control," Chase countered.

The doctor smiled, gesturing for the orderlies to do something. Chase watched as they strategically placed electrodes along his body. The orderly who called himself Grausam grabbed his arm and injected an orange liquid into his bloodstream. Chase inhaled angrily through his nose. He was getting a little tired of the different medications forced into his body. "I thought you said this was done without drugs. What is this?"

"It's called maldominorex. It enhances your senses and makes you more receptive to the conditioning," Dr. Caultin said, making a note on his PDL.

"In other words, it strips any mental capabilities I have." Chase pulled against his restraints. "Is this what you did to my wife?"

Dr. Caultin's tone changed to a patronizing singsong. "Just relax and keep your eyes on the box."

Chase closed his eyes in defiance. There was no way he'd comply with these evil men. If they thought he would, then *they* were the ones who needed to be locked away in a crazy house.

"Being difficult only makes it worse," Dr. Caultin murmured in his ear.

After a moment, Chase felt two tiny pinpricks near his temples. He roared with aggravation as his eyes popped open. His lids felt rigid and he couldn't shift his gaze, as hard as he tried. His eyes were focused on that box.

"Muscle constrictors." Dr. Caultin grinned, holding up his hands in Chase's line of sight to reveal two tiny devices on his fingertips. "You forget, Mr. Leighton, I have absolute control."

"Of my body, perhaps. But not my mind. And never my heart," Chase said through gritted teeth.

"So passionate and poetic. But we shall see about that. Dim the lights, please," the doctor said, stepping back as he moved the box contraption closer to Chase's face.

Chase concentrated on taking even breaths. He would not let this get to him, no matter what they did. He had to maintain control. He had to—

The box flashed a teal-blue light and emitted an earsplitting squeal. The electrodes issued a searing, burning pain that permeated his skin.

Chase stiffened as the electric shock blazed through his bones. When it finally subsided, he leaned limply against the restraints that held him and panted. His eyes wanted to close, but they were focused on the box. The box. The—

Flash of teal blue light from the box. Earsplitting squeal. Searing, burning pain emitted from the electrodes.

Flash of blue light. Squeal. Pain from the electrodes.

Flash. Squeal. Pain. Whimper.

Flash. Squeal. Pain. Whimper.

Flash. Squeal. Pain. Cry.

Flash. Squeal. Pain. Cry.

Flash. Squeal. Pain. Cry.

Flash. Squeal. Pain. Scream.

Flash. Squeal. Pain. Scream.

Flash. Squeal. Scream.

"Excellent. He anticipated the pain without it being administered," Dr. Caultin explained to the orderlies. "His brain is doing the work for us."

What? No—

Flash. Squeal. Pain. Cry.

Flash. Squeal. Pain. Scream.

Flash. Squeal. Scream.

Flash. Squeal. Scream.

"Release him," Dr. Caultin ordered.

Grausam and his orderly pal, Moyenne, moved the box out of the way and pulled the electrodes from Chase before they unstrapped him. He had very little strength left, but he managed to stand on his own. He shrugged off Moyenne as Dr. Caultin instructed them to move back. "Mr. Leighton, can you hear me?"

"Yeah," Chase growled. He wanted to lynch Caultin.

The doctor moved closer. Chase knew the man was taunting him. They had no interest in rehabilitating the inmates. They were torturing them. And from the way Chase now felt, they were creating monsters.

"Want to hurt me yet, Mr. Leighton?"

As much as he wanted to, Chase refused. He stared at the doctor, still unable to close his eyes. Caultin moved closer, again murmuring in his ear, "You can end this. Show us what you can do with your gifts. Dismantle the remote with your mind. You can do that, right?"

Chase glared at him in silence. He wasn't about to disclose the nature of his gifts, let alone demonstrate them. They had been bestowed upon him by the Creator King to serve His purposes. Sure, he'd been stupid with them after he found out about Trista, and his relationship with the Crown was in question, but he knew deep in his heart that the Crown would never forsake him. The Legacy could destroy him, for all he cared. He would never allow them to use his gifts for their objectives.

Dr. Caultin smiled, staring at him. "You know, Mr. Leighton, I was fortunate enough to be in the observation room during your wife's surgery. Dr. Terces is my mentor. But I don't think he had her under deep enough anesthetic. She twitched as he cut into her skull."

With a snarl, Chase leapt toward the doctor. Caultin lifted a small remote into Chase's view. The smile on the doctor's face turned dark as he pressed the button.

Flash of teal-blue light from the remote. Earsplitting squeal.

Vicious, biting pain flattened Chase. Tearing at his uniform, he collapsed breathlessly on the floor. He heard an agonized cry and realized that it had come from him. Oh, by the Crown, they *did* have control over him.

Caultin squatted next to him, smiling up at the orderlies, who stood nearby. "Schedule conditioning maintenance for him every other day. But for now, he's ours. Lower his daily dosage. His bedtime sedative should still be administered.

"Mr. Leighton, can you hear me?" Dr. Caultin asked him again.

Chase grunted his response. The pain had left him weakened and confused.

"Every staff member is equipped with these remotes. We're granting you a bit more freedom, but if anyone feels you are crossing a line, they have permission to use the remotes. Do you understand?"

Chase understood. Instead of using the numbing control of drugs, they were using the piercing control of pain. As he had thought before, the Legacy never intended to release them back into normal society. They planned to manipulate the Ghost prisoners for their own use.

"You're ... you're going to ..." he stammered, his lungs groping for breath.

"What, Mr. Leighton?" the doctor goaded. "Tell me what I'm going to do."

"Turn us ... on our own people ..." Chase finished.

With a wide smile, Dr. Caultin nodded. "Indeed. That is the idea. We have to understand you first, though. Your gifts, your boundaries. I'll pull you apart if I have to. But now that you've guessed our intentions, we'll have to schedule you for further treatments. We can't have you thwarting our plans."

The orderlies and Caultin laughed as Chase dropped his head back down to the floor. He didn't know how much longer he could resist. Nor how much longer they would allow him to. They were finding ways of getting to him. *Trista …*

◆

Day 9357 PLR: Atrum

"You guys know what you're doing?" Britt asked, looking between Cole and Cam. He pressed his fingers against the brown goatee adhering to his chin and upper lip. The color matched the dye he'd used to change his reddish hair to a dark brown. The disguise may not have been necessary, but it helped Britt get into the role he was about to play.

"Why didn't you just grow one, man?" Cole stroked the full beard he sported. He'd purposely not shaven since the meeting with Armand. Britt thought he looked like a savage cave dweller.

"It's itchy," Britt replied, leaning back in his chair. "And Laney doesn't like it."

"Laney doesn't like what?" his wife asked, stepping from the fresher. She had just gone in to change from her normal comfortable togs into a sleek, form-fitting suit. Her long, dark curls spilled over the fine gray material. She captured them in her fist and skillfully wrapped them into an elegant chignon.

Britt pointed to his mouth, which earned a disapproving grimace from Laney. "Ugh. You're right. Laney doesn't like it," she replied, pinning her hair in place.

Cam chuckled, shaking his head. He wore only a thin moustache under his nose. He tossed Britt a small vial of adhesive. "You're losing your left side," he said.

Britt frowned, whipping a mirror from a small bag at the center of the table. He worked quickly to get the goatee secured. "All right, so …" he murmured, tucking the glue into the bag. Laney grabbed the mirror from him and applied a coating of deep-red lip color.

"Cam and I are inspectors from the Tzigane shipyards. You're our super, who is in some serious hot water with the head of the shipyards, Madame Vaisseau." Cole pointed toward Laney as he rattled off the story they'd fabricated with Armand. "We were expecting the *Halcyon* to come to us, but instead, by some crazy mix-up you created, it came here to Atrum."

"Overcrowding," Britt supplied the answer to the mix-up.

"Overcrowding," Cole mumbled.

Brendan called from the cockpit, "We're docking."

The ship's smooth course jerked and jolted as it entered the awaiting bay. Laney scampered to a seat and strapped in while the men gripped the arms of their chairs, waiting for the craft to land. The shaking subsided just as Brendan eased the small shuttle into the receiving area of the docking bay and lowered it to the floor.

"Clear," he confirmed. "We're now awaiting airlock closure in five, four, three, two, one."

"You're up, Laney. Knock 'em dead." Cole smiled, rising from his seat to straighten out his uniform.

Laney pushed to her feet, adjusting the wide-shouldered jacket she wore. Britt cleared his throat, gesturing to the hats Cole and Cam were supposed to wear. They situated the caps on their heads as Brendan stepped from the cockpit, joining the small crew. With a final nod, Britt lowered the stair unit, allowing Laney to storm from the shuttle.

The first docking assistant she encountered got off easy. Laney tossed him a few pallads and said in a thick accent, "Refuel her, and keep her warm. I don't intend to be long."

"Y-yes, ma'am," the young man said, scurrying away to prepare the ship for refueling.

Laney lifted her chin, sinking fully into the haughty persona of Madame Natalia Vaisseau. Armand insisted that it was a hefty gamble to throw Laney into that role, but hopefully, if she played the right cards, no one would bother to check until after the fact. After all, Tzigane was across the system from Atrum. And all the computer entries would reflect their story. Armand would make sure of that.

"Does anyone work here?" Madame Vaisseau asked loudly, glancing around the quiet docking bay.

A mechanic and his buddy ducked out from another shuttle across the strip. The mechanic wiped his hands on a rag. "Uh, I can help you," he said. "You gotta realize, you just came in. When the lock is open, you know, most of us like to breathe, so we scatter until the bay is pressurized again."

Madame Vaisseau glared at the mechanic, pressing her lips together in a most displeased manner. "I need to speak with Silas Buque. Immediately," she insisted.

The mechanic snickered, glancing to his partner. With a sly grin, he said, "Sorry, ma'am. No one sees Mr. Buque. Best I can offer you is my supervisor."

Laney narrowed her eyes, folding her arms gracefully over her chest. "Then I suggest you get on that."

The grin turned into a broad, rebellious smile. "He's at lunch. But, uh—I could show you his office." He winked at Laney.

Britt forced himself to stay the course and not lay into the jerk. He could see that the kid was a bully and a lascivious rat. It grated against Britt's honor to let the boy speak to his wife that way.

"Hmm," Laney said, unwrapping her arms to play mindlessly with her fingers. A dizzy, flirtatious smile tickled her lips as she stalked slowly toward the mechanic. "That *does* sound rather inviting. You have such strong hands. May I … look at them?"

The mechanic grinned at his friend, who smacked him in the arm with an excited whoop. He stepped closer to Laney, holding out his oil-stained hands, palms down, toward her. She took them in her own flawless ones, admiring them. Interlacing her fingers between his, she whipped them around with a snarl, squeezing them with a tight vise grip. Britt could see the pain flash through the kid's face. *Way to go, Laney.*

"Tell me you were joking," she spat into his face.

"I was," the mechanic whimpered. "I was joking."

"Now, we're going to do this in a very professional manner. Do you understand?"

"Y-yes, ma'am."

"Call your super. Tell him Madame Vaisseau is here from Tzigane to clear up a little matter with Mr. Buque. I expect him to be down here within five minutes. Got it?"

"Yes, ma'am."

With a shove, Laney released the mechanic. He fell back against his friend, and the two of them darted off toward a section that looked to be offices. Laney brushed her hands together, sharing a disgusted look with Britt. He felt like hugging her, but resisted. Instead, he whispered, "Good job."

She paced between the men, her heels sending impatient clicks reverberating through the bay. Before long, an overweight man in a uniform too small to contain his waist came stumbling toward them.

"Madame Vaisseau?" he asked.

Spinning a crisp, controlled turn, Laney eyed the man. "And you are …?"

"Sam Lang, ma'am. I-I supervise the mechanics in the receiving bay." He proudly gestured back toward the bay, like she wouldn't know what he was talking about otherwise. "We, um, we weren't told that you were coming."

"No. When I learned of this little mishap, I gathered those involved and headed this way immediately."

"Excuse me, ma'am, but, um, what mishap?"

"That's for Mr. Buque and me to discuss, thank you."

"I'm sorry, ma'am, but, um, I…I can't bother Mr. Buque."

Laney stepped forward, tilting her head. "I assure you, this is important Legacy business, and your obedience in this matter will be rewarded. Should you choose instead to obstruct the dealings here, you will find yourself smack in the filthiest, most terrifying cell the Justice Center has to offer."

"He's a … he's a very busy man, ma'am." Lang nervously scratched at the back of his scalp.

"I understand. He and I both run large, crucial operations. And you are wasting my time by arguing. Mr. Arger," Laney turned to Britt, "perhaps you can redeem yourself yet. Go back onboard and contact the Atrum Zenith base. Have them dispatch an arresting squadron immediately."

"No." Lang waved his hands in front of him to stop Britt. "No, Mr. Arger, that won't be necessary," he insisted. "I-I'll see what I can do."

Lang waddled back toward his office, leaving Laney and the others alone once again. She moved back to the group, murmuring, "That was odd."

"I imagine Mr. Lang has something going on up here that he doesn't want Zeniths finding out about," Cam whispered.

"Fear is a pretty powerful motivator," Cole said, his eyes following Lang.

"How you doing, Laney? You okay?" Britt asked.

She nodded. "I'm fine. I don't like how reluctant they are. Do you think they are checking out our story?"

Brendan shook his head. "No. If they were, we'd be in an office, answering more questions. I think it's just what Cam said. They're hiding something up here that they just don't want anyone to know about. Perhaps some kind of private operation."

"You're doing great, though." Britt smiled, hoping to encourage Laney. "Keep it up. They seem to be buying it."

Lang reappeared at the entrance to the office wing and gestured for them to join him. Britt guessed that he didn't want to make the eighth-of-a-squant trip across the bay again. In character, Laney rolled her eyes and indicated that the men should follow her. Her boots clicked even more loudly than before. Britt admired her talent.

"Mr. Buque can meet you in his office in a couple of hours," Lang panted. "In the meantime, he invites you to take advantage of our employee lounge on the main deck."

Laney's expression revealed bridled rage, which unleashed with the tone in her voice. "My associates and I traveled three days across the system. The least he could do is meet us down here."

"I quite agree." A voice spoke quietly behind them.

Britt spun around, as did the others. A tall man, hemmed in an aura of protection by two larger, bulkier men, stood behind them, seeming to appear from nowhere. Lang waddled around Laney. "Mr. Buque, I went through the proper channels ..." he professed.

Silas Buque was an interesting conundrum. His manner and dress reflected a stylish elegance, but he looked hard and worn, like an old space sailor who had seen far more than any normal person should ever have to deal with. He nodded to Lang. "I have eyes and ears all over the yards, Sam. You know that."

"I bet you do," Cole muttered.

Britt shot him a look to shut him up. Buque stepped toward them, once again drawing Britt's attention. Buque's eyes studied Laney, probably looking for a flaw.

"I didn't expect you to be so alluring, Ms. Vaisseau. Your creative use of the colorful language in your communiqués suggests a more ... experienced woman," Buque said.

"Don't be fooled by appearances, Mr. Buque. I am indeed more experienced than perhaps I seem. But I haven't time to discuss personal representation. I have more pressing issues, namely the *Halcyon*," Laney answered, her words snapping with tension.

"You'll have to refresh my memory, Ms. Vaisseau. We have many ships passing through here every day." Buque smiled, aiming his darts directly at her. "We *are* the most popular shipyard in the fleet."

"Only because of your location," Laney replied.

Britt was thankful that Armand had briefed them on the long-standing conflict between the shipyards. Atrum had been the Legacy's first official shipyards, but with their growing fleet, Atrum was no longer enough to support the ongoing needs. Several years ago, they had annexed to the opposite rotation near Tzigane. Natalia Vaisseau had only recently taken the helm of the Tzigane yards, but her loyalty to her home world was fierce as could be. She had a reputation of being stiff-necked and steel-handed. She wouldn't take insults from the likes of her competitor.

"And because you've been established for a longer period of time," she finished, meeting Buque's gaze evenly with no sign of intimidation or fear. "But that's all about to change."

Lang watched the two chat back and forth before he ducked behind Buque's wingmen. Britt shifted a bit closer to Laney. He couldn't help it. Instinct kicked in. The move was enough to distract Buque from the verbal duel.

"You speak of the Ghost ship," Buque said, lifting an eyebrow.

"Yes," Laney confirmed.

"It's in confinement, awaiting inspection."

"It should be in confinement in my yards."

"Then why is it here?" Buque asked, taking slow, measured steps from his bodyguards. "We received it thirteen days ago."

"You received it by mistake," Laney answered, following him with her eyes. "We had a slight issue with overcrowding, and my yard manager, Mr. Arger here, erroneously rerouted the Ghost ship to you."

Britt lowered his gaze sheepishly. He was supposed to play the part of the repentant, brainless yard manager who blew it big time.

"Why did you drag him along? Why not dismiss him?"

"That's my business, Mr. Buque. Give me my ship."

"What's in it for me?" Buque answered.

"Excuse me?"

"You heard me." Buque crossed to Laney, standing just inches from her. Britt seethed inside. "Impounding a Ghost ship is a pretty prestigious thing. If handled appropriately, it adds to the credibility of the shipyard. I'm not letting this go without proper compensation."

Britt watched as Buque's trim fingernail trailed along Laney's arm. He chewed the inside of his cheek. His eyes flickered toward Cole, who also stared intently at the tasteless suggestion. Was everyone up here after just one thing?

Laney didn't bat an eye. "Perhaps we should go somewhere to discuss this more privately."

Fury erupted through Britt. He had to remind himself to trust his wife. Still, he didn't like the idea of her being alone with the worm that stood before them. "Madame Vaisseau," he started.

"Mr. Arger." She turned to him, silencing him with invented anger in her eyes. The purse of her lips revealed her confidence in her next move. "I imagine that Mr. Lang could show our inspectors and the pilot the location of the *Halcyon*."

Lang's questioning gaze darted to his employer. Buque gave a subtle nod of approval. Britt could see the look of smug satisfaction on his face. He wanted to punch him.

Looking at Brendan, Cole, and Cam, she ordered, "Go ahead and board the ship. Prepare it for transport back to Tzigane. You will receive launch permission from control when Mr. Buque and I have reached an adequate agreement."

She angled her head back toward Britt. "Wait for me on the shuttle."

Britt bit his lower lip as he stared at Laney. *Don't do this. Don't walk blindly into this man's territory. He will trample you.*

Squaring her jaw, her cool gaze turned into a demanding glare. "I said wait for me on the shuttle."

"Yes, ma'am," Britt whispered, bowing his head.

He watched as Buque settled his hand on Laney's back, leading her toward a long, dim corridor. The goons followed, much to Britt's dismay. He knew that was sealing Laney's fate. Cole clapped him on the shoulder just before Lang told them to follow him. Britt swallowed hard and headed back to the shuttle as Laney disappeared.

◆

"Go," Laney said, breathing heavily as she slid into the copilot's chair.

"What?" Britt asked, straightening up in his chair. He'd been stewing in a funk ever since reboarding the shuttle. He hadn't even heard Laney until she was right next to him.

"Go now," she insisted, pulling the mesh harness over her head. "Brendan has the *Halcyon* up and out. Cole and Cam are scouring it for tracking devices. We don't have very long."

"What did you do, Laney?" he asked, revving the shuttle's engines.

"Let's just say that Mr. Buque and Madame Vaisseau's relationship will need some work from this point on."

"I want details," Britt demanded as he opened the link to communicate with the shipyard's operators. "After I get permission from control."

"Blast control. Just go!" Laney ordered. "Airlock should be opening in three seconds."

Gritting his teeth, Britt shut down all communication and gripped the thruster control. He lifted the shuttle off the ground, his fingers scrambling to the throttle. The shuttle zoomed down the prep strip and into the sanctuary of space. Laney seemed to calm a bit as the distance between them and the shipyards grew.

"What happened in there?" Britt asked softly. "Or do I want to know?"

Laney pressed back against her chair and rolled her head toward him. A smile crept onto her lips. "You're worried."

"Tell me, Laney." Britt didn't feel like playing games. For all he knew, that creep had had his paws all over her.

"He took me to his private quarters. Before I was allowed in, his men patted me down and took my slayer, which I expected. But then I got him alone," she murmured, holding up a tiny glass vial. "Who knew the man liked to relax with a mixed drink before he talked business?"

Shifting the shuttle into autopilot, Britt took the vial. "What is this?"

Laney shook her head. "Something Cole gave me before we left. Made Mr. Buque sleepy awfully quickly, though. I was able to tie him up in a chair and send out a few orders from his DDL before he really started snoring."

Britt clasped the vial in his palm, laughing. "You never cease to amaze me, Laney."

She punched his arm. "I can't believe that you didn't trust me."

Before she retracted her hand, he grabbed it, placing a gentle kiss on her fingers. "You, I trust. Him, not so much."

"Let's just get home," Laney said. "I want to see Redic's expression when he sees the *Halcyon* pull in."

Britt smiled, unable to hide the pride he felt toward his wife. "Wait until he hears about your performance. He'll want to send you to the *Straightjacket* as a doctor."

"I think I'd be more convincing as an inmate." Laney grinned, sliding her hand into Britt's.

CHAPTER 13

DAY 9394 PLR: THE STRAIGHTJACKET

Chase stared at the certificates on the wall beyond Dr. Caiman. Graduate of the Ossia Institute with a focus in medicine. Highest honors in his class. Two residencies served with a Dr. Reid Terces, both on Crenet, but one in an ExMed facility. Where he learned the treatment procedures he and the staff used here on the *Straightjacket*, no doubt.

The doctor watched him, tapping one end of his pen, then flipping it through his fingers to tap the other. Chase's eyes dropped to the hypnotic motion. It was a good thing he was restrained. The pen tapping was terribly obnoxious. And after the weeks of torment, Chase would have loved to obliterate Dr. Caiman.

"I understand that you are making progress." Dr. Caiman spoke, glancing down at Chase's file spread across the desk before him. It was small talk. Caiman was stalling.

Still, Chase said nothing. He'd learned it was best to keep quiet. He blinked at the doctor, waiting for the assessment to come to an end.

The door opened behind him. Chase startled at the unexpected sound, then chided himself. Dr. Caiman smiled and wrote something in the file.

Probably a note about Chase's reaction to the door. That would mean another round of treatments, counseling sessions, and drug therapy, undoubtedly beginning with a concentrated, injected sedative at bedtime tonight.

Dr. Caiman lifted his gaze to greet the woman who had entered, bringing along with her more torture for Chase. Chase swallowed, staring straight ahead as Dr. Sainne took a seat next to him. The hydralily perfume she wore nearly made Chase gag. It wasn't necessarily a bad smell, but he'd grown to associate it with the mental torture they disguised as treatment. And Dr. Sainne might have been considered attractive, with her medium-length, jet-black hair and violet-colored eyes. Might have been, had she not been so merciless.

"Excuse me for running behind, Dr. Caiman. I had a particularly difficult patient this afternoon," she said.

"Anything I should be concerned with, Doctor?"

Chase was almost surprised that he asked. Dr. Caiman usually maintained a hands-off policy. He rarely interacted with the inmates, although he often observed them. From what Chase could tell, his main duty was to consult with the other doctors on treatments. He'd recently begun these assessments, meeting with each inmate and their main doctor for a brief amount of time. The inmates all wondered why.

Dr. Sainne answered, "He's just resisting every step of the way. Only makes it more difficult for himself." She laughed a bit, shaking her head lightly as if she were discussing a rebellious toddler. "One of the electrodes actually burned him during his shock treatment."

Chase forced himself to take steadying breaths. Maybe Caiman would scold Sainne for this blunder, or even modify their procedures to treat the inmates with a bit more dignity. Dr. Caiman simply raised an eyebrow in question.

"It's that Ben Reiger," Dr. Sainne said, flipping her hand about to wave off the air of concern. "Completely his own fault. The orderlies did everything according to the book. Mr. Reiger thrashed about excessively, dislodging the electrode."

Chase bit the inside of his cheeks to keep from exploding with anger. Ben was one of his crewmembers. Husband. Father. Gentle, loving man who passionately believed in the Ghosts' cause. He'd dedicated his life to serving the Ruler Prince, becoming a Lumen years prior. Chase remembered the day, although he had been very young. Aram led the ceremony, which was followed by an exciting celebration. Chase had seen Ben harden since they'd been onboard the *Straightjacket*. It would take years to undo what had been done to him, if it could ever be undone.

"I wouldn't bother making a note of it," Dr. Caiman advised. "Things like this don't need to go into our records."

"Yes, sir." Dr. Sainne smiled, placing the charts she held on her lap.

Hands-off. Caiman didn't care about their dignity, or well-being, or even their rehabilitation. Chase had foolishly placed the tiniest hope in the man before him. Foolish, indeed. He wouldn't make that mistake again.

"Well," Dr. Caiman leaned back in his chair, twirling his pen between his fingers, "we are here to discuss our treatment progress with Mr. Leighton."

"Yes." Dr. Sainne sighed, glancing toward Chase. "The conditioning was successful, as Dr. Caultin reported. We have yet to have to use the remotes on Mr. Leighton, as he is a shining example of an inmate. His behavior is respectful, and he demonstrates improvement with each treatment." Her words were tinged with disappointment, as if his good behavior was a bad thing.

Dr. Caiman sighed, shaking his head and clucking his tongue. "I'm afraid that won't do, Dr. Sainne. We need to broaden our scope. Take him to the very edge of reason and beyond. I want to analyze his spectrum. At what point does he give us a negative response? How far do we have to push him before he lashes out?"

Don't react. Don't react. Chase tasted blood as he chomped hard on his cheeks to keep control.

"We did see him lash out a bit with the conditioning," Dr. Sainne reminded the other doctor.

"But it wasn't enough," Dr. Caiman said, leaning over his desk. "Dr. Terces is expecting my report on mental manipulation without the use of implants. He's so far been successful with the hunter technology. That experiment to mainstream his MRP patient into normal society is going well. He wants a behavioral control program without the implants, though."

The doctor rose, rubbing his chin as he walked the length of his office before turning back to Chase. "What is it we have to do, Mr. Leighton? How do we reach you?"

Chase lowered his eyes and gritted his teeth.

Caiman crossed to him, leaning down to speak into his ear. "All you have to do is show us your abilities. Let us connect you to our monitors, slip into your Logia trance—or whatever it is you do—and demonstrate your power."

Chase remained silent. They would have to kill him. He would never allow the Legacy to learn anything about the Logia through him. Never.

Caiman straightened up, staring down at Chase. "Increase his receptor meds. I want him on two hundred units of nexletum and one hundred and fifty units of decessus."

Resisting the urge to comment, Chase took another focused breath. The medications and levels Caiman had prescribed would dope him into a vegetable state. Not exactly what Caiman initially discussed with Dr. Sainne.

"I want him on a strict therapy routine. Schedule him for three treatments a day, cycling through each of them. Assign a couple orderlies to him and him alone."

"Yes, sir," Dr. Sainne answered, making notes as Caiman spoke.

"And finally, during his free time," Caiman leaned on the arms of the chair that held Chase firmly to it, inches from Chase's face, "I want him witnessing his men going through the shock treatments. He may endure whatever torture we throw at him, but I doubt that he'll be able to handle it when Ben, or Nic, or even old Joe convulse under the excruciating voltage that will ravage their bodies and minds."

Unable to take anymore, Chase jerked against his restraints. Caiman pushed back, chuckling. "Good, Mr. Leighton. Very good." He returned to his desk and pressed a tiny button near his DDL.

"Dr. Sainne, I personally will oversee Mr. Leighton's new treatment program, which will begin immediately," Dr. Caiman said as he took his seat and resumed twirling the pen. "You can expect to see results within the week."

"Yes, sir," Dr. Sainne said, rising as Grausam entered Dr. Caiman's office.

Dr. Caiman greeted him with a nod. "Mr. Grausam, please escort Mr. Leighton to the CBT room. Dr. Sainne will be there momentarily to administer Mr. Leighton's new medication regimen. I will allow a bit of time for it to take full effect before I begin." Caiman's gaze fell to Chase. "Make sure he's tightly secured."

❖

Day 9420 PLR: Revenant

The polished hull of the *Halcyon* captured Seraph's heartache and guilt in its reflective chrome and cast it back upon him with a somber heaviness.

He had walked the length of the ship and now stood at its nose, looking up toward the viewport of the bridge. He half-expected to see Chase's grin shining down on him, ready to launch some goofy plan that was sure to get them in trouble. Instead, the *Halcyon* remained dead cold. It had been grounded since Brendan landed it weeks earlier, bringing it home from Atrum.

In the mirrored metal, he saw Echo standing behind him. With her golden tresses and penetrating blue eyes, her beauty was a shocking contrast to the dark worries that plagued his heart. She had made no sound as she approached, yet Seraph wasn't surprised to see her. He dropped his gaze to the floor, pulling himself together. He should have known better. Echo could already sense his feelings.

She slipped her arms around him, cradling him in a loving hug. "Stop that," she scolded gently. Her heart saw much deeper into his soul than he'd like to admit.

He reveled in the sunshine of her adoration. She expected nothing from him. She loved him without condition. It was more than he could give himself at the moment. "I'm responsible for both of them," he said, staring up at the ship again.

Her eyes met his in the reflected image. "Your dad sent out Trista, at her insistence. You tried to stop her," Echo reminded him. "And Chase … well, Chase was just being stupid."

Seraph shook his head. "No. He was being a husband." He gently grasped her hand and pulled her around him into a protective embrace. "Any of us would do the same."

Her fingers caressed his arm as she leaned back against him. "You miss him."

"He's my best friend. No … more than that. He's my brother. Of course I miss him." Seraph rested his head atop hers. "I can't stop imagining what he must going through."

Turning in his arms, Echo gazed up into his eyes. "Terrible as it is, Seraph, I know he can handle it. Chase is courageous and stubborn. He's an excellent captain. He cares about those men as if they were his family. Perhaps that's why the Crown chose him for this situation."

"I hate to think that the Crown would *choose* to put *anyone* in such a situation," Seraph countered.

"You know what I mean," Echo said. "You've experienced your share of broken moments, and you've grown through them. The Crown will use this to strengthen not only Chase, but all of us. We just have to trust that Chase will do something soon."

"It's been two and a half months, Echo." Seraph bowed his head as he answered softly. "He should have already done something. I'm afraid he's so incapacitated that he will be unable to fight this. That he'll die out there."

Her arms tightened around him as if she were trying to squeeze encouragement into him. "Don't write him off just yet. Give it over to the Crown. You don't have to bear this burden."

"Until they are both safe at home—or at peace with the Crown—I do," Seraph said sadly, scuffing his shoe along the floor like a lost, scared child. "Before he left, Chase asked me if we should consider … killing … Trista if she cannot be restored."

Her mouth opening in a quiet gasp, Echo stared at him in astonishment. "You said no, of course."

Seraph gave an anguished nod. "But I'm beginning to understand his position. Leaving them to the devices of the Legacy is far crueler."

"Seraph, think about what you are saying. If the Crown wishes to end their suffering in such a way, He will handle it. He will not force their friends to make that kind of horrific decision. His compassion is greater than that. Be optimistic, Ser," she finished in a whisper.

He knew she understood, but it was the first time he'd actually put voice to the thoughts that now tormented him. As a leader of the Ghosts, and particularly as Redic's son, he was expected to display a thick skin. But here, with Echo, he could lay his fears bare before her. "I can't. My dad can be optimistic. Everyone else can be optimistic. I have to be real. I know what the Legacy is capable of doing. I saw it firsthand."

"And you know what the Crown is capable of doing," Echo said. "You saw *that* firsthand, too."

Pulling back from her, Seraph walked to the barrier that separated the ships' fields. He leaned against the concrete, crossing his arms over his chest. "He's abandoned us, Echo."

"Has He?" Echo, who had followed him, stared at him with passionate fervor. "I've seen miracles that are absolutely unexplainable. I've participated in them. And now I'm starting to wonder if this is about Chase and Trista at all. I'm starting to wonder if the Crown is using this to reach *you*."

Out of frustration, Seraph closed his eyes and pressed his fingers to his forehead. "I didn't mean that. It just … it feels like that sometimes. Like He just up and left, walking away in disgust to leave us measly humans to fester on our own. When I look back and think that He could have ended the Legacy rule as soon as He returned from the dead ..."

Echo moved closer, taking his hand from his face to hold it in her own. "The Crown has a larger plan, Seraph. We have to believe that." With her opposite hand, she touched his hair, stroking it tenderly. "Had He fixed everything then and there, would we have met? This situation with Chase and Trista is just another chapter in His book. The story has just begun, and it's going to have a breathtaking ending once His glory is fully revealed."

Allowing the truth of her words to overtake his doubt, Seraph tilted his head to kiss her wrist. "How do you know just what I need to hear?"

"I know a little about how you think," Echo answered, smiling playfully.

They shared a chuckle as Seraph stood, taking Echo in his arms again. After a moment, he kissed the top of her head. "You're right," he murmured. "You're right. Thank you."

"Seraph!" Cam called out from the entrance to the bay before running toward them.

Seraph shot Echo an apologetic look as he slid his hand into hers and led her to meet Cam. "Everything okay?" he asked, resuming the mantle of leader.

"Remy's been trying to raise you," Cam said, nodding a polite salutation to Echo. "We're meeting in the Turret. There's been a casualty reported from the *Straightjacket*."

"Not—"

Cam shook his head. "No, not Chase. None of ours, in fact." Although the bad news held some promise, an air of tension hung in his tone.

Breathing a sigh of relief, Seraph gripped Echo's hand. He smiled a gentle farewell. "I'll see you in a bit, all right?"

She squeezed his fingers, her eyes boring into him. She said much more than her response, "Of course," silently reminding him to keep their conversation in mind.

Seraph gave her a nod as he walked away briskly with Cam toward the center of the base. "Any names given?" he asked.

"One I didn't recognize," Cam answered. "He had a strong affiliation with the Legacy, but for some reason, they were disgruntled with him enough to ship him off to the *Straightjacket*."

"So then why are we meeting? They killed one of their own. That's not anything new."

Cam glanced at him, maintaining their expedited gait. "The reported cause of death. The list is frightning. If it's any kind of indication of what our guys are going through, they're in big trouble."

Seraph pressed his lips together and picked up the pace to jog with Cam toward the Turret. Cam's report confirmed his fear. Poor Chase. What were they going to do?

CHAPTER 14

Day 9448 PLR: Crenet

Another day. Krissa stared at the ceiling above her, her fists crumpling the blanket between her fingers as the alarm blared on her link. She'd had the dream again. It was better than the nightmares of the Ghosts, though both carried the same haunting feelings. Wandering through a cozy apartment with fresh white walls, trimmed in deep crimson, that nestled not only her, but a man she knew as her husband, and a child. It made no sense to her. But the images soon dissolved into the ugly brown water spots that discolored the bumpy white ceiling tiles. Exactly how Krissa felt. Dirty. Used. Worn. She had to find the motivation to get out of bed.

Taking a breath, she remembered the appointment she had scheduled with Legacy Placement Services. Today was the day she would tell her boss, Finnegan Streuben, that she would no longer be working for him. It was a long time coming, but recent events had solidified her decision.

Streuben could be a good boss when he wanted to be. When it served his purpose. He kept her so busy that she didn't have time for friends or even venturing out much. Not that she had any friends or any desire to go out. Not since her sister, Lila, disappeared. And especially not since the Ghost incident.

It was easier to keep to herself. Besides, the Legacy provided her every need, including meals and a place to live.

She sat up, catching a glimpse of her reflection. Limp brown hair, cut square at her chin. Her bangs were getting a little long. She blew them out of her eyes. Dull, lifeless eyes. Pools of brown, just like the muddled ceiling above. Glancing at the clock, she calculated that she had a little extra time before Streuben expected her. She intended to be early in order to speak with him about her resignation. But she could spare a few moments to shower and fix herself up a little. Streuben would definitely know something was going on if she showed up looking nice.

The meager heat of the shower felt good, but it didn't wash away the uneasiness she felt. Was she pinning too much on the idea that getting out of her job would make her life better? It had to. She hated her job. She was good at what she did, which is why the Legacy placed her as a systems analyst. And it had taken her a long time to realize that it wasn't just Streuben who made her miserable. It was the actual job.

She stared at the mirror, her hair dripping into the sink below. "I quit," she said, practicing the speech she'd thought up several hours ago as she tried to ease into sleep. "I've been at this a number of years, and I just don't have the heart for it anymore. I hope you'll understand." She lifted a rusted pair of scissors and snipped a few hairs from her bangs.

With a nod, she smiled politely at her reflection. The smile faded into her normal expression of apathy. Yeah, it would do. Streuben wouldn't expect a whole lot of flowery words and emotion. For a moment, she entertained the notion that he might beg her to stay, but she was easily replaceable. He reminded her of that on a daily basis.

Crossing to her closet, she pulled out her service uniform and slipped it on. It was too big, but she'd rather it be too big than too small. She rolled up the sleeves, which went against Legacy policy, and slid a belt around her waist. The Legacy insignia on her chest curled out. The patch had been sewn on wrong and warped the entire cut of the top.

Running her fingers through her drying hair, she sat on the bed to tug on her boots. Mundane, tedious tasks. She remembered why she rarely bothered taking the time to get ready. Once more looking at the clock, she sighed. It was time to go. Just one last thing.

Lifting a small gray metal case from the table next to her bed, she examined the lettering on the instruction label. Since the surgery, she'd been taking the drugs that Dr. Terces had prescribed. Four different pills—two white ones twice daily, as well as a large green one in the morning and a blue one in the evening. And the red ones when necessary. She still, on occasion, felt lightheaded, and dealt with blurred vision and confusion, which all too often led to a raging headache. It had been a while since she'd experienced that, though. The pills, particularly the fast-acting red ones, were supposed to help with those symptoms, but she wondered if she even needed them anymore. Well, she would take the pills *with* her in case she began to feel strange. Today was a new day. She wasn't about to start it drugged.

She tucked the pill case in her uniform pocket, grabbed her tool pack near the door, and paused to run through a quick mental check. The little room was in order. Her bed. A chair. A dresser. A closet. She didn't have much, nor did she need much. She only came here for a few hours to sleep between jobs. Perhaps all that would change today. A tiny smile of hope crept onto her face as she pulled the door closed behind her.

The short walk to Streuben's office was invigorating. Of course, living at the heart of Reticulum kept Krissa from needing her own form of transportation. She stood at the bottom of the steps that led into the building, staring up at the cold gray brick wall. As impenetrable as Streuben himself. Giving a resolute nod, she climbed the stairs and entered the building. Streuben's office was really nothing more than a tiny room on the first floor, down the right corridor. Just outside the door, Krissa took a breath and straightened her uniform before marching in.

The office held far more than it should. The cramped space was even tighter, with rows of dull gray filing cabinets that lined the ochre-colored walls. Over the years, the patterned wallpaper had curled and peeled back and now licked the ceiling. The glue had stained the walls the sickly yellow color. File boxes stacked on top of the cabinets blocked the one dusty window that allowed a bit of sunlight to filter through. More boxes cluttered the floor, making it difficult to find stable footing. Just like her apartment, the whole space seemed to be tinted with a dingy brown oppression.

The desk sat at the center of the room, with two chairs in front of it. Next to Streuben's functional DDL, an ancient defective one took up a good portion of the desk, which was also littered with papers and files. Behind the desk, a workspace counter jutted out from the wall, encumbered with DDL parts, wires, tools, and other gadgetry. A large map of the system was stapled to the wall above, thousands of tiny red pins stabbed into various locations. Busy as they were, Krissa had never asked why they didn't have a receptionist of some sort. Streuben had always handled the entire operation.

"Miss Carlisle." Streuben spun around in his desk chair to greet her. "I see you got my message."

Finnegan Streuben might have been handsome once. He was probably close to twenty years older than Krissa. Greasy black hair that was too long for a man his age fell down across his eyes, which were colorless. Krissa imagined that they had been blue long ago, but had taken on the cold, fish-like stare when the Legacy sucked his soul from him. Tight, pale skin made his eyes bulge slightly and pulled his mouth back in a sneer. Instead of the Legacy uniform that he made Krissa wear, he wore an ill-fitting, wrinkled suit. Like he had anyone to impress.

"Message?" Krissa asked, standing at the edge of his desk. She didn't want to sit. If she sat, she'd lose her courage.

Streuben supported himself on the mess of his desk. "I asked you to be here first thing. I have an assignment of dire importance."

An assignment. Blast. "I—" Krissa started.

"And the commander of that last ship you did …"

Crinkling her nose with a puzzled expression, Krissa sank into one of the chairs across from Streuben's desk. He wasn't going to let her get away easily. "The *Haulaway*?"

"Yes." Streuben smiled, pointing at her. "He had nothing but glowing remarks about you."

"I'm surprised," she mumbled, rolling her eyes.

The commander of the *Haulaway* apparently misunderstood her job. She was there to service the computers, but he assumed she would handle matters that were more of a personal nature. She left him with a black eye, locked herself in the operations room, fixed the computer issue, and waited until they reached the shipyards. She promptly debarked, three days early, without so much as a word to the commander.

"You finished the job way ahead of schedule," Streuben said, settling back in his chair as he clasped his hands together and rested them on his thick middle.

"Mmm," she answered in a sigh. The *Haulaway* incident had been the final factor in her decision to change careers.

"You were requested for this assignment." Streuben spun his PDL around for her to read.

Krissa picked up the device and scanned the requisition. "The *Straightjacket.* Sounds lovely." One of the Legacy's prison ships. They'd received a batch of new programming that no one could figure out. They wanted a retrograde to return to their old stuff, which seemed to work just fine.

"One hundred percent safe," Streuben reassured her as he rocked in his chair. "All of the inmates are thick in the midst of treatment, and the staff is in complete control."

Peering at him over the PDL screen, Krissa asked, "Why me?"

Streuben gave a little shrug. "You're fast. You can root through the problem and analyze what they need before anyone else. The less time spent in a place full of crazy people, the better."

"Yeah, that's my philosophy too," Krissa said, returning the PDL. She sat back in her chair, eyeing Streuben. "I came in here to quit."

"Quit?" Streuben scoffed, shaking his head. "You can't quit."

"I have an appointment with placement services," Krissa explained. She certainly *could* quit. And she would, too. He wasn't going to talk her out of it.

He leaned forward, narrowing one eye and lifting the opposite eyebrow. How did he do that? "Did you take your meds this morning?" he asked.

Shoving her hand in her pocket, she lowered her gaze and said, "That has nothing to do with it." Her fingers closed around the pill case.

Streuben stared at her for a long, uncomfortable moment. "After this assignment," he said, turning his attention to the PDL. His fingers bobbed along the keypad. He was ignoring her. Intentionally.

"I don't want the assignment," Krissa murmured. She felt like a rebellious teenager on the verge of a tantrum. Why wouldn't Streuben listen to her?

"If you don't take it, I will report you as absent without official leave." He tossed out the threat with a casual air.

AWOL? Krissa frowned, crossing her arms over her chest. "I'm not Zephyr or Zenith."

"No, but you're a servant of the Legacy," Streuben paused to glare at her, "unless you've forgotten."

Krissa bowed her head, staring at her fingers. He always had a way of making her feel small. She hated when he brought up the monkey on her back. She hated him.

In a meek whisper, Krissa argued, "I was exonerated."

"Perhaps, but—"

Anger heated her words, giving her a bit more gumption. "And you were the one who assigned me to that ship, anyway."

"But you were the one who *completed* the assignment." Streuben stabbed at his desk with thick finger, hissing, "Really, Carlisle, I don't want to have this argument every time something doesn't go your way. You should have been the one to recognize their Ghost encryptions and report them to the Legacy."

"I *did* report them," Krissa said in an effort to defend herself.

"After you fixed the comsys issue and told them that the ignition flux was the problem. You allowed them to escape," Streuben reminded her. He shut down the discussion with an order and dismissal. "An empty crew transport is leaving fleet headquarters tomorrow at oh-six-hundred hours to retrieve the master-sergeant. Be on it. That will be all."

Tears threatened Krissa's eyes with a sharp sting. She stood stiffly and headed for the door. She didn't want him to see how he'd upset her. And after all this time working under him, she should have known better. He was simply a jerk.

"Oh, and Carlisle …" Streuben said, causing her to turn back. "I expect the report of your daily duties at precisely nineteen hundred hours, an hour before the end of your shift." He smirked before returning his eyes to his PDL. "They are listed on the UV datalog as usual."

Krissa bit her tongue as she exited the office and headed back to the street to access Streuben's utility vehicle. It was definitely time to leave.

"I'm glad you could make it in today, Krissa," Dr. Terces said as he closed the door behind him. He examined her chart, then smiled up at her.

Krissa had completed her assignments for the morning, and was about to report back to Streuben to ask him to bump up her afternoon appointments when he linked her with a crucial message from Dr. Terces. The doctor had requested that she stop by his office as soon as possible. Streuben seemed remarkably understanding, slathering her with words of compassion and sympathy. Most out of character for him.

Terces's office was located at the top of a structure adjacent to the Justice Center. In fact, the buildings were connected by a bank of lifts. Krissa knew that her initial surgery had taken place in the medical ward of the JC, as it was the hospital to where she'd been transferred from Quintus after passing out. Still, for some reason, being so close to the JC made her nervous.

Krissa fidgeted uncomfortably on the edge of her examination chair. She hated doctors, even though Dr. Terces and Dr. Aftal had shown her nothing but kindness. "My boss shifted around my assignments today to allow for some time with you. He said when you spoke with him, it sounded urgent."

Dr. Terces sighed, taking a seat next to Krissa. "Quite, I'm afraid." He frowned, looking as if he was searching for careful words. "I—have you been taking your medications as prescribed?"

Good grief, did Streuben report her? She hadn't answered him when he questioned her this morning. Releasing a sigh, Krissa leaned forward, resting on her knees. She didn't want to tell anyone, but her doctor had asked her point-blank. She had to admit the truth. "No. But I haven't felt any ill-effects."

"And you probably won't," Dr. Terces said, "but you have second growth, Krissa." He held up a PDL for her to see. The image was an internal scan of her brain. A dark cloud muddled a portion of the image. "I really didn't understand why the dizziness and disorientation continued to linger until we took that scan last week."

Krissa blew out another heavy breath. "What is it?"

Dr. Terces shook his head. "Without going in, I can only make educated guesses. But for now, I'm going to give you different, stronger medications. Hopefully, we can keep it from growing further and doing greater harm to you."

A frightning cold descended upon Krissa. She wrapped her arms around herself as she looked up at Dr. Terces. "Wh-why don't I feel it?" she asked.

"You do, Krissa. The feelings you've described on previous visits. The headaches. The blurred vision. The strained memory. Those are classic symptoms of such a growth," Dr. Terces explained.

"Is it—" she began to ask, but couldn't bring herself to do so.

"Terminal?" Dr. Terces finished for her. "It could be. But if you follow my instructions and faithfully take your meds, we should be able to manage it."

Krissa felt shaken, but she had no one to talk with about this except Dr. Terces. And Streuben. Streuben would probably somehow blame her for her body's incompetence at fending off such illness. "What about removing it? Like before?"

Dr. Terces shook his head. "This one is inoperable, Krissa. Too intertwined with central nerves and brain functions. I'm sorry," he added in a whisper.

Nodding, Krissa tightened her hold around herself. She hadn't expected this kind of news. The day had started with such hope, but as it went on, that hope had been stripped away. Discouraging thoughts ate at her.

"These medications that I'm giving you are pretty strong, and they'll take some getting used to. Can you take some time off?" Dr. Terces asked.

Krissa frowned. "I have an important assignment in the morning."

Dr. Terces nodded. "All right. I'll talk with Mr. Streuben about you taking off at least the rest of the day. I think it important for you to go home and rest. The initial dose will take effect immediately, but you should be functioning normally within a few hours."

There was no way Streuben would let her take time off. Or if he did, he'd increase her workload later to make up for the lost time. Krissa started, "Streuben won't—"

"As long as you make that appointment in the morning, I doubt he'll take issue with my orders. I'll talk to him. He'll agree. I promise. Don't you worry about that," Dr. Terces insisted. "And I think we should increase our visits from biweekly to weekly. I want to keep a closer eye on you."

Krissa nodded, removing the case of pills from her pocket. "Here're the old meds," she said, offering Dr. Terces the small metal box.

"Thank you," he said, rising as he took the case from her. He moved to the far wall of the spacious office, which held a set of cabinets above and below a working countertop. Removing a large bottle from the top cabinet, he measured out several tablets and placed them in the case. He selected three more bottles and poured out more pills from each one. He placed a new label on the front, hand-writing the instructions for her.

"This should get you through the week. Take all of them three times daily," he instructed. "The red capsules, the capustatim, can be taken as often as you need when your symptoms appear. That's what you've been taking. They are quick releasing and should help you almost immediately. If you have any trouble with any of these, aside from this afternoon, I want you to link me. The reason I say not this afternoon is that this is going to take you out of commission for a bit. That's why I'm sending you home. You need to be in bed."

"Sounds wonderful," Krissa muttered, taking the case from him. Maybe she would just not take the new pills. How would he know, anyway?

"I am required to witness your first dose. And I have an injection that has to accompany it. The liquid dosage just makes your body a bit more receptive to the new combination of the therapeutic drugs. After I administer that, I'll have Nurse Fiara see you home."

Of course. He'd make certain she took it.

"And don't think that you can just stop taking these like those others," Dr.

Terces said as he turned his back to prepare the medication he was about to give her. "The drugs will be attacking that tumor, trying to reduce its growth rate. You'll suffer through a severe withdrawal, even after taking just the initial dose." He stepped to her side, looking down on her. "These are serious meds, Krissa. You can't play with brain meds."

Krissa nodded again. Good thing Dr. Terces wasn't a pitchman. His selling technique was really lacking.

He held out his hand, a large, plain white pill, a smaller yellow tablet, and a green capsule resting on his fingers. His other hand offered a small cup of water. With a sigh, Krissa took the pills and the cup. Why did she feel like she was being condemned to death?

"Take them, Krissa," he advised, standing over her with his hands on his hips. She hadn't even taken the drugs, yet he seemed to grow before her very eyes. "Compliance."

Reluctance slowed her movement as she lifted the pills to her lips. For an instant, she wished Lila were around to help her. Even just to talk to. But no. She was alone. Completely alone. The pills tasted bitter—like regret mingled with dread—as she washed them down with a swig of water.

"Good," Dr. Terces said as he returned to the countertop. He crossed back to her with a syringed needle in his hand. "Tilt your head, please."

He held her face with his hand as he settled her head against his leg. "You can close your eyes," he whispered, brushing her hair back from her neck.

She squeezed her eyes shut as she felt the needle prick her skin. The rush of liquid spewed into her veins, catching Krissa's breath as heat burbled in her bloodstream. Dr. Terces held her for a moment before he removed the needle. "Finished," he said.

Leaning back against the hard padding of the chair, Krissa shuddered as the spotless ceiling danced above her. She heard Dr. Terces call for Nurse Fiara, but after that, all she heard was her heart pounding in her ears. The heat in her blood turned to ice and back. Her mind spun as her breath raced. And she didn't remember how she got home, but as she opened her eyes, the stained ceiling loomed on top of her, closing in like the lid of a casket.

CHAPTER 15

Day 9452 PLR: The Straightjacket

The line for meds moved along at its normal pace. The routine was always the same. Orderly Taub would call out the list of who was to receive their prescribed dosage. The inmates were expected to line up to accept them from Droga, who doled out the various pills. Those who could anyway. The debilitated inmates had their meds delivered to their rooms. It had been just the previous week when an excruciating overdose experience that nearly ended Chase's life drove Dr. Tuscane to suggest that they give him a break. They made little progress, no matter how hard they pushed him.

He'd mostly recovered, but he immediately stopped taking the meds. Which meant he had to employ every ounce of self-control to conceal the withdrawal symptoms he experienced to keep the doctors from catching on. Which meant facing the torturous treatments without the comforting numbness of the drugs.

Chase stepped forward and lifted the pills from the tray, his eyes on Droga, who watched him closely. As part of the charade, he threw his head back as he popped the pills into his mouth. He picked up the cup and took a sip, but carefully worked the pills under his tongue.

"Check," Droga muttered.

Chase opened his mouth to prove it empty. Droga grunted and waved him on as Taub checked him off the list. Chase crossed the room, and while his back was turned, spit out the pills and shoved them in the pocket of his uniform.

Dr. Caultin whipped into the room, speaking privately with Taub and Droga. They shared a tense, heated conversation before the doctor returned to the corridor that led to the offices. Droga made a face at the doctor's back as Taub stepped forward.

"They are going to take blood from all of you tonight while you're sleeping to run a levels check, so if you think you're fooling us by not taking your meds, think twice," Taub announced to the inmates.

The declaration didn't faze Chase. He measured his steps carefully before sitting down at a table. All part of the ruse. Across from him, Church's good eye bored into him.

"You good?" Church growled softly. It was code for *Did you swallow the drugs?*

"A little parched," Chase responded. That meant *I fooled the orderly.*

Behind them, Hart, another of the staff, activated the Bands screen. Several inmates settled themselves on the lumpy couch as their drug-induced stupor took hold of their minds. Chase calculated that he and Church had another ten or fifteen minutes before they'd have to start faking theirs. Until then, they could communicate cryptically under the observant eyes of Plastar, Zermel, and Craser—burly orderlies who monitored the inmates from the edges of the room—and Dr. Tuscane, the doctor on duty.

Church nodded, sliding a Ruli card toward Chase. Ruli was an illegal game, but that didn't seem to matter out here. Fittingly, they never had full decks onboard. The royalty cards were always missing. Today, however, the card in front of Chase was the king.

Chase snatched it up quickly. Church continued to stare at him. As dealer, he slid another card toward Chase. The dark meets light card. Chase understood that to mean that the men were ready to make their move tonight. It would have to happen before the level checks.

Another card came his way. Emerald twelve. Midnight was the time of the shift change, when the entire staff, numbering twenty in all, would be engaged in a briefing. The level checks would happen prior to that, but more than likely, the doctors and staff would review them during the briefing. The inmates could make it work, though. They could still pull it off. Chase bowed his head in a slow nod.

The ruby marquis and the drat cards slid into place before him. Paired together, Chase presumed that meant there would be bloodshed and death. Considering their time on the *Straightjacket*, the men were hungry for revenge. It turned his stomach, but was there any other way? There had to be.

He peered up from his collected hand of cards to see a disturbing smile on Church's lips. The treatments were obviously getting to him. They were getting to all of them. That's why he and Church had risked the whispered conversation two days ago, snippets of sentences implying that it was time to do something. They had decided to take over the ship, regardless of consequences. If nothing else, perhaps their dying voices would be heard throughout the Legacy.

Chase returned the drat card. Yes, he wanted to make the escape from the suffering, but he wouldn't hurt anyone to do it. Nor would he allow his men to do so. He selected the sapphire baron and the diamond duchess from his hand and placed them before Church. He hoped that with the symbol of the baron's chalice and the duchess's sword on the cards, Church would understand that he intended to round up and imprison the staff. The blue of the sapphire and white of the diamond meant the blanket of space and its glittering stars. They would place the staff on the next shuttle that arrived and ship them all back to the Legacy. Chase focused his energies on Church and whispered a prayer that his friend got it.

Church nodded, then lifted an eyebrow. He ran a hand over his stubbly cheek and looked beyond Chase. They were being watched. Church's careful expression warned him clearly.

Keeping up the pretense of the game, Chase reached for the Ruli deck and took a card. He slipped it into his hand and slid the King card back to Church. Confirmation. The plan was set.

As Chase returned his gaze to his hand, Church stood, tossing his cards on the table. He grumbled several swear words before he toppled the table in a mock dispute. All planned. They didn't want the doctors to know they were working together. Chase jumped up and spun around as Church stormed toward the inmates' corridor.

Zermel and Craser stepped into Church's path, asking what had happened. Church stumbled back from them, but not before Zermel grabbed his arm. Chase moved toward them to explain, but Craser pulled out a remote and flashed it in Church's face. Church cried out as he collapsed on the floor. The squeal affected each of the inmates, including Chase. He closed his eyes as brain-induced waves of conditioned pain took over his body. Whimpers and howls twittered throughout the room.

Once he recovered, Chase opened his eyes. A single card in his hand took him by surprise. The Prince. It had appeared from nowhere. The reminder of the Prince's presence diminished Chase's anger over the way the orderlies had treated Church. The Crown was still in charge.

He dropped the card on the floor. Dr. Tuscane marched toward him, a slight smirk on his face. Chase bowed his head, raising his hands in surrender and submission.

"Mr. Leighton," Dr. Tuscane said, touching Chase's arm, "why don't you head on into your room? I'll come get you for your ECT in a few moments."

Blast. He'd forgotten that he was up for shock therapy. He should have taken the drugs. They would have helped mask the pain of the electricity a bit. His hand rested on his pocket as he considered taking them. No. He couldn't be cloudy tonight. Church and the others were relying on him. And soon, he'd be free.

◆

The crew transport was really just a small shuttle, which fit perfectly in the starboard docking bay of the *Straightjacket*. The bays obviously were not built to accommodate larger crafts. Krissa was only allowed to carry her tool pack, but Streuben assured her that she wouldn't need a lot. It was, after all, a software issue.

After waking just hours following the dose of medication she had been given, she'd felt no more ill effects. Well, perhaps a little lingering dizziness, but that was almost normal for her. She'd taken the first round of medication just before boarding, stomaching a bit of protein paste to avoid nausea. The pills must have made her drowsy, though, as she slept in regular patterns through the majority of the automated flight, waking to eat and take the next round of meds. She never slept this much. Hopefully, once she focused on the assignment, she would be able to stay alert.

The master sergeant greeted her, introducing himself as Sergeant Cord Brewster, Zephyr Force. Confident almost to the point of being cocky, Brewster must have been trying to make up for his short stature. Krissa stood easily a head taller than him. And while he should have been in full uniform appropriate to his rank, he wore dark slacks and a white tunic. Black stubble poked through his shaved head, giving the skin a grayish pallor. The rules must be a little more relaxed when in the presence of lunatics.

Brewster led her from the two-level bay into the receiving zone of the facility. They entered a storage area before passing through an engine room, where a lift was waiting to take them to the above decks. He gave her a brief rundown of the ship operations that now were run completely by the staff. He was the only nonmedical officer left onboard, and his tenure was up as of today.

The lift emptied out into a spacious conference room. A thick slab of varnished wood took up the center, surrounded by a good number of gray cushioned chairs. A strip of matching wood ran the length of the conference room, single binding cuffs attached to lengths of chain every so often. Brewster mumbled something about the doctors and staff, but Krissa's attention was trained on the Bands screen that hung on the wall. Someone had left it on, and a report concerning recent Ghost activity flashed images that troubled her for some reason. Brewster crossed to the screen and shut it off, cursing the Ghosts as he did so.

A dull ache skittered through Krissa's head. Once she got to the control room, she would dig out her capustatim. Before the ache compounded into something worse. She couldn't risk a blinding headache while on duty out here.

The control room, which housed the main computers, lay between the staff quarters and the inmates' area. A long corridor separated the two areas. Both entrances were capped with sealed fire doors. Brewster indicated that those were an added security measure.

Large gray panels had been pulled from the obsolete mainframes, leaving the control room in a state of absolute disarray. Wires and cables were strewn across the floor, tangled into crazy jumbles. Some were even cut, stripped of their protective coating. It looked as though someone who really didn't know what they were doing had come in here, bludgeoned the poor computers, and in a tantrum, left them to fix themselves somehow.

The computers were rather quaint, to say the least. Krissa had heard that the ship had just gone through a remodeling, and she wondered why the computer upgrade wasn't done then. Of course, the upgrade hadn't worked, which was why she was here. It was not for her to question why. It at least supplied her with a job. For now. She just wished that she didn't have to deal with someone else's mess.

"I can't offer you any accommodations, Miss Carlisle. We have a full staff, and I don't think you wish to lodge with the inmates." He chuckled as he stared at her, clearly waiting for her reaction.

She gave him a polite smile, which took some effort to cover her anger over the way the computers had been treated. "I hope no accommodations will be required."

Brewster nodded, clasping his hands behind his back. The move puffed out his chest, transforming his stocky build into that of a plucky rooster. Was he trying to impress her? "I hope not as well," he replied. "As soon as you are finished, we both board that shuttle and head out of here." He looked about the wreck of a room. "If you need anything, there is a link here, next to the door. I am required to seal the door when I leave."

Krissa pulled a garbled knot of wires from a chair before settling into it. May as well see how bad the situation actually was. She tapped the console into an active state. "I understand. Thank you," she said.

The sergeant didn't move. Krissa hoped that he wasn't under the same mind-set as the captain of the *Haulaway*. She lifted an eyebrow, silently wishing him away. "Did you have a question?"

"No, just curious. And anxious," he added with a grin, taking a step closer to her. "I've been up here for three and a half months, and I'm ready to get home."

"Mmm," she said, coloring her face with a disapproving frown. "I work best on my own. And I would like to get done with this just as quickly as you."

"Yes." Brewster's now nervous gaze flickered toward the door and down the hallway. "Yes. The quicker, the better."

"All right, then. I'll alert you if I need something, or when I am done," she assured him in a firm tone. *Take the hint, man.*

Sergeant Brewster nodded, clicked his heels, and spun around to leave. As promised, the door slid shut behind him, leaving Krissa alone with the bungled computers. She rolled her eyes as she set to work, delving into the very heart of the digital systems. Her first order of business was to send an arrival report to Streuben. And then she hoped she'd have no more interruptions.

CHAPTER 16

The nightly sedative had been administered. Due to Chase's recent reprieve and impeccable behavior, he'd been promoted from the injection the doctors called somnoctis to the pill variety. And he'd fooled the orderly as he had before, slipping the pills under his tongue. A few other prisoners were still given the injections, but Chase remained confident that the more alert inmates could overtake the staff. His clarity of mind had allowed him some time in prayer, which helped greatly as well.

Lying deathly still in his bed, Chase listened as Dr. Caiman spoke with Sergeant Brewster just outside his room. "It's time for our staff shift change. I'd like to debrief the orderlies and doctors for a few moments, twenty minutes tops. The inmates have all been given their normal dosages and are asleep. I want you to stand guard," Caiman said.

"Sorry, Doc. I'm not part of your staff," Brewster replied snappily. "Besides, I'm outta here in just a few minutes, hopefully. There's a shuttle with my name on it docked in the bay."

Perfect. Chase hadn't counted on a shuttle being onboard already. The plan was to hold all the doctors and staff in the conference room, but it would definitely secure the inmates' chances of successful escape if they could go ahead and get the staff off the ship. Chase held his breath and continued to listen as the conversation took a nosedive into an argument.

"I'm asking you kindly," Caiman's tone implied anger. Chase had heard it before. "Just sit here at the orderlies' station. That's all you have to do."

After a moment of silent standoff, Brewster hissed, "Fine. But you know that your staff is going to have to step up and handle things from now on. I'm not staying any longer than I have to, and I'm definitely not planning to come back."

"If I don't relieve you before, link me when it's time for you to go," the doctor said, evidently not pleased with Brewster. Chase heard the click of his shoes as he marched down the hall, followed by grumbling from the master sergeant. The sigh of a cushion and the shrill squeak of the chair's frame told Chase that Brewster had taken a seat at the orderlies' station as instructed.

Chase lifted his head, his eyes catching movement in the room across from him. Church was ready. It was time.

Carefully climbing out of bed, Chase met Church's gaze across the hall. Church held up a syringe full of orange liquid. Ben Reiger, Church's roommate, still received the injected sedative. The second dose, normally administered in the middle of the sleeping hours, had been left in their room. Whether it was procedure or laziness on the part of the orderlies, Chase felt like celebrating. They would use it to take down Brewster.

With great care not to make even a whisper of a sound, Chase pulled the sheet from his bed and slunk into the hallway. Their rooms were closest to the station, so they didn't have far to go. Church gripped the syringe and positioned himself in a crouch, ready to pounce the moment Chase grabbed Brewster. Church gave him a nod of encouragement.

Finally deciding that speed outweighed stealth, Chase made his move. He darted the few feet down the hall, ducked into the station, and whipped the sheet around Brewster's head, covering the master sergeant's mouth and nose with the fabric. Church shot out of his room like lightning and pricked the needle through the sergeant's tunic and into his arm. The man squirmed and wriggled in Chase's grasp until the sedative took hold.

Church took over at the station, disengaging the observation system. "In case they decide to take a peek from the conference room," he whispered.

Chase nodded as he lowered Brewster to the floor. "Good thinking. Brewster said there's a shuttle in the bay."

"Thank the Crown," Church said. "We can go home."

"The shuttle's probably not big enough to hold all of us." Chase tapped his fingers on the station's countertop. "Besides, I want to blow the ship. No one else needs to suffer this way. We send the staff and Brewster on autopilot back to Crenet, arrange a rescue with the Ghosts, and set the self-destruct as we leave."

"I want to go home, Chase," Church replied, his jaw squared with impatience.

"We will, Nic. I promise." Chase bent down to remove Brewster's access card. "He's got to have weapons in his quarters. I'm going to have a look. If we're armed, we have a better chance of overpowering the staff."

"Be quick. We may not have much time," Church said, glancing down the corridor toward the conference room.

Chase stood, meeting Church's gaze. He offered a hand. "You're with me?"

Church grasped Chase's fingers and nodded resolutely. "All the way."

"Keep watch," Chase said as he moved toward the common area that led to the stairs.

Using the appropriated access card, Chase snuck into the stairwell. The lift would cause too much racket and probably tip off the doctors. Instead, he tripped lightly down the stairs. Brewster, obnoxious as he was, had been rather generous with information regarding the layout of the ship. His loose lips often bragged about his accommodations on the lowest level. Chase dashed through a maze of corridors, circumventing the kitchen and laundry facilities. Finally, he tumbled into a hallway that ran parallel to the catwalk above one of the docking bays. Through a heavy airlock window, he could see the shuttle. He'd been right in what he had told Church. It looked small, perhaps a five or maybe a ten-passenger maximum capacity vessel. Fitting twenty staff members, plus Brewster, wouldn't be an easy task. Once the other inmates got involved with the takeover, Chase would set some of the more technical-minded on making adjustments to the life support systems to accommodate the entire staff.

Past the complement of empty crew quarters, he found the ladder that led to the first deck, which housed the private cabin of the master sergeant. Brewster's access card granted him entry to anywhere on the ship. Chase found what he was looking for in Brewster's quarters, though. Several fully charged slayers were strategically placed in the top drawer of his bureau, while two equally charged stingers stood on either side of it, almost as if they were decorative. The weapons probably would be no match for those evil remotes, but the men would just have to face the conditioned pain. The reward of freedom would be worth it.

Making sure the safety was set on each weapon, Chase carefully tucked the slayers under his arm. He carried the stingers and placed them against the wall before he climbed up the ladder. After situating the guns on the floor above, he leaned down and retrieved the stingers. He had to hurry. The staff meeting would break up any minute, and they had to get men into position.

Church was waiting for him at the top of the stairwell. Chase passed off the stingers, then presented the guns as he took the stairs two at a time. "Lancaster and Torin are standing by," Church confirmed.

"All right. I want them armed with the slayers, as well as you and me. Are there any others lucid enough to handle a stinger?" Chase asked as they moved back to the common area.

"I would trust Declan and Newell," Church answered, activating the stingers.

Chase released a breath, gripping his slayer. "That's six up against twenty."

"There are more who will put muscle behind us. Like Reiger. We just gotta get the drugs out of them."

Chase nodded. "Rouse who you can. Tell them to stand by. I think we should raid the conference room. Don't even give the staff a chance to come out."

"I agree," Church muttered as Lancaster and Torin met them in the hall.

"Captain, we got Brewster tied up," Torin reported.

"Good work. Let's get our friends ready for a battle," Chase said, handing off the slayers. "Take the guns off the safety. And gentlemen, no bloodshed, if possible. I want each of those doctors and orderlies to walk out of here alive. Have everyone assemble in the common area. We strike in five."

"Aye," came from the three men.

Chase nodded, darting back into his room. His roommate, Joe Weller, was the oldest member of his crew. Joe'd also had the hardest time taking the treatments. Chase felt so guilty about what had been done to him, and about his condition. But he also knew that old Joe would want to be in on the takeover.

"It's time to go home, Joe," Chase whispered.

The old man lifted his head, blinking at Chase. "It is?"

"We're taking the ship. Meet in the common room."

"Yes, sir," Joe said, pushing back his blanket.

Chase ducked out again, glancing down the hall toward the conference room. No sign of the staff yet. He clutched the master sergeant's card and opened the drug pantry that sat inside the orderlies' station. Scads of sedatives and other drugs filled the shelves. "Help us to be merciful," he whispered in prayer as he moved back into the hallway.

More men filtered from their rooms with mixed expressions of confusion, joy, and anxiety. Chase caught Church's eye as Church brought Declan and Newell past the stragglers to the end of the hall, where the strong master sergeant lay wrapped in the sheet, taking a nice snooze. Torin and Lancaster quickly joined Chase and the others.

Looking back at his men, Chase watched as Joe stepped out with his severe limp. Chase gave a nod of confirmation. "Listen up," he said in a hushed tone. "I'm taking Caiman. Church, I want you on Caultin. Lancaster, take Sainne, and Torin, take Tuscane. Declan, Newell," Chase looked to the two crewmembers, "low-grade stings to anyone who raises a remote."

His eyes shifted to Duncan, another of his men. "Duncan, lowest drawer of the middle cabinet, you'll find a supply of binders. Give those without a weapon a single dose of somnoctis—on the third shelf of the pantry—and a pair of binders. We'll bring the doctors and orderlies out one by one. We drug them, cuff them, and lead them to the staff lift.

"Marlen, Simmons, Decker, Stone, I want you to escort them down to the bay. Two of you to one staff. Keep them separated until they are on the shuttle. Start with Brewster here." The men weren't members of the *Halcyon* crew, but Chase recognized Marlen from the *Vanguard*. The others were in Ghost service. He knew they were all trustworthy and reliable.

"Joe, you and Kern get on down to the bay. Secure each staff member as they are brought onboard the shuttle," Chase said to the old man and another before turning to the rest of the men standing around. "If I find out that you've used anything but somnoctis, there will be repercussions. We are not to seek revenge on these people. We are to focus only on our freedom. Is that understood?"

The men grumbled acknowledgment. Chase made eye contact with Church, who nodded once. Lifting his slayer in the air, Chase whispered, "Let's do this," as he crept toward the conference room.

He took a deep breath, closed his eyes, and shot another arrow-prayer of protection and guidance to the Ruler Prince. The electricity from this afternoon's treatments still coursed through his blood, making him edgy and nervous. His shaky fingers tightened around the slayer's grip, ready to pull the trigger, but hoping that wouldn't be necessary. He would have been far more comfortable with a reliable queller in his hand. Swallowing hard, he stepped back and kicked open the door to the conference room.

"Everybody stay seated!" he shouted, waving the slayer about the room as wide, panicked eyes stared back at him. Dr. Caiman stood at the head of the table. Chase ordered, "Caiman, take a chair."

Church and the others filtered in, moving to their assignments. Church wasted no time. He dug his slayer into Caultin's back, ordering him to his feet. Dr. Caultin looked at Caiman, who instead of following Chase's order, reached for his pocket.

"Don't even think about it," Chase said, raising his slayer in a dead aim at Caiman. "We want to be kind, but I will not hesitate to end you if you so much as *try* to hurt my men any further."

Church escorted Caultin to the door, placing him in the hands of a waiting inmate. He straddled the doorway, slayer trained on the remaining staff, but observing the treatment of Caultin. Nodding toward Chase, he moved back into the room.

"What about you, Leighton?" Caiman asked.

"What about me?" Chase growled back.

"I think you're bluffing. You've already demonstrated that you're a strong leader and are willing to protect your men," Caiman sneered, taking a step toward Chase. "But what if I hurt you?"

Chase stood his ground, staring down Caiman. Why did this man elicit such fear from him? Caiman's eyes pierced his very soul. Chase's resolve nearly wavered as Caiman closed in, his fingers now encircling his remote.

An angry shot split the distance between them. Chase blinked, looking toward his first officer. "Enough," Church barked to Caiman. "You no longer hold any power over us."

Caiman squared his jaw, and in a most exaggerated way, pressed the button on the remote. Chase managed to avoid the light, but the squeal still shocked him with mind-bending pain. *Don't give in to it.* He ground his teeth as he made eye contact with the others. They too were fighting the effects of the conditioning.

Knowing that Caiman expected to conquer them easily, Chase stumbled toward him. He lowered the gun, feigning surrender. As Caiman reached for it, Chase snapped into action, batting away the remote. He then lifted the weapon, aiming between Caiman's eyes.

"It's over, Doctor," he growled, silently struggling with the desire to pull the trigger.

"Chase," Church murmured softly, drawing Chase back to a proper, principled mind-set.

Dropping the slayer to his side, Chase grabbed the scruff of Caiman's collar. He shoved the doctor into the hallway, where Stone jabbed a needle into his arm. Two others caught the doctor as his knees buckled. "Get him to the shuttle," Chase muttered.

A sharp cry called Chase's attention back to the interior of the conference room. One of the orderlies, a particularly malicious man named Vencer, lay on the floor under Newell's stinger. Meeting Chase's questioning gaze, Newell explained, "He grabbed for his remote, sir."

Chase nodded. "He can wait. Let's get the rest of these folks out of here."

The men worked together, getting each of the doctors and orderlies out of the room and in line for the sedative. With only two of the staff left, Chase ran a hand over his face. Suddenly, he felt tired and overwhelmed.

Church stepped to his side, his slayer lowered. "You did it, Chase."

"We did it," Chase corrected him. "Torin, I need you to head down to the docking bay. That shuttle won't carry the entire staff comfortably. Do what you can to make it better. And reset the autopilot course for the farthest point it will reach. Take who you need."

"You got it," Torin answered, surrendering his slayer to Chase as he left.

"Church, you finish up here. I'm going to hide the guns," Chase said.

"We might need them, Chase." Church frowned, a little too hesitant to relinquish the power he'd regained after it had been stripped from him during his time on the *Straightjacket*. Chase understood. He felt the same way, which was the precise reason why he wanted the weapons hidden away.

"Negative. I don't want anyone to have easy access to any weaponry. I also want the drug pantry secured. I'll put Simmons on that," Chase replied, collecting the slayer from Lancaster and the stingers from Declan and Newell. "I will see the shuttle off on my way back up. Tell the men that they may move into the staff quarters. You guys," he gestured to Declan and Newell, "I want you to seal off the treatment wing. And Lancaster, when all is done here, get down to the bridge, and try with all your might to link Rev One, or any Ghost ship within range."

"Yes, sir," Lancaster answered.

"Church, finish up in here, and meet me in the bay in a few moments," Chase said, taking the slayer from his first officer.

"Yes, sir," Church replied.

They were free. And while freedom tasted sweeter than ever, the obstacles loomed large before them. Chase would need to consult with his officers to formulate a plan. But first they had to make sure the staff was sent far away. As he'd said, he wouldn't allow them to hurt his men ever again.

CHAPTER 17

Krissa reached for the link near the door of the control room to contact Sergeant Brewster. The door slid open. Odd. The master sergeant had sealed it when he left. He should have had to unseal it before it opened again. She shrugged, returning her eyes to her PDL. She made a couple more notes before glancing up. With the ruckus she'd heard a little while ago, she expected to see the corridor full of activity. It was just as empty as before. *Perhaps the inmates are rioting.* She laughed softly to herself.

It had been a long night, but she had managed to put some order back into the room and find the source of the facility's computer issues. Straightening it out took the longest, but she soon discovered that the retrograde was unnecessary. She had a long list of recommended fixes and upgrades that would actually work. Approval would have to come not only from the head doctor, but also from Streuben. She'd already sent the report and requisition his way. The install would take a few more hands to finish in a reasonable amount of time. But now, she needed something to eat and her medication. She'd been so wrapped up, she'd forgotten to take one of the doses.

Tucking her PDL under her arm, she moved into the corridor. She heard raucous laughter from the conference room across the way. She looked around for any sign of Legacy personnel, but still found no one. With a frown, she headed toward the laughter.

A sizable crowd of men were talking, laughing, and carousing playfully through the wide room. One even jumped up on the table, shedding the top of his blue uniform to reveal a plain white tunic underneath. They appeared to be celebrating. Krissa's eyes darted about, searching for anyone in a Legacy uniform. She swallowed hard as she realized why the men were celebrating. They—the inmates—had indeed taken over the *Straightjacket.*

Someone across the room locked eyes with her and shouted, "Hey! There's another one!"

She scrambled to back out of the room, but several of the men grabbed her before she made it very far. She screamed as her PDL was batted to the floor. A pair of hands seized her neck and pinned her against the wall. She couldn't breathe.

"You're new," the man said. His blue eyes glinted with unrestrained ire.

Krissa gasped, trying to squirm from his grip. She had no plans to fight or even run. There was nowhere to go. She simply wanted to fill her lungs. She nodded quickly, hoping that her answer would earn her release.

His grasp tightened, accompanying his demand, "Were you hiding?"

She shook her head this time, feeling her eyes bulge as the lack of air started to affect her.

He curled his fist around the collar of her uniform and lifted her off the floor. She panted rapidly as her lungs tried to compensate for lost breath. "Talk," he ordered.

"I-I'm a systems analyst," Krissa answered quickly, hoping for mercy, "here to assess the computer needs for the facility."

A tilt of his head narrowed his eyes. "You're not a doctor?"

"No."

He glanced toward several of the men who had taken interest in her. She followed his gaze and looked at each of the men in turn. "Do you know what we did with the doctors?" the man holding her asked with a malicious grin. The other men snickered with both callousness and craving.

"I don't," she whispered. Fear had taken her voice.

With a snarl, he tossed her into the waiting arms of the men. They tore at her uniform, ripping off the Legacy paraphernalia. Fists pummeled her, fingernails scratched her, and teeth bit her. She cried and screamed, trying to block them, but there were just too many. The surrounding men cheered as the others beat her.

"Let's kill 'er!" one shouted.

"No! Torture her," another man said, baring his teeth menacingly as he ripped one of the uniform tops and wound the strip of cloth around his hand. "Slowly. Like they did to us."

She scuttled across the floor as three men backed her against the wall again. A fourth wheeled an ominous-looking machine toward her. She clung to the wall, unable to keep herself from shaking. Her eyes hurt, and the swelling from the beating threatened to close them before she would be able to see what was going to happen to her.

"Enough!"

The room went quiet, and Krissa's instinct curled her into a tiny ball. She covered her head and whimpered. After a moment of silence, Krissa forced an eye open. A man with blond hair and a patch over one of his eyes stood between her and the crowd of leering prisoners. He pointed toward the machine. "Take that out of here," he ordered. "Back to your duties. We have to prepare."

Her champion spun around, lifted her arm, and secured it to one of the binding cuffs attached to the wall. She was taken aback by a long scar that led up his cheek and trailed behind the patch. "It's all right," he whispered, kneeling at her side as the inmates moved on to carry out their orders, although a few of the men lingered. "No one's going to harm you."

She stared at him, shuddering a breath every few seconds. Was he serious? She reminded herself that she was now shackled to a wall on a prison ship for the criminally insane. By the Crown, was he going to ravage her?

Her bones would not stop trembling. She closed her eyes in a futile effort to calm herself. The men had possibly obliterated the entire staff of the ship, and now she was bound in a room with the man who appeared to be their leader. Tears fell across her cheeks. "P-please don't hurt me ..."

The man sighed softly and shook his head. His fingers wrapped around a card that lay next to her. "Is this your identifier?" he asked.

"Yes," she whispered.

He pushed himself to his feet, still holding her identifier, and looked at the remaining men. "Torin, Lancaster, meet me in Caiman's office. Marlen, close down the room and watch over her. I want you on guard outside the door. The rest of you have your assignments. This room is now off limits, and no one is to touch this woman. She is our prisoner, and under Ghost protection as of this moment. Understand?"

Ghost. Terror gripped Krissa as a twitch of fire stabbed her brain. The men grumbled and shuffled through the room. A cough lodged in her throat. She regretted it immediately, throbs of pain working through her limbs. Her face scrunched up in agony as her head fell back against the wall.

Krissa had almost fallen asleep when she saw the man with the wild, angry eyes standing over her. He had been the one who pinned her against the wall. Before she could make a sound, though, he dropped to her side and gripped her face, covering her mouth. "We don't want to scream, do we?"

He held up some sort of sharp-looking instrument. It was hard to make out in the darkened room, but Krissa could tell that whatever it was could cause pain. She shook her head under his powerful hold.

"Good girl."

The man worked quickly to unbind her from the wall. He sat her up as he produced a new pair of cuffs. Encircling her wrist, he pulled her arm behind her back and secured it to her opposite hand. "I want you to come with me," he said gruffly in her ear.

"Where—"

He pressed a finger to her lips and shook his head. Grabbing her elbow, he helped her to stand up, then led her through the conference room and down the familiar corridor. They stopped at a massive door, and the man, glancing back over his shoulder, fished an access card from his pocket. The area beyond the door lay in shadow, only emergency lighting lining the carpeted hallways. As the door slid open, the man pushed her through.

Taking her arm, he guided her through what appeared to be a recreational area. Tables, chairs, a lumpy sofa, and Bands screens were set up in various places. He paused in front of another sealed door, again looked back, and applied the access card. Instead of sliding, this door opened inward. He held the door open while placing a strong hand on Krissa's neck to shove her into the room. The spring-loaded door closed behind them, and the man used the card to lock it once more.

Krissa glanced about the room, trying to figure out why she'd been brought in here. It resembled Dr. Terces's office, in that one wall held a panel of cabinets with a countertop. A recessed light provided a dim nuance to the room. A second man stood behind a mobile console of some sort. Centered in the room, the stark white sheets of a medical table picked up most of the light.

The man removed her binders, chucking them on the floor behind him. "Get on the table," he said gruffly.

Krissa blinked, his words making a flash of memory reverberate in her head. She chalked it up to déjà vu, and rubbed the wrist that had been shackled longest. "You're crazy," she said, her eyes flickering toward the door. The man blocked her only means of escape.

"Get on the table," the man repeated with a measure of force, stepping closer. His stature towered over her in a most threatening way.

She ducked around him and bolted for the door. He was faster. Grabbing her elbow, he spun her around. His powerful touch ripped a frightened scream from her. Without much exertion, he snatched her up in his arms, carried her to the table, and slammed her onto it. She swatted at him, wriggling and struggling, but he didn't seem to care. He worked deftly to strap her to the table.

The other man in the room came forward, holding a bunch of wires. Krissa cried out again as she tugged on her arms and legs, now inhibited by the restraints. She was completely at their mercy.

Both men worked to affix the wires to her body. Krissa realized they were electrodes. Oh, by the Crown, they were going to put her through shock therapy, weren't they? The night with the interrogators burned in her mind. Krissa shrieked with panic, "Help! Someone, please!"

The man clapped his hand over her mouth, pinning her head back against the table. He waved the sharp object madly in front of her face. "I told you to be quiet."

Tears surfaced in Krissa's eyes as the men finished their task. One of them stood at her side while the other one moved behind the console. "Why are you doing this?" she asked in a nervous whisper.

"Because it was done to us. For no reason. And you're one of them," the man answered, lifting his hand to signal the other man to begin.

Krissa felt a tingle in her arms and legs before the heated pulse of electricity tracked through her. Every muscle stiffened, and her breath evaporated. The release left her dry-mouthed and weak. Nightmares of horrific interrogation rods clawed at her, plaguing her from deep within.

The man paced toward the console. "Kern, increase voltage by five percent."

He walked back to her side and nodded. The familiar sensation tingled again, then tore through her veins. Her back arched off the table as she screamed in pain. When it stopped, she fell back against the table, her head rolling lazily to the side. "P-p-please," she whimpered.

"Increase by ten," the man ordered. "Again."

"I don't know how much more she can take, Ben," Kern said.

"Increase by ten," Ben insisted, glaring at Kern.

Krissa shut her eyes and cried as the violent shock ruptured her bones. A relentless vortex kept her suspended in agony. After the electricity died down, she felt herself twitching. Every movement brought reminders of the pain.

She heard a loud thud against the door, then a muffled voice shouting, "Ben!" She must be imagining things.

"Increase by ten," Ben didn't seem to hear the sound. His eyes were on Krissa. He signaled Kern once again.

Krissa shrieked as the preliminary tingles sent tiny electric stabs into her skin. The current surged through her, silencing her instantly. She had no energy nor breath left for crying. Her body shook with rigidity.

◆

Chase sat behind the desk, scrawling his plan on a tablet of paper. He'd conquered the urge to ransack Caiman's office by focusing his attention on the second part of their escape. Still, the ridiculous display of diplomas behind him taunted him. He recalled his mission by murmuring a soft prayer. Reassurance, peace, order came from the Crown. Besides, destroying someone else's belongings wouldn't help the situation.

He knew what needed to be done. It was just a matter of visualizing it and getting everyone else organized. And most of the men, while excited about the possibility of going home, were too on edge to focus. Not to mention that he'd lost a lot of their trust while searching for Trista. He'd have to earn that back. First step was asking their forgiveness.

He peered up as Lancaster, Torin, and Church entered the office. He was relieved to see them, but a little anxiety crept into his thoughts. The men closest to him had followed him this far. Still, he felt the need to apologize.

"Gentlemen," he acknowledged, gesturing toward some chairs that surrounded a circular table in one corner of the room. He grabbed his pad and moved to join them. As he sat, he looked each one in the eye. "Let me start by saying that … I'm sorry. I know that I did you a great disservice in the weeks prior to our detention. And I hope that I will one day regain your trust as your leader."

"Chase, none of us are thinking about that right now," Church said. "We appreciate the gesture, but I think your move in taking over the ship and working to get us home has solidified that trust. Maybe I shouldn't speak for the men ..." he added, motioning toward the other two.

Lancaster nodded with exaggeration. "You're dead on, Church. Cap, none of us care about any of that. We'd follow you into the blazes if you asked us."

Chase chuckled. "I hope that won't be necessary, Hal."

"I concur," Torin said. "And that's the general consensus I get from the rest of the guys, too."

With an appreciative sigh, Chase smiled at his officers. "Thank you. I needed that assurance." He placed the pad on the table, readying his pen for further writing.

The men exchanged concerned glances, which caught Chase's eye. "Tell him," Lancaster whispered to Church.

Sitting back in the chair, Chase rested his arms on the chair and clasped his hands over his middle. "What's going on?" he asked, looking between his men.

Church slid an identifier across the table toward him. The image was of a young woman with short brown hair and eyes that he couldn't forget if he tried. Oh, by the Crown ...

"Trista," Chase whispered, lifting the card closer to his face. The card read, *Krissa Carlisle*. "Where did you get this?" he demanded.

Church rubbed his chin before he met Chase's gaze. "She's onboard, Chase," he said quietly.

Surprise and shock stole Chase's breath. "Where?" he insisted, rising to head to the door.

"The men took her prisoner, Cap," Lancaster said.

Church stepped between Chase and the door, shooting Lancaster a disapproving scowl. His look softened as he stared at Chase. "She's safe, Chase. She's alone, locked in the conference room. Marlen's watching over her. I know you want to see her, but we need to get on this plan. We're working against time."

Chase swallowed hard, nodding as he stared at Krissa's identifier. Why the Crown would choose to bring them back together when he was so broken was beyond him. And as much as he wanted to see her, he had to ask himself if he was ready to do so. According to previous reports, she wouldn't remember him. Could he take that kind of hurt?

"You're right, Nic." Knowing she was safe helped make the decision.

Chase moved back to his seat, placed the card on the table, and pulled the pad before him as he sat. "Hal, you alerted the Ghosts?"

"I've tried, Cap. I can't hack into their system. They've locked it up tight," Lancaster answered.

"Keep trying," Chase said, resting the pad over top of Krissa's identifier. He would lose his resolve if she kept staring at him. "Once we get in, we need to send out signals across the board to throw off any approaching Legacy ships. I also want all passcodes changed. I don't want the Legacy to gain remote access to our systems."

"Yes, sir," Lancaster said.

Chase turned to his ship operations officer. "Wes, report on bay status."

"Assuming the Ghosts would send a shuttle large enough to accommodate all of us, there's no way it would fit in the bay," Torin replied. "We're going to have to get creative."

"Suggestions?"

Torin placed a roughly rendered map of the bay in front of Chase. "There is a docking pad atop the ship, but any landing shuttle has to have special mating equipment. Our ships won't have that. So ... all I can find are these aft supply hatches, which empty into the receiving zones on deck one. From what I can make out from the records, a delivery ship docks behind the *Straightjacket* and places the supplies in the hatch. It's somewhat pressurized to accommodate certain items, but not enough for any of us."

"So we would need to create some sort of airlock that we can travel through," Chase murmured, thinking aloud.

"Yes, sir," Torin replied. "That will require welding equipment and other hardware, which I can probably find in the bays. I'll also need some men to supply the labor."

Chase nodded his approval. "Get on it. Take able-bodied men, whomever you need. As Church said, we don't have a lot of time."

"Chase, we've got bigger worries than creating an airlock. No doubt that shuttle full of staff will arrive somewhere shortly. When that happens, the Legacy will be on the move. The ship isn't armed. We can't go up against any part of the fleet," Church said.

Chase bit his lip. He knew all of that. But he still had to cling to the hope that they would succeed. "We've made it this far, Nic. Let's deal with that when and if it comes to it."

Church sighed, shaking his head as he sat back in his chair. "We'll need those weapons. I'm not dying without a fight."

That's what Chase was afraid of. He trusted Church completely, but adding weapons to the mix could be dangerous. Should one person crack, they might all be killed in a heartbeat. The last few months had changed them. Hurt them. All of them. That couldn't be denied.

"I'll get them," Chase answered carefully, "when the time comes. But we'll have to be selective with who gets one. I would place my confidence in any of those men out there under normal circumstances …"

The officers all nodded, knowing exactly what Chase was saying. Still, the expression lingering behind Church's good eye worried Chase. Being the *Halcyon*'s medic, Church had always been compassionate and caring. Chase just might have to remind him of that.

"All right, I—" Chase said.

The door slid open, allowing entrance to a panicked Marlen. "Mr. Church, sir, I'm so sorry!" he cried.

Nic and Chase rose at the same time. "What is it, man?" Church asked.

"Ben. I just got up for a minute. I was hungry. When I came back, she was gone, and Ben …"

Chase didn't wait another second. Muttering a curse, he pushed past Marlen and darted for the sealed-off fore section of the ship. He didn't know exactly where Ben Reiger had taken Trista, but he had a pretty good idea. He just prayed he wasn't too late.

CHAPTER 18

In an instant, it all ended. Weak and exhausted, Krissa crumpled against the table, her eyes open just enough for her to see. The man with the patch, who had proclaimed her a prisoner, now stood behind the console, fiddling with something. A fourth man, tall and dark-headed, stood in the center of the room, his hands raised. Part of the doorframe was crumpled. They must have kicked in the door. Ben moved behind her and said something. She couldn't understand, but it sounded like he was yelling.

The taller man lifted his hands warily. "Let her go, Ben."

She felt cold metal flick against her neck as Ben hissed, "Not a chance, Captain."

The taller man stepped closer. His movements were slow and cautious. Krissa sucked in a breath as the metal pierced her skin. She flinched, causing the object to cut her. "Ben …" the man—the captain—said, offering a hand.

"She's one of them," Ben whispered.

"Look at her," the captain pressed, his tone soft and persuasive. "She's frightened and hurt. She has no power over you." The captain took another step closer. Krissa felt the object pull away a bit.

"She'll pay for what they did," she heard Ben growl, suddenly snapping. He held up the object within her line of sight, and she saw that it was a scalpel. He arced it down toward her neck again.

Before she could scream, the captain plowed into Ben and held him against the wall with a single fist. He wrestled the scalpel from Ben's hands, allowing it to clatter on the floor. Compassion tinged with anger colored his words. "I know they hurt us, but that does not give us a right to do the same. You're not thinking clearly, Ben. Get it through your head."

Ben peered at Krissa, and she could have sworn she saw remorse pass over his features. Clarity seemed to return to him. He mumbled an apology as the captain pulled him into an embrace. Something else was murmured between them. Something Krissa could not hear.

Krissa's body twitched again, causing a whimper to escape her. The captain released Ben with a sturdy pat on his back and told him and Kern to leave. As they exited the room, the captain and the man with the patch moved to her side.

"Are you all right, miss?" the captain asked. They both worked to remove the electrodes as quickly as they could.

She moaned, her lips unable to yet form words. Their hands worked gently, finally releasing her from the table restraints. A strong arm lodged under her shoulders and sat her up. "That's quite a question. Of course you're not all right," the captain muttered to himself.

Distraught green eyes sought hers, probably looking for some sign of lucidity. "Can you hear me?" he asked as he tucked her hair behind her ear. His fingers remained intertwined with the strands.

Her body shuddered again, but she managed a single clear nod. She frowned, finding deep frustration in the fact that she couldn't control the shuddering. And the headache didn't help. If she could get her arms to cooperate, she'd retrieve her pill case from her pocket.

The captain's face crinkled with sympathy. "The twitching is normal. It will go away in a few moments. Just relax and be patient."

The man with the patch placed a medkit on the table next to her. He worked efficiently, handing the captain a compress, which he snapped in the middle to activate before he placed it against her eye. It was icy cold, but felt good. The other man dabbed at her other injuries, cleaning her up a bit before he applied a bandage of some sort to her neck.

"Aah dii doo itha," she tried to speak, but her tongue was as rebellious as her arms. Again, the déjà vu struck. Those words were all she could think to say.

"I'm sorry," the captain leaned closer, "what was that?"

Krissa frowned more deeply and concentrated on her words. "I-I di-dn't do … annny … thiiing," she finally stammered as another spasm rattled her limbs.

The captain nodded, a sad smile touching his lips. "I know." He glanced at the man with the patch. "Church, would you please go get some water for our guest?"

Church mumbled, "Aye," and left.

Water. Yes. Water would be good.

The captain lowered the compress as he caught her gaze again. He stared at her with the strangest expression. It was one of recognition, familiarity, yearning. Krissa could see that there was something he wanted to say, but he must have thought better of it because he quickly blinked it away as he spoke.

"I hate to say that what just happened to you," he paused, lowering his eyes, "was merely a misunderstanding. I know that you were—are—in a great deal of pain, and I don't wish to belittle that fact." The green eyes once more met hers. Conviction and sincerity flooded his features. "But Ben Reiger is really a decent guy. He … well, we've all been treated pretty poorly over the last few months.

"You probably don't even know what's gone on here. I'm only going to tell you because I think it's important for you to know, no matter where your loyalty lies. All of us are Ghosts, miss. Most of us are followers of Prince Ternion."

"He's d-dead." Her teeth chattered, joining the torrent of pain that surged through her head. Oh, great. Where was that water?

Now his eyes flickered a haunting sorrow, concern for … her? "No," he replied. "No, He's very much alive. We've seen Him. But now is not His time. He will come again. That's a story we can talk about later." The captain erased the worry from his features, replacing it with a serious look before he continued. "The Legacy sentenced us to this ship—this *asylum*, as they put it—to 'rehabilitate' us. No rehabilitation was ever necessary. The treatments that they gave us were nothing more than disguised torture. Just like what Reiger did to you. I wish I could say that we weren't affected, but as you can see—" the captain gestured toward the door, "—we were."

Krissa eyed him closely. He seemed to be the honest sort. Either he was telling the truth, or he was so completely batty that he fully believed every word he'd just said and could convince others to believe it, too. "So you're n-not crazy?" she asked.

The captain raised his hand, starting to touch her hair again. Krissa probably wouldn't have thought much about it had he not stopped himself, crushed his fingers into a fist, and dropped it to his side. Regret hung on his brow as he gritted his teeth before answering, "No. Not at all. And I hope that once I get my men back home, we'll be able to repair what's been done to them."

"W-what about you?" she whispered.

The mantle of responsibility seemed to flow from him in waves of equal parts power and humility. It was obvious that he cared for the men he worked with. The captain bowed his head. "My men come first."

Why did he keep referring to them as such? "*Your* men?" Krissa asked. "What does that m-mean?"

"I am their leader," the captain said, looking at her as if she should know what he was talking about. "Their captain. Half of them are my crew."

Too many questions came to mind, but the ache in her head had intensified to an uncomfortable level. She stuck with easy ones. "And the other half?"

"Prisoners of the Legacy," he answered.

"And you're all G-G-Ghosts?" Why did her body refuse to settle down? She looked away as embarrassment lit her cheeks aglow.

The captain's response carried tones of empathy. "Not all of us, but most. We lost one inmate about a month ago—a result of a terrible treatment gone wrong. So those who weren't Ghost before are now."

Krissa dropped her head into her hand, rubbing her forehead. The ache spun things into a dizzying whirlwind of confusion in her mind. The pain of the last hour reminded her of the night long ago that she'd spent with the interrogators. And for some reason, Reiger now seemed to play in that memory. If they all weren't Ghosts from the start, then maybe ... "Reiger ... w-was he an interrogator?"

"No. No, Ben's always been part of my crew," the captain said softly, a frown knitting his forehead. His hand settled on her arm as he replaced the compress against her eye. "Are you all right?"

How could she answer that? She was no longer in the clutches of that madman, but her head pounded furiously. And she couldn't think straight. Oh, and she was now a prisoner of the Ghosts. Streuben would love that, wouldn't he? With her record, she'd probably be in a world of trouble when—and if—she got home.

"A little mixed up, I guess," Krissa finally whispered. "What do you p-plan to do with me?"

The captain smiled sadly at her. "You were an accident. We didn't know you were here, and we certainly didn't expect to have a prisoner." He sighed as he paused in thought, lifting his eyes to the ceiling above. "I think it best that you stay close to me. I don't want anything else like this to occur."

"How can I trust that you won't do the same?" Krissa asked. She didn't wish to insult the man who had saved her, but she couldn't forget that he was an inmate, too, regardless of how rational and caring he appeared.

The captain frowned again and took a steadying breath. Taking her hand, he placed it against the compress to free up his. He then reached into his pocket and produced a small device, holding it up for her to see. "The doctors conditioned our brains to react to the blue light and a terrible sound that these remotes emit. One press of this button," he said as he pointed to the tiny red circle, "the light switches on, the sound goes off, and I'm on the floor."

Krissa swallowed, whispering, "How cruel."

"It's the only one left onboard. I kept it in case things got out of hand." The captain stared at the device and shook his head, looking as though he couldn't believe he had done so. His countenance changed as he snapped back into leader mode, lifting his gaze to hers. "You hold on to it. If I—or anyone else—tries anything," he paused, this time taking in a shaky, uncertain breath as he passed the remote off to her, "you use it."

She nodded, eyeing the gadget in her hand. She hoped she would never have to turn it on this nice man. She frowned once more as she realized that she didn't know who he was. Shouldn't she? That nagging sensation of not quite knowing what she thought she should know returned, along with a fresh rush of throbbing.

"May I ask your name?" Krissa asked.

The captain bit his lip, sorrow filling his eyes as he pressed them closed. "Leighton. Chase Leighton. Captain," he said quietly, His wary gaze strayed to the remote. She watched as he swallowed before lifting his eyes to her. His anguish was now fully concealed behind an isolated, professional manner. "I'd prefer it if you called me Captain."

The throbbing swelled into an unbearable gush of agony, taking away all sense. She moaned, gripping the table under her. The remote clattered to the floor, along with the compress pack. The pain eventually subsided, leaving her breathless. "He chases ghosts," she whispered, her eyes locking into a distant stare.

As awareness resurfaced, she felt his hands on her shoulders. She looked about the room, trying to process where she was. A full bout of trembling overtook her before she eased into an acceptable state of control.

"What was that?" the captain asked, still holding on to her.

What was what? With lingering puzzlement, she shook her head. She started to slip the remote into her pocket, but found her hand empty. That made no—oh, wait. It fell on the floor. The captain bent down to retrieve the remote, placing it in her open palm. His eyes followed it the entire way to her pocket before rising to meet hers.

The moment was awkward. She couldn't get a reading on him; so many emotions ran through his eyes. And she had things to do. She had to report back to Streuben. The mess. The control room was a mess. No, she's taken care of that. She needed water. Where was that guy whom the captain had sent to fetch water? She had to take her medicine. Oh, no ... her meds. Maybe that would help her line of thinking straighten out. Right now, she felt all over the place.

"I'm Krissa," she said, hoping to break the uneasiness. She even lifted her hand in a polite gesture, as she had seen others do.

The captain closed his eyes and sighed. "I wish you hadn't told me that."

She lowered her arm. Had she done something wrong? "Why not?" she asked.

"It's a lot easier to think of you as just a prisoner—an object, if you will—if you don't have a name." The captain frowned, staring at her. "But now, you're a person. And my head fills in the blanks. You're a daughter. A sister." His voice softened, "Maybe even a wife."

Krissa bowed her head. Her ears buzzed with static for a moment as the world around her disappeared. Clarity returned, along with freedom from the pain. *Verify the programming.* She lifted her chin, looking at him. "Was a sister," she said. "A long time ago."

The captain held up his hand, shaking his head. "Don't tell me anything else. Please."

"What did you do to the doctors?" she asked. She didn't want to know, really, but he didn't seem the type to kill without guilt.

Rubbing a hand over his face, the captain stepped back a bit. "After we overpowered them, we put them in the transport shuttle and set the autopilot. We did leave one unbound, in case there was an emergency of some sort."

They may as well have killed them. The crew transport wouldn't accommodate the full staff. It was only meant for two or three passengers. Surely a ship's captain would know that. "That shuttle isn't equipped to handle that many people," she said, hoping for some form of substantiation.

"We unloaded what cargo there was, knocked out a bulkhead or two, and my men made some adjustments to the engine and life support," the captain explained.

"Oh," she murmured. They thought of everything. At least they had found a humane way of dealing with the staff. They could have—

"Sure, only a few had a secured seat, but we tried to give them better chances than they would have given us. A few of my men would have loved to get them ... well, in here." He gestured to the table and the console across the way. "I couldn't let that happen," he added in a whisper.

"You don't have to explain," she said, trying to comfort the man who now held her fate in his hands. "I get it."

The captain shifted uncomfortably, pacing away from her toward the door. He said, "I suppose we should figure out what to tell the Legacy."

"They aren't coming?" she asked.

He nodded, resting his hands on his hips. "Oh, they're on their way. I've been working with our communications officer to get a spurious signal to the approaching ship to throw them off while we try to raise the Ghosts. We're having a bit of trouble getting into the system."

Krissa frowned, pain pressing into her head once again. Just when she thought it was over. She could easily help the men get into the system. But wouldn't that be betraying the Legacy? Would they consider her a Ghost by doing so? They were ready to tag her with that label so long ago.

"No matter," he said gently, shrugging his shoulders as he crossed back to her. He scooped up the compress and offered it to her. "This has probably taken a pretty heavy toll on your body. And Church told me that the men hurt you before ... this."

Church. The man with the patch. The one who went to get water. "Where did he go, anyway?" she asked as she took the pack and held it to her forehead. "I could use that water."

"I said that to get rid of him." The captain chuckled a bit. "He knows me well enough by now to understand my code. Let's get you someplace safe for you to rest, and we'll see about some water, all right? Want to try to walk?"

The captain held out an arm while keeping one at her back. She scooted off the table, and as soon as her feet touched the ground, her knees buckled. His arms grabbed her before she hit the floor. "It's all right," he said, reassuring her. "It takes a minute."

She held on to him, allowing him to be her strength. After a few moments, she was able to steady her legs and take a wobbly step. She felt ridiculous. It was like learning to walk all over again. Like when she had the surgery—

"Good," the captain said, interrupting the vortex of dark thoughts. He kept an arm under her elbow as he led her to the door.

They walked in silence down the corridor, heading the opposite way Ben had brought her. Various doors labeled with initials dotted the walls. He led her through the darkened hall. Emergency lighting lined the path and cast a greenish hue along the walls. Two doors loomed at the end, "Isolation" pasted to the metal in thick, black lettering. She couldn't help but feel frightened, despite the gentleness of the captain, who continued to guide her.

"Why are there no lights in this hall?" she asked.

The captain stared straight ahead. "This is the treatment wing. We've shut it down, and I have a couple of guys working to seal it off completely. None of us want to come down here."

Krissa nodded. Made perfect sense to her. She shuddered as she thought back to the horror she had just experienced and how the men had dealt with that on a daily basis. No wonder they were angry and hurt.

As they approached another long corridor, the captain pointed down a hall that ran perpendicular. "Those were our rooms. This," he gestured to the area they were walking through, "was staff access to the inmates' rooms. We've all now moved into the staff's quarters. We want to sleep in beds without restraints."

Krissa closed her eyes and swallowed. What had the Legacy done? She'd never seen them in such an evil light. They were the ruling faction. The government that led its people and provided for her. As long as she could remember, it had been that way. She just accepted them and never really thought about it.

The captain turned, led her through a short corridor, and turned again. More doors, this time without labels. "Doctors' offices," the captain said.

The hallway ended at a thick fire door. Two access panels were mounted to either side. "Staff quarters. Requires two different access cards to enter," the captain said as he placed an identifier against the panel closest to him. "We kept the doctors' cards," he explained with a guilty grin.

The panel lights changed from red to green. He leaned in front of her and repeated the motion with a second card on the opposite panel. Its light patterns did the same. The door shifted outward with a hiss and slid to the side, allowing them entry to the staff wing.

Krissa followed him through another set of corridors. The ship was a pretty good size, as far as she could tell. Maybe she was just tired. They finally stopped at the end of the hallway. A double door blocked their way, along with another access panel. The captain pressed the card to the panel and waited until the doors split and slid open.

Gingerly and with a failed attempt to conceal his hesitance, he helped her into the cabin. An enormous, comfortable-looking bed was anchored against the wall, along with a broad desk, a table, and a few chairs. A wide viewport opened the far wall to the breathtaking stars. Under it, parallel to the bed, a gray leather sofa spanned the length of the glass. A decorative archway branched off from the room, leading to what appeared to be a fresher and a closet. The whole room was luxurious, especially compared to her little apartment back on Crenet.

"These are my quarters," the captain said, gesturing for her to get on the bed. "You'll stay here."

"Um …" Krissa stammered, glancing around nervously. She wasn't sure what he expected exactly, but she was starting to feel nervous. Vivid memories of the *Haulaway* played in the back of her mind.

He smiled and tilted his head. "You still have the remote, remember?"

That's right. She let him lead her to the edge of the bed. With care, he pulled back the blanket and sheet as she shook off her boots. He then offered a hand to help her slip under the covers. How grateful she was for this unexpected hero.

"Um, I, uh—need to talk with Church, but I'll be back. I want you to stay in here, and if you don't mind, I'll seal the door for your added protection," the captain said, situating the covers around her.

Before she slept, she needed her meds. It had already been too long without them. She'd skipped the midday dose. She couldn't afford to skip another. "I have medication," she said, reaching into her pocket to produce the case of pills.

"What's it for?" the captain asked, sitting next to her on the bed as he took the case to examine it.

"Well, that's really none of your business," Krissa answered, sinking back against the pillow. The softness of the bed certainly was winning out over her resolve to stay awake to take her meds.

The captain frowned, dropping his hands and the pill case to his lap. "You're right. Sorry. Do you need it now?"

Krissa nodded her response, unable to form cohesive thought. She hadn't realized how tired she was. She just wanted to close her eyes …

"All right," the captain whispered. "I'll go get you some water, and I'll be right back."

"Where will you sleep?" she murmured, drifting somewhere between the wooziness of fighting exhaustion and being fully defeated by its enticing power. She opened one eye to see him smile with an air of affection.

"Don't worry about me, miss," he assured her gently as he stood.

Perhaps it was utter fatigue, but he had won her over. She felt she owed him something for his compassion. After all, he'd rescued her and treated her with dignity and grace. She could at least—

"Cogstar Q Seven," she said with a sleepy yawn.

"I'm sorry?" he asked, a bit of a laugh in his words.

"It's the passcode that will allow you into the system. Cogstar Q Seven." She forced her eyes open to look up at him. "The initial letter of Crenet, each of Crenet's moons, and the number seven. Seven moons."

The captain released a heavy breath. Regret saddened his eyes. "Thank you," he said, leaning over her.

Krissa allowed her eyelids to close as he tucked the covers up to her chin. His fingers brushed her hair back from her face. The move was sweet and soothing, easing her into a restful slumber. She almost hoped that he would stay ...

CHAPTER 19

Chase stormed into what used to be the staff lounge. He marched to the table at the center of the room and whipped out a chair. Plunking down on it, he dropped his head into his hands as he rested his elbows on the table. "Blast," he muttered into his arm.

Something clunked on the table in front of him. He could smell the kaf scent wafting on a ripple of steam. It normally would have been a comforting smell, but he was shaken at seeing and interacting with Trista. Krissa.

"It's her, isn't it?" Church asked, taking a seat at the table.

Chase grabbed his hair with his fingers and sighed as he ran them through his unkempt locks. "Unless I really have gone mad … it's her," he whispered. "She doesn't remember me."

"It hasn't even been a year, Chase." Church kicked back in his seat, resting his foot on his opposite knee. "She has to remember."

"No," Chase answered, ringing his hands around the cup in front of him. "No, they did something to her, Nic. Redic knew and warned me. We got reports from inside saying that her memory was scrubbed. Looks like they took everything."

"Scrubbed? Why didn't you tell me?" Church asked.

Chase picked up on a hint of insult, but that was to be expected. Church was his first officer and had gone with him on many expeditions in search of Trista. Chase owed his friend an explanation, but he really didn't have it in him.

"I don't know," Chase replied. "I think I was hoping that it wasn't true."

Church nodded slowly with sympathy as he positioned his mug on the table. "Weird coincidence, though. We scour the system looking for her, and she shows up out of the blue? Here, of all places."

"It's no coincidence. It's the King's timing," Chase murmured, still wondering how he was managing not to give in to the insanity that threatened to strangle him. "He provided the right circumstances for us to get her home. I just hope that He'll help her remember who she is on her own. No one's brain should be messed with." Chase gritted his teeth, remembering his own experience with that.

Church grabbed his cup as he began to rise. "I'm sorry, Chase."

"What are these?" Chase asked, slapping Krissa's medication case on the table.

Dropping back into his seat, Church cradled the case in his hands as he examined it. He opened the case, spilling a few capsules and tablets out onto the table. He picked up each different pill one at a time, sniffed it, and rolled it around for further inspection. "I can't make out the label. Are they hers?"

"Yes." Chase sighed.

"Did you ask her what they were?"

"She said it was none of my business."

Church grunted. "Well, your guess is as good as mine. This one," he pointed to a large white pill, "I don't know. These two," he said, gesturing to the others, "look like inhibitors of some sort. I think they're the same thing they gave us those first few weeks. These little red ones ..." He just shook his head.

"Does she need them?"

"I can't answer that with the little interaction I've had with her, Chase. Besides, I'm just an emergency medic. I don't have the proper training to diagnose that."

Chase pounded his fists on the table, sloshing kaf from the cup. He calmed himself before he spoke again. "We've either got to convince her to go with us when our friends get here, or take her as a prisoner."

"You think Brax can do something to help her?" Church asked, returning the pills to the case.

Chase shook his head again. "But I bet Seraph can, even though he's denied it. I'm just going to have to watch myself closely. If I say one wrong word, I could destroy her."

"You're her husband, man. Surely you could reach her. Help her recall something."

"I'm going to try, but I can't just announce it to her."

"Why not?" Church lifted an eyebrow as he drained his cup.

"The report indicated that …" Chase released a heavy breath, frustrated with not knowing what step to take from here, or even how to begin to explain the situation. "She belongs to the Legacy. To ExMed. They altered her. Physically. It wasn't a forced understanding. It wasn't a brainwashing. Some very bad things could happen."

"She belongs to the Ghosts, Chase. She belongs to you. And above all else, to the Crown," Church reminded him.

"I know," Chase said. Dropping his voice, he added, "She's suffered through so much. I don't want to hurt her any more."

"I know you don't want to risk it, Chase, but reminding her of who she is might be just what she needs. You might break through," Church replied, pushing up to his feet.

"No," Chase said. "I looked into her eyes. They aren't Trista's eyes. She just has this … blank, vacant stare. She's in far more trouble here than any of us thought." He held up a pointed finger toward Church. "And you're going to have to watch it, too. Not a word."

Church nodded, grabbing his cup. "I'll be careful. You're going to have to keep up the prisoner pretense, or she'll get suspicious."

"I know." Chase nodded. "I know."

Before Church dropped his mug in the sink, he turned back, looking at Chase. "You know, they may not be Trista's eyes. The blasted Legacy may have changed her inside and out. But that girl's soul is still in her somewhere. I fully believe it. And I fully believe that it's up to you—given this coincidence, or the King's timing, or whatever you want to call it—to reach her."

Chase stared at his friend as he delivered his cup. Church nodded once, giving Chase a quick salute. "I'm going to see how I can help Wes," he murmured as he slipped through the door.

Astonishment roared in the silence of the lounge. Chase had never considered that there was a part of Trista that the Legacy couldn't touch. Seraph had alluded to it, now that he thought about it. The Crown had touched her soul. It was her soul that belonged to Him. And blast it if Church wasn't right. Perhaps Chase could indeed find a glimpse of her soul and use that to reel Trista back to them. It would have to be done with prudence and care. Timing would be essential.

Terces sat down at his desk, rubbing his forehead with his hand. The day had started to catch up with him. One of the doctors under him had been careless with a patient, which resulted in the loss of the patient's life. Terces had spent the entire afternoon covering for the doctor, fielding pervasive questions from the agencies, and basically cleaning up the mess. He'd more than likely face the same thing tomorrow, as after further investigation, the agencies would probably have more questions.

The Bands screen burbled in the background. Aftal always liked to have it on. Terces had gotten so used to it that he'd usually tune it out. Today's report, however, caught his attention. Details were sketchy, but a tiny shuttle full of Legacy service members from one of the prison ships, the *Straightjacket*, had been intercepted by a Zenith outpost in the Vetus rotation. An investigation was underway. It appeared that the inmates had rioted and overtaken the ship.

Leaning over his desk, Terces's eyes caught sight of Krissa Carlisle's file. He'd meant to link her earlier in the day, to see if she'd had any noteworthy reactions to the new medications he'd put her on. He pulled her file closer and opened it as he glanced at his watch. Still within reasonable hours. Surely she wouldn't be sleeping. Not with the minimal required hours that the ITCs needed to recharge.

He turned to his DDL and accessed the link program. The speaker buzzed in response, but before long, the DDL connection diverted to Streuben's link. Terces waited, tapping his fingers in rhythm on the desk. Finally, Streuben picked up.

"Go."

Terces rolled his eyes. The man was obnoxious. They should have sought out someone with a bit better breeding. But better breeding led to higher level of principles, which led to more questions. When Streuben had seen the offered pallads in exchange for his employment of Krissa, he'd swallowed his questions.

"Where's my patient, Mr. Streuben?" Terces asked, forcing himself to be tolerant.

"Who is this?" came an irritated demand. If Streuben had really known who it was, he would have been far more respectful.

"I'm certain you can figure that out, Mr. Streuben, a smart man like you. Where is Krissa?"

A loud clunk on the other end of the link told Terces that he had indeed caught Streuben at a bad time. More shuffling noise irritated Terces's ear until Streuben said, "Sorry, I dropped my link. She's on a job."

"I'd like to speak with her. Check in on her with her change in medication."

"She's out of personal link range," Streuben answered, "out in the Vetus rotation."

Terces froze. He stared at the link, hoping that Streuben wasn't about to tell him what he somehow already knew. "Where exactly, Mr. Streuben?" he whispered.

"Um, some ship called the *Straightjacket*." Streuben replied. "She's already reported back to me that it's a fairly easy job, but she'll require assistance."

Terces ignored him as he scattered the files on his desk to find the information about the *Straightjacket*. A thick brown folder deep within his bottom drawer held every detail he would need. He plopped the folder in front of him, flipping through its pages. Approved treatment procedures. Doctor biographies. Finally, what he was looking for—a list of incarcerated inmates.

Leighton, Chase. Ghost affiliation, Logia.

Terces pressed his lips together and squeezed his eyes closed, attempting to withhold the deluge of anger that threatened to burst forth. He clenched his fists as he took several breaths, in and out, calming himself. This was bad. Very, very bad.

"We're in worse trouble than that, Mr. Streuben," he eventually said. "Get down to the JC now. Meet us in the conference room. I'll authorize your clearance with the front reception desk."

"All right, Doc," Streuben said before Terces closed out the link.

Terces sat back in his chair. Cyndra would be livid. How could a blunder like this happen? Aftal would tell him to trust in the programming. And he should be able to do just that, but something still worried him. He wasn't completely confident in their work. Not just yet. He'd have to reach Krissa before Leighton tried to reach Trista. He slammed his fist on the desk and picked up his link to alert Dr. Niveli.

CHAPTER 20

Krissa woke, feeling a quite a bit better. Even though she'd been without her meds for longer than she should, the headache had disappeared. Her stomach growled with hunger, but that was manageable. She stretched as she got her bearings, only to find one arm shackled to the bedpost. Nice. She tried to wriggle her arm free, then caught the captain's gaze. He sat at the desk, watching her.

"Don't trust me, huh?" she asked, trying to change to a more comfortable position. With the cuff around her wrist, she found it difficult to move.

"Whether or not I trust you, you're still a prisoner, miss. You belong to the Legacy. I can't deny that, no matter how much I would like to," the captain said softly.

She dropped her head back against the pillows with a sigh. She could hear him move, and as she turned her head, she met his piercing stare. He now stood at her bedside.

He'd cleaned up since she last saw him. His dark brown hair had been trimmed, and he had shaved. The loose-fitting prison uniform had been completely shed, exchanged for a pair of tan trousers and a cream-colored tunic. He'd rolled up the long sleeves, giving him an air of casualness, regardless of the obvious tension in his body language.

"How long did I …"

"Just a couple of hours. I thought you might sleep longer," he said.

"I don't require much sleep. At the most three, four hours. But I do need my medication," she said, dropping her eyes from his.

"What do you do with your time?"

He was trying to distract her. "I work. Some travel is required, but mostly I fix my computers. My meds, Captain, please."

"You don't have any friends? Hobbies?"

"Captain, I need to take my medication," she repeated firmly.

The captain knelt down next to her. "No, you don't. Whatever they told you about those pills is a lie."

Krissa frowned, shifting to sit up a bit more. "I have a condition that requires *those pills*." She emphasized the last words to mimic his. She was a prisoner, not a child.

Staring at the covers, the captain filled his lungs and released the air in a careful breath before he explained, "Whatever condition you might have will not change with those drugs. Those are inhibitors that mess with your brain. We were all given those when we first arrived to repress any clear thought that we might have. The Legacy used those to manipulate us."

Krissa sank back into the pillows again. Inhibitors? Dr. Terces had convinced her that those pills would attack the growth in her brain ... Wait a minute. Why did she believe this guy? She'd only known him for—

His eyes snapped back to hers. "Why did you give me the passcode?" he asked.

Krissa frowned. She really didn't know how to answer him. When she'd given him the passcode, she was exhausted and perhaps not in her right mind, considering what she'd been through. Had he cuffed her to the bed then, she certainly would have kept her mouth shut. But in hearing his story and those of the men's suffering, she had felt sorry for him. Them.

"Pity?" she replied with a hint of question.

The captain nodded, his lips turning down to match her frown. "Don't do it again," he ordered calmly.

She pushed up on one elbow, her brows creasing with aggravation. "I'm sorry. A-are you angry with me for helping you?"

"Only because that puts me in a situation."

"How so?"

Rolling back on his heels, the captain rose, pacing to the end of her bed. He turned back as he spoke, "I don't know whether to trust you and take you into protective custody, or send you back to your people." He seemed to choke on that last part.

So she was nothing more than property.

"Do I have some choice in the matter?" she asked, glaring at him.

In an instant, his expression softened. He crossed back, this time sitting on the bed next to her. "I'd like to offer that, yes, but when you dole out information like that, I can't very well send you back to the Legacy. They'll string you up for treason."

Krissa sighed again, bowing her head. "You're right," she admitted.

"This room isn't wired," the captain said, glancing around before looking back at her. "I made certain of that. But the other rooms have cameras and microphones everywhere. We're trying to disconnect them from the watchful eye of the Legacy, but until then, you cannot offer up anything else. All right?"

She nodded, lying back to stare up at the ceiling. When did helping someone become such a burden? She found herself wishing she were back in her apartment. Or even Streuben's office.

"Why are you looking out for me?" she asked before turning her eyes back to the captain.

She saw a bit of color drain from his face. He blinked rapidly as he sought for an answer. "I believe in honor, miss. It's the code I live by. And I've seen what the Legacy can do to those who oppose them." The captain lowered his gaze. "I don't want that to happen to anyone else."

"Mmm," she replied.

The silent friction lingered between them. Krissa watched him for a moment before looking away again. He seemed to hold a secret that he so badly wished to share with her, but for some reason or another, couldn't. Oh, blazes, maybe he was planning to blow up the ship as an affront to the Legacy. Would she still be on it?

"Will you come with me?" the captain asked quietly, saving her from her downward spiral of fear and anxiety.

It took her a moment to figure out exactly what he was asking. Did he mean immediately? Or did he mean when and if they were rescued? She settled on an answer that required further details.

"Depends on where you're taking me," Krissa said, adding an edge of wariness to her voice. If he planned to take her to one of the treatment rooms, she certainly wouldn't go willingly.

The captain smiled as he stood. "Wise girl. I need to address the men in the conference room. I'm giving them a rundown of what's happening, and I'd like you to be in on it. Just so that I don't have to repeat myself."

With great care, he leaned across, removing the binding cuff from the bedpost. Strong arms helped her to sit up. "I'm going to keep these on you," he said.

"Why?" The cuff was uncomfortable and starting to hurt.

"Remember what I told you about the surveillance cameras?" he asked as his eyes fixed on hers, intent and cautious. "If things go down in a bad way, I want you to be able to say that you had no part in what we were doing. That you were indeed a prisoner the entire time."

His concern for her well-being after the fact negated her worry over the idea that he might blow up the ship. Thankfully, Krissa sighed, reluctantly offering her other hand for binding.

"It won't be much longer," the captain murmured, his fingers tender and skillful as they clasped the binder around her wrist. "I'm sorry to have to put you through this."

"Could be worse, I imagine," she said, standing next to him.

"Could be much worse." He grinned at her, nudging her arm. "We could be lunatics or something."

She laughed softly, realizing that she hadn't done that in a long time. This mysterious captain put her at ease. His presence alone was reassuring. He took her elbow and led her toward the door. "I like your smile," he said as they moved into the corridor.

"Captain!" A boisterous shout burst forth from a sturdy, red-headed man who nearly plowed through them. He beamed excitedly. "I've got Rev One on link."

"Great, Hal. Good work," the captain said with an encouraging smile. "Krissa, this is Hal Lancaster, my communications officer."

Confusion passed over Lancaster's face. "Um, Cap, isn't she—"

"Krissa," the captain said, his tone as insistent as his gaze. "She's a computer specialist for the Legacy."

"Systems analyst," Krissa corrected quietly.

The captain gestured toward her with a nod. "What did Rev One say?" he asked, changing the apparently uncomfortable subject.

Every ounce of joy sapped from the man in an instant. "Well, we're only able to broadcast PLF signals. She won't do much more than acknowledge me. I've tried to explain, but she said she needs your security clearance before she will establish a secure channel with us."

"All right," the captain said. "Let's go."

Lancaster led them to the lift and allowed them to step inside before he did. He pressed the button, without the use of an access card, Krissa noted. The captain smiled at her. "Since we were able to get into the ship's systems, we eliminated the need for the cards in high-traffic areas."

Krissa nodded. She knew he was grateful, despite his earlier scolding. And even though the Legacy would probably wallop her with a pretty nasty sentence if they found out she had helped them, she didn't regret it.

The captain guided her down the long catwalk above the bay, following behind Lancaster. A group of men worked together on something along the aft wall of the bay. Krissa couldn't really tell what they were doing. One of them waved as they crossed over. The captain waved back, ushering Krissa along.

The bridge took up the majority of the front part of the second deck. It looked like it would accommodate a full crew—a generous pilot and copilot workspace along the main helm console, a separate communications area, and several other monitoring stations. Krissa eyed the helm. A small section along the console was lit up, but the rest of it was completely dark.

Lancaster slid into the communications chair, slipping a headset over one ear. He left one side off, probably to hear the captain's orders. His nimble fingers danced over the comsys, adjusting the mic close to his mouth. He pointed to the mic affixed to the console. "They're both hot," he said.

"All right," the captain replied. "Raise them again. No visuals."

As they waited for the response, he offered her a small smile. She gestured toward the helm. "Why don't you just pilot the ship back?" she asked quietly.

"A full complement of crew access cards is required. The doctors were trained for ship maintenance, but not flight. This ship was intended for nothing more than sticking us out here, completely isolated," the captain answered, positioning himself behind Lancaster.

Static piped through the communications channel as Lancaster said, "Rev One, come in. Rev One, do you copy?"

The three of them held their breath as a long moment of silence carved away hope a bit at a time. Krissa wasn't sure why she was hoping that they would make a connection. She should be in complete support of the Legacy, including its reasons for imprisoning these men. But some underlying feeling told her that everything that had occurred on this ship was wrong. So it was all right to root for these men to return home safely.

A female voice responded with a crisp coolness. "You've connected to a private-use signal, Legacy. Be advised that further use of this channel will result in the disabling of your communication system."

"Remy, it's Chase," the captain said over Lancaster's shoulder. "Security clearance Alpha Twelve Serenata Trista Eight Leighton."

Krissa bowed her head as her headache suddenly returned. She pressed her fingers to her forehead, trying to convince it away with a little massage. The ache partnered with the hunger in her belly, which momentarily stripped her of her composure. She stumbled back a step, gripping the copilot's chair.

"Captain Leighton was arrested three months ago," the female responded. "That information could have been taken from him."

"*Soli Deo Gloria*, Remy," the captain declared with a sense of urgency. "The King reigns, the Prince has risen, and the Companion is among us."

Krissa's headache surged with great power, causing her to close her eyes and press her palm against her forehead. Nausea crept into her stomach, threatening to take her down. She'd lost track of how long she'd been without her medication. She'd definitely need to take a dose. Soon.

"Stand by, Captain. We're encrypting now," the woman said.

A gentle hand touched her arm. Krissa opened her eyes to see the concerned stare of the captain. "Are you all right?" he murmured, holding her firmly.

"Headache," she whispered. "I still haven't taken my meds today."

The captain frowned. "You also haven't eaten anything. I'll have Church look you over. Take a seat," he said as he eased her into the chair.

She closed her eyes again, leaning her head against the leather backing. "Church, I need you on the bridge," she heard the captain say, she guessed into a link.

The woman's voice filled the bridge again. "Go, Captain. We're secure. Ghost One is listening."

"As you probably know, we're on the *Straightjacket*. We've taken the ship, but it's anchored somewhere in the Vetus rotation, and we have no way to fire her up. My full crew, plus some, are onboard, and we need rescue immediately," the captain said.

"Prisoners?" a man's voice asked.

Krissa's head pounded. She knew that man's voice. Was it Dr. Terces? She doubled over her legs, trying to see if a change in position might make the pain stop.

"Just one," the captain replied.

"Of value?"

"To me," the captain answered quickly. "You might recognize her name. Krissa Carlisle."

Silence overrode the room. After a moment, the man spoke again, "We'll dispatch the *Fool* immediately. Have you seen any Legacy activity?"

"We sent the staff and last remaining crew member in a shuttle on autopilot back toward Crenet. I'm expecting contact at any time," the captain said.

"It all makes sense now," the man said as if he'd just comprehended something most puzzling.

"The shuttle didn't make it to Crenet, Chase," the woman explained. "It was picked up by a Zenith outpost on the other side of Venenum."

Another surge of pain. Blazes, would it ever stop?

"And we've caught wind of a warship dispatched to the Vetus rotation. Likely heading your way," the man added. "Where is the *Fool*, Remy?"

"In orbit around Quintus," the woman—Remy—answered.

"I'll have Gray drop whatever they've got going on and get to you. How many onboard, did you say?" the man asked.

"Thirty," the captain said. His tone turned somber as he corrected himself, "Sorry. Twenty-nine former inmates. Plus the one prisoner."

"We'll make it happen. See you at home, Chase. Ghost One out."

Krissa gripped the arms of the chair, digging her fingernails into the soft leather to counterbalance the throbbing. She tried to remember to take steady breaths, but she was reduced to sucking in air as her muscles tensed with pain. It now ran a constant course from her head into her neck and shoulders.

"Yes, sir," the captain replied, relief in his voice. "Thanks, Remy."

"Crownspeed, Chase," the woman said. "Rev One out."

◆

"Good work, man," Chase said to Lancaster as he turned toward Krissa. Blast. Color had completely drained from her face, leaving her pale and shaky. She looked awful. He fought the urge to scoop her up and whisper promises of making everything okay again.

Instead, he gave Lancaster an order. "Hal, head up to the conference room and tell the guys to stand by. We'll be just a minute."

Lancaster mumbled, "Aye," as he swiveled around in his chair and headed out.

Moving closer to her, Chase said gently, "You're not looking so good."

"I'm not feeling so good," she muttered shakily. "Please, let me have my meds."

The meds. She apparently relied quite heavily on them. Believed in their power, just as the Legacy intended. They had taken their hold on her.

"Church," Chase growled into his link, "where are you?"

At that precise moment, Church jogged onto the bridge. "Sorry, Chase. I was working with Torin. We were trying to get a crucial piece together, and I just couldn't get away."

Chase nodded, gesturing toward Krissa. He hated the helplessness he felt. He hated keeping her at such a distance. Maintaining the pretense of unfamiliarity and nonchalance was grating on him. "She's not feeling well," he said.

Church knelt down before Krissa, looking into her eyes. He slid his hands along both sides of her face as he examined her. Chase envied him.

"What's wrong, miss?"

"Terrible headache. Dizziness," Krissa groaned. "I need to lie down ..."

Church nodded, pressing along her forehead. "Here?"

"A little," Krissa said.

Church passed his hand along the back of her skull. "How about here?"

Krissa moaned softly, pressing her eyes closed.

Gritting his teeth, Chase looked away. He couldn't bear seeing her in pain. If only he were big enough to crush the Legacy.

"She needs the meds, Chase," Church said, interrupting Chase's thoughts. "We can get her off of them when we have access to the right resources, but for now, she's just going to suffer if we don't allow her to take them."

No. He wasn't about to surrender to those meds so quickly. He gestured for Church to join him in a private conversation, but first offered Krissa a reassuring smile. "Hang tight right here a moment, okay?"

Closing her eyes, she nodded a bit. Chase guessed that her head hurt so much, she just didn't want to move a lot. Poor girl. If he could, he would take that pain from her in a heartbeat, even if it meant inflicting it upon himself instead.

Bowing his head close to Church's ear, Chase asked. "Why give her those pills? I thought you said they won't do her any good."

Church shook his head. "Whatever the Legacy did to her wasn't as thorough as perhaps they hoped. My guess is that her brain is still firing connections, but they are somehow being blocked. That produces a headache. Triggered by a memory or something familiar, I'd guess."

With a grimace, Chase glanced over toward Krissa. Her forehead creased with frustration, and occasionally she'd flinch with pain. Her eyes held an underlying panic.

"So we have to league up with the Legacy to keep her from hurting," he said.

"For now," Church replied. "But I imagine if we were to get her to a Logia restorer, like you suggested, they should be able to heal her. At least, that's my thought."

Chase frowned. "I don't like this. Not one bit."

"You want her to suffer?" Church asked, looking toward her.

"She's done enough of that already," Chase hissed. He wasn't angry with Church, and he knew that Church would recognize that. Oh, but he'd like to get his hands on those doctors who did this to Trista. Krissa.

"Exactly. It's not hurting her as much as it hurts you, Chase. She doesn't remember you. She has no idea. All she knows is she gets a headache when she doesn't take those pills. She doesn't know that they strip her down and make her brain malleable for whatever evil the Legacy decides to use."

"It keeps her from me," Chase whispered. "You don't know how I ache to just hold her."

"I can imagine," Church said, patting Chase's arm. "Hold on a little bit longer."

With a heavy sigh, Chase surrendered the pill case to Church. "She hasn't had anything to eat," he murmured as Church fiddled with the case to open it.

"Can you take these on an empty stomach?" Church asked, turning back to Krissa.

"The red ones. That's what I really need right now. They ..." She rolled her head back to lean it against the chair again. "... they act quickly."

Church selected a single red capsule from the case and offered it to her. Chase turned away partially to speak with Joe via link, but he still kept his eye on Krissa. She took the pill, gulping it down. Hopefully, relief would soon be on its way—if the pills really did as the Legacy doctors had promised her. Church then closed the case and folded it into his hands.

"Why doesn't he want me to take them?" Chase heard Krissa ask.

"Well, we've only seen them used for more sinister purposes. It's hard to see past the bad when they might do a little good." Church smiled sadly. "I'm going to let the captain hold on to these, but he'll let you have them as you need them, okay?"

Chase murmured his requests softly to Joe, who acknowledged him with a simple, "Aye, Captain." He then stepped back to Krissa and Church. "Joe is scoping out the food pantry. I think all that we've got left is some protein paste," he said with a note of apology. "Even the staff supply is limited."

"And I suggest a cup of téchaud. The heat will help," Church advised, patting Krissa's knee. He handed off the pill case to Chase.

Offering her a hand while pocketing the case with the other, Chase smiled encouragingly. "Come," he said. "Joe's going to meet us in the conference room."

She took his hand, pulling herself up next to him. "Thanks," she murmured. Already she looked better. At least a little steadier on her legs.

Chase shrugged, his eyes falling to their intertwined hands. For the first time, he realized her ring was gone. The beautiful golden wedding band he had given her. There was so much he wanted to say. So much he couldn't say. He swallowed the lump in his throat that his emotions had built up. "The, um—the men are waiting for me," he reminded her.

"Yes," she said, falling in line behind him and Church as they exited the bridge to walk back through the ship.

Each step thudded with anger. Chase focused his gaze straightforward. He'd have to spend some time alone tonight, seeking the presence of the Crown. Thoughts of revenge were keeping him at a dangerous distance, and he needed to release the festering anger before it overtook him. He wondered just how far his forgiveness threshold would be tested before this was all over.

◆

Never in a human being had Terces seen the shade of red that now colored Admiral Niveli's face. He had accompanied Cyndra to the conference room, promptly berated Streuben for the reckless oversight regarding Krissa, and then asked for a strategic plan of action that he could relate to the Tribunal, if necessary. He expressed his desire to keep this incident quiet, but should the Tribunal catch wind of an issue, he wanted to be prepared.

Terces paced the length of the conference room. He'd feel better if he could at least make some sort of contact with Krissa. "We have to find out her condition. Have you heard *anything* from her, Streuben?" he asked.

The greasy man fished his PDL from his pocket. "Like I told you, the last report I received from her, she had fixed some of the issues with the ship's computers, but requested approval for assistance in completing the job."

From his seat at the head of the table, Niveli lifted an eyebrow. "And the issues?"

"Nothing that puts the ship at risk," Streuben answered. "The networked computers received an upgrade that didn't take. Ship operations are completely separate."

Cyndra sighed audibly, crossing her arms as she leaned against the long black table. "Let's just blow the thing. We eliminate two ExMed projects, but we can recover from that easily."

The admiral shook his head. "That craft cost the Legacy a pretty pallad."

"That was the original plan if things went sour, Altus," Cyndra reminded her husband with a shrewish sneer.

"Only to be authorized by those of us who run the fleet. I'm not letting a mere thirty men take down a ship as valuable as that. No, my dear, we have to figure our way out of this one."

Aftal, standing near the doorway with his hands in his pockets, said, "I heard on the Bands that a warship is on its way to the Vetus rotation."

It was the admiral's turn to sigh. "They aren't supposed to report on warship activity. But yes, the *Vanquisher* changed course after we received the report from the Zenith outpost that the staff shuttle had been intercepted."

Terces gazed out the window, looking over the Justice complex. Krissa was the key here. For reasons he could only imagine, they hadn't sent her along with the staff on that shuttle. That meant that either Leighton had recognized her and would try to make her remember, or that they had killed her. He hoped that wasn't the case, although it would alleviate the intense situation a bit. He had a lot riding on her.

"I have to get to Krissa," he said.

Cyndra stared at him through his reflection in the glass. "It may be too late for her, Reid. She might be dead," she said, echoing his thoughts.

Terces rubbed his chin, turning back to resume pacing. "Not if Leighton was onboard."

"Not if he *recognized* her," Aftal suggested. "She's different, Reid. She looks different, acts different."

"He's her husband. He'd recognize her," Terces insisted.

"And what if he has? And what if he's tried to reach her? Her brain could be beyond repair," Cyndra argued flatly.

"I have to find out. If they escape that ship and word gets out on this experiment before we're ready to go public with it, we'll have an uproar on our hands," Terces said. "We have to retrieve Krissa and then terminate those inmates."

"How do you suggest we go about that, Doctor?" Admiral Niveli asked, clasping his hands over his middle. His tone was snide and sarcastic. Understandable. Terces had just stated the obvious.

"Get me on the *Vanquisher*," he said, stopping just a few steps from the admiral.

Niveli chuckled, shaking his head. "It's halfway to the Vetus rotation by now, if it hasn't already entered it."

"I'll take a personal shuttle," Terces said, meandering as he calculated his plan. "I'll rendezvous with the ship. From there, I can try to make contact with Krissa. She will do as I tell her, but she must hear my voice."

"I don't know if the vocal imprints will be the same if they are broadcast," Dr. Aftal said. "Her reaction might vary, or it might have no effect at all."

"We have to take that risk," Terces said. "Once I'm onboard, we can dock a smaller shuttle on the *Straightjacket* itself with a squadron of Zeniths and infiltrate the craft. I can at least secure Krissa before we execute the inmates."

"That just might work," Admiral Niveli said.

Terces crossed to Cyndra, leaning over the table as he spoke with her. "I want the *Straightjacket* doctors with me."

"They are being questioned, Reid." Cyndra lifted her chin, much like an angry child on the verge of a tantrum. "And I'm still uncertain as to disciplinary action."

"I understand that you want to punish them for what happened aboard that ship—"

"It should never have happened. We had procedures in place to prevent things from getting out of hand," Cyndra snapped.

"You don't have to get defensive, Cyndra. I know. But I need those doctors. Caiman, at the very least. The mere sight of them might shake up some of those inmates. Caiman knows the ins and outs of each of those men. We need him," Terces carefully explained.

Cyndra rolled her eyes, shaking her head. "All right, but it's against my better judgment."

Terces looked to the admiral. "Can you make that happen?"

Admiral Niveli nodded, rising. He slapped his palms against the table. "I'll send the order to the *Vanquisher* immediately. You, in the meantime, get over to fleet headquarters. I'll have a shuttle waiting."

Terces nodded, pointing to Streuben. "Stay in close contact with me. I want word the moment you hear from Krissa."

"Of course," Streuben answered.

Terces pushed back from the table, marching for the door as he spoke. "I'll be in touch as soon as I evaluate our situation. Aftal, relegate all subjects to other ExMed wings. I want the lab clear upon our return. I imagine we'll have quite a lot of work ahead of us."

Aftal gave a silent nod. Terces bowed his head to him in respect as he exited the conference room. His legs couldn't carry him to fleet headquarters quickly enough.

◆

The men, twenty-nine in all, Krissa now knew, chattered with each other in small groups. When she entered the large room with the captain, the men quieted and sat down. Some leaned against the walls. Krissa caught sight of the man named Ben. He wouldn't look at her. He kept his eyes on the captain. And that was perfectly fine with her.

The captain situated Krissa in a chair against the wall. He glanced to a corner of the room and then back to her binders. Following his line of sight, she saw a camera mounted on the ceiling. It was all for show. She dropped her gaze as he stepped back and spoke quietly with Church.

Church nodded. His eyes fell on Krissa, and he nodded again. The captain was obviously talking about her. She blushed, fighting her curiosity to know what was being said. He patted Church on the back, who then took a seat next to Krissa. The captain stepped forward, speaking loud enough for everyone in the room to hear.

"The *Fool* is on its way," he said. While the announcement should have been joyful, his words carried a more somber tone.

A cheer went through the air, regardless of the implied warning. The captain raised his hands to quiet them. "I know you're all excited to get home, but we have to come up with some contingency plans. The Legacy has also dispatched a warship."

"A warship? For this tiny vessel?" Torin asked. "They'll incinerate us in a heartbeat."

The captain shook his head. "I don't think so. There's something of value onboard that they won't let go of so easily." He looked at Krissa.

Heat tinged her cheeks. She wasn't valuable. What was he talking about? She was terminal. Expendable. The Legacy would just as soon open the airlock and let her walk home as to send a warship to rescue her.

"And the *Fool*, Chase? There's no way it can bear the weight of thirty extra men," Church argued.

"I've spoken with Ghost One," the captain replied. "He's assured me that they will get us home."

Krissa shuddered as a stinging twinge tingled through her brain. She had taken the medication. The pain should have evened out. She slumped down in the chair, earning a nudge from Church.

"You okay?" he whispered.

She nodded in response, returning her focus to the conversation.

"How long do we have, Cap?" one of the other men asked.

"Two, maybe three days," the captain answered, pacing a few steps back and forth. "That warship is coming from the Novus rotation. The *Fool* is coming from this side of Crenet. But it's quite possible that the warship will outrun the *Fool*."

"So what do we do? Just give up?"

The Captain shook his head again. "Not a chance. We fight. We take up arms if necessary. Torin, drop the airlock project. The bays are big enough to accommodate the *Fool*, although it will be tight. We're going to need to clear one out. Get whatever cargo may be lying around up in the air with netting and such. Guys, he's going need some strong men to help on that one. Volunteers?"

Nearly every hand shot into the air. There were a few left, those who looked sickly or tired. Regret and sorrow lined their faces. Krissa pitied them.

"Good. Gentlemen, you are dismissed to the port bay. The rest of you, try to get some sleep. When things start going down, there will be no time for exhaustion." The captain gave a casual salute before moving to Krissa's side again. "Would you like to go back to my quarters, or would you like to stay with me?" he asked.

Krissa watched as the men moved out of the room. Her eyes fell on Reiger, and she couldn't help the shudder that coursed through her. She had always preferred being alone, but right now, she wanted to remain in the protective presence of the captain. Still, she knew he was busy and had much to do before the ships arrived. She shrugged uncomfortably. "I don't want to be in your way."

"You're never in the way," he answered tenderly, a strange look in his eyes. "Come on."

CHAPTER 21

After the meeting, the captain led her to the kitchen on the second-deck level, where Joe, as he was introduced, waited with a plateful of protein paste. The old man apologized repeatedly as she tried to tolerate a couple of spoonfuls. The entire ship was low on rations. The captain linked Lancaster and had him check the requisition logs. Apparently, the *Straightjacket* was due to receive supplies at the end of the week. Without the usual dosages of medications, the men were hungrier, and thus eating more.

The captain made her a cup of téchaud and led her toward the aft of the ship. He opened a door that led to a wide workroom. It spanned from port to starboard and housed extra parts, tools, and repair equipment. He gestured to a far corner, where some sort of device in a large black casing waited. Krissa, cradling her cup in her hands, crossed the room and sat on the floor on one side of the device, while the captain settled on the other side. He pushed back the sleeves of his tunic and started to work.

The tools he required, along with a stack of oil-stained rags, were laid out between them. Placing the cup of téchaud in front of her, she assisted by handing the tools to him when he needed them. The cumbersome chains clinked together, reminding her that she probably shouldn't be helping.

"I really thought you guys were just a bunch of lunatics," Krissa said, toying with a wrench the captain handed back to her. "I mean, isn't that why the Legacy put you away?"

"Do you believe … everything the Legacy does … is right?" the captain asked between grunts. She couldn't tell what exactly he was working on, but it was giving him some difficulty.

"Well, no, but …"

"But what?"

"I don't question it. It's how things are."

The captain poked his head around the casing to look at her. "Why? Why don't you question it?"

She stared at him, her mouth open to say something, but the words wouldn't come. She wanted to tell him of her past, but she still felt unsure. "I learned my lesson a long time ago … about questioning the Legacy."

She had piqued his interest. He tossed a rag on the ground and rested the tool on it. "What happened?"

Krissa turned her eyes on the wrench and flipped it in her hands. "Nothing," she answered lightly, hoping he'd catch on and change the subject.

No such luck. He supported his weight with his arm as he leaned further around the box. "You're hiding something from me," he pressed.

She shrugged, her nerves forcing an anxious smile on her face. In a swift move, the captain gently grasped her fingers and the wrench in one strong hand. As she looked at him, he urged in a softer, more convincing tone, "Tell me."

"M-my sister disappeared several years back. She was accused of turning … Ghost," she whispered, her gaze locked on his.

The captain listened intently, still holding her hand. She dropped her eyes to stare at his fingers as she continued. "It was my fault, really. I-I took an assignment that turned out to be a Ghost ship. I did the work before reporting them, which enabled them to make their escape before the Zeniths arrived. I was arrested and questioned. Spent an entire night with the interrogators. I …"

There was nothing more to say. She had blocked the memory quite a while ago. After years of nightmares, she had to do something. But this was the first time she'd spoken of it with anyone. Aside from the occasional argument with Streuben.

"Several years ago, you say?" the captain asked. She could tell that he was puzzled by the way he cocked his head and narrowed his eyes.

Krissa nodded.

The captain's bewildered look turned to one of question, but he released her hand and finally changed the subject. "What about your parents?"

Shrugging, Krissa resumed playing with the wrench. "I lived with my sister. She was the only family I knew."

The captain let out a slow breath. He seemed to want to say something, but chose differently. Ducking back behind the box, he hid his face from her as he said, "I'm sorry, Trista. It sounds like you've been through a lot yourself."

The wrench clattered to the ground as a surge of pain stiffened Krissa. She shook it off, recovering quickly enough to respond, "Krissa."

"Hmm?"

"M-my name is Krissa. You called me Trista."

"I did?" he asked, angling his head enough to look at her again.

She nodded, but decided to drop the argument. "I haven't really been through that much. I've dealt with it. I live a life that I despise, but I can't change anything about it because of the circumstances that follow me due to someone else's paranoia."

The captain wiped his hands on another rag. "Your sister. Was she …?"

"A Ghost?" She shook her head. "No. No, she followed Prince … well, you know, for a time, but that fizzled out. She was going through a rebellious stage," she added with a scoffing giggle.

"And you have no idea what happened to her?"

She shook her head again, frowning. She thought she had put this all behind her, and here he was, drudging it up again. Replacing the wrench in its spot, Krissa folded her hands in her lap.

"What was her name?"

Why did he want to know? She was gone. It was over. Still, Krissa felt compelled to tell him. "Lila. Carlisle. I kept the last name, despite my legal representation's advice to change it."

The captain chuckled. "See? Even you can defy the Legacy."

She grinned, picked up a rag, and tossed it at him. He laughed again, tucking his head back around the casing. "I think I've heard … that name in my circles …" he said as he resumed working. "I'll ask around."

"It's all right, Captain. I grieved her. And I've put it behind me." Krissa picked up her cup of téchaud and took a long sip to finish the hot liquid.

He peered toward her from the other side of the box. "If there was the slightest possibility that my family might be alive somewhere, I'd want to find them. I'd probably do everything I possibly could … to find them."

Krissa bowed her head, fidgeting with her ring finger. "We're two different people with two very different lives."

His mouth fell open a bit as his eyes fixed on her hands. Just an instant later, he shook his head and returned his attention to his job. "I suppose you're right," he murmured.

She didn't understand why he seemed so shaken all of a sudden. Best to change the subject. Again. "What is it you're working on?" she asked.

"A generator," the captain answered quickly. "We changed the passcodes throughout the ship to keep the Legacy out of its internal system, but if they find a way to shut us down, I don't want to lose life support."

"Oh," Krissa said. "They'll shut down your comsys too."

"I know. I'm still thinking through how we'll handle that one."

With very little effort, Krissa could resolve that issue. She'd already revealed too much just by giving the captain the passcode into the system. But she also now had the choice to go with the men, if they were successful in escaping. She snuck a glance toward the captain. He seemed so kind and gentle—not at all the way had she pictured Ghosts. She'd always been told how evil the Ghosts were. That they killed people and blew things up, just because they disagreed with the Legacy.

She suddenly found herself wondering about his background. "What about you? The way you said that just now ... about finding your family ... Do you not have any ... family?" she stammered, a bit uncomfortable now.

She heard a tool clatter on the floor. Slipping around the giant casing to check on him, she saw him staring at the floor and rubbing his forehead. He looked distraught.

"Are you all right?" she asked.

"Fine," he said, pasting a smile on his lips. She could tell it was false. He continued on with his story. "Um ... well, my grandfather was a member of Prince Ternion's Praesidium."

Krissa pressed her fingers to her forehead as another eruption of pain throbbed through her skull. She clenched her teeth, trying to keep her face from revealing her suffering. The captain returned his focus to the piece of machinery he'd been struggling with. It still gave him difficulty. He paused, resting his arm on his knee and looking at the floor as he finished, "When the Legacy took over, they killed him and my father. During the attack, my mother was able to escape and get me to safety. She died moments after handing me off to the man who raised me."

His story nearly made Krissa forget about the ache in her head. She stared at him in awe. "You're making that up."

The captain shook his head, meeting her gaze. "I wish I was."

"Why did they ... I—why did they kill them?" she spluttered, her heart finding deep issue with this.

"They were subjects of the Ruler Prince. Loyal followers. They weren't about to bow down to the Legacy and the evil Tribunal."

Krissa gasped, both in fear and in pain. Those words alone could get the captain executed. He spoke with such freedom and passion. And her headache now flared in constant bursts. She pressed her fingers against her brow, still trying to mask the hurt.

He smiled softly. She'd done her job. He must have thought that she was indeed simply fearful of his words. "You can speak freely here, Trista," he said, inducing another swelling of torment. "I'm not going to report you. Even after you take off."

That wasn't funny. "Krissa," she reminded him through gritted teeth. "You forget, Captain. I'm still your prisoner."

"The time will come, Krissa," the captain replied, making an obvious point to use her real name. "You're going to have to make a choice." He looked at her with a distant sadness. "Keep on the way you're going, or find a new path. Something you should know about your precious Legacy. They put us here. Innocent men who burn with the desire to see freedom and honor return to our system. Execution would have been much kinder and far more merciful. We've been onboard for close to three months now, and the things that were done ..."

The captain paused, dropping his hands in his lap as he bowed his head. Krissa watched him close his eyes and murmur something. She knew the moment was not for her. He was praying.

When he finished, he picked up his tool and resumed working on the machinery in silence. She scooted to his side, remorse filling her on behalf of the unsympathetic Legacy. "Here," she whispered, sliding the remote across the floor toward him.

He lifted his eyes to hers. "But—"

"No. I don't want it anymore."

"Trista," he murmured.

She blinked, staring at him as the fire burned through her skull. He kept calling her that—Trista—but somehow, regardless of the accompanying pain, it didn't matter. With his kindness and compassion, he'd shown her an entirely different side of the Ghosts she'd grown to fear. As his gaze lingered, she felt an uncomfortable wave of heated nausea pulsing through her middle. She dropped her eyes and held her head.

"Thank you for trusting me," he whispered.

"It's the least I can do, Captain," she whispered back.

The captain smiled again, moving closer to her. "Call me Chase. I mean, if we're forgoing all rules of war and enemy etiquette, we may as well be friends."

"He chases ghosts ..." Krissa muttered under her breath, flinching slightly.

She lifted her chin with a smile, trying to ignore the pain. Evidently, she couldn't hide it from him anymore. He grimaced as he pulled her medicine case from his pants pocket and opened it to retrieve the pills. "I'll find you some water," he murmured, handing her two of the red capsules as he pushed himself to his feet.

Krissa opened her eyes to the lush accommodations provided by the captain. Chase. She smiled as she thought about their conversation hours ago. After she took her medication, he suggested that she come back and lie down a while. He escorted her back to his quarters and even removed the chained cuffs to allow her a more comfortable rest. The sleep had benefited her greatly. She now felt refreshed and relaxed. Ready to tackle anything.

Carefully displayed on the table next to her was a change of clothing, a small basket of shower items, and a PDL. She lifted the handheld device and powered it up. A note from the cap—no, *Chase*—awaited her.

"Thought you might appreciate a shower and some fresh clothing. I'll check on you in a bit. Stay safe—Chase."

Considerate. She returned the PDL to its place on the table and then picked up the clothing to shake it out. The cut of the lavender tunic was stylish and feminine, complementing the dotted print of the short white pants. She wouldn't have chosen such an outfit for herself, but it was very pretty.

She laid the pieces aside on the bed and grabbed the basket. It contained a gel soap, hair cleanser, and lotion, all scented with hydralilies. A compact with an array of neutral-toned cosmetics was also in the basket, next to a small brush and comb. All such frilly things. She couldn't help but smile a little.

Did she really give Chase the impression that she was so ladylike? Or was it all that was available to him? She imagined he'd found it in one of the staff's or crew's quarters. Still, the gesture was very sweet.

Rising with the basket from the bed, she collected the clothing and headed for the fresher. It had been such a long time since she'd showered; she knew it would add to her relaxed state of mind. Amid the stressful situation, the moment of tranquility was most welcome. She would have to express her gratitude to Chase later.

She took her time, enjoying every drop. The fragrant soaps left her smelling like an overgrown garden, but she didn't mind so much. It would wear off after a bit, anyway. It was just nice to feel clean again.

The clothes were a size too big, but Krissa was used to that. Her uniforms never fit. She had almost grown accustomed to the bagginess. And with the ties sewn on either side of the tunic, she was able to make it look a bit more fitted.

Working quickly, she added touches of color to her eyelids and lips. She began to put a little on her cheeks, but as she admired her reflection in the compact's mirror, she noticed that she really didn't need any. There was a new glow about her. She smiled, nearly liking what she saw.

Krissa startled as someone pounded on the door. Seconds later, it opened. She wasn't expecting Chase back so quickly, but as she looked up from her seat on the bed, she saw that it wasn't him. Ben Reiger stole into the room. He closed the door behind him and marched to the bed. She held her breath as frenzy stiffened her limbs.

"The captain sent me to fetch you. The *Fool* is almost here, and he wants you in the bay." He stared off to the side for a moment before he took a knee at her side and bowed his head. "But I cannot go on without offering you my humblest apologies. I ... was not ... myself."

He struggled with the words, and Krissa could tell he was broken. The apology was honest and raw. How could she not accept?

"I forgive you," she murmured with a whisper of uncertainty.

Ben grabbed her hand, offering her a teary-eyed smile. "Thank you."

The move took her by surprise. She nodded, not really sure how to react. Would he attack her again? Chase had assured her that he was normally gentle and caring. She had to trust his judgment. And she'd never seen such passion and fervor in someone, aside from Chase. She had to give it to the Ghosts. They sure believed in what they were fighting for.

Holding her gaze, he snapped a cuff around her wrist. Panic tackled her as she chided herself for trusting him. She would scream this time. She wouldn't let him do to her what he'd done before.

"It's all right," he said quietly. A heavy shame weighed down his tone. "I'm not doing this to hurt you. I'm sorry, but it's the captain's orders. It's for your own good."

So quick to judge. Krissa closed her eyes momentarily, hating that she had assumed the worst. She looked back at Reiger. "I'm beginning to wonder about that," she said as he helped her to stand.

"If the Legacy sees you unbound, they will question your loyalty," he reminded her. "Smart of the captain to be protecting you like that."

She nodded as he led her from the room. She knew that the Legacy would question her loyalty, regardless of whether or not she was bound. She just wondered if her loyalty was still true to them, or if things were changing in her heart. The protection of the captain had been unexpected, but now she found it most welcome. The picture he painted of the Ghosts was far more inviting than what she'd seen of the Legacy. But as she had told Chase, life under the thumb of the Legacy was all she knew. Could she walk away from that?

CHAPTER 22

"Church! The *Fool* is in the rotation, closing in on Maeror," Chase announced at full volume as Reiger and Krissa met him along the starboard catwalk above the bay. He must have just come from the bridge. "Good. Did you see Church as you came this way?"

"No, sir," Reiger answered. "We had to wait a few minutes for the lift."

"Then he's probably taking the generator down to the engine room," Chase thought aloud. "All right, Ben, I want you to head down to the port bay and check with Torin to make sure it's completely clear. See if he needs anything."

"Aye, sir," Reiger said, handing Krissa off to Chase.

He smiled gently at her. "You look like you feel better."

"Much. Thank you for the—"

"Captain!" Lancaster called out from the far end of the catwalk.

Church dashed toward Krissa and Chase from behind. Chase greeted him with a nod and led them down the catwalk to catch up with the breathless Lancaster. "Cap, there's another ship on the approach. It's the Legacy warship."

Church muttered a curse as Chase closed his eyes. After a moment's thought, Chase looked at Lancaster. "Raise the *Fool*. Have them contact the warship with Legacy codes. Tell them to be discreet, but to come up with an excuse to get close to us."

"Aye," Lancaster acknowledged as he dashed back to the bridge.

Chase turned to Church. "Generator's in place?"

"Standing by," Church answered. "I tried connecting it, but it's dead as can be. It's not going to do us much good."

"I know," Chase said with a solemn nod. "All right, from here, I want you to get the men to—"

"Captain!" Lancaster shouted out. "The warship is hailing us!"

"Come on," Chase growled. He led Church and Krissa toward the bridge at a jogging pace.

The image of a callous-looking officer in full Zephyr regalia glared at them from the wide Bands screen above the viewport. "I am Commander Valach of the Legacy warship, the *Vanquisher*. I order you to surrender now, Ghosts."

A roar of pain snuck up on Krissa, causing her to sway back a step. Church steadied her by grabbing the chain between her wrists, wrapping it around his hand. Surely, it was a calculated move, intended to demonstrate their power to the Legacy.

"We're not about to do that, and you know it," Chase replied. "We have a hostage."

Krissa frowned as Church pulled her toward Chase. She peeked at the screen, then lowered her eyes. Regardless of how the inmates had grown on her, she didn't like being used in their negotiations.

"Prove to me that she's not a Ghost."

Lowering her chin, Krissa tried somehow to elude the threat of another headache. There were important things to focus on here. She couldn't be bothered or sidetracked by the relentless agony.

Chase fished her identifier from his pocket and held it up for the commander to see. He took Krissa's arm and brought her forward, positioning her face next to the identifier. "I'm sorry," he whispered in her ear, as her chains rattled with the weight of captivity.

"She's a worthless hostage, Leighton," Valach sneered. "It's really too bad that you didn't keep someone of more value."

Krissa flinched with pain, then looked up at the commander, unable to hide the hurt she felt from his words. How cold-blooded could one be? Church yanked her back and firmly sat her in a chair.

"We refuse to surrender, Valach. You may as well take action against the ship," Chase challenged. He had to be bluffing. Had to be.

"The Legacy wants the *Straightjacket* intact, Leighton. We'll wait you out. Don't doubt it," Commander Valach promised.

Krissa pressed her hands to her head, massaging her temples. It didn't really help, but it was still a comfort. Chase muted the link and angled his head toward Church. He masked his mouth with his hand to prevent Valach from reading his lips. "How are we going to get the *Fool* through?"

"They're our only chance," Church responded. "I'm surprised Valach hasn't blown us to bits already."

"They want something," Chase murmured.

"Yeah, but what?"

"Me."

Church scoffed with a chuckle. "You're a great captain, Chase, but—"

"I'm Logia, Church," Chase admitted, glancing back toward Valach. "And they know it."

Krissa took a breath as Church stared in silence at his captain. The surprise offset the pain this time. And she couldn't believe that Church didn't know. Chase sighed, unmuting the link. "We're low on provisions, Commander. My men are hungry. There's a ship within the rotation on the way. Allow it to dock, let me feed my men, and then I will go with you willingly."

"Denied." Valach turned his eyes back to Chase. "I'm not a moron, Leighton. No doubt you've contacted your Ghost friends, and they've sent a boat to retrieve you."

Trying to make the fire go away, Krissa doubled over her knees. The pain hadn't been this bad in a long time. And Chase was too wrapped up in the dire negotiations to notice that she needed her medication. She would endure it. There was no other option.

"That boat," Chase said, his tone tense with anger, "is a Legacy ship, Commander, on a routine supply run. Check the logs. You'll find it there."

Commander Valach gestured to one of his men nearby, keeping his gaze steady on Chase. The friction and hostility between the two authorities was unnerving. Krissa found that she was holding her breath as her eyes darted between the Legacy officer and Chase.

Church distracted her slightly as he knelt at her side. "Are you all right?" he asked in a whisper.

She nodded quickly, intent on Valach. As a representative of the Progressive Legacy, he should have demonstrated decency, integrity, and honor. Instead, she saw heartlessness, insensitivity, and abject cruelty. Could it be that her heart had changed so much in the presence of the Ghosts? Or were her eyes no longer blind to the truth of what the Legacy stood for?

"Confirmed, Commander," the crewman answered.

Red anger passed over Valach's face as he stiffened. "No supplies until you comply. Surrender."

Steady and even, Chase continued with his attempt to bargain. "Let the ship through. After my men get a good meal, I will surrender to you, with the promise that they are free to go."

Valach smirked at him, clasping his gloved hands behind his back. Superiority rolled off him in stifling waves as he responded, "Free?" He gave a snide chuckle. "You are all criminals. Including your hostage."

Chase narrowed his eyes. "I don't think you heard me, Valach," he said. "I will go *willingly*."

The officer scrutinized Chase for a long moment before he stepped back, stalking to his command chair. He sat down, crossed one leg over the other, and said with a sneer, "We have plenty of time, Leighton. Plenty of time."

Krissa closed her eyes, running her hand through her hair to rub the back of her skull. Every time the commander said the captain's name, the pain surged. The connection made no sense to her. Why would her head hurt—

"But to show you my mercy," the commander continued, "when that ship arrives, I will allow it to dock with the supply hatch, provided it transmits authorized Legacy codes. The hostage is to be the only one to have any form of interaction with the crew. Do you understand?"

"Understood." Chase nodded before terminating the link. He turned to the others on the bridge. "The supply hatch. Blast! Hal, raise the *Fool*. Tell Cam to get someone on knocking out the proper coding sequence."

Krissa rose, breathlessly fighting the pain as she moved to one of the consoles. She pulled up the LUM, and using her passcode, accessed a deeper intranet level. The question of her loyalty seemed to have been answered.

"What are you doing?" Chase asked.

"First, I'm shielding your comsys," she said as she stared at the screen, her fingers dancing across the keypad. She ignored the annoying chains. "Standard procedure dictates that they will remote in and try to block your transmissions. I can at least buy you a little time before they figure out how to crack this program."

It was an easy fix, and if the *Vanquisher* crew had any wits about them, they'd be able to get in relatively quickly. She accessed a program in Streuben's database and installed it in the ship's computers. It meant a complete betrayal of the Legacy. They would be able to trace exactly who executed the install.

"And now I'm finding the codes you need. I can get to them a lot easier than your people," she said, her eyes scanning the lists of ship's logs.

"I told you, no more helping," Chase said softly, placing a hand on her shoulder as he looked at the screen.

"Mm-hmm," Krissa murmured as she zeroed in on the codes. "There you go."

Chase straightened, patting her gently in thanks. "Hal, transmit these to the *Fool* using the Rev link. Alert Cam to our little white lie, and tell him that we don't know how much longer we'll be able to communicate. If he has any questions, patch him through. I'll be on deck one, engine room."

"Yes, sir," Lancaster responded.

"Church, with me," Chase said, offering his hand to Krissa. Evidently, he wanted her to go with him as well.

She stared at his fingers a moment before she swiveled around in her chair to take them. The moment was quickly approaching, and she felt torn. Of course, she had just cemented her fate as a criminal, as Valach had already accused her of being. Taking Chase's hand, in her mind, meant more than just standing up. It was full acceptance of him.

His grip tightened around her hand, pulling her to her feet. Church followed them as Chase led them back into the ship. They clambered down the ladder to the lower deck. She could tell that Chase was nervous and tense. The edginess about him made her uncomfortable.

"Nic, head on to the bay. Grab Torin, and get back on that airlock. It's going to need an independent power supply. Make sure that it's not routed into ship power in any way. I need just a minute," Chase said, staring at Krissa.

Church said nothing, but nodded and dashed down the corridor. She watched him go before she looked back at the green eyes that held her locked in their gaze. Breathe, she reminded herself.

"Trista," Chase whispered, "I need you to tell me what to do."

Her knees shook as the pain again anchored in her brain. Once it passed, she glanced up at him. "Krissa," she corrected him again. "You said no more helping."

Chase smiled through his concern. "Now you listen to me."

She shrugged, the chains clattering together. His nervousness was rubbing off on her. It was getting hard to play it cool when all she wanted was to feel safe again.

"No." He frowned, looking away. He seemed to have some difficulty finding the right words. "You've helped us several times now. And I need to know ... do you wish to go with us?" He lifted his eyes to hers. "Do you want to turn Ghost?"

She whimpered and cringed as the pain swelled. As she bowed her head to catch her breath, he took hold of her elbow. "Do you need your meds?" he asked.

"I don't want them," she murmured, straining to regain control over the chaotic twinges. Squeezing her eyes closed for a moment, she took in a slow, calming breath before looking at him once more. "Do I have to decide that right here? Right now?"

Chase frowned, his hand reaching up to touch her hair. As before, he stopped himself short of actually touching her. "Soon," he said, dropping his hand to his side. "And you have to be absolutely certain. There's no going back."

Krissa lifted her bound wrists toward him. "Is this how I'll be going? As your prisoner?"

With a sigh, Chase stared at the cuffs before stepping toward her. He reached into his pocket and removed the key. Swiftly, he unlocked both cuffs and freed her, tossing the binders on the floor. "No. You go of your own free will."

"I—" Krissa paused as the ship shook once, the lights snapping off with a fading whir.

"Blast!" Chase shouted. "They've gotten into our system. Shut us down."

Krissa began to float as the ship's grav control died away. She clung to the wall, blinking in the blackness. She couldn't see anything, but she could hear Chase's breathing. "Are you all right?" he whispered, his fingers brushing along hers.

"Yes," she answered, gripping his hand.

This time, his fingers found her hair. He caressed her cheek before pulling her close. "Stay safe," he said.

She felt something click deep within her brain. Shadows, whispers, blurred images swam around her, haunting her with feelings she couldn't quite grasp. She moved into him, finding glimpses of the sanctuary she so desired. "Always ..." she replied automatically.

A hand torch suddenly blinded them from the end of the corridor. Krissa squinted, lifting a hand to shield her eyes from the light. Chase did the same. The brightness brought up distracting memories of waking up in the hospital. Why had she been there? The headaches. The tumor. He said it was a tumor. Dr. Terces ...

"Captain, we've lost all power!" Reiger shouted through the eerie silence of the lifeless ship.

Chase nodded, pulling back from Krissa. "Thanks, Ben. Can you lower your light?"

"Oh, sure," he answered, dropping the beam to the floor.

"Come with us," Chase ordered Reiger as he led Krissa down the corridor. "I need to get to the engine room and connect the generator."

"I can do that for you," Reiger offered.

"No. I need to do it. But you can fetch the supply of hand torches in the storage area and pass them out. I especially need you to get one to Church and Torin. They should be in the port receiving zone," Chase said as they swam along the air into one of the large docking bays.

Reiger's light flashed over the void contained by the bay. The area appeared much bigger than when she first arrived. The floor seemed to sprawl on endlessly. Long arms shot off the railing of the catwalk above, anchoring large nets that held lighter cargo. Of course, it was all floating weightlessly, looking more like balloons than netted masses. The rest of the standard docking equipment and instruments had been pushed along the outer walls, lashed with heavy cords.

Krissa couldn't shake the confusion that muddled her head. How had she ended up here? The last thing that she remembered—operating room. She'd fought off the technicians ... No. They had overpowered her. They—

Chase directed Reiger to one of the storage rooms. He took the light from the man and asked Krissa to hold it so that the beam spread widely enough to dimly cover the room and its compartments. She did as he said, staring down at the shaft of light. Chase and Reiger both worked quickly to find the box that contained the hand torches.

"Captain!" Church shouted from a nearby location. "We're in the dark down here!"

She knew that voice. She blinked as an image of a blond-haired man nodded toward her. He stood aboard a ship. A large ship with a shiny chrome hull ...

"We're working on it, Church!" Chase shouted back as Reiger pulled a hefty crate from a smaller compartment. He popped it open to reveal a load of hand torches. They started to drift out of the box, but Reiger closed the lid quickly enough to contain them.

"Excellent, Ben," Chase said with a nod. "Go ahead, and get those lights to everyone. But like I said, Church and Torin first."

Chase took Krissa's hand again and pulled her toward the docking bay. "Hang on to that," he said, pointing to the hand torch.

Lost in the vision now, she caught her reflection in the mirrored hull of the ship. Long brown hair ... Long hair? She lifted her hand to touch the hair cropped short at her neck. The operating room. They'd shaved her head ...

"Captain ..." she said, trapped in confusion.

"Chase," he insisted, dashing to the far corner of the engine room. The large black box he'd worked on earlier sat in front of two green metal panels.

"Chase," she repeated in a whisper. "He chases ghosts ..."

"Hold up the light," he said before asking, "What?"

The light wavered about as she stumbled toward him. Chase grunted, trying to get the box into position. "Here, plug these in." He handed her several cables and pointed to the sockets between the panels.

She stared at him, holding the cables in one hand and the light in the other, but she couldn't think for the life of her why she was here. The dull ache throbbed through her brain, pressure beating on her skull to get out. She gritted her teeth and forced herself to breathe.

"Trista, I need you to plug those in," he urged.

"Krissa ..." Wasn't she? That's what they'd told her ...

"Hey. Hey, are you all right?" he asked, moving into her line of sight.

"He chases ghosts," she mumbled again, gazing into his eyes.

Chase grabbed her shoulders, staring back. "Trista?"

That's who she was. Trista. Oh, by the Crown ...

"Chase." She blinked, releasing the light and the cables to hold on to his arms. "Where am I?"

"Who am I talking to? Krissa or Trista?"

"Trista ..." She dug her fingernails into his skin as the pain surged. She couldn't stand it anymore. A cry ripped from her as she curled her knees into her chest.

Chase pulled her close. "Hold on, Trista. Stay with me." He pushed her hair back from her face, looking into her eyes with a smile. "I love you," he whispered.

"Wh-what's hap ... pened?" she gasped, squeezing her eyes closed.

"Oh, baby, it's a long story. I—" He stopped short, then cried, "Trista?"

She felt her body shake violently. Her head jerked from side to side before her muscles tensed to rigidity. She clawed at him, trying to draw any hint of breath. He held her, tears in his eyes. His mouth moved, but she heard nothing.

Within moments, she saw Church appear next to her, like an angel of mercy. The men hollered at each other before Chase shoved several pills between her lips. He held her as Church forced water into her mouth and clamped her jaw closed with his hand.

"Swallow," he mouthed.

She struggled against him, trying to pull her head away. She didn't want the pills. She wanted the pain to cease. She wanted Chase to take the hurt and the fear away. She wanted …

A calm ebbed over her, stripping away the confusion and replacing it with structure. Uncertain peace massaged away the pain, numbing her mind into the logical configuration of computer modules and mechanics. Reason swept emotion under the rug, tucking it away into frozen recesses. Everything became clear again. Krissa opened her eyes, seeing the captain and his first officer bobbing in the air before her and watching her with great concern.

"Captain," she whispered.

His hopeful expression fell, betraying his frustration and anguish. "Who am I talking to?" he asked softly.

"Krissa, Captain," she answered. That was puzzling. He knew who she was.

The captain bit his lip and hung his head. Church patted him on the arm before he moved away. She noticed that her tunic felt wet. "What happened?" she asked.

"Nothing," the captain muttered.

"You developed a headache," Church explained, glancing at the captain. "We gave you your meds, and now you're fine."

The captain shook his head, grumbling angrily as he swam back to the box. Oh, yes. They were hooking up the generator to supply power to the life support system. She collected the hand torch and the cables that now spun freely close to the ceiling. As she plugged in the cables, she heard the captain speaking with Church.

"It was her," the captain said.

"I don't doubt it. But we have to tread carefully, Chase. She was seizing and going into shock. You can't do that to her," Church said.

Krissa flinched slightly at the mention of the captain's name. The razor of pain dissipated quickly, though, now that she'd had a dose of her medication. She wondered what they were talking about. Church had said she'd developed a headache, but now he accused the captain of doing something to her. She began to feel a little wary.

"I didn't do anything to her," the captain argued. "She surfaced. Something brought her back."

She silently plugged the cables into the sockets along the wall, glancing over her shoulder. Church caught her gaze, holding up a hand to quiet the captain. The captain was obviously upset. He turned away from her. What had she done?

"Torin and I almost have the airlock in place. Another five minutes or so. Without grav control, it's taking longer. I'll come back and help you with this," Church said, gesturing to the box.

"No. It doesn't work," the captain said. "But I can make it do what we need it to do. You'll have grav control back in a few seconds."

Krissa frowned as Church nodded and moved back toward the docking bay. She was alone with the captain, and that made her a bit nervous now. He approached her with a sense of hesitancy, a mix of anger, sorrow, and bitterness lining his face. He nodded approval as his eyes caught sight of the plugged-in cables.

"I, uh, need a moment," he said, an edge of uneasiness tainting his words. "There was another box of hand torches in the storage compartments. Take ours and fetch another one."

"You'll be left in the dark," Krissa said.

"I'll be fine," the captain answered a bit snappily.

Pushing herself away, Krissa murmured, "All right."

"I'm sorry," the captain whispered as he pulled himself behind the box. Krissa turned and floated quickly from the room, but not before she heard strains of a tormented prayer. She wished she knew what she'd done to offend the captain.

CHAPTER 23

The hand torches splayed pools of lights across the barren crew cabin. They met here—the officers, the captain, and Krissa—to discuss the next steps in relative privacy. The location was ideal, suggested by Church—deck two, right across from the bridge.

Krissa anchored herself to the doorway, watching the captain. His drawn face told of his exhaustion and frustration as he sat holding on to one of the bunks. She hadn't seen him sleep, or even take a few minutes for himself, since he'd saved her from Reiger nearly two days ago. Concern for his well-being sprang up in her heart.

"All right, we've got a direct power source to the life support system, so there's nothing to worry about there," the captain said, looking at each of his friends. "What else do we need to cover?"

"The airlock is complete. It was an ordeal trying to hook it up to battery power, but we got it. Once we connect with the *Fool*, our men can crawl along that conveyer belt safely," Torin answered.

"The *Vanquisher* has control of the *Straightjacket*, correct?" Church asked.

The captain nodded.

"Then we're sunk," Church replied. "All they need to do is drop the airlock of the port bay. That would seal us off from the receiving zone and prevent us from getting out."

"I can—" Krissa said quietly.

"Lights would be nice," Lancaster added.

She tried again. "I, um—"

"We may have to do this without lights, Hal," Church argued.

Lancaster frowned. "Grav control?"

"I tried to bring up both lights *and* grav control, but neither worked," the captain said.

"I'd start praying now," Torin added.

Krissa grabbed a hand torch that drifted toward her and pushed off the doorframe. Without a word to any of them, she moved out of the cabin and crossed the corridor to the ladder that led to the first deck. She'd almost grown accustomed to the darkness, but the chill that it left in the air was becoming unbearable.

The silent engine took up the majority of the lowest deck. She skirted the edge of the room and made her way to where the captain's generator sat, now bolted to the floor. She pulled herself down behind the engine's master control unit and tugged off a panel that concealed its inner workings. She unplugged the main power cable, then swam back out to search for a tool pack.

"What are you doing now?" the captain asked, floating next to her. He must have followed her after she left the room.

"Taking care of business," she said, moving to scan the area for anything containing tools. A nearby box gleamed under her light, promising the very treasure she needed. She skittered toward the kit and unlatched it, rummaging through the suspended tools for the right one.

"This is *my* business," he answered, grabbing her hand firmly.

She looked up at him, meeting his gaze. "Let me do this."

"I can't. You've already done too much."

"They don't have to know."

"They *will* know. They know everything that you do. They may even see everything that you see, or hear everything that you hear. I don't know the extent of their hold on you," the captain said.

Krissa dropped her eyes, shaking his hand away. "Then the consequences are *my* business, Captain," she said, selecting a slender tool with a flattened end.

"Why are you back to calling me that?"

"Calling you what?"

"I asked you to call me Chase," he said, sounding offended.

Offsetting a heartbeat of pain by holding her breath, she glanced at him. "I don't recall that conversation."

She moved back to the control unit and pulled herself under it again. Popping the socket cover off, she pulled three delicate wires and re-routed them to the auxiliary supply line, which should have been connected to the generator, if things were done correctly. Replacing the cover, she grabbed the power cable and plugged it back in. The master control blinked to life.

"Trista," the captain pleaded softly.

The name earned her another scraping pain deep within her head. Muscles in her neck tensed as she fought off the ache. She pushed herself from the floor, brushing off her knees as she swam in front of the master control. Her fingers went to work, first bringing the lights online, then grav control. Tools and equipment rained down through the room. The sensation was jarring, but as her feet touched the floor, she took a seat on the attached stool. She turned her focus on the grand airlock.

"I'm going to seal the outer bay doors to prevent them from docking a shuttle full of Zeniths, or at least delay it until they can figure out my override signature code," she said.

The captain's hand rested on her back. "Thank you," he whispered.

She shrugged out of his grasp as she rose. Collecting the tool to return it to the box on the floor, she nodded. "Just don't tell anyone. I may yet be able to defend myself when they start asking questions."

He took her hand and pulled her close. "Don't go back to them," he begged in a husky tone.

Krissa blinked, caught in the captain's gaze. "Captain, I—"

He lifted a hand to her cheek, caressing it tenderly. "Please," he whispered again, leaning in to place a gentle, heartfelt kiss to her lips.

Taken aback, Krissa pulled away, staring at him. She didn't know what to say. She felt as though her heart had stopped. The relentless headache pierced her skull again. She pressed her palms to her brow, shuddering as the dizziness wrenched the pain into place.

"No. No, they can't take you away again," the captain said, placing his hands on her shoulders.

Krissa stumbled back from him, running into the metal panels that covered some of the engine operation units. Squeezing her head, she tried to relieve the pressure. "The tumor must be getting bigger," she cried.

"Tumor?" the captain asked as he closed in on her.

"That's why I …" she paused, whimpering, "… take the medication."

She slid down the panels to the floor, resting her head against the cool metal. Her head felt like it might burst at any time. The pain flashed down her spine, immobilizing her.

The captain knelt next to her, a look of absolute helplessness on his face. He started to touch her, but held back. "W-we just gave you a dose, Trista, back in the bay. I don't want to give you more," he said, worry trembling his voice.

"It's not working," she cried. The agony of the pulsing ache rendered her weak and worn out. She just wanted it to end.

"Captain! Valach is hailing again," Lancaster called out.

"He can wait!" the captain roared.

"He's furious that we have lights. He's threatening to fire on us."

The captain pounded his fist against one of the panels, muttering a soft curse. He squeezed Krissa's hand and placed the pill case at her side. "I'm sorry. I'll send Church in to help you. I'll be back as soon as I can."

Krissa nodded, closing her eyes. She forced calming breaths into her lungs, counting backward from one hundred. Focusing on numbers helped. Numbers were pure. Honest. Emotionless. Ninety-one, ninety, eighty-nine, eighty-eight …

"How did you override the system, Leighton?" Valach demanded as Chase walked onto the bridge.

"We have our ways," Chase answered, equally as livid as the commander on the screen. His anger went beyond the cat-and-mouse games they were playing, though. The image of his wife in deep, constant pain fueled his rage. They were completely to blame for that.

Valach stalked in a predatory pace back and forth, his hands clasped behind him. "You've lost the supply ship, Leighton. My mercy has its limits."

"I don't doubt that. I wasn't about to let my men freeze to death out here."

"You could surrender," Valach retorted.

"I already gave you my conditions."

"And I am now denying them," the commander sneered. "I hold the power here, Leighton."

Chase crossed his arms over his chest. "I imagine that your superior officer won't like explaining to the Tribunal that you killed the Logia they've been searching for."

Valach glared at him. Chase had hit the nail on the head.

"I want to speak with your hostage."

"She's currently unavailable at this time," Chase snapped.

"Now, Leighton. Her doctor is here and wants to check on her *condition*." Valach stepped aside and allowed a silver-haired man in a white lab coat to join him on the screen. Chase couldn't help but notice that Dr. Caiman stood just behind them.

"Mr. Leighton, I'm Dr. Reid Terces. I've been caring for your wife, Trista, since she was brought in to us. It's very important that I have a word with her. Please. Her health is at risk. She has a brain tumor that is growing rapidly and could devastate her at any time," the doctor said.

Chase blinked, staring back at Terces. Here was the man who had taken his wife from him. He bristled when the doctor said Trista's name, his tone carrying an air of familiarity in regards to her. "It's not true," he growled, avoiding Caiman's intent stare.

"It's very true, Mr. Leighton. Perhaps you've noticed strange behavior in her. Confusion, disorientation, headaches, personality fluctuations."

"You created that," Chase said. He recognized the calm, convincing manner with which the doctor spoke. Caiman had used that approach often to lure the inmates into disclosing information they shouldn't have.

"No, Mr. Leighton. Her identity as Krissa surfaced after I saved her life by removing one tumor. But a second growth is what is affecting her."

"You took her memories."

"I had to, Mr. Leighton. The growth was eating her brain."

Chase stared at the floor, wanting with all his heart not to believe what the doctor was saying. They were all so good at telling lies; it was hard to comprehend the truth. And part of him wanted to hold to the hope that the Legacy wouldn't have subjected Trista to unnecessary torment merely to entertain their whims.

"I don't know what you were told, Chase," Dr. Caiman now spoke, the edge of persuasiveness lilting in his voice. "But Trista needs Reid's attention and care. Please let him provide it. He is familiar with your wife's case, whereas your Ghost friends are not."

Chase stumbled back, glaring up at the screen. "You ..."

"I'm only here with your wife's best interest in mind, Chase," Caiman reassured him. "I'm not angry about what happened between us. I understand that your instinct to survive drove you to overtake the *Straightjacket*. And I'm not here to harm you or your men. I wish to appeal to your sense of responsibility as a husband to this young woman. She is in dire need of medical attention."

"I ask only to speak with her, Mr. Leighton." Dr. Terces spoke again. "I'm not asking you to turn her over to us just yet."

They were right. Seraph's words came to mind, heaping doubt onto the already tenuous situation. His friend wouldn't be able to help Trista. And if Seraph couldn't, certainly Brax couldn't either. "Give me ... just a moment to ..." he whispered.

Dr. Terces nodded, peering toward Valach. Caiman also nodded his approval. "Thank you, Chase," he said.

Slipping into the corridor, Chase crossed toward the entry of the crew quarters. "Church! I need Trista on the bridge, please," he said, swallowing hard. The question of whether or not he was doing the right thing beat him up inside.

After a few seconds, Trista scuttled into the hallway to join Chase. "Is everything all right?" she asked. She seemed perfectly poised and lucid. Back to Krissa. He'd lost her ... again.

"Did Church—" Chase gestured back down the corridor.

"I took another dose of my medication, Captain," Krissa answered mechanically. "I feel much better."

Chase gritted his teeth and gripped her hand. The blasted meds imprisoned her with such distance. It broke his heart, especially when she had been so close to coming back to him. And now, he was about to present her to that evil doctor. But it was for her good, right? And what if she really was sick?

"Someone wishes to speak with you," he muttered, directing her toward the bridge.

Lancaster gave him a respectful nod as they re-entered. Chase knew that meant his officer was behind him. He was grateful for the encouragement. It was enough to keep him going in this tough moment.

Krissa gasped softly as she spotted Dr. Terces on the screen. She stepped from Chase's side, centering herself before Terces. He greeted her with a warm smile. "Miss Carlisle, how are you feeling?" he asked.

Still full of suspicion, Chase watched Caiman closely. It was surely a crafty, strategic move to bring him along. They must have been expecting to recapture the inmates. Silently, Chase vowed that he would die before that would happen.

"A little disjointed, but overall, I am well," Krissa answered in her dutiful tone.

"I need you to focus, Miss Carlisle," Terces said. "Keep your eyes on me, please. Compliance."

"Stand by to kill the link, Hal," Chase murmured softly. His eyes darted between Krissa, the doctors, and Valach, wondering just what they were up to. Krissa blinked, her eyes steady on Terces, almost as if she were in a trance. But it was Caiman who made the move. He raised a disturbingly familiar device within view and pressed its button, flashing a teal-blue light into Chase's waiting gaze.

Agony gnashed into his muscles, screaming along with the sound from the remote, but he resisted as much as he could. The hypnotic light flickered in constant torment, finally tugging Chase to the ground. But even after he closed his eyes, the squealing continued to torture him. He writhed, trying to make the pain stop. Next to him, Hal cried, also affected by the seemingly innocuous light and sound.

"Miss Carlisle," Terces's voice piped in louder than before, "listen carefully. I have news of your tumor. I need to get to you for treatment. It's growing faster than I thought."

Krissa blinked, glancing between Terces and Chase. Unable to move from the floor, Chase strained to keep focused on her. A look of confusion clouded her face. She was fighting a difficult internal struggle.

Terces pressed on, "I need you to shut down the ship so that we can get to you."

"I—"

Chase grasped her ankle, looking up at her pleadingly. Perhaps he could still sway her. She blinked again, returning her eyes to Terces.

"Just power down the ship, Krissa," Terces insisted. "We can allow the supply ship to dock, and I can get onboard to help you. Compliance."

"The supply ship ..." Chase groaned, looking at the screen.

"That supply ship doesn't dock until you power down," Valach said as Caiman flashed another mental bomb toward Chase.

"Don't ..." Chase gurgled in pain. It was too much. His head fell back against the ridged metal floor as his body seized with anguish.

Krissa stepped in front of Lancaster and Chase, shielding them from the cruel box. "Stop it," she demanded. "You're hurting them."

"Krissa, shut down the power," Terces ordered, his voice turning more forceful. "Compliance."

She turned her back, kneeling next to Chase. "Are you all right?" she asked, ignoring the seething doctor.

"Compliance!" Terces shouted.

Chase nodded, squeezing his eyes closed again to regain a bit of self-control. "We'll shut down the power when the supply ship is within range—" he said to the commander.

"It's within range, Leighton," Valach answered. "We're waiting on you."

Pushing up to his knees, Chase bowed his head as he tried to catch his breath. Powering down would allow the warship to dock a shuttle, as Krissa had suggested. It would allow other means of infiltration. That's what Valach and the doctors wanted. Their time to escape would be short. Too short. "Fifteen minutes," Chase growled, ending the transmission.

CHAPTER 24

The captain forced himself to his feet with some effort. Krissa stood nearby, ready to assist him, but couldn't help but be a bit frightened by what had just occurred. She was reminded that he was a Legacy prisoner and condemned to an asylum for the insane. Not exactly a comforting feeling.

After helping Lancaster to a standing position, he took her arm and led her back to the crew cabin. "Join us, Hal," he ordered.

Church stood when they entered, a look of concern on his face. Torin glanced between the two. The captain shook his head and lifted a hand toward them. "I'm fine," he muttered. He was understandably short and gruff. "Hal?"

"Just want to get home, Cap," Lancaster said quietly.

With a resolute nod, the captain ran a hand over his chin. "We don't have much time. They'll be on the ship in a matter of moments. Church, Lancaster, get the men to the port bay. We're going to have to make this quick. Real quick. The ship will go dark, but as soon as you hear the *Fool* attach, I want you to open that airlock and begin transferring men. Torin, you head on down to the bay. Get it as close to ready as you can. We'll meet you there."

Church jumped up, clapping the captain on the shoulder as he and others brushed past them. Krissa heard Church already barking orders into a link. The captain took Krissa's arm. "Come on," he said.

"Where are we going?"

"The staff had a supply of slayers hidden in the master sergeant's quarters on the first deck below. I'm guessing they wanted options in case things went awry." The captain shook his head as he chuckled with a sense of irony. "We used them when we took over the ship. I locked them up to prevent an incident."

"You think it's going to come to that? The use of deadly weapons?" she asked.

The captain sighed softly, his demeanor changing from the hurt leader back to the kind Chase. "It might," he murmured. "But by the Crown, I hope not."

Krissa stiffened, digging her fingernails into her palm to counter the twinge that burst in her head. She was getting tired of the unyielding pain. It seemed that no matter what she did, it returned. She doubted her doctor would be able to help her. Terces had already said the growth was inoperable. It was just a matter of time now before it conquered her completely.

Pausing next to the ladder, the captain gestured for her to go first. She climbed down and waited for him. The deck was dark. The captain patted the wall along the ceiling and found the emergency lighting switch.

"How did you know about this supply?" she asked.

"Just a hunch I had. I knew that we wouldn't be able to take the ship without some display of power. I hoped that the master sergeant had some weaponry. Turns out I was right," the captain said, leading her to a door a few steps down the hall. "Brwester had a weapons storage box in his closet that contained several more slayers. I hid the guns and stingers we used to take over the ship in the box and then cut the power to this deck because I didn't want someone else to find them. If one of those guys snapped …"

Krissa stood back as he jiggled the door loose. She was thankful that he left the hypothetical situation to silence. Her imagination ran with it, but she managed to block the wild, frightning thoughts before they went too far. He slid the door aside and stepped into the room before he offered her a hand.

Taking his warm fingers in hers, she moved into the room. He was trembling, but whether it was fear or residual effects from the remote attack a few moments ago, she couldn't tell. She waited near the door as he rummaged through a closet on the far side of the room.

"How are you at lifting heavy things?" he asked between grunts.

"I can handle it," she said.

He lugged out a wide metal box that was obviously too heavy for him to carry alone. "I'll just need help getting this into the bay."

Moving quickly to assist, she grabbed a handle mounted to the far end of the box. He did the same, and together, they carted the crate into the hallway. It clattered against the grated floor. "This is ridiculous," the captain said, dropping his side as he straightened to his full height. "The box weighs much more than the slayers. Take them out, and carry as many as you can down to the bay. Safety should be set on all of them."

After he popped the latch on the crate, she collected three guns and scampered down the corridor to the port bay as he instructed. With great care, she lay each of the weapons on the floor. She turned, heading back for more. The captain gave her a nod. She noticed he carried five slayers. "There are twelve total. Grab a couple more. I'll be right there," he instructed.

Krissa dashed back down the corridor to fetch the other guns. She heard the captain immediately behind her. "I'm not bothering with the stingers. I don't want to have to get that close," he said as he bent down to hand her two of the weapons.

"I don't blame you," she said.

Rising slowly, he eyed the slayers in her hands. "I hope we won't have to use these," he murmured.

"I don't understand," Krissa said with a tilt of her head. "I thought Ghosts were careless renegades."

The captain lifted his gaze to her, frustration in his eyes. "We believe in freedom, Trista. And we're followers of Prince Ternion. Violence is a last resort."

His words walloped her with a nasty crack of lightning through her brain. She clutched the slayers as she stumbled back against the wall. After she caught her breath, she looked at him, ignoring the worry in his expression. "But you blow up stuff ..." she said, continuing the conversation.

"Like I said," he answered, heading toward the bay. "Last resort."

She trotted behind him, delivering the weapons to the bay floor. The ugly black guns lay there like frozen snakes, each stamped with a Legacy symbol and number. Hopefully, she wouldn't be called to take up the arms. She'd never shot one.

"One last thing," the captain said, moving back to the corridor. "Will you help me?"

"What is it?"

He looked up at the wide entry. "I want to seal this off. Find something to wedge under the door that will allow us enough room to crawl under."

Krissa pointed to the metal gun box. "How about that?"

"Yes," he said, "Perfect."

They ran to either side of the box, carrying it the rest of the way down the hallway. It really wasn't that much lighter without the weapons in it. Situating it against the wall, the captain stood, looking into her eyes. "Don't suppose I could talk you into waiting on the other side for me? Just in case that box doesn't hold?"

That would be the smart thing for her to do. But she didn't want to leave the captain to defend himself against a shipload of angry Zeniths. Besides, if the panel didn't work, she might be able to figure something out. "If it doesn't, we'll find another way," Krissa said.

He gripped her hand, pulling her toward the operation panel on the wall. Using the master sergeant's access card, he pressed his finger to the sensor and dropped it. The door complied, matching the speed of his movement. Krissa jumped as the bottom connected with the metal box, sending a reverberating *clang* through the bay and the corridor.

They both breathed sighs of relief. With a hesitant look in his eyes, the captain stepped closer to her. "Are you …" He ran his hands over his face, looking down at her. "I want you to stay safe, Trista," he whispered.

Always. The pressure pounded deep within. She pressed her fingertips to her temples as she backed away from him. "Why do you keep calling me that?" she asked.

The captain frowned, reaching a hand out to her. "It's your name." His words were careful. Measured. Deliberate.

She stared a moment before she shook her head. "I-I've told you, my name is Krissa."

A haunting sorrow filled his eyes as his upper body slumped with the weight of a burden Krissa knew nothing of. He grabbed her hand. "They took everything from you, didn't they?"

"Wh-who? I-I don't understand." The wall sprang up behind her, trapping her in his path. She had nowhere else to go.

"Trista," the captain said, his tone softening. She bit her lip in reaction to the pain as he continued, his hand over his heart. "You have to trust me. I can't tell you the things I want to tell you to make all of this right. But I have friends who can help. They can help with your memory, with your …" He had difficulty getting out the words. "… b-brain tumor. Please come with us."

Krissa glanced down the long corridor. "My whole life is Legacy," she said.

"Look at what they did to us," the captain pleaded. "You saw me on the floor up there. Do you really want to be a part of something that cruel?"

Of course not. Krissa wanted to cry. The life that had led her to this very point had become so unsatisfying. Between Streuben and Dr. Terces, she had no identity of her own. Her options were limited, though. She was Legacy. They owned her. And suddenly she could no longer stand it. But did she really have a choice?

"And your sister, Trista," the captain pressed. "We can help you find her."

She bent forward in pain, grasping his hand for support. Her palm lodged against her skull as she looked up at him. "I told you, I put that behind me."

He steadied her, holding her shoulders in his strong hands. "You can't put lost family behind you. I don't think she's dead. And I don't think she abandoned you years ago."

Krissa suddenly felt weak and overcome. The promises he made were most appealing. Freedom—from her life, from the pain. Her head pounded and throbbed. She was grateful for the grip on her shoulders. It kept her from falling to the floor. "They will take me to the interrogators," she cried in a whisper.

"I won't let them, Trista," the captain assured her. "I'll keep you safe. I promise."

Beyond the grinding ache that now settled in her head, Krissa made the mistake of looking directly into his gentle gaze. His eyes held more than friendship and hope. They held a deep, penetrating love. Something far more than what a captor should feel for his prisoner.

"Come with me. Please," the captain begged once more, the urgency in his voice escalating. He stared at her, his eyes searching hers. "You really don't remember me? Not even the slightest bit?"

She blinked, holding on to his arms. Confusion swept through her fatigued and beaten brain. "What are you talking about?" she whimpered.

The captain lifted a hand to her hair, gently running his fingers through the short strands. "They cut your hair. They took you away from me ..."

She untangled from his arms, sliding along the wall. As means of comfort, she kneaded her ring finger. "I—"

He moved with her, his eyes boring into her. "You wonder why I call you Trista. That's what I called ... my wife. She disappeared—"

The back of her skull raged with a mix of misery and excruciating sparks. "No," Krissa said, shaking her head.

"—close to a year ago," the captain continued, raising his voice over her denial. "The Legacy captured her and used her for their vile purposes ..."

"You're crazy," she muttered, pushing him away.

"She always played with her wedding band," he added, gesturing to her hand. "Trista, I know your sister."

Everything seemed to stop for an instant. Another flicker of pressure smacked her back into reality. She stared at him, bursting with exasperation. "Why are you doing this?"

The captain swallowed and bowed his head. "Lila is a good friend of mine," he said, his words obviously guarded as he revealed more and more. "And my sister-in-law. She's the first officer of the Ghost ship the *Vanguard*. She's married. To Sterling Criswell. They have a son named Blane."

Putting a good arm's length between them, Krissa pointed at him. "You're turning my story against me."

"Trista—" he said, pleading as he took hold of her outstretched hand.

"I'm not her!" she shouted, shaking him off.

He grabbed her arms and pulled her close as she collapsed against him, sobbing. A crackling inferno once more blazed through her skull, muddling her thoughts into blurred memories of who she might have been. "I'm not ... her ..." she gasped.

Slowly, he lowered himself to the floor, holding her in his arms. "I have no reason to lie to you."

"You're in a facility for the insane, Chase ..." she whispered. It felt so natural calling him by his first name.

He stroked her hair, consoling her with the comforting rhythm. "You've said yourself that I'm not a lunatic. Trust me, Trista," he implored as he held her close. "I have proof that you're my wife, but it's all back at the Reserve on Revenant. When I was processed, the Legacy took the reminders of you I carried with me."

"Why do I ..." Krissa paused, resting against his strong chest. She allowed the question to come out, even though a part of her still didn't believe him. "Why do I not remember?"

"The Legacy hurt you," Chase said cautiously. "Somehow, they've erased your memories and embedded ones that they created. That's why you don't remember your parents."

"My parents died from the illness on Gravatus," she replied.

Chase pulled back a little to meet her eyes. "There was no illness on Gravatus. That whole thing was contrived by the Legacy. It was a biological assault disguised as a vaccine, given as a means of control. But your parents, Antin and Kylea Carlisle, were never there. They faithfully served Prince Ternion. They were imprisoned by the Legacy for some time before they were executed. Lila raised you—"

"No." Krissa pushed herself away, but Chase held fast.

"Yes. Lila raised you on Revenant, under the protection of the Ghosts."

"I've never worked for the Ghosts," she insisted.

"Aram Zephaniah, the only father I knew, brought me there so that I could serve under Redic Clairet. That's how we met. We fell in love, and on one beautiful, sunny day, under the shade of the subluce trees, you agreed ..." Chase paused, fighting back tears. "... you agreed to be my bride."

Krissa choked on a sob, shaking her head. The pressure pounded against her skull. "This isn't right. I need my medication ..."

"That medication controls you, Trista. I've seen that in just the last few hours." Chase grasped her neck, trying to make eye contact with her. She dropped her head between her knees to avoid his gaze as he told the rest of the story. "You went out on a mission and never came back. By the Crown, Trista, I did everything in my power to get to you, but I couldn't. The Legacy had you, and they were bent on making an example of you. We heard everything from you being imprisoned to you being executed. My world crumbled in that instant. And when we found out that you were in service as a systems analyst—"

Pressing her palms against her forehead, she cried, "It's not possible ..."

"—we tried to make contact. Redic himself set up the job and asked specifically for you. We knew it would be close, but we had to try. Britt Lockhart, my colleague and friend—*your* friend—tried to get you to recognize him."

He chases ghosts ... "They left," she whispered, lost in a stare. "They launched early."

"Only because the Zeebs were on their way to arrest them."

"They arrested me instead."

"They took you to the interrogators and 'freshened' your memories," Chase said, pushing her hair from her face. "And Trista, that wasn't several years ago, before Lila 'disappeared.' It was close to five months ago."

Krissa started to feel sick to her stomach. She cradled her torso in her arms as she bent over herself. Chase placed his hand on her back. "Trista," he murmured.

She exploded, shaking off his hand as she leapt to her feet. "Don't touch me."

"Trista ..." He stood, watching her with wide, innocent—honest—eyes.

Violent trembling rattled her from deep within her bones. "I came here to do a job. And I end up finding out that not only are the inmates *not* crazy, but *I* am? And that I had a life I know nothing about. I'm married ..."

"Trista ..." He stepped toward her, his arm reaching out toward her again.

"Stop calling me that!"

He froze, intense hurt passing over his features. "I love you, Trista," he whispered.

She collapsed on the floor, curling into a tiny ball. The grate below helped to ease the tension in her head as she slammed her fists against it repeatedly. Chase knelt at her side and grabbed her hands to keep her from hurting herself further. His strength wrapped around her, cradling her close to him.

"You know, don't you?" he whispered.

"I don't ... remember ..." she cried. "But yes ... I know."

Chase kissed her forehead as he returned to stroking her hair. "I'll help you to remember. I promise. We'll find a way." He smiled down at her.

She closed her eyes, pressing her cheek against his chest. Her crying left her with shuddery breaths, but Chase didn't seem to mind. He lifted her to her feet. "I would love to sit and hold you for hours, but we only have a few more minutes. Come with me. Please. Let me help you get that life back."

Her answer was a mere nod. Uncertainty distracted her, along with wishing that the buzzing in her ears that now joined the intense pain in her head would stop. Her brain felt like a rock, skipping along the surface of the pool of reality. Maybe the captain—Chase—would help her find solid ground.

His tender eyes urged her to follow. "Come on," he murmured as voices echoed through the docking bay on the other side of the lowered door.

CHAPTER 25

Krissa and Chase crawled under the door and into the docking area, then jogged toward the aft of the ship, where Church met them. The group of men waited along the outer wall of the receiving zone. Chase gave them a courteous nod as he spoke with Church.

"I've got twelve slayers over there. Take one. Make sure Lancaster and Torin are armed. The rest, I leave to your discretion."

Church glanced in the direction of the weaponry. "You don't have one," he commented.

"I don't want one," Chase responded. "Trista, go on down to the receiving zone. Stick close to Ben."

She couldn't leave him now. Not when she'd decided to place her trust in him. "I want to stay with you," she said. "Please."

With an apprehensive sigh, Chase grabbed her hand, still talking to Church. "I have to pull the plug on the ship's power, which means Valach's warship will take control. When that happens, I imagine this corridor's airlock is going to close down to allow a shuttle to dock. If the Legacy remains true to their word—which I doubt, but I'm going to give them a little hope and credit here—the *Fool* should attach. Get the men through that portal. We'll get there as soon as we can. I might need you to cover us."

"You got, it Chase," Church answered, moving to grab a slayer. "Torin! Lancaster! Declan! Newell! Over here, now!"

The men dashed over, following Church to the opposite end of the bay to retrieve the weapons. They each picked up two or three and headed back to the waiting group. Chase pulled Krissa to the far wall, striding quickly across the bay to a control unit.

"Blast," he murmured, looking at the readout on the console.

"What is it?"

Chase ran a hand over his chin. "They've already landed a shuttle on the emergency docking pad on the roof deck."

Panic erupted through her. "Are they coming in?"

"Not yet. We still have control of the ship. But once I shut us down, they'll be able to connect." Chase stared at the computer. Krissa knew he was trying to figure out what to do.

"That won't give us very long ..." she murmured.

"I'm not worried about that." Chase lifted his eyes to hers. "I'm worried about getting you back across this bay if that airlock opens. Getting you to safety."

Krissa stepped away, crossing to a long panel that ran the length of the bay doors. Curling her fingers under it, she ripped off the lowest section, exposing multiple bands of different-sized wires and cables. She scanned the area around her for something to slash them. Amid a small pile of clutter against the wall, she spotted an old, rusted wire cutter. "Hand me that," she said.

Moving quickly, Chase grabbed the cutter and passed it to her. "What are you doing?" he asked.

She pushed back several heavy cables, reaching for a grouping of wires. Closing her eyes for just one moment, she took in a calming breath. She angled the cutter along the wires and snipped. With the rustiness of the tool, it took a couple of tries, but eventually she hacked through. The indicator lights along the sides of the bay doors went dark.

"Disabling the airlock. This door won't open," she said with an air of triumph. Short-lived, though, as she had a couple of other ideas in mind. And they had to hurry. They were already out of time.

Chase shook his head, smiling in amazement. "Thank you," he whispered.

Sliding in front of the control console, she brought up the ship's system. "I would just shut down the lights, but I imagine they are monitoring power across the board."

Nodding in agreement, Chase leaned with one hand against the unit. "Can you tell if the *Fool* is close to docking?"

Shifting to a proximity readout, Krissa pointed to the nearby ship. "They came through. It's ready to connect."

Biting his lip, Chase nodded again. "All right. Shut us down."

"One thing first," Krissa said. "I may not be able to do much, but I can at least keep this kind of thing from happening again."

She accessed the master ship control and selected the self-destruct mechanism. Her personal code wouldn't allow her to set it, but she'd had access to the master sergeant's and the head doctor's codes. Inputting both confirmed the order. She set the timer for fifteen minutes, hoping that would allow all the ships to put some distance between them and the *Straightjacket*. Her final move was encrypting the sequence, so that it would take at least that long for someone else to figure it out before they could reset it.

Chase bowed his head. Seeing his softer side, Krissa knew that he hated the idea of destroying things, particularly when lives were at risk. But she also knew that his time on this ship had been devastating to his spirit. This was the opportunity to save others from the same fate.

As she looked across the bay, her eye caught sight of the raised door. They'd have to dislodge the box before they shut down the power.

"Chase," she said, running to the door.

He cursed under his breath as he took off after her. She wrapped her fingers around the handle and yanked, but to no avail. Pushing her aside, he tugged on the handle, unable to budge the stuck box. She watched as he repositioned himself and tried again, but the box wasn't going to move under the weight of the door.

Directing her to take the handle, Chase moved to the center of the door. His eyes locked on hers. With a nod, he gripped the bottom, took a breath, and tried to lift the door. Wrapping both hands around the grip, she planted herself and wrenched the box back and forth, shimmying it slightly. His face turned deep red with exertion as he put more effort into his lifting. She could see the strain and tension in his neck. Pulling with all her might, she fell back with a cry as the box finally gave way and slammed into her. Chase leapt back as the door crashed to the ground.

Shaking out her hand, she got to her feet. He rushed to her side, taking a hold of her elbow as she rose. "Are you all right?" he asked.

Her knuckles were torn up from the box's assault. "I'll be fine," she murmured, pressing her hand to her mouth. "You?"

He answered with a nod. "I want you to start for the receiving zone, Trista."

"I'm in this with you, Chase," she replied with insistence.

"I'm not losing you again," he answered, staring into her eyes.

"You need me to shut down the ship."

He shook his head. "I can do that. But when I do, it's going to fry the system. They won't be able to bring us back online. And it might even detonate the self-destruct, setting it off before the timer runs out."

So that was why he looked so upset when she programmed the self-destruct. It wasn't because of remorse or hesitation. It was because it now jeopardized their chance of escape.

"It's okay," he reassured her. "I'll be right there. We're going to have to get across in the dark, but we'll do it together, okay?"

She nodded, moving toward the receiving zone. Glancing back toward him, she saw that his eyes remained on her. He placed his hand on the control console and closed his eyes. A popping sound followed by several sparks came from the unit before everything around her went dark and she floated upward. "Captain?" she called out.

"I'm coming," he said.

She felt him wrap an arm around her. A klaxon mounted above sounded a severe warning throughout the bay. He held her close as they made their way through the bay. The dark was maddening. "Oh, my King, help all those men to get onto the *Fool* and protect us," he said.

"Church!" Chase shouted through the silent darkness.

"They're docked, Chase!" came the distant reply. "We're seconds from opening the portal."

"Good," Chase whispered. "And they say good-byes are hard."

Krissa cried, pressing her head against his chest. The headache cracked against her brain, taking away reason once again. With the flurry of activity, she had managed to ignore the brutal pain. But now her adrenaline was spent, and she started to slow down.

"Hey." Chase paused a moment. "Are you okay?"

"I—"

In an instant, they fell, sucked down to the floor. The sudden application of gravity took Krissa's breath from her. As she pushed up, a prickly feeling slunk down the back of her neck. Chase gasped, yanking on Krissa to shield her with his body. "Concussion blast! Get down!" he shouted.

The ship rocked forcefully. Krissa tried to hold on to Chase, but she tumbled from his grasp and with a groan, landed hard amid a scattered stack of pallets. They hadn't made it very far. Church seemed squants away. Her head spun with confusion, dizzied with knocking her head against a wooden crate. Chase said he'd fried the system ...

"Let's go!" she heard the echo of Church's cry off the bay walls. He had managed to open the portal and start filtering the men into the getaway ship.

Chase dashed to Krissa. "Are you all right?" he said as he cleared away the debris around her.

"You—the grav control—"

"They must have connected the shuttle's power to ours. Come on!" he shouted.

"Freeze, Ghosts!" an unfamiliar voice hollered.

A single Zenith stepped out onto the catwalk above. He lodged his hand on the rail and leapt over, landing in a crouch in front of Chase and Krissa. His slayer hung from a strap over his shoulder, but the look on his face as he slowly straightened to his full height told her that he had a much worse weapon that he intended to use. "No. Not the remote," she said.

Images of Chase writhing on the floor of the bridge propelled Krissa to her feet. Before the blue light flashed from the Zenith's hand, she launched herself toward him. He scrambled to take hold of his slayer, but Krissa's surprise maneuver kept him from doing so. She pummeled him with her hands as he tried to fight her off.

The thrumming of boots caught Krissa's attention. She glimped up to see Zenith after Zenith running into the bay on the catwalk. They all had slayers trained on the men below. Dr. Terces led in a team of Zephyr soldiers, barking orders at them not to hurt her. Church and Torin had joined in the mayhem, aiming their slayers at the first Zenith. Chase swore softly as he planted his fist in the Zenith's jaw and grabbed Krissa around the waist in one swift move. "Come on," he growled.

Blasts rained down on them, lighting up the floor in rings of flames. "Let's go!" Church shouted at Chase, jerking his head toward the portal. A sinister bolt from a slayer made contact with Church's shoulder, sending him careening into the wall with a pained cry. Krissa noticed the captain had grabbed one of the slayers and shot back at the Zeniths.

With a loud burst, Krissa felt fire pulse from her skull through her veins. She cried out, releasing Chase's grip as she hobbled a few rigid steps, then fell in a contorted twist. Looking up, she saw Terces holding a slayer aimed at her.

He pulled the trigger, but no shot came forth. However, a fresh wave of pain stripped her every thought and breath, and deafened her ears. Chase stepped toward her, then looked up with horror on his face.

She followed his gaze, only to see a netted load of crates plunging toward her from the ceiling. Everything in her desired to get clear of the falling weight, but her body wouldn't obey. Torin and Church left their posts at the portal and tackled Chase as the crates crashed down on Krissa. She screamed before allowing herself to go completely limp, giving up.

"Trista!" she heard Chase cry as her ears cleared with a ringing tone.

She rolled her head around to see Church and Torin pulling Chase through the portal. He reached toward her and fought against his own men, but the two were strong. Another shot smacked fire on Chase's leg. His face wrenched with anguish, and she watched his men wrestle Chase until they were out of sight. At once, she felt panic and relief. He, at least, had made it. He was safe.

A Zenith knelt at her side, jamming a slayer against her skull. "You're under arrest, Ghost."

"I-I'm not a ..." Krissa murmured, trying to find her breath.

"Save it for the Justice Center," the Zenith replied as several others surrounded her.

Krissa closed her eyes, only to see Chase's frantic expression lingering in her thoughts. Why did he care so much? Dizziness joined the throbbing ache as her memory began to fail her. *He chases ghosts.* The captain. Chase. No, the captain ... was a Ghost, and she was a servant of the Legacy. It was—

She gasped in pain as the net was lifted from her legs. The soldiers worked efficiently, not giving the first thought to her comfort. They shoved a stretcher under her, which sent fresh waves of throbbing from her legs up her spine. A restraining strap crisscrossed over her, tighter than it needed to be.

"Be gentle with her," Dr. Terces ordered, stepping into view.

"We don't want her to try anything, Doc."

"Of course not," he said, looking down at her as the team expanded the legs of the stretcher to roll at waist level. She saw a new evil in his eyes. He shook his head, clucking his tongue. "I'm very disappointed in you, Miss Carlisle."

"You shot—"

"Caiman," Dr. Terces said to someone across from him. "Give me that dose of somnoctis."

"Don't drug me," Krissa demanded. "You've already done enough ..."

A different doctor moved to her side, handing off a syringe from a medkit. Dr. Terces lifted it, tapped the ampoule, and despite her pleas, plunged it into her neck.

"Sleep, Ghost," one of the Zeniths muttered.

She winced and continued to protest, but soon found herself swirled in nightmares of the captain—no ... Chase—being just beyond reach. *He ... chases ...* She fought the torrential current to warn them, "The self-destruct ..." Only a few moments left ... *He chases ...*

CHAPTER 26

Church gave Chase a final jerk, plunging onto the deck of the *Fool*. "Seal it!" he ordered Torin, as he still wrestled with his captain.

Torin slammed the airlock closed, shouting to Brax above, "That's it! We're all in!" He keyed in a sealing sequence on a panel next to the airlock.

"No! No, Brax!" Chase hollered, shrugging off Church as he leapt to his feet. "We're not!" Blast it! Trista hadn't made it through. He had to go back for her.

"Go!" Church ordered, tugging Chase away from the sealed airlock.

Chase clung to the metal hatch, but collapsed to the ground as the ship shifted under him. He'd been so close. He'd almost had her. Just a few more seconds … Hopelessness brought tears to his eyes. Pounding his fist on the deck, he cried, "No!"

"Leighton, I need you on the bridge. Now." Cam's voice echoed off the metal cargo hold through the ship link.

Church moved to his captain's side, offering him a hand. "I'm sorry, Captain," Church said with a tone of regret, but also resolve. "I did what I had to do to protect my commanding officer. That's my duty."

Chase stared at Church's hand for a moment before he took it and pulled up. He nodded silently in sorrow as he limped toward the metal ladder that led to the bridge. He understood Church's position, but he'd also spent too many days apart from the woman he loved. Not to mention, he had just left her in the clutches of those who could do her the most harm.

Cam greeted Chase as he entered the bridge with, "About time. That warship is aiming all it's got at us, and I need you to take care of it."

Chase sank into the copilot's chair. "I really don't care," he murmured, staring out of the viewport.

"Then why did you drag us out here?" Cam asked with a glare. Rarely seen anger flashed in his eyes. "You're just going to let your men die? After all that you've been through? You're going to let *us* die? That's awfully inconsiderate, Chase."

"I don't need you to lecture—"

"Oh, but you do," Cam insisted. "You're not thinking beyond yourself."

Chase bristled, "Get off my back, man!"

Cam stared at him with wintry intensity. "We are going to be shot down, Chase. Maybe captured. Did you not have enough fun in the Legacy's care the last few months?"

"Trista didn't make it through the portal!" he blurted.

Blowing out a breath, Cam shook his head. "I'm sorry," he replied, softening his tone. "I know it's hard. But use it, Chase. Let the Crown use it. If you make it home alive, you'll have the chance to try again. But if you die here, you condemn her to a lifetime with the Legacy."

Chase bowed his head, dropping it into his hands as he leaned on his knees. He'd tried not to blame the Crown through this, but someone had to take responsibility for the topsy-turvy circumstances. He'd done everything he possibly could to save his wife. "The Crown," he muttered in a scoffing tone. "The Crown took her from me ..."

"The Crown wants you to stay strong!" Cam said with force as a loud noise, followed by a fierce jerk, shook through the ship. "Come on, Chase! You know better than this, man!"

Chase glanced up toward the viewport. A furious red pulse shot out from the warship, aimed directly for the *Fool*. The ship rocked hard to the starboard side, setting off a frantic beeping sound. Cam's hands flew across the console, trying to regain control.

"She can't take much more, Chase. Please," Cam begged. "Do it for Trista."

Closing his eyes, Chase reluctantly slipped into a prayerful state, first begging forgiveness for not only his failure, but for his wavering faith. He then concentrated his efforts outside the Ghost vessel to reach the giant, attacking warship. His thoughts traveled into the heart of the enormous ship, finding a crucial fuse that tripped a surge, enough to overload the ship's weapon function. The system shut down, but it would be an easy fix for their techs. No doubt they'd find it quickly, but not before the *Fool* would make its escape.

"Go," he murmured to Cam.

"Thank you," Cam responded, shifting the *Fool* into its course and traveling speed.

Chase sat back as the ship moved along. He had to take some comfort in the fact that they were no longer prisoners of the Legacy and that they'd survived months of torture. But as the distance grew between him and Trista, bitterness set in. He'd have to do something drastic. And soon.

Brax dashed onto the bridge. "I picked up chatter on the comsys. The *Straightjacket* is imploding. They are trying to evacuate as quickly as they can, but the engine core is unstable and corrupting quickly. The warship is concerned with putting adequate distance between them."

Heavy pressure crushed Chase's lungs. By the Crown, he'd forgotten that Trista had set the self-destruct mechanism. Another million prayers flew from his heart. *Please protect her.*

"We're not going to make it. The *Fool* isn't fast enough to escape those shockwaves," Cam said, scanning his gauges and monitors. He looked at Brax, a solemn expression on his face. "Alert Rev One."

Gritting his teeth, Chase leaned forward and placed both hands on the console. He would not let them suffer at the hands of the Legacy any longer. A fervent, heart-wrenching prayer echoed through him as he focused on getting the *Fool* to safety. He'd trust that the Crown would take care of Trista, one way or another. The *Fool* shuddered with the strain as its engines blazed with supernatural heat.

"Chase ..." Cam said, a hint of warning in his tone.

"We're going home," he whispered.

As he closed his eyes, a grand pathway opened before him. He saw it with complete clarity. Adding a prayer of gratitude, he aligned the ship's course to match that of the pathway. The *Fool* quaked as they entered the aperture, sweeping memories of Chase's life with Trista—and without—through his thoughts.

In a split second, they had reached the other side, allowing the *Fool* to settle into its normal operational speed. Chase crumpled against the chair, exhausted and shattered. He'd never accessed a pathway, other than the one between Viam and Revenant, and honestly, he had no idea how he'd happened upon this one. The Ghosts hadn't even known if other pathways existed. It had been speculated, but no concrete evidence had been secured. Clearly, the Crown had aided in their escape.

"We're in the Aevum rotation, on approach to Viam," Cam murmured in astonishment.

Brax stood, frozen between the pilot's and copilot's chairs. "I, uh ... I'll a-alert Rev One," he said, stepping back toward the communications room.

With a look of bewilderment, Cam started, "How—"

"It wasn't me," Chase whispered between panting breaths. "Don't ask. I don't know." He wrapped his arms around himself and closed his eyes again. It was too much. Too much.

Krissa opened her eyes to the sterile white of a medical area. She lifted her head and tried to sit up, but her arms were bound in straps on either side of the bed. An IV had been stuck into her right arm. The room had three other beds, but no other patients, at least that Krissa could tell.

"Just stay where you are," a male's voice said from her side.

She glanced over to see an officer staring at her. He held a PDL, and his Zenith insignia read, "Lt. Blouter." She'd seen him before. On the street outside her apartment. Near Dr. Terces's offices. She took a breath, resting her head against the pillow. Maybe her memory of the lieutenant was just another mind trick.

"She's awake," he said to someone else.

Streuben stepped into her line of sight, a smirk on his face. "Welcome back, Krissa. Heard you turned Ghost on us."

She closed her eyes with a frown. "I didn't."

"She's my prisoner. I'll do the questioning," the officer said.

"She's my employee. Was ... my employee."

"You want to interfere with her case? I'll be happy to have you in chains next to her."

After a moment, Streuben shrugged. "Fine. She's yours. Carlisle, consider yourself fired." He walked away before Krissa could say anything more, leaving her alone with Blouter.

The lieutenant moved closer to her bed, still sitting in his chair. "Krissa Carlisle, you are currently being detained on a medical ship. You are considered a prisoner, but for now, you are in the custody and care of your doctors. Do you remember why?"

Krissa turned her head away, staring at the next bed. "Of course I remember why. I was attacked by Zeniths."

That wasn't true, really. It was Dr. Terces who had held the weapon that didn't shoot, but somehow wracked her body with enough pain to drop her to the floor in a heartbeat. She still didn't understand that. He was supposed to be helping her.

"And why was that?" Blouter asked.

She shifted her eyes back to him. "I was taken prisoner by the Ghost inmates of the *Straightjacket*."

"They took no prisoners," Blouter responded, scratching his eagle beak of a nose. "They sent the staff on a rendezvous course with a Zenith outpost."

"They sent the staff on a shuttle set on autopilot," Krissa corrected. "I was assigned to fix their computer issues. Ask Streuben about that. I was working in a private room when the riot happened. I heard nothing. It wasn't until after the shuttle had been launched that they discovered I was onboard."

Blouter blinked rapidly. "The rescue squadron said that you were trying to make an escape with them."

Rescue squadron? That was a nice way of putting it. "What else was I supposed to do?" Krissa asked.

"Why didn't you attempt to contact the Legacy before the escape?"

"I told you, I was a prisoner."

"Were you bound the entire time?"

"Well, no ... but—"

"Then you could have found a way."

"I—"

"It seems to me, Miss Carlisle, that you were aiding and abetting the Ghosts, which puts you in league with them," Blouter stated, making a note on his PDL.

"I wasn't—"

"That's a rather serious charge, Miss Carlisle." The officer stood, pocketing his PDL. He glared down at her. "The Legacy will determine your fate."

Krissa bit the insides of her cheeks as she frowned. "Nothing I say will change anything, will it?"

With a self-satisfied smugness, Blouter folded his arms over his chest. "Bring us Leighton."

Did she hear him right? "What?"

"The rescue squadron reported that Chase Leighton tried to get to you after the net fell. You betray Leighton to us, and you'll be free to return to your duties."

Krissa closed her eyes as the scene filled her head. The flashing, deadly slayers. The battle between the Zeniths and the Ghosts. The gentle captain, straining to reach her. He'd called her Trista. Said he loved her. Or was that just part of the nightmares?

"I have no way to contact him," she answered quickly. "And even if I did, we have no connection. He doesn't care about me. I was just his prisoner back on that ship." She didn't know how much of that was truth, but at this point, she had to believe it.

The lieutenant smirked. "Too bad, then." He turned and crossed the length of the room.

Krissa looked up at the ceiling, thinking about what the officer had said. Leighton had only kept her close because she was his prisoner … right? His sense of honor caused him to keep her close in order to protect her from the men who might wish to harm her. But that was only because he felt people should be treated with dignity. All people. She wasn't special.

Recalling her final moments aboard the *Straightjacket*, Krissa tried to remember everything Leighton had said and done. The kind words. His insistence on getting her to safety. The pain on his face as the two men pulled him away. Was that just honor or something more? She would probably never know.

Blouter returned with Dr. Terces in tow. The officer stood at the end of the bed, his arms again crossed over his chest in a most arrogant fashion, as Terces wheeled a chair to her bedside. "They are expecting the report, Doctor," Blouter said.

"It won't take but a moment," Terces responded, reaching for a nearby cart. "I take it that the questioning has already led you to your conclusion."

"Indeed. But confirmation is required."

"Dr. Terces," Krissa said, her pulse accelerating. The last time she saw him, he had looked so cruel and menacing. Her base instinct told her to flee, but she couldn't move.

The doctor pulled a large metal device from the cart and settled it on the pillow around Krissa's head. She watched in horror, wondering exactly what they were going to do. She tugged on the restraints and thrashed about as much as she could. Over her protests, she heard Terces call for assistance.

Two technicians—she recognized them from her recovery time following her initial surgery—marched to either side of her bed and held her still as the device made contact with her skull. Frightning images flickered in her head as she remembered fighting with the two. The blond one had been gentle at times, but the darker-haired man was brutal.

The doctor unfolded metal plates from each side of the device. They were secured against her shoulders and kept her from twisting her head around. Five pins shot forward and made contact with her temples and forehead. Another drilled into her head from above. They felt warm against her skin before they pulsed with heat, which caused her to cry out in panic.

Terces stared at something on the apparatus, then glanced up at Blouter. "You have confirmation. She's been breached, but it's still repairable."

"I'll make my report," the officer snapped before he spun around.

"Link Admiral Niveli, and tell him to call a board meeting. Before you spew your report to the public, I'd like to cover a few things among us," Terces said.

Jutting his tongue into his cheek, Blouter shook his head and walked off. He muttered something about ExMed's botched procedures.

Dr. Terces signaled the technicians. "Matlen, go down to the pharm. I want twenty units of maldominorex, thirty units of imperactium, and fifty units of deleouxor. They will question those amounts, but assure them that I will monitor the reactions personally. Berreks, tell Aftal that we'll be on our way up to the lab momentarily. I want to use the handling keep. We already have her in the shroud."

They both moved off as Krissa looked up at the doctor. "What are you doing to me?"

"Nothing you need concern yourself with," Terces answered, pressing a button on her bed to make it recline to a fully horizontal position. He then reached for something else from the cart. "Open your mouth, please."

He was going to hurt her somehow; she was sure of it. She clamped shut her jaw, but the doctor squeezed her cheeks between his fingers and pressed his palm against her chin with such force that her mouth opened. He slipped a plastic piece between her teeth and worked it down into her throat, despite her gagging and crying. Jamming a tube to the end of it, he then placed a mask over her mouth and nose. Her chest rose and fell in robotic rhythms. She remembered this. The breathing apparatus. The technician had been much more careful before, though.

Matlen returned with a small hypodermic and two larger ones. Krissa nearly fainted at the sight, but the forced, even breathing kept her panic from overcoming her. Terces eased one needle at a time into her intravenous port and injected the liquids. The gush of each dose burned through her blood.

"Take her to the lab. I'll meet you there. And then I will let you know when the IIS deletion process is finished. She'll need some time in recovery before she undergoes the restructuring stim," the doctor said.

Deletion? "No!" Krissa screamed into the mouthpiece as she jerked on her restraints. She knew no one would save her or even show an ounce of pity. Her heart plummeted as she thought of Chase. If she ever saw him again, she wouldn't remember him. Twice now, she had lost him, and she never even knew it.

"Just relax, Miss Carlisle," Dr. Terces said, patting her arm. "This will all be over soon."

CHAPTER 27

Armand's eyes flickered between the doctors as the called advisory board meeting began. He noticed a bitter tension between them. Dr. Niveli, in fact, completely disregarded all welcoming formalities, quickly introducing Dr. Terces again. The Spokesman was unavailable, apparently relying on the reporting of Admiral Niveli. The screen, split in four squares, captured Finn Streuben, Gib Blouter, Dr. Terces, and Dr. Aftal. The younger doctor looked away nervously, keeping an eye on his monitors as he participated in the meeting. The four were aboard a medical shuttle en route to Crenet from the *Vanquisher*.

"We, um, had to do quite of bit of work this time. And I'm not sure how long it will hold up," Dr. Terces explained to the group of Legacy officials. His manner had changed quite a bit. Armand could detect an edginess. The doctor's lifework was crumbling around him. The image of Krissa popped up on the individual DDLs as before.

"Following our last routine visit, Krissa went out on assignment to the *Straightjacket*. We are not sure how the failure in communication occurred, but she never should have been anywhere near that ship. While she was onboard, her husband, Chase Leighton—who had been sentenced to treatment aboard the *Straightjacket*—led a riot, and the inmates overpowered the staff. Krissa remained as his prisoner."

"Did he heal her?" Dr. Niveli asked quietly, her lips hidden behind her steepled fingers.

"As stated previously," Admiral Niveli answered with a condescending tone, "his gifts, fortunately, do not include healing,"

"But in being reunited with him, some breaching did occur," Dr. Terces amended. "I don't think she remembered anything distinctly, but I believe she had an idea that something wasn't right. She experienced … fluctuations. That's the best term I can come up with to describe what's happening."

"Both Commander Valach, of the engaging warship, and Dr. Terces indicate that she tried to protect Leighton. She disregarded a fail-safe in the programming, defying a direct command. And it looked as though, had she escaped, she would have gone with the inmates to the Ghosts," Admiral Niveli added.

"But thanks to the professionalism and efficiency of our Zenith Brigade and Zephyr soldiers, Krissa was apprehended and delivered to us. We immediately began to work with her to try and salvage some of our effort," Dr. Terces said. "She resisted us at first, but we were able to repair the breach, and she is undergoing IIS as we speak."

The report turned Armand's stomach. He had heard from Redic about the goings-on with the *Straightjacket*, and how the *Fool* would be participating in a recovery mission. He'd also heard from the Legacy reports that the *Straightjacket* had been destroyed, and apparently the Ghost ship with it, as there was no trace evidence of it.

"How are you obscuring this encounter?" Zak Sinclaire asked. His tone was terse and impatient. Exactly how Armand felt.

Dr. Aftal spoke from the screen. "In our previous restructuring, Krissa had had an encounter with the Ghosts that led to a frightning night with the interrogators. It was a bandage of a repair to synchronize events that had occurred."

Admiral Niveli jumped in. "She had been sent on an assignment, unbeknownst to us, to a Ghost ship on Pavana—an attempt by the Ghosts to recover her. She completed the assignment before reporting the ship as Ghost. When the Zeniths raided the bay, the ship made its escape and left Mrs. Leighton behind."

He spoke of Britt's attempt to reach Trista. Armand bit his lip as he thought of how close they had been, and how terribly they all had felt when they'd met failure. As long as he had been with the Legacy, it was still odd to hear the flipside perspective.

"Let me be clear here, though—no breaching occurred at that time," Dr. Terces said. "But we had to instill a fear of the Ghosts, in case similar incidents were to take place. She was accused of aiding the Ghosts, interrogated, and released. The interrogation was enough to affirm her loyalty."

Blinking, Armand crisply said, "My associate asked about this latest incident, Doctor."

"Yes," Dr. Terces said with uncertainty.

Dr. Aftal covered abruptly. "We are retaining most of her memories of the experience, including her exchanges with Leighton. We are taking advantage of these exchanges, though, to make him out to be a bad guy in her eyes. He imprisoned her. He used her to gain footing with the Legacy. He even ordered his men to torture her with the treatment devices."

"But none of that is true," Zak said, filling in words that the doctors intentionally left out.

"No. From what we can tell, Leighton treated her with compassion and care," Dr. Terces answered Sinclaire, irritation now evident in his tone. "She was completely taken with him, which goes against our structured parameters. We established a block of all chemical and electrical impulses that would lead to romantic feelings of any nature."

"They became romantically involved?" Kalislyn Carter asked. From what Armand knew of the Elite representative, the question made sense. She had the reputation of being quite a gossip.

Dr. Terces raised his hands to stop the onslaught of speculative questions. "No, but feelings of trust and interest were evident."

"We are currently skewing her memories of two men—Leighton, and another who really did attempt to torture her. If she sees Leighton face-to-face, she will not recognize him. And if he attempts to help her recall the events, and somehow breaches her again, the memory of fear will resurface," Dr. Aftal explained. "In the end, Mrs. Leighton will emerge from the restructuring remembering the assignment and the incident, but in her memory, the Zenith Brigade freed her from the clutches of crazy, evil men and returned her to the life she thinks she has always known."

"We plan to heighten her reaction to the pain inducers as well. Any mention of certain words pertaining to the Ghosts and her husband will immobilize her with pain," Terces explained, his lips tightening with determination. "I will be the only authorized person to access the inducers and alleviate the pain."

"Mr. Streuben, we are asking that you take her on again. The medical shuttle will arrive back here on Crenet in three days. Krissa will be expected to show up at your office the next morning," Admiral Niveli said. "You will be compensated, of course, to maintain the illusions and keep a watchful eye on her."

"Extra compensation, I hope. I already have clients asking questions," Streuben answered. "And I want her to treat me with more respect. Make her more docile."

"Noted." Niveli replied. "We'll take care of it."

Streuben nodded his gratitude.

"Perhaps a new employer should be solicited," Lady Saxby suggested. "If you wish for my money to continue to support this project, I suggest you find someone else to babysit the subject. It seems that Mr. Streuben cannot mind which assignments might place her in jeopardy."

"Now, look—" Streuben said.

"Why are you bothering with this, gentlemen?" Zak Sinclaire asked with a raised voice, overriding the battle. "It seems an awful lot of trouble for one former Ghost who serves in such an inconsequential way."

Dr. Terces looked toward Admiral Niveli, who leaned back in his chair, rocking slowly back and forth. "Mrs. Leighton is an example to the Ghosts. They are most certainly watching her, and perhaps her experience will teach them a lesson. We had hoped somehow to reach Chase Leighton through her, which remains a possibility in the future."

"And at this point, it is quite possible that Mrs. Leighton's brain can take no more," Dr. Terces said solemnly. "I came close to losing her during this last round of stimulation."

By the Crown ... "And if that's the case?" Armand asked.

"She will effectively be brain-dead. We would pull all life support and let nature take its course," Dr. Terces replied.

Zak shook his head, folding his arms over his chest. "This procedure should have remained banned. That is my recommendation at this juncture."

Several others on the advisory panel whispered to each other or voiced their agreement. Armand kept his eyes on Terces. He could tell the doctor was withholding information. He just hoped that Trista wasn't already gone.

Admiral Niveli raised his hands. "Now just a moment. Dr. Terces didn't say that was the case. We've invested a lot—*you've* invested a lot," he gestured to the ladies of the Elite across the table, "and we're going to see this through."

Pressing a pointed finger to the table, Zak stood. "We established the Progressive Legacy with the ambition of providing a bright and glorious future for the people of the Circeae System. Instead, we are wreaking havoc with whimsical, experimental torture disguised as medical procedures. It's an alarming and frightning way to control people. I have issue with this, doctors."

"Would you be touting your righteousness were the Spokesman here, Captain?" Admiral Niveli asked, glaring at Zak. "It sounds as though you are in support of the Ghosts."

"Quite the opposite, Admiral." Zak straightened, lifting his chin with pride. "I believe in the Legacy, and I believe that you and ExMed are misrepresenting our interests."

Niveli stared in anger as his wife touched his arm. "We created this board with opposition in mind, dear. Remember that," she murmured. Uncharacteristically quiet, she was.

The admiral nodded, looking down his nose at Zak. "Thank you for your input, Captain Sinclaire. It will be noted," he said curtly.

Zak bowed his head, glancing toward Armand as he sank into his seat. Armand released the breath he'd been holding. He had to give Zak credit. That had been a bold and courageous, albeit unwise, move.

"Any other ... opposition?" Admiral Niveli asked, looking about at the silent members of the advisory board. "In that case, we will convene again in one month's time. You are dismissed. Dr. Terces, I'd like a private word with you, please."

Armand rose, moving out of the room with the others. He'd meet with Zak later. He had to get this news back to Revenant immediately.

As soon as the *Fool* touched down, Chase stood to debark. Cam insisted that he wait until the landing report was made, which irked Chase. He flopped back in the chair, tapped his foot in the most obnoxious way he could, and stared at Cam. Eventually, and without losing his patience one little bit, Cam gave a nod, dismissing him. Chase dashed out of the ship and, ignoring the searing pain in his leg, marched past the men who were receiving care. He made eye contact with Church, who immediately shrugged off a medic and followed Chase as he strode toward Redic, Seraph, and Remy.

"Did the *Straightjacket* blow?" Chase demanded.

Redic stepped forward, narrowing his eyes. "Slow down, son," he advised, placing a firm grip on Chase's shoulder.

"Did it blow?"

Seraph gave a silent nod. His expression said too much, but Chase refused to believe that Trista hadn't made it. He'd trusted the Crown, after all.

"What about Trista? Krissa?"

Remy cleared her throat. "Chase, this isn't the time—"

So she *was* alive! "You have to let me go back for her," Chase insisted.

"Not a chance, Chase," Redic answered with a growl. "The *Halcyon* crew is grounded. You all need medical attention."

"With all due respect, sir, I don't care about me," Chase replied. "I care about my wife."

"We are quite aware of that, Chase, but if I have to, I will confine you to quarters under guard. You are not going right now, and that is final," Redic said. Looking beyond Chase, he called to Cam and Brax. "Gentlemen, I'd like to see you in the Turret. Seraph, Chase, please join us."

Chase sighed, then nodded to Church. If Redic wouldn't agree, they'd go out on their own, like before. But this time, they'd be successful. "Go get your shoulder checked out," he said to Church. "And then stand by. I'll meet you at my shuttle."

"Disregard that order, Mr. Church," Redic commanded. "Go get checked out, and then proceed to your quarters. You are on temporary relief of duty, as is your entire crew."

Chase glanced at Seraph, who answered with a slight shrug. So Redic was trying to make it impossible for him to pursue Trista. Again. Well, he'd have the freedom to confront Redic in the Turret. And he'd let Redic have it there.

The men walked in silence to Redic's office, although Chase was about to burst. They were wasting precious time. Time that allowed that doctor and his cohorts to hurt Trista. To take her away. He shuddered as he thought of the last few moments on the *Straightjacket*. How very close he had been …

Redic allowed Remy to pass first before he entered. The others followed. In the Turret, most of the Crew waited. The Logia were out, as well as Brendan and Stu. On various runs, Chase guessed. As the men and Remy took their seats, Redic turned on Chase, his fists supporting his weight as he leaned over the table.

"What were you thinking, going out on that run, Chase?" Redic roared. "I ought to strip you of your rank."

Taken aback, Chase held the leader's gaze as he rose to his feet. Redic's anger fueled his own. "You weren't moving on it, sir. While the Legacy hacked away at my wife's brain—"

"I do not have to defend my authority, which you blatantly disregarded—"

"You didn't listen—"

"You've acted like a child since she was taken—"

"If you'd sent me to begin with—"

"You landed yourself and your entire crew in a nut house!"

"You, of all people, should understand my resolve in seeing this through! I will not lose her like you lost Caelya and your kids," Chase said, realizing immediately how damaging his words were. He slowly sank into his chair as regret settled on his shoulders.

Redic stared at Chase, stunned into silence by his words. Everyone in the room seemed to hold their collective breath. Remy cleared her throat as she slid a PDL before Redic. The leader took his seat, dismissing the argument with a sudden irate lull. Chase dropped his chin and stared at his lap. He shouldn't have said that about Caelya and Redic's children. He would apologize later. And to add to his guilt, the wound on his leg began to pulse with a grueling inferno.

"We just suffered a sloppy rescue of an even sloppier mistake," Redic said softly. "I am angry, gentlemen. I'm thankful that *almost* everyone made it home safely, but I am angry."

Armand's quiet voice piped through the PDL link Remy had activated. "I have news of Trista," he said.

Chase straightened up, trying to catch a glimpse of Armand's image. It really should have been enough to know that she was alive, but the same old obsession returned. He had to bring her home. Redic nodded, giving Armand permission to proceed.

"She is currently on a medical shuttle, undergoing the restructuring procedure again. The shuttle is en route to Crenet and is scheduled to arrive within three days. If all goes well, she is supposed to report to her employer, Finnegan Streuben, the following morning."

Clenching his fists tightly, Chase closed his eyes and pounded the arms of his chair. They would completely strip her down to nothing. The first round had already impaired her. Now she was enduring it all over again. Poor Trista.

"They nearly lost her," Armand continued. "Terces said he didn't know how much more her brain could take, and it was possible that through this second restructuring, she could slip into a state of brain-death."

Chase shot out of his chair and hobbled to the wall. By the Crown, they had really hurt her. There was no stopping it. No protecting her or saving her. It had already been done. They had taken her away from him again, not just physically, but mentally and emotionally as well.

"Is there any chance of reversal, Armand?" Brax asked.

"As before, they said it was a permanent change, but Niveli asked if Chase had healed her. I don't think the doctors are banking on Logia interaction. I don't know what you all might be able to do, should you encounter Trista. But be warned. They've upped the tamper-proof triggers on those devices. Any interaction, at any level, could kill her."

"We still have to try to reach her," Seraph said.

"I would do it sooner rather than later," Armand advised. "And your best bet is going to be through Streuben. He won't expect us to try again so soon."

"Then we set up another assignment for her," Redic murmured, already focused on the new plan. "Chase, Seraph, I want you to take this one."

Chase spun around, looking at him. Really? After insisting on grounding the crew and the things Chase had said, Redic was going to send him out?

Redic answered his unspoken question with a nod. "Trista needs you. Your gifts. You can shut those things down. Seraph, you and Selah ..." He paused, lowering his eyes. Chase knew that Redic was about to put his most precious treasure on the line for this rescue. "You and Selah can help in the restoration."

"Thank you, sir," Chase said, his brows furrowing with contrition.

"But this is the last-ditch effort," Redic said, staring at Chase. "If this fails, you won't get another chance. We have to let her go."

"I understand." Chase ran his hand over his stubbly chin, grateful for the opportunity, but fearful of what was to come. "I understand completely."

CHAPTER 28

Day 9458 PLR: Crenet

Krissa opened her eyes slowly, blinking as her world came back into focus. Her little apartment—which wasn't much, but it was home—surrounded her with familiarity and comfort. She'd just had the strangest dream. An assignment had led her to an asylum, where she was taken prisoner by rioting inmates. They carried slayers and threatened her with interrogation rods. She shivered under her blanket. It seemed so real.

"Carlisle." Her link crackled with activation.

Streuben. She wasn't late, was she? She'd been sleeping an extra couple of hours the last few nights. Close to a week ago, Dr. Terces had informed her that the tumor had entered a new stage. She was to check in with him every other day. He increased her dosage of capustatim and gave her stronger medications to try to counteract the growth. They did nothing to help the constant, raging headache she now felt.

Pushing back her cover, she sat up and reached for the link on the table next to her bed. "Yes, Mr. Streuben?"

"You have your clearance paper yet?"

Clearance paper? Krissa sat up. On the little table next to her, a red certificate of clearance from the interrogators. It wasn't a dream. It happened. It really happened.

"Yes," she murmured, lifting the certificate in her hands to read it. Her brain felt like mush, which made it difficult to hold on to reality. The certificate was the evidence she needed to cement the dream into fact.

"Good," Streuben responded. "I have a list of assignments for you. Can you come in early?"

"Yeah," she muttered. "I've got nothing better to do."

"Good girl. See you in a few minutes," Streuben said.

Krissa stood, the rush of dizziness swirling her mind into confusion. Her vision blurred with white light. She squeezed her eyes closed until the numbing dizziness passed. Pressing her fingers to her forehead, she surveyed the room. "Where do I keep my clothes?" she asked herself.

A small dresser sat in the corner near a closet. Well, that made sense. Clothes in a dresser. She crossed the room and opened one of the drawers to select a lavender—no. No, that wasn't right. When had she ever worn lavender? This drawer contained only two Legacy uniforms, both the same color, size, and style. She really didn't need anything else. This was her life, after all.

She dressed quickly, shaking off the strange sensation that nibbled at the back of her mind. Going to work would help. She could focus on her assignments and not have to think too much about anything else. Maybe she could even shake that haunting dream. No, it wasn't a dream. Another gaze at the red certificate confirmed that.

After tugging on her boots, she folded the certificate into her pocket, grabbed her personal tools that always sat near the door, and headed for Streuben's office. It wasn't far, and Krissa made it within five minutes. Streuben would be pleased. Funny—she had heard his voice telling her that she was fired. Must have been part of her dream.

But it wasn't a dream.

She rubbed her eyes and pressed her fingers to her forehead again. Her skin felt moist and clammy, although heat raced through her veins. She had to pull herself together. Climbing the stairs of the office building, she moved inside, wishing for a different job. A different life.

Streuben sat behind his desk, barely glancing up as she walked in. He held up a finger and gestured for her to sit. "Yeah, well, I can't promise anything, but I can try to fit you in sometime today." He spoke into a private link.

Krissa silently dropped into a chair, listening to the other end of his conversation. Streuben always turned up the volume as high as it would go. The small speaker and a hiss distorted the clarity of the voice, but it sounded like a man begging for assistance with his ship's PDL integration system.

"Okay. We'll do what we can," Streuben said, flipping a pen into his hands to scribble a note on a small pad. "It will probably be toward the end of the day, and extra fees will be tacked on for the short notice."

A gush of thanks and the promise of a hefty tip poured through the link. Krissa knew the tip would go to Streuben and not the SA who actually did the work.

"Very good. Yes." Streuben closed the connection, looking Krissa up and down. "You're fast."

"Didn't have much else to do today." Krissa forced a smile to her face. "What have you got?"

"Clearance paper," Streuben demanded, holding out his hand.

Krissa pulled the folded red square from her pocket and placed it in his hand. The way he eyed her made her feel rather uncomfortable. She hadn't done anything wrong. He stared at the certificate before him.

"So you're free and clear?" he asked.

Krissa nodded. The last few days or so were fuzzy in her memory, but she chalked that up to the time with the interrogators and the disturbing news from Terces. Luckily, her memory kicked in. "After watching the surveillance tapes from the ship and considering the report from the interrogators, the judge decided that I did everything I could have possibly done, and that I was never in league with the Ghosts."

"And so now you're coming back here ..." Streuben lifted an eyebrow.

"You called me," Krissa retorted. Not wise, she figured, as she needed him. She bowed her head with shame and swallowed her pride. "I need a job, Mr. Streuben."

"If I remember correctly," Streuben leaned back in his chair, waving the clearance paper back and forth, "you were going to quit."

He was really going to draw this out, wasn't he? She wouldn't beg, but she might have to come close. Blast it all. "I was wrong about that. This is good job, and you're a good boss. Besides, no one else will take me on. Not even with the clearance," she admitted, gesturing toward the certificate.

Streuben nodded, eyeing the paper again. "Don't know that I should, either."

Krissa took a deep breath. She hated that her life was in this man's hands.

And she hated that he toyed with her as such. But she had nowhere else to turn. It was either this or— Well, she didn't know what else.

With a grunt, Streuben lowered the paper and turned to his DDL. "I got something that just came in. It's a dumpy little ship. Not like what you're used to doing. But I suppose I could add it to your list."

Krissa nodded with feigned eagerness. So this was how it was going to be now. She'd get stuck with all the lower-rung assignments. But it was a job, right?

Streuben passed her a PDL, which contained the full layout of duties. "Can you handle all that?"

Krissa read over the assignments. She'd certainly be busy. Most of the fixes seemed fairly easy, though. Rewiring jobs and such. And every job was within the walls of Reticulum. She rested the PDL on Streuben's desk. "Yeah, I can do this."

"All right." Streuben returned his attention to his DDL, situating the keypad in front of him. He typed for several moments before looking over the screen at her. Impatience and annoyance tainted his face with an ugly expression. "What are you waiting for?"

Krissa blinked as she lowered her eyes and rose. The confusion had resurfaced. "Sorry. I'm a little out of it today." She reached for the PDL.

Streuben's fingers snatched the PDL from her grasp like a greedy child grabbing the last piece of candy. "This is mine. I'm synchronizing the list with the UV computer. Really, Carlisle, it's like you've never done this."

Stepping back toward the door, Krissa frowned. "Sorry," she murmured under her breath as she headed for the door. UV computer. What was the UV computer? She tried to remember, but nothing was coming.

"That last shuttle is docked on the outskirts of the city. Apparently, they're stranded and waiting for assistance." Streuben rolled his eyes, obviously feeling no sympathy for his needy clients. "They can wait until your list is complete, though. And I want you to charge 'em double."

"Doub—?"

"You heard me," Streuben cut her off as he stood, smoothing out his violet-colored suit. It seemed like it might have been black long ago, but had faded with age and wear. As he crossed to one of the filing cabinets to pull out a mirror, she noticed that his pants rode high along his ankles. He looked ridiculous. "Now get moving. The utility vehicle is waiting outside. I've got important people coming in, and I don't want them to see you here."

Utility vehicle. Of course. UV.

He waved her toward the door. Some things never changed. But she owed him for taking her back. "Thanks, Mr. Streuben," she whispered.

He grunted again, walking back to his desk. His focus settled on the DDL. As she walked from the office, Krissa wrapped her arms around herself, realizing that he was the closest thing to a father that she knew. And how very little he really cared about her. Just one word of approval ...

Why was she thinking such sentimental thoughts?

Settling into the tiny UV, she closed her eyes. "Focus, Krissa. Get it together," she scolded herself. Her mind brought up images from the dream she'd had—the inmates who'd captured her. In the dream, they felt more like friends. And one of them held her fascination. She couldn't make out his face, but he called to her. She shook her head. "It was just a dream," she reminded herself. She forced herself to remember how frightning they were in reality.

She rubbed the tears from her eyes and keyed in the coordinates to the first assignment. The UV's engine burped purple-gray smoke before it died out. After three more tries, she finally got the old heap to ignite. It was definitely going to be a long day. Maybe she should have just stayed in bed.

◆

Chase stared at the small craft docked across the prep strip. They'd done a good job. The shuttle was swift and in top running condition, but with the help of Church, Seraph, Cam, and Brax, it now appeared decrepit. Grease would probably never forgive them for damaging the body the way they had, regardless of the fact that they had stolen it from the Legacy fleet. Chase was sure that they'd all be in for logging hours on repair duty when they returned. If they ...

Seraph crossed from the docking field, gesturing back toward the ship as he took a seat next to Chase on the rickety space crate. "Pretty authentic, don't you think?"

"It'll do," Chase answered, dropping his eyes to his mud-crusted hands. He'd spent quite some time caking dirt and water along the viewport. It couldn't just be slopped on, as it was their getaway vessel and he would have to see clearly to pilot them home.

"It's going to work, Chase. You have to believe that."

Rubbing at the mud, Chase shook his head. "It's not that, Ser. I'm questioning why I took it this far."

"You love her," Seraph answered.

"You're right. You're absolutely right. I do … love her." Chase looked up at his friend. "But I put her before the Crown. And I've hurt my friends, my crew—" Running his dirty fingers over his hair, he shook his head. "Blast, the things I said to your dad …"

"He's heard worse." Seraph smiled a little. "He's strong. And understanding, particularly in this situation."

"We spoke just before we launched. I apologized, and he forgave me. Graciously."

"Then it's time to forgive yourself and let it go."

Chase pushed off the crate, pacing a few steps away and back. "Are we doing the right thing here, Ser?"

"Approaching Trista? Trying to bring her home? Only you can answer that, man," Seraph replied. Chase could sense a hint of annoyance, which was perfectly reasonable. He had asked many people to risk a lot for this one dicey chance.

"She's precious to me. And I know that many others back at the Reserve care about her. But if this fails—"

Seraph stood, pointing at him. "That's what's behind this, isn't it? You're afraid that we won't be able to reach her."

Chase froze, whispering, "I don't know that I can take coming so close again."

Placing a hand on his shoulder, Seraph squeezed with gentle reassurance. "This isn't about us, Chase. You keep forgetting that. Echo had to remind me. The Crown is working through this, and we need to place our trust in Him."

Chase closed his eyes with a nod. "Run me through the plan," he said.

"I will, and then I think you need some time alone. You need to get your heart in the right place." Seraph launched into the full explanation. "Cole is getting into makeup as we speak. He'll act as the elderly caretaker of the shuttle and keep watch for Trista. You and I wait in the cockpit while Cam, Brax, and Selah wait belowdeck on the *Fool*. Cam wants to keep Selah as protected as possible. I'm sure you understand that. Once Trista arrives, Cole alerts Cam, who will then deliver Selah to us. Cole hops on the *Fool*, and they head for home.

"You try to disable the chips in Trista's brain while Selah and I stand by. If Trista needs medical care, Selah will try to restore her. If she needs mental reconciliation, I'll be there. You fly us home."

"And if she—" Chase wanted to ask about a contingency should Trista die, but couldn't bring himself to put words to the question.

"We'll handle that if it comes to it, Chase," Seraph answered, a frown lining his brow. "But try to have a little faith. If you do this for your own purposes on your own strength, you will surely fail. And Trista will be the one to pay the price."

Chase nodded. Seraph was right. Again. He had to put his faith beyond his own abilities and trust in the One who could handle the situation.

"We still have some time before she's scheduled to arrive," Seraph said. "Why don't you get onboard, clean up a bit, and then close yourself up in the sleeper cabin? I'll make sure you're not disturbed. That will give you a while to seek the guidance you need."

"I don't know—"

"That wasn't a request from your friend, Chase. That was a direct order from your commanding officer." Seraph pointed and jerked his head toward the ship. "Dismissed."

Chase noticed the smile in Seraph's eyes. He'd tried to hide it behind the stern look he used, but Chase saw through the facade. He grinned, shaking his head. "You look just like the old man," he said with a chuckle.

Throwing a punch against Chase's arm, Seraph broke into a laugh. "Get on the ship."

The two walked together in silence to the shuttle. Chase was grateful for Seraph's presence and leadership. Optimism began to rise again, and gave Chase hope for a fresh start. He just prayed that the fresh start included his wife.

CHAPTER 29

"All right, describe for me again how she acted," Dr. Terces said, sitting across from Streuben. He sat on the very edge of the seat, not wishing to get too comfortable in the filthy rathole of an office. After receiving a flustered message from Streuben, Terces had decided it would be best to meet with him to find out more details.

"She was scatterbrained something awful, Doc. She didn't remember routines. Gazed off into space a lot." Streuben shook his head. "It's like she went cuckoo." He said the last word with a singsong tone, followed by a nervous chuckle.

Terces glared at the repugnant man behind the desk. Streuben obviously didn't understand the gravity of the situation. Yes, there was a distinct possibility that they would soon lose Krissa, but all the more, it meant that Terces's career with ExMed could come to an end. After the last board meeting, he had met with Admiral Niveli and the Tribunal. They expressed their displeasure over the incident with Krissa and the *Straightjacket*, as well as all the backpedaling ExMed had to do. Terces was demoted from ExMed and ordered to terminate the project, but he was able to convince the Tribunal to give him one more chance with Krissa. This time, however, failure would be absolutely unacceptable. If things turned messy, Terces might not only lose his position, but his life.

"Where is she?" he asked through clenched teeth.

"Gads, Doc, I gave her a whole list of assignments."

"Where?" he demanded.

Streuben pushed the blanket of papers around on his desk, finally coming up with a PDL. He beat on the screen with his stubby fingers. "Uh ..." He dragged out the syllable until it grated on Terces's nerves. Streuben found the answer before Terces attacked the man's jugular vein. "Here."

He plunked the PDL down on top of the loose pages. Terces scanned the list, which sent Krissa all over the city. Streuben was apparently trying to make this as difficult as possible.

"Link her," Terces ordered.

"That goes against my policies, Doc—"

Rising, Terces leaned over the desk, getting into Streuben's face. "I don't care about your policies. Link her now!" he shouted. His patience wore too thin with this man.

"Um ... I—"

Streuben's link buzzed under the mountain of files. As he searched for it, the folders and papers slid off his desk, amassing into a new jumbled heap on the floor. Terces closed his eyes and counted to five before Streuben finally came up with the device. "It's her," he said.

"Mr. Streuben, sir?" Krissa's voice came across the link. She sounded uncertain. Lost.

Terces shook his head and whispered, "Don't tell her I'm here."

Jamming a finger into his ear, Streuben rocked back in his chair. "What is it, Carlisle?" he asked.

"Well, the good news is that I've already knocked out half of the list."

Streuben erupted, "Only half of th—"

"It's taken a whole lot longer than I'd wanted it to," Krissa explained. "I'm having trouble focusing, and my head is throbbing nonstop."

Terces frowned. Things didn't sound good for Krissa. And he didn't know what else he could do for her. Perhaps the Tribunal had been right. Terminating the project was probably their safest—and best—option. And he'd rather accept a subordinate position in the hospital than be killed by the Tribunal.

The crass man picked his teeth with the finger that had just been in his ear. "Sounds like you're making excuses, Carlisle," he said.

"Oh, no. No. But I'm at the Zenith recruitment office and—"

"You're only on that one, Carlisle? What's taking you so long?" Streuben scolded.

"Look, I'm just behind today. I'm not thinking clearly. And I need your help," she said softly.

"My help?" Streuben's tone implied that he was far from pleased.

Terces mouthed, "Find out more." He was anxious to hear what boggled Krissa's mind. If it was something complex, then there might be hope.

"Yeah, okay," Streuben said with a sigh. "What's going on, Carlisle?"

"It's a rewiring sequence on a processing unit. The wires are jumbled together and it looks like someone tinkered with it at some point, maybe trying to fix it. The patching looks wrong, but I can't remember where to begin. The colors are red, green, yellow, blue, white, black," Krissa explained.

Closing his eyes, Terces shook his head again. Even *he* knew how to solve that issue. They had indeed tampered too much with her brain.

"You should be able to do that in your sleep, Carlisle." Streuben sucked on his teeth, examining his fingernail.

"I know," she answered with dismay, "but I can't remember."

"Okay." Streuben's tone changed to one of almost pity as he straightened up in his chair. "The sequence is yellow, green, blue on top. White, red, black on bottom."

"Thank you," Krissa said. A long moment of silence led Terces to assume that she was proceeding with Streuben's instruction. "That's it. The DDL sparked right up."

"Tell her to come back here," Terces murmured quietly. "Immediately."

Streuben nodded, staring at the doctor as he spoke into the link. "Maybe you should head back to the office, Krissa. I'll give your assignments to someone else."

"Um, I'm close to that last docking bay assignment," Krissa replied with an air of determination. "Let me at least take that one, okay?"

Terces placed a single finger over his lips, then pointed to the link. In response, Streuben silenced his end to allow them to speak freely.

"Docking bay?" Terces asked.

"Some stranded ship linked this morning, needing assistance."

"Where?"

Streuben shrugged. "Some old bay that's hardly used anymore. Near the old Logia sector, on the opposite side of the Castellum ruins."

It would be a good part of the city to take care of the dirty business. A simple mix of her prescriptions, at higher levels, would provide a lethal dose.

Because of her medical history, no one would think to investigate beyond the initial pronouncement of overdose on her part as cause of death.

Terces nodded his approval, gesturing again to the link. "We'll meet her there."

Activating the link with a wary eye on the doctor, Streuben said, "All right, Carlisle, how about if I meet you there?"

"There's no need ..."

Pounding his fist on the desk, Terces gave another forceful nod. If Streuben backed down, they would miss a prime opportunity to rid themselves of a growing problem. They had to get to Krissa. Straightaway.

Streuben answered with a silent raise of his hand, assuring Terces that he had the situation under control. To Krissa, he sweetened his words with gentleness and concern. "In case you need help, you know. And then I can make sure you get home safely."

The response carried hesitation and uncertainty. "O-okay, sure," Krissa said. "See you soon."

"That you will," Terces murmured as Streuben offered his farewell salutation to Krissa.

Tossing the link on the desk, Streuben lifted an eyebrow. "What's the plan, Doc?"

Terces paced in front of the desk, fidgeting with his fingers as he walked. "I must stop by my office for a moment. Do you have transportation?"

Streuben kicked back in his chair, plopping an enormous foot on the desk. "Only my personal—"

"Forget it. You ride with me. It's time to resolve the problem," Terces said as he moved toward the door. He flashed a wad of pallads, triggering Streuben to scramble quickly from his seat. "Do exactly as I tell you, and your return will be far greater than what you've seen from the Legacy."

A sinister smile slunk across Streuben's lips. It was even more disconcerting with the accompanying amusement that danced in his eyes. Perhaps Terces had picked the right man after all.

The ship, if it could be called that, was on its last legs. Krissa found herself wishing that she had an escort or even a personal stinger. The docking bay was in a neglected area, and there didn't seem to be a soul in sight, but it was creepy nonetheless. Streuben's presence would be a comfort at this point.

She knocked on the rusted ramp and waited. How was it that she felt safer among a group of imprisoned lunatics than here on Crenet? She briefly entertained the question of whether Streuben had set her up for something worse than she had faced on the *Haulaway*. Of course not, she told herself. He wouldn't be coming to meet her if he had.

The ramp lowered, slowly at first, with a harsh, rusty squeal. As gravity took over, the metal walkway clattered to the ground. Krissa startled at the loud sound, then peered up the ramp. "Hello?"

"Come on in," an older man's voice floated from within.

She gingerly stepped on the ramp, hoping that it would hold her weight as she climbed aboard. The inside of the ship wasn't much better. Exposed wiring and gritty dirt lined the walls. These people must be expecting her to perform a miracle.

"I'm here to—"

"Yeah, yeah," the older man's voice said. Where was he? "What you're lookin' fer is in the cockpit. Up th' ladder."

Krissa swallowed and turned to see a half ladder that led to a door with peeling paint. She shuddered to think about what condition the cockpit was in. Gripping her tool pack, she climbed up and opened the door. The cockpit was mostly dark. The viewport was covered with grime, allowing very little light through. Krissa sighed as she tried to determine where to begin.

"You came."

Krissa blinked in the dark. The male voice sounded familiar, like a distant dream of childhood before more vivid memories start taking shape. His arms encircled her in a tight, warm embrace. She stiffened and held her breath as her tool pack fell to the floor. She'd been right, whether Streuben set it up or not. This man expected something from her that she wasn't willing to give.

"Please, sir ..." she said, struggling against him.

"Sir?" the man said, withdrawing a little. "Trista, it's me."

Stabbing pain in her head sucked the air from her lungs. A soft groan slipped between her lips, but she covered quickly by saying, "M-my name is Krissa. I'd prefer to keep our interaction on a business level, if you please. You may call me Miss Carlisle."

The man dropped his arms to his sides. She heard him take a slow breath. "They took you away completely this time, didn't they?"

Krissa's instinct kicked in, telling her to step back. Distance was good. Safe. She tucked her hair behind her ear before her hand nervously fiddled with her ring finger. "I don't know what you're talking about," she answered. Part of her told her to flee, but something else made her stay.

"Oh, by the Crown," the man muttered, his eyes darting about in frustration.

The headache surged again. "P-perhaps I should be going ..."

The man grabbed her hand and pulled her into a passionate, frantic kiss. The surprise tingled through her nerves, and she pounded her fists against him, but soon found herself relaxing into it. Something about him stuck in her brain. Something in the far reaches of her mind ...

He pulled back, holding her at arm's length. "Anything?"

She took a shaky breath. She wasn't sure what he was expecting from her. "Um ..."

"Trista, try to remember me. Please." The man lifted his chin and spoke to someone else, "Please, my King."

He jerked her into another fevered kiss. The heated throbbing sent waves of pain crashing through her head. Snapshots of memories flashed in her thoughts. Images captured in time. The Ghost base she called home. The sister she thought she'd lost. The man who'd pursued her heart and eventually laid claim to her as his wife. The man ... Leighton. Chase. Chase!

"Chase!" she cried before even more vicious pain ripped through her skull. Her entire body stiffened as every muscle went rigid with fire.

◆

Chase grabbed Krissa, jerking her to him. Her eyes had rolled back into her head, and he couldn't get her to respond. "Seraph!" he called out, unsuccessfully trying to calm his panic.

His cry must have been enough to rouse her. She looked up at him. The lively expression normally glowing on her face had drained back into the drone state. "Wh-what ... are you doing?" Krissa demanded. She pushed at his chest, wriggling in his arms.

He'd lost Trista again. Blast!

"Let go of me!" she shrieked.

Seraph hopped into the cockpit and marched to the couple. He placed a hand over Krissa's forehead, closing his eyes. Chase had to tighten his grip to keep hold of her. She screamed, trying to pull away from both him and Seraph.

"I can't do it, Chase," Seraph said, looking at him. "I can't even get close enough to tap into her memory."

Krissa yanked on her arms, breaking free. Chase tackled her, but not before she found her link and pressed her alarm to call in Zeniths. Adrenaline took over as he pinned her to the floor. Seraph knelt down next to them.

Cole, still under his mask of heavy wrinkles and a set of dirty coveralls, poked his head into the cockpit. "*Fool's* landed. Cam said he caught word of a shuttle full of Zeniths on its way. A personal shuttle has also requested permission to dock near us. I'm tagging out with Selah," he said hastily, disappearing again.

"You have to do it, Chase," Seraph insisted. "I can help you. With Selah on her way, we can care for Trista, but you have to disable those chips."

"It could kill her," he whispered, looking down at the wide, frightened eyes of his wife.

"Let me go!" she whimpered, fighting against him.

"The fluctuations are already taking their toll, Chase. You're going to have to choose," Seraph said softly.

Chase studied Trista's face—the warm and tender brown eyes, now frenzied with panic and fear; the delicate cheekbones and nose, heated with anger; and the lips whose smile could melt him in a heartbeat, now crying and pleading with him to release her. Seraph was right. He had to do it.

He wedged his hand behind her head, his fingers closing around the base of her skull. He closed his eyes, lifting a prayer to the Ruler Prince. In an instant, he could sense the inner workings of the tiny chips that had stolen all of Trista's memories. She swatted at him, but he couldn't fight that now. His battle was much more involved.

Using his mind, he disabled the first chip with relative ease. The second one gave him a bit more difficulty. It touched crucial tissue that aided in Trista's everyday function. As he rendered the chip inoperative, it sent out shockwaves through Trista's brain.

"No!" Chase cried, feeling her seize beneath him.

"Keep it together," Seraph advised. "Selah is here now. We'll take care of Trista. Just do what you need to do, Chase."

Swallowing hard, Chase focused on the third chip. He could tell that this chip was different from the others. It seemed to have a higher level of function, more powerful. And she was more dependent on it, too. "Stand by," he whispered to Seraph and Selah. He had no idea what the reaction would be.

He directed his full effort into the chip. The bio-interface relay ran deep, but Chase managed to sever the connection. Trista's body shook and jerked in his grasp. Chase heard himself gasp, then Seraph reassure him, "It's okay, Chase. She's safe. Keep going."

He found a cache that retained Trista's memory. "By the Crown," he whispered as he plowed through the data path, releasing the flood of memories back into Trista's brain.

"Slow down," Seraph said. "She's going into shock. Selah—"

Opening his eyes to connect with Seraph, Chase murmured, "That's it. It's done."

"Then back off and let us take over." The look on Seraph's face worried Chase.

Chase reluctantly released Trista, scampering back against the console. Her limbs sprawled lifelessly on the metal floor while brother and sister Logia swathed her head in a gentle healing glow. He added his own selfish prayers as he watched, begging the Crown for mercy and grace.

Cam's voice tore him from his focus, shouting an order over the ship link, "Chase, you need to get in the air. We've got a regiment of Zeniths en route to the bay."

"I—" Chase stammered. He was frozen with fear over Trista. She wasn't moving ...

"Chase, do it!" Seraph hollered. "We didn't come this far just to get caught by Zeebs."

Misery wrapped Chase in a chokehold. His eyes remained fast on Trista. If she ever awoke from what he'd just put her through, would she remember anything? Would she even be able to function?

"Do it for Trista," Seraph pleaded softly over his shoulder. "At least get her home."

That was the inspiration Chase needed to move. With another brief prayer, he replaced the fright and anxiety with resolve and purpose. Unlike before, they could at least take Trista physically away from the Legacy. He climbed into the pilot's chair and ignited the thrusters.

Connecting the ship link, Chase asked, "Cam, are you up?"

"On our way," Cam answered, along with licks of static. "Tell Selah I'll see her at home." Chase could tell that last part wasn't intended for Selah. It was an order for Chase to return Cam's wife safely to Revenant, regardless of the situation.

"Will do," Chase acknowledged. "And thank you."

Chase watched for a more few seconds as Selah and Seraph hovered over Trista. Her face and head were still bathed in a faint, white glow. Whatever they were doing to help her certainly was taking a lot longer than he'd ever witnessed. But he had to trust that the Crown would now show favor.

He input the course for Viam and lifted the ship off the ground. Easing it out of the docking bay, his eyes caught sight of a bunch of confused Zeniths surrounding Dr. Terces and another man. The doctor raised his hand, shaking his fist toward the shuttle. His face snarled with anger and resentment.

"Blast you, Doc," Chase whispered as he pulled back on the throttle.

CHAPTER 30

The waiting area of the medbay was quite possibly one of the most disturbing places Chase had ever been, and that was saying a lot considering his sentence on the *Straightjacket*. But just in the last day or so, since landing back on Revenant, nearly everyone had come by to wish him the best. That was most frustrating. He wasn't the one needing the well wishes. It was his wife.

Seraph and Selah had done all they could. By the time they entered the Pathway heading home, Selah was exhausted. Seraph was, too, but he said he couldn't leave Trista in the state she was in. After that news, once they had cleared the Pathway, Chase pushed the shuttle to its limits to get to Revenant. Remy even told him that she'd nearly ordered the shuttle to be shot down because he'd disregarded the requests for clearance codes. Redic, however, recognized the mannerisms of the pilot.

When Lila and Sterling came to see Trista, they had spent some time crying with Chase. It was good. Necessary. Even before Chase was imprisoned, he'd never truly grieved the loss of Trista.

But now he sat alone, elbows on his knees with his head hanging, on a bench made of three metal chairs welded together. He'd been in with Trista, but the constant beep of her heart monitor drove him crazy. Seraph and Brax both assured him that it was only a precautionary measure. That she was fine. That she was just resting. But each beep reminded him of his failure and incompetence as a husband to protect his wife. Brax promised to alert him as soon as she awoke, provided that he get some rest. Even so, he couldn't go very far from her, certainly not across the Reserve to their quarters.

With a heavy sigh, he opened his eyes. A pair of black boots stood before him. He lifted his head and sat back to see Redic Clairet looking down as him. Oh, he wasn't in the mood to be reprimanded. Hopefully, Redic knew that.

"Any improvement?" the leader asked in a hushed tone.

"Not really. Seraph comes by every couple of hours, and Brax has her hooked up to all sorts of monitors. The slightest movement and the nurses' station will light up like a post-ECT inmate on the *Straightjacket*," Chase muttered.

"I know you're trying to be funny, but that little wisecrack really wasn't." Redic sat down next to him. "I understand Brax removed several other devices from her forehead."

Chase nodded. "Said he thought they were used to emit some kind of painful signal to her brain."

"Terrible," Redic growled. "You've been dealt a rotten hand, Chase."

"I don't need you to tell me that, sir," Chase said, glancing at him. "With all due respect."

Redic shrugged, his brow falling with a frown. "Do you remember the conversation we had just after Trista's memorial service?"

"The pep talk?" Chase broke a sarcastic grin.

"That's the one," Redic said with a gentle chuckle. "I told you not to choose vengeance."

"I remember. I have to be honest, sir." Chase paused as he leaned on his knees again. "That's what kept me from obliterating the doctors and the staff."

Redic matched his stance, offering a PDL to Chase. "You're a stronger man than I, Chase."

Chase examined the PDL. There wasn't anything extraordinary about it. In fact, it looked like an older model, which really was nothing more than memory storage. "What is this?"

"You know, sometimes a little vengeance is unavoidable," Redic straightened up again, planting his hands on his knees, "particularly if it prevents others from suffering at the hands of those who have already done tremendous damage."

"Sir?" Chase asked, still not sure what the old man was getting at.

"Armand, Zak, and I did some digging. We found highly unfavorable information on all of the doctors involved in the *Straightjacket* fiasco, as well as some dirt on the doctor who maltreated Trista. Unethical treatment of patients. Abhorrent practices. Concealed deaths. All covered under the guise of ExMed." Redic pointed to the PDL in Chase's hand. "The information will be delivered to the Agency of Justice, by way of a Zephyr officer, within the hour."

Chase stared at the PDL. Redic was fooling himself. The Legacy took care of its own. "Forgive me, sir, but the agency won't prosecute. They're all protected."

Redic shook his head, pointing to the device. "These details come from private, individual documents that escaped ExMed reports. While the ExMed policies are quite liberal in their handling and treatment of patients, I think the agency, as well as the Bands media, will find that these particular doctors were far beyond the permissible bounds."

The news astounded Chase. As a Logia, he couldn't bring himself to wish poor fortune on anyone. These doctors were enemies of the worst kind. And yet their determined fates were about to be played out, the retribution plain and visible for Chase to see. He battled with satisfaction, instead offering up prayer for the men who had altered his world.

Carefully wording his question, Chase gazed down at the floor. "Does this measure of vengeance allow for confrontation?"

Redic blinked, obviously puzzled by Chase's question. "I suppose it does."

By the Crown …

Chase rose, clutching the PDL. "Permission to make a quick personal run, sir?"

Chewing on his bottom lip, Redic stood, narrowing his eyes. "Take Church. And come home this time," he said, deadly serious.

Acknowledging the order with a salute to Redic, Chase stepped back, nearly running into Brax. "Keep an eye on my girl," Chase said, pointing at him.

"Um, she's not going anywhere," Brax responded, curiosity in his tone.

Redic patted Brax on the back as they disappeared into Trista's room. Chase turned, dashing down the hall toward the docking bay. He'd link Church along the way. If he didn't go as the moment propelled him, he'd never leave Trista's side. And he had an important appointment with a particular doctor.

◆

DAY 9462 PLR: CRENET

The study at the Terces home was dark, as the doctor preferred it to be. It was his place to think, to study—his sanctuary. On Crenet, it was nearly impossible to find a quiet, shaded spot, but with the thick custom drapes lining the tall windows, he could shut out the relentless sunshine and the bustling craziness, and focus or even just relax. He closed the door behind him with a soft click and crossed the shadows to his desk.

Pulling out the cushioned chair, Terces sank into it, resting his head against the back to stare into the void. He'd lost his most important subject. He should have known that Leighton would come after her again. Streuben should have been far more watchful. But it was all too easy to lay the blame at Streuben's feet. Terces should have kept her closer.

The Tribunal wanted success. That's why he'd pushed Trista so hard. He needed the affirmation of the Tribunal. Affirmation meant more power. More money. More security. And now ...

Taking in a cleansing breath, Terces forced calm into his thoughts. He'd dealt with setbacks before. No doubt he'd encounter them again. He'd just have to do some quick thinking to find his way out of this one.

Leaning forward, Terces snapped on his desk lamp. His eyes immediately flew to the figure standing next to the desk. He hadn't heard anyone in the room with him, so it startled him when the light shone on Leighton's furious expression.

In absolute silence, Leighton leaned over the desk, placing his hand palm down on the wood. When he straightened up, Terces noticed three tiny devices against the grain. The ITCs. More specifically, Trista's ITCs.

"Did you—" He began to ask if the Ghosts had surgically removed them from Trista's brain. That would have killed her instantly.

Leighton didn't answer the question directly. Instead, he glared at the doctor and said, "Never again."

"How did you get these?" Terces asked, scooping up the devices with his fingers.

"There are many things you will never know, Doctor." Leighton's eyes bored into Terces, rattling him with discomfort. "But I want you to know this. Trista lives and breathes, and will continue to do so until her Creator King, the Crown, calls her home to eternity. And I pray for your immortal soul that you will take a knee before Him by the time you breathe your last."

That sounded like a veiled threat. "And do you plan to have a hand in that?" Terces asked, his voice turning meek with a sudden fear.

Leighton shook his head. "That is not for my choosing. I am Logia, and as such, I forgive you for what's been done. But it is within our power to stop you, and that's precisely what we've done."

Meeting his gaze with a cold, even stare, Terces asked, "What do you mean?"

Stepping back near one of the windows, Leighton gestured toward the door of the study as a bell rang, alerting Terces to the arrival of someone at the front door. "That is a squadron of Zeniths coming to arrest you, Doctor. While I can guarantee that your life is safe from my hands, I can also assure you that your career is over.

"A judge has given a recommendation that you, your cohorts here on Crenet, and the team of doctors from the *Straightjacket* experience 'rehabilitation' in the mines of Ferus. You will make your restitution to those you've hurt by laboring for the Legacy," Leighton said.

Terces searched for delight or gratification in Leighton's eyes but only saw a haunting sorrow. "You don't wish for us to suffer in the same manner as you?" he asked.

Once again, Leighton shook his head. "I don't wish for you to suffer at all, sir. I only wish for swift justice."

"How can you say such things?" Terces demanded, a raging anger at Leighton's noble reaction boiling under his skin. He lifted the ITCs in his hand. "After we did this? After you experienced the *Straightjacket*?"

"Perhaps you'll be led to understand someday," Leighton replied. "The answer doesn't lie in me." He raised his eyes, murmuring a quiet prayer.

A knock at the door drew Terces's attention. He turned, his pulse quickening as fear of what awaited him gripped his heart. If what Leighton said was true ...

"Sir, there are several Zeniths here with me, insisting that they speak to you," Terces's butler said through the door.

Terces's chest rose and fell with panicked breaths. He whipped back around toward Leighton, but the room was empty. Glaring down at the ITCs in his hand, he crumpled them in his fist and threw them across the room with an outraged cry. The door fell open as Zeniths burst into the room, slayers cocked and aimed.

It was over.

EPILOGUE

DAY 9467 PLR: REVENANT

Trista opened her eyes to a white wall. It was quiet. Much quieter than the last time she had awakened. There had been a regular, steady, beeping sound, but now there was just silence. Peaceful silence, too. Nothing frightning. Nothing disconcerting. She blinked as her gaze fell to the velvety burgundy blanket that encompassed her. She knew this. She was home. On Revenant.

Sitting up quickly, she looked about, catching Chase's joyful, disbelieving stare. His hair had grown longer, and stubble shadowed his chin. His green eyes held a new maturity about them. The experience had certainly changed him. Every bit of her breath left her lungs. He was the only thing she cared about. The only person she wanted to see.

He climbed onto the bed next to her, his hand sliding across her cheek as he stared into her eyes. "Are you …?"

Relief flooded into her heart. Her mind retained a clarity that helped her to know that this wasn't just a dream—being in the same, safe place with her husband, whom she fully recognized. A prayer of thanks lifted from her heart.

Pressing against his hand, Trista nodded. "I'm fine," she whispered.

"Do you … remember?"

"All of it," she said, her eyes meeting his. "It's a little overwhelming, but it's all there. You were shot …"

Chase pulled her into his arms, holding her close to him. "All taken care of. Are you in any pain?"

As she rested her head against his chest, she shook it a bit. "Not at all."

"*Soli Deo Gloria*," Chase murmured, pulling back to look down into her eyes again.

She smiled at him, completely taken in. Even his scent comforted her. "I've missed you," she whispered.

"Oh, you don't know the half of it!" Chase chuckled a bit, kissing her forehead. "Redic is waiting. And Brax has a few questions. Are you up for that?"

"Only if you stay with me," Trista answered, winding her fingers around his tunic. She didn't want him very far from her, especially now that they'd been reunited. "And if I get some time alone with you."

"Baby, you got it." He smiled before speaking into his link. "Remy, send him in."

The door cracked open, allowing Redic to enter. He smiled with warmth and affection at the couple. She'd never been so glad to see him.

"It's good to see you again, Trista," he said as he settled in the chair Chase had occupied when she first awoke.

"Thank you, sir. It's good to be home," she replied, shifting to lean a bit more on Chase. He slipped an arm around her and cradled her close to him.

"I imagine so." Redic kicked his foot onto his knee, his eyes on Trista. "Seraph recommended that we move you here to a more comfortable and familiar spot. Said it might help you ease into an awakened state."

"Tell him thank you from me," Trista replied. "It was certainly more heartening than a medical facility."

The older man nodded, eyeing Trista. "Now, I'm giving you an order. No more runs for a while. You're grounded," he added with a paternal smile.

"I accept. Wholeheartedly," she said, resting her head against Chase's shoulder.

"When you're feeling better, I'd like you to address the Crew. Tell us what you know about what was done to you. We want to prevent it from happening to someone else. All right?"

"Yes, sir."

Redic patted her blanketed foot gently before he rocked forward and stood. "Chase, the Crew is meeting in the Turret this evening. I expect you *not* to be there. I'll have Remy send you the minutes."

"Thank you, Redic," Chase said.

As Redic was about to step out, Brax threw open the door, striding in with a PDL and a folder. "Good afternoon, Mrs. Leighton. I trust you're feeling better," he said, nodding a greeting to Redic.

"Much," she said with a smile. Brax was always good at making her laugh.

"On your way out?" Brax asked of Redic.

"Yes," the leader confirmed.

"I'd like you to stay," Brax said before turning to the couple. "I have some interesting news on Trista's condition."

That didn't sound good at all. "Condition?" Trista asked nervously, glancing to Chase.

"Just a medical term. I like to throw them out here and there. Makes me sound like I know what I'm doing," Brax rattled with a grin and winked at her.

He splayed the folder on the end of the bed and tossed the PDL to Chase. "When you first came in, Trista, I ran a brain scan. Just wanted to be thorough. Chase told me that you were in treatment for a brain tumor?"

Chase squeezed her hand. He must have known that the question upset her. Really, she wanted nothing more than to forget about the horrible events. But for now, she'd rely on Chase's strength to give her leadership the answers they sought. "That's what Dr. Terces said, yes. It was all fabrication, though, right?" she asked, even though she knew the truth.

"Oh, yes. I confirmed that with the scan," Brax said. "But what I found interesting was this …" He pointed to the dorsal view of the brain scan. "No sign of any kind of entry. No indication of surgery. No damage. Nothing. Your brain is in perfect health," he announced with a smile.

"That's impossible," she whispered in astonishment.

"That's the Crown," Chase answered, staring at the information on the PDL readout. He seemed equally amazed. "Are you sure, Brax? I know there was damage done."

Brax shrugged, lifting his eyebrows. "I can run a second scan if you'd like, but the evidence is right here," he said, gesturing to the folder containing the brain scan.

"No," Trista answered quickly, recoiling into Chase's protective arms. "I don't want anyone to …"

Chase kissed her head and held her close. "It's okay," he murmured, squeezing her in reassurance.

Redic looked up from the folder, clearing his throat. "Then I say you release the young lady with a clean bill of health, Brax. We praise and thank the Crown for what has been done." He smiled, pointing at her. "You're a miracle, Trista."

"Thank you, sir," she whispered.

"Come on, Braxford. It's time to leave these two alone. They've been separated long enough," Redic said as he stepped to the door.

Brax rolled his eyes as he gathered up the folder and took the PDL from Chase. "I hate it when he uses my full name," he grumbled.

Trista laughed softly as the men left the room. Chase pulled her closer. He held her to him, stroking her hair. "I'm so sorry, Trista," he said. "I never would have left you there alone ... It destroyed me to leave you on that ship."

"I know that, Chase. And it's done. Finished. Behind us," Trista replied, lifting her gaze to his. "I'm here. With you. And that's all that matters."

He smiled down at her. "You're right." He squeezed her tightly. "You're right," he whispered a second time, pressing another kiss to the top of her head. "I'm not letting you go again."

"You better not." She closed her eyes, snuggling into his side. She didn't want to think anymore. She didn't want to go anywhere or do anything. She just wanted to be with her husband, close and connected. It had been too long, as Redic said.

"The Legacy took a year from us," she murmured.

"A year that I fully intend to make up," Chase said, slipping a beautiful new gold band on her finger as he pressed a kiss to her lips.

- **access card**—key card allowing entry to sealed rooms.
- **Agency of Justice**—bureau overseeing law and proceedings throughout the Progressive Legacy.
- **Agency of Medicine**—bureau overseeing medical concerns throughout the Progressive Legacy.
- **Bands**—Legacy media.
- **candlestick house**— a network of safe houses for the Logia
- **comm room**—communications room.
- **comsys**—communications system.
- **cradle**—ExMed equipment, fully functioning life support unit.
- **The Crew**—group of twelve advisors to Redic Clairet who assist in the leadership of the Ghosts.
- **Crepusculum**—gifted persons opposed to Prince Ternion.
- **Crownspeed**—farewell salutation of the Lumen and Logia.
- **CS**—computer specialist (term used by the Ghosts).
- **datadisk**—portable information storage.
- **DDL**—digital datalog, a computer.
- **ECT**—electroconvulsive therapy.
- **eternity**—Lumen/Logia's equivalent to heaven.
- **ExMed**—Experimental Medicine, a Legacy-approved branch of the Agency of Medicine, in which medical experiments take place.
  + **acquisition**—reception area of new ExMed subjects.
- **field**—docking slot for ships in a docking bay.
- **Ghost symbol**—tEU.
- **Ghosts**—group of freedom fighters, consisting mostly of Lumen and Logia, who oppose the Legacy.
- **hand torch**—flashlight.
- **he chases ghosts**—unexpected glitch in Krissa's "programming."
- **Holy Book**—the Lumen/Logia equivalent to the Holy Bible.
- **hunter**—biomechanical/cyborg bounty hunters employed by the Legacy.
- **hydralily**—a flower indigenous to Pavana.
- **identifier**—identity information card.
- **ignition flux**—crucial component to the proper functioning of any ship.

- **interrogation**—intense, brutal questioning of a suspect.
  - ✦ **interrogation rods**—equipment used to get answers; long electric rods of varying sizes and lengths.
  - ✦ **preliminary**—initial stage of interrogation; questioning performed without the rods.
  - ✦ **stages 1–5**—levels of approved interrogation; questioning performed with the rods.
  - ✦ **truth sleep**—drug-induced trance in order for the interrogation to be effective.
- **kaf**—coffee.
- **Legacy Placement Services**—employment agency.
- **lift**—elevator.
- **link**—communication device.
- **Logia**—gifted follower of Prince Ternion.
- **LUM**—Lexical Upload Matrix, source of information for the system provided by the Legacy.
  - ✦ **intra-LUM**—restricted access LUM, used by Zeniths, Zephyrs, and other officials.
- **Lumen**—dedicated follower of the Crown.
- **Medications**
  - ✦ **anisceptrum** (*Latin "sceptrum"—rule, authority, "anima"—breath, life, soul*)—inhibitor agent used by ExMed.
  - ✦ **capustatim** (*Latin "caput"—head, "statim"—instant*)—quick-releasing pain reducer.
  - ✦ **decessus** (*Latin—retirement, withdrawal, departure, death*)—control agent used on inmates.
  - ✦ **deleouxor** (*Latin "deleo"—erase, "uxor"—spouse*)—memory block agent.
  - ✦ **imperactium** (*Latin "imperium"—control, "peracto"—complete*)—inhibitor agent used by ExMed.
  - ✦ **maldominorex** (*Latin "mal"—bad, "dominor"—dominate, "rex"—king*)—control agent.
  - ✦ **mensviscus** (*Latin "mens"—mind, "viscus"—heart*)—inhibitor agent used by ExMed.
  - ✦ **morisentia** (*Latin "moris"—will, inclination, "sentential"—thought,*)—inhibitor agent used by ExMed.
  - ✦ **nexletum** (*Latin—death, ruin, annihilation*)—control agent used on inmates.

- **proceptum** (*Latin "proceptum"—accept*)—used with MRP as antirejection drug.
- **serenidor** (*Latin "serenus"—serenity, "nidor"—vapor*)—gas given to Trista prior to surgery.
- **somnoctis** (*Latin "somnus"—sleep*)—sedative.
- **torstatim** (*Latin "torpeo"—numb, "statim"—instant*)—instantly numbs muscles.

- **MRP (memory restructuring program)**
  - The patient is anesthetized for the surgical procedure, but must remain awake for the IIS. Once the process is completed, the memory of the IIS is deleted. Parts of the brain retain echoes of deleted memories. Fabricated memories, or "programming," from the IIS must contain pieces of that information so that the patient doesn't encounter neural dissonance. Side effects of the MRP include headaches, dizziness, confusion, and disorientation. All MRP patients, although mainstreamed into society, are monitored closely by the medical community—given false diseases and medical issues to keep them on a short leash.
  - **auditory program control**—trigger words used for control.
  - **handling keep**—life support system used while patient is undergoing the surgical portion of the MRP.
  - **IIS (intracranial impulse stimulation)**—the reprogramming of the patient's memory structure.
  - **ITC (integrated transmuter circuit)**—surgically implanted device, often used for hunters, that contains encoded memories, and, using two telescoping wires, activates the intracranial impulse stimulation (IIS) needed to accept the memories as true. One ITC is routed to the hippocampus of the brain, another is routed to the temporal lobe, and a third is routed to the frontal cortex. (The third ITC was not standard practice in the initial trials—which all led to fatalities. Upon further research, it proved to be crucial.)
  - **pain inducer**—electronic devices that emit a painful signal when tripped by certain words or phrases.
  - **programming**—encoded information/memories issued by the Legacy.
  - **technicians**—assistants.
  - **shroud**—apparatus used to initiate IIS, often while the patient

is still in the keep. Encircles the patient's head, secured by metal plates that set against the shoulders. Six pins make contact with the patient's skull—three along the brow, one at each temple, and one at the crown. Three base receptors at the back of the skull interact with the ITCs. The pins pulse with heat as they make contact with the wiring deeply embedded within the skull, allowing the doctor to activate stimulus or determine regression or breaching of previous endeavors. A computer monitor along the band of the shroud guides the doctor, allowing him to access, delete, and create memories.

- **navsys**—navigational system.
- **pandemic on Gravatus**—deadly illness that killed millions, rumored to be the result of Legacy testing of biological agents.
- **passcodes**—passwords.
- **Pathway**—a wormhole provided by the Crown and used by the Ghosts. Its coordinates are classified, and a mystery to the Legacy.
- **PDL**—personal datalog.
- **pharm**—pharmacy.
- **PLF**—Progressive Legacy Fleet.
- **PLR**—Progressive Legacy Rule, date designation incorporated by the Legacy
- **prep strip**—craft taxiing area in docking bay; leads to the launch deck.
- **Prince Ternion's Praesidium**—panel of twelve advisors that aided Prince Ternion.
- **prison transport**—prisoner transportation from the Justice Center to prison ships.
- **processing**—entering a suspect into Legacy criminal database.
- **Progressive Legacy**—ruling faction of the Circeae System.
- **protein paste**—standard tubed food for Zephyrs/Zeniths.
- **queller**—stun gun.
- **reconciliation**—the Logia gift of mental healing.
- **restoration**—the Logia gift of physical healing.
- **Ruli**—illegal game similar to poker; banned for its use of royalty cards.
  - ✦ **dark meets light**—special card.
  - ✦ **diamond duchess**—nobility card in the diamond suit.
  - ✦ **drat**—card that can eliminate a player.
  - ✦ **emerald twelve**—card in the emerald suit.

- ♦ **king**—royalty card.
- ♦ **prince**—royalty card.
- ♦ **ruby marquis**—nobility card in the ruby suit.
- ♦ **sapphire baron**—nobility card in the sapphire suit.
- **run**—Ghost missions, assignments.
- **SA**—systems analyst, term used by Legacy. Same as a computer specialist.
- **seal override**—device that hacks ships' seals.
- **slayer**—standard weapon (gun) issued to Zeniths/Zephyrs. Can wound or kill.
- **sleeping hours**—sleep period during the system's standard twenty-four-hour day.
- *Soli Deo Gloria*—To God be the Glory, Logia/Lumen phrase.
- **squant**—unit of measurement for distance.
- **stinger**—device resembling a cattle prod.
- **téchaud**—tea.
- **"The King reigns, the Prince has risen, and the Companion is among us."**—Lumen/Logia password.
- **Zeeb**—Ghost nickname for the Zenith Brigade.
- **Zenith Brigade**—policing force.
- **Zephyr Force**—military armed forces.

ASYLUM PLACES

- **Aevum rotation**—one of three stars of the Circeae System.
- **Archet**—a moon of Crenet.
  - ♦ **hidden Logia base**—following the execution of Prince Ternion, the Logia fled to a hidden area, knowing that they would soon be hunted.
- **Atrum**—a planet in the Vetus rotation, where Legacy shipyards are located.
- **Caelum**—a planet in the Aevum rotation.
- **Crenet**—the central planet.
  - ♦ **Regiam/Reticulum**—the royal city/the main city.
    - ▪ **Justice Center**—detention center, ExMed facility, courthouse.
    - ▪ **fleet headquarters**—base of operations for the Legacy fleet.

- **Doppel**—the Twin Planet in the Aevum rotation, mostly farmland.
- **Ossia**—a moon of Crenet.
  + **Ossia Institute**—an Elite institute specializing in medical practices.
- **Gravatus**—a moon of Crenet, famous for its pandemic at the rise of the Legacy.
- **Maeror**—a planet in the Vetus rotation.
- **Novus rotation**—one of three stars in the Circeae System.
- **Pavana**—a planet in the Aevum rotation.
- **Quintus**—a moon of Crenet.
- **Revenant (Rev)**—a hidden planet beyond the Aevum rotation.
  + **The Reserve**—the Ghost base on Revenant.
    - **docking bays**—located on the south end of the base.
    - **northwest atrium**—a private area intended for relaxation and meditation.
    - **central atrium**—the heart of the base, gathering place.
    - **operations room**—base of operations for the Ghost faction.
    - **medbay**—medical wing, located just north of the docking bays.
    - **The Turret**—private conference room for the Crew, adjacent to Redic's office at the north end of the base.
    - **The sacrarium**—the place of worship for the Lumen and Logia, located on the west end of the base.
    - **observation deck**—area in operations room, intended specifically for monitoring Legacy activity.
- **Soubrette**—a moon of Crenet.
- **Tzigane**—a planet in the Novus rotation, where Legacy shipyards are located.
- **Venenum**—a planet in the Vetus rotation.
- **Vetus rotation**—one of three stars in the Circeae System.
  + **Zenith outpost**—anchored station within the rotation.
- **Viam**—a planet in the Aevum rotation, closest to the hidden planet of Revenant.
  + **The Junction**—location on Viam where Ghost ships always stop prior to entering or just after exiting the Pathway.
  + **bay B 1230**—docking bay where the Ghosts try to contact Trista following her capture.
    - **Field 102**—the specific spot where the Ghost ship docked.

- The *Bastille* (*any prison or jail, especially one conducted in a tyrannical way*)—a Legacy prison ship.
- The *Halcyon* (*calm; peaceful; tranquil*)—a Ghost ship captained by Chase Leighton.
- The *Haulaway*—a small Legacy ship.
- The *Lambent* (*brilliantly playful*) *Stallion*—a Ghost ship captained by Britt Lockhart.
- The *Oubliette* (*a secret dungeon with an opening only in the ceiling*)—a Legacy prison ship.
- The *Straightjacket*—a Legacy prison ship, specifically for the criminally insane.
  - **ACT (acceptance and commitment therapy) room**—one of the approved treatments for the *Straightjacket*'s inmates, located on deck three.
  - **CBT (cognitive behavioral therapy)**—one of the approved treatments for the *Straightjacket*'s inmates, located on deck three.
  - **control room**—the heart of the *Straightjacket* where the ship's computers are located, located on deck three.
  - **ECT (electroconvulsive therapy)**—one of the approved treatments for the *Straightjacket*'s inmates, located on deck three.
  - **staff quarters**—luxurious part of the ship that houses the staff and doctors, located on deck three.
  - **inmates' row**—small section of the ship, consisting of rooms where the inmates bunk, located on deck three.
  - **MS quarters**—the master sergeant's room, located on deck one.
  - **docking bay**—areas on both sides of the ship where smaller ships can dock, located on decks one and two.
  - **crew quarters**—nice part of the ship that houses the crew, located on deck two.
  - **emergency docking pad**—space at the top of the ship where a craft could land.
  - **isolation**—a small room where inmates are placed when they display poor behavior, located on deck three.
  - **doctors' offices**—private offices for the doctors, located on deck three.

- ✦ **engine room**—the operation center of the *Straightjacket*, located on deck one.
- ✦ **receiving bay**—area where supplies are loaded into the *Straightjacket*, located on deck one.
- *Valor's Fool*—a Ghost ship captained by Cam Grayson.
- The *Vanguard* (*the foremost division or the front part of an army*)—a Ghost ship captained by Brendan Faulkner.
- The *Vanquisher* (*to conquer or subdue by superior force*)—a Legacy warship.

Asylum Characters

- **Dr. Aftal** (*"fatal" rearranged*)—Legacy, ExMed doctor.
- **Mr. Arger** (*German—severe*)—Legacy, supervisor of Tzigane shipyards, Britt's disguise.
- **Berreks** (*"berserk" rearranged*)—Legacy, technician under Terces.
- **Zenith Lieutenant Gib Blouter** (*"big trouble" rearranged*)—Legacy, Zenith commander who keeps an eye on Krissa.
- **Master Sergeant Cord Brewster**—Legacy, last crewmember aboard the *Straightjacket*.
- **Bruiser**—Ghost, traitor.
- **Silas Buque** (*Spanish—ship*)—Legacy, head of Atrum shipyards.
- **Dr. Adam Caiman** (*"a mad maniac" rearranged*)—Legacy, *Straightjacket* head doctor.
- **Antin and Kylea Carlisle** (*mentioned only*)—Lumen and servants of Ternion, Lila and Trista's parents, deceased.
- **Krissa Carlisle (02C1917)**—Legacy, Trista's new Legacy identity.
- **Kalislyn Carter**—Legacy, member of the Elite.
- **Dr. Caultin** (*"lunatic" rearranged*)—Legacy, *Straightjacket* doctor.
- **Nicodemus (Nic) Church**—Ghost, first officer and medic of the *Halcyon*, inmate on the *Straightjacket*.
- **Clairet kids** (*mentioned only*)—Morgan, Halley, Corrin—deceased. Selah and Seraph survived.
- **Caelya Clairet** (*mentioned only*)—Redic's deceased wife.
- **Echo Clairet**—Logia, Ghost, wife of Seraph.
- **Redic Clairet (Ghost One)**—member of Prince Ternion's Praesidium, founder of the Ghosts, father of Seraph and Selah.

- **Seraph Clairet (Ghost Three)**—"Junior," Logia, Ghost, son of Redic Clairet, husband of Echo.
- **Craser** (*French—crush*)—Legacy, orderly aboard the *Straightjacket*.
- **The Creator King**—the Father component of the triune God of the Logia.
- **Blane Criswell** (*mentioned only*)—Ghost, son of Sterling and Lila.
- **Lila (Carlisle) Criswell**—Ghost, first officer of the *Vanguard*, wife of Sterling, Trista's sister. Legacy records list her as deceased.
- **Sterling Criswell**—Logia, Ghost, husband of Lila, brother of Echo.
- **Harlan Cromley** (*mentioned only*)—Logia, Chase Leighton's grandfather, member of Prince Ternion's Praesidium, deceased.
- **The Crown**—the Triune God of the Logia.
- **Decker**—Ghost, inmate on the *Straightjacket*.
- **Seth Declan**—Ghost, crewmember of the *Halcyon*, inmate on the *Straightjacket*.
- **Droga** (*Spanish—dope*)—Legacy, orderly aboard the *Straightjacket*.
- **Lem Duncan**—Ghost, crewmember of the *Halcyon* inmate on the *Straightjacket*.
- **Stu Engrell (Ghost Two)**—Ghost, friend to Redic Clairet, member of Prince Ternion's Praesidium.
- **The Eternal Companion**—the Spirit component of the triune God of the Logia.
- **Brendan Faulkner**—Ghost, former Legacy pilot, captain of the *Vanguard*.
- **Nurse Fiara**—Legacy, nurse in Terces's office.
- **Frisco**—Ghost.
- **Interrogator Gamead** (*"damage" rearranged*)—Legacy, interrogator who questions Krissa.
- **Grease** (*mentioned only*)—Ghost, former Legacy, head mechanic.
- **Grausam** (*German—cruel*)—Legacy, orderly aboard the *Straightjacket*.
- **Barrett Grayson**—Logia, son of Callum Grayson.
- **Callum Grayson** (*mentioned only*)—Logia, member of Prince Ternion's Praesidium.
- **Cam Grayson (Fool One)**—Ghost, Captain of *Valor's Fool*, husband of Selah.
- **Selah (Clairet) Grayson**—Logia, Ghost, wife of Cam, daughter of Redic.

- **Quinn Grayson**—Logia, Ghost, son of Cam and Selah.
- **Hart** (*German—hard*)—Legacy, orderly aboard the *Straightjacket*.
- **Belle Hughes** (*mentioned only*)—Ghost, wife of Brax.
- **Braxford Hughes (Fool Two)**—Ghost, first officer of *Valor's Fool*, husband of Belle, head medic for the Ghosts.
- **Jared Kern**—Ghost, crewmember of the *Halcyon*, inmate on the *Straightjacket*.
- **Halden (Hal) Lancaster**—Ghost, communications officer of the *Halcyon*, inmate on the *Straightjacket*.
- **Sam Lang** (*German "langsam"—slow*)—Legacy, supervisor of Atrum shipyards receiving bay.
- **Chase Leighton (Logia Three)**—Ghost, captain of the *Halcyon*, husband of Trista, inmate on the *Straightjacket*.
- **Dorsey Leighton** (*mentioned only*)—Logia, Chase Leighton's father, deceased.
- **Sasha Leighton**—Logia, Chase Leighton's mother, deceased.
- **Trista (Carlisle) Leighton**—wife of Chase Leighton, Ghost, Legacy Prisoner 1183721. *See also* **Krissa Carlisle**.
- **Britt Lockhart (Mr. Hazelton, Mr. Arger, Elite One)**—Ghost, captain of the *Lambent Stallion*.
- **Laney Rose Lockhart (Madame Natalia Vaisseau)**—Ghost, wife of Britt.
- **Zephyr Lieutenant Commander Armand Lyria**—Legacy, Ghost spy.
- **Vivienne Lyria**—former Ghost, wife of Armand.
- **Avalyn Marari (Logia Two)**—Ghost, former member of Prince Ternion's Praesidium.
- **Marlen**—Ghost, crewmember of the Vanguard, inmate on the *Straightjacket*.
- **Matlen** (*"mental" rearranged*)—Legacy, technician under Terces.
- **Moyenne** (*French—mean*)—Legacy, orderly aboard the *Straightjacket*.
- **Thad Newell**—Ghost, crewmember of the *Halcyon*, inmate on the *Straightjacket*.
- **Admiral Altus Niveli** (*"live in" rearranged*)—Legacy, Zephyr official.
- **Dr. Cyndra Niveli** (*"live in" rearranged*)—Legacy, ExMed doctor.

- **Plastar** (*Spanish—crush*)—Legacy, orderly aboard the *Straightjacket*.
- **Benjamin Reiger**—Ghost, crewmember of the *Halcyon*, inmate on the *Straightjacket*.
- **Cole Rose (Elite Two)**—Elite Two, friend of Britt Lockhart.
- **Dr. Sainne** (*"insane" rearranged*)—Legacy, *Straightjacket* doctor.
- **Lady Mischa Saxby**—Legacy, member of the Elite.
- **Simmons**—Ghost, inmate on the *Straightjacket*.
- **Zephyr Captain Zakaris Sinclaire**—Legacy, Ghost spy.
- **The Spokesman**—member of the Tribunal.
- **Stone**—Ghost, inmate on the *Straightjacket*.
- **Finnegan Streuben**—Legacy, owner of a computer repair service, Krissa's supervisor.
- **Remy Sullivan (Rev One)**—Ghost, assistant to Redic Clairet.
- **Taub** (*German—numb*)—Legacy, orderly aboard the *Straightjacket*.
- **Dr. Reid Terces** (*"dire secret" rearranged*)—Legacy, ExMed doctor.
- **The Ruler Prince**—the Son component of the triune God of the Logia.
- **Prince Ternion**—The Ruler Prince, deceased and resurrected.
- **Wesley (Wes) Torin**—Ghost, second officer and operations of the *Halcyon*, inmate on the *Straightjacket*.
- **The Tribunal**—leadership of the Legacy consisting of the Spokesman, the Magistrate, and the Fulcrum.
- **Dr. Tuscane** (*"nutcase" rearranged*)—Legacy, *Straightjacket* doctor.
- **Madame Natalia Vaisseau** (*French—ship*)—Legacy, head of Tzigane shipyards, Laney's disguise.
- **Commander Valach**—Legacy, commander of the warship *Vanquisher*.
- **Vencer** (*Spanish—vanquish*)—Legacy, orderly aboard the *Straightjacket*.
- **Joe Weller**—Ghost, crewmember of the *Halcyon*, inmate on the *Straightjacket*.
- **Aram Zephaniah (Logia One)**—Logia, Ghost, Chase Leighton's adoptive father, member of Prince Ternion's Praesidium.
- **Etta Zephaniah** (*mentioned only*)—wife of Aram.
- **Zermel** (*German—crush*)—Legacy, orderly aboard the *Straightjacket*.
- **Lieutenant Ziebleman**—Legacy, Zenith who delivers Trista to ExMed.

CPSIA information can be obtained at www.ICGtesting.com
Printed in the USA
LVOW051308290413

331370LV00002B/272/P